THE WHOLE TRUTH

Also by James Scott Bell

Fiction

Deadlock

Breach of Promise

Presumed Guilty

No Legal Grounds

Sins of the Fathers

Circumstantial Evidence

Final Witness

Blind Justice

The Nephilim Seed

City of Angels (coauthor)

Angels Flight (coauthor)

Angel of Mercy (coauthor)

A Greater Glory

A Higher Justice

A Certain Truth

Glimpses of Paradise

The Darwin Conspiracy

Nonfiction

Write Great Fiction: Plot and Structure

THE WHOLE TRUTH

JAMES SCOTT BELL

3841

 ZONDERVAN®

ZONDERVAN.com/
AUTHORTRACKER
follow your favorite authors

ZONDERVAN®

The Whole Truth
Copyright © 2008 by James Scott Bell

Requests for information should be addressed to:

Zondervan, *Grand Rapids, Michigan* 49530

Library of Congress Cataloging-in-Publication Data

Bell, James Scott.
     The whole truth / James Scott Bell.
       p. cm.
     ISBN-10: 0-310-26903-2
     ISBN-13: 978-0-310-26903-8
     1. Lawyers—Family relationships—Fiction. 2. Threats—Fiction. 3. Fathers and
daughters—Fiction. 4. Teenage girls—Fiction. I. Title.
PS3552.E5158N62 2007
813'.54—dc22
                                          2006033493

Printed in the United States of America

---

08 09 10 11 12 • 10 9 8 7 6 5 4 3 2 1

This is a novel about brothers.
I dedicate it to mine.
Tim and Bob, this one's for you.

Sin has many tools,
but a lie is the handle which fits them all.

Oliver Wendell Holmes

THE WHOLE TRUTH

PROLOGUE

They put Robert in Stevie's room when Stevie started getting night terrors. He was five and the terrors came hard one night when he woke up sure that a monster was trying to get him. He woke up screaming in the dark and when no lights went on he screamed louder because he thought the monster heard the screams and would try to kill him *now*.

His mom flicked on the light that first time, and Stevie saw through sleepy eyes his older brother, Robert, seven, rubbing his own eyes with his hands. He was in his train pajamas. Stevie would never forget that. All those years later, he would think of Robert in his train pajamas wondering why his little brother was screaming.

The terrors came three nights in a row. The third night was the worst and Stevie wet the bed and cried.

Stevie's dad yelled at his mother the next night. Stevie could hear them in the kitchen, arguing, like they usually did. His dad yelled, "You're not putting Robert in that room with the baby bed wetter."

His mom yelled right back at him. "You're not the one who has to get up! You don't even hear him, you're so bombed. Robert's going to sleep with him for a while, and that's the way it's going to be."

Then Stevie heard a noise and thought it was somebody falling hard to the floor in the kitchen. He never found out if it was his mom or his dad.

Robert didn't have a problem moving in with Stevie. The little house in Indio had three bedrooms. Four if you counted the living room as one, because that's where his dad slept most of the time. He'd drink beer and watch TV and usually fall asleep with the TV on.

That first night, Robert said he'd tell Stevie a story. That was way cool. Stevie loved his big brother, because he was athletic and fearless. Stevie wanted to be like Robert in every way, even wishing his brown hair was sandier like Robert's, and his eyes blue.

And he loved hearing Robert tell stories. Robert could tell the best ghost stories. But tonight Stevie hoped he wouldn't tell one of those, because they were too scary. Then Robert said he was going to tell a monster story and Stevie said maybe not, and Robert said just hang on and listen.

"Once upon a time," Robert began—the room was dark except for the moonlight, and Robert's bed was close enough for Stevie to touch with his foot—"there were two baby monsters. Their names were Arnold and Beebleobble."

Stevie cracked up. *Arnold* was a funny name, but *Beebleobble* was even funnier. Funny names for monsters. A funny monster story, he could deal with.

"One was green," Robert said, "and one was blue."

"Which one was green?" Stevie asked.

"Arnold. Beebleobble was blue."

"Cool."

"Listen to the story."

"Okay."

"One day Arnold and Beebleobble decided to go to the store. Arnold wanted some peanut butter and Beebleobble wanted some gum. So they went into the store, and the man screamed, 'Monsters!' and ran out of the store. But Arnold and Beebleobble didn't want to scare him. They were friendly monsters. They just wanted some peanut butter and some gum."

"Was anybody else in the store?"

"No. So Arnold got some peanut butter and Beebleobble got some gum and they left without paying for it. Then the police came and said, 'Why did you scare that man?' and they said, 'We didn't mean to. We don't want to scare people. We just want to get something to eat. We have money.' So the policeman scratched his head and said to the man, 'If they have the money then everything's okay.' And the man said, 'I guess so. I'm sorry. I thought they were trying to scare me.' So they paid him and went home and ate the peanut butter and chewed gum."

Stevie smiled in the moonlight. "I didn't think monsters did that."

"They were baby monsters," Robert said. "They didn't know about scaring people yet."

That night Stevie didn't have the terrors.

A week later, at kindergarten, it occurred to Stevie that Robert told the story that way just so he wouldn't be afraid of monsters trying to get him.

The terrors never came back. Until the night of the shattered eyes, when the real monsters came.

It was good to have Robert in the same room when Mom and Dad were fighting. Robert would say, "Don't worry. They'll get over it."

Then Robert would tell another story about Arnold and Beebleobble. And even though Stevie could still hear the voices yelling in the kitchen, he'd get lost in the stories about the two baby monsters and everything would seem all right.

Of course, Stevie knew that Robert was Dad's favorite. Robert could throw a baseball almost across the park. He was built like Dad, strong and stocky. Stevie took after his mom, who was kind of skinny.

Lots of times Dad took Robert to the park to play and left Stevie at home.

Once Stevie cried about it and his dad took him outside and whacked his butt with a piece of kindling.

The night of the shattered eyes started with a hot wind from the desert. It blew into Stevie's room like a pair of hot gloves, pressing his face. Stevie's window looked east toward Highway 86 and across the valley, to the brown desolate mountains, sun-baked in the distance. There wasn't much but undeveloped land between the house and hills. Sometimes Stevie thought they lived at the end of the world. Because all he could see from his window was a whole lot of hot nothing.

This night, there was something on the wind. Stevie tried to tell Robert about it.

"It's hotter," Stevie said.

"It's not so bad," Robert said. "Sleep on top of the sheets. Sleep in your underwear."

"I will if you will."

"Okay."

In the darkness they took off their pajamas. Stevie wore underwear under his pajamas like Robert did.

Then Robert said, "Once upon a time, Arnold and Beebleobble decided to sleep on top of their cave. They looked up in the sky. They saw a shooting star. Some of the shooting-star dust fell on them and made it so they could each have one wish and it would come true. Arnold wished he could go to an Angels game. Beebleobble wished he could fly to the moon and back. And they got their wishes."

Stevie thought about that. "Know what I'd wish for?"

"What?"

"That I could throw as good as you."

"You can if you practice."

"I tried."

"Tomorrow I'll practice with you, okay?"

"'kay."

With the wind blowing outside, Stevie fell into a calm sleep. Deep like the desert night.

He woke up with a rough hand over his mouth. Pressing him down. Maybe it was Robert playing a game. But it wasn't. It was something big.

A monster.

Stevie tried to scream, but the monster pushed on his mouth. The monster had no face. Stevie heard something by the window and knew there was another monster in the room. Getting Robert.

The no-face leaned down and Stevie smelled cigarettes, and that both relieved and frightened him. He was sure it was a man now, not a monster, but what was he doing to him? And Robert?

The man was wearing a ski mask. It was too hot to wear that, so why was he?

The man in the mask whispered. He had a scratchy voice. "Don't make a sound, you hear me?"

Stevie tried to nod his head, but the man was holding his face hard.

"If you make one sound I'm going to kill you and your brother. I'll kill you right now."

Stevie tried not to cry but couldn't help it. He wanted Robert. He wanted his mom. Even his dad. Anybody.

"So you listen good. I'm gonna be right outside this window, and if you move, if you make any sound—quit crying!"

Stevie couldn't stop.

"Quit crying or so help me I'll kill you both."

For Robert, Stevie thought. *Stop crying or they'll hurt Robert.* Stevie closed his eyes and sucked in air through his dribbly nose. It took him a minute, but he stopped crying.

"Good," the man whispered. "Now here's what you do. You turn over and put your head in the pillow. If I hear you make a sound or call out anything, you're going to be dead, you and your brother. You understand?"

Stevie nodded.

The man slowly took his hand away. "I'm gonna be there all night. Not one sound. Now turn over."

Stevie did as he was told. If he did what the man said, then Robert would be okay and so would he. They would get to live.

Oh God let us live. Oh God don't let them hurt Robert. God God please.

Stevie started to cry again but made himself stop. They would kill Robert if he made a sound.

Oh God don't let me make any noise. Make them go away and don't let Robert get hurt.

He had to go to the bathroom. But if he moved they would kill Robert. He had to go to the bathroom so he did it in the bed.

This was worse than nightmares. He remembered the nightmare he had before Robert told him stories, and one of the monsters took his bear and broke the eyes, shattered them. The bear looked at Stevie with shattered eyes. The eyes accused him. *Why did you let it happen?* the shattered eyes said.

Tonight was like that for real. Stevie couldn't help Robert. Only God could help him. Stevie could only lie in the bed and not cry.

Shaken awake.

Jolted out of sleep. Somebody clutching him. Hurting his shoulders.

Mom.

She was shaking him and yelling, "Where's Robert?"

Scared, Stevie thought it was a dream. But the room was full of light and he felt the wetness and smelled it and knew it was real. Like last night was real.

"Answer me!"

Like she was mad at him.

He didn't answer. Didn't want to make a sound. What if they were outside the window?

Now his mom was really crazy and tears were in her eyes.

"Answer me, will you!"

If she was yelling then maybe it was okay to talk now. "Outside! Look outside!"

"Outside *where?*"

"The window!"

His dad charged in. Must have been right outside the door. Ran to the window and looked out.

He turned back to Stevie, face red. "Whattaya mean *outside?*"

"A man! He had a mask. He was gonna kill us!"

His mom and dad didn't say anything. They looked at each other the way people did sometimes in movies. Not knowing what to do.

"Where's Robert?" Stevie said.

"Oh, honey." His mother sat down on the bed and hugged him. "Frank, call the police. Hurry."

Stevie let himself cry now. He saw Robert's train pajamas on the floor.

The police came. A lot of them. It was confusing. Everybody was talking to him, asking him questions, making him go over and over things. Stevie started sucking his thumb again. He clung to his mother.

She told the police not to make him talk anymore, that he had told them everything.

Other people came. Stevie knew they were people from TV. They had cameras and microphones.

Stevie's mother wouldn't let the people in the house.

Finally, when it was dark, the people were gone. But the house wasn't the same. Something had changed, and it wasn't just that Robert wasn't there. It was that Robert wasn't there because of Stevie. He wasn't there because Stevie didn't say anything. The man in the mask didn't stay outside the window. He just said that to scare him.

There was a moment when Stevie knew all this instantly. One look was all it took.

One look from his dad. They were sitting at the kitchen table. Too tired to eat. Mom had heated up some Tater Tots for Stevie, and he ate some, but not all of them. His parents were silent, looking down at the table.

And then Stevie saw his father looking at him. The look bore into Stevie like fists. It was a look of disgust. His father hated him. Stevie was sure of that now.

Stevie ran from the table into the bathroom and threw up and cried.

His mom came in and cleaned him up.

His father didn't come. His father didn't speak to him for a week.

Eight weeks later, Robert hadn't been found. There was no ransom note. No contact of any kind.

Stevie managed, from snippets of conversation, to piece together that the police thought a group might be involved. They called it a "religious cult," and Stevie wondered what that was. He asked his mom once and she just shook her head like she didn't want to answer.

A couple of times he heard the word *pervert* and wondered if that was something else, but he was afraid to ask.

His father was drinking a lot of beer and stuff from a bottle. He stayed away from the house for days sometimes. When he came back he and his mom yelled at each other.

He wouldn't talk to Stevie.

When Stevie looked at his father, he thought something was taking Dad over. A bad thing. All because of Robert. What Stevie had done to Robert.

And then one day the bad thing took over completely. The day they found out Robert would not be coming home. Ever.

His mom told him it wasn't his fault. And a doctor his mom took him to also said it wasn't. The doctor, a nice lady, even got Stevie to say out loud that he knew it wasn't his fault Robert had died in a terrible way.

But Stevie didn't believe it. He knew better.

Stevie also knew that he was why his dad went away. He never saw his dad again.

When Stevie turned six he found out that his dad was dead. And learned a new word. *Suicide.*

He hated the sound of it. It was an evil-sounding word.

A word he couldn't get out of his head.

PART 1

ONE

"Mr. Conroy?"

Steve heard his name. Like someone calling from the front of a cavern with him deep inside. Inside, where his thoughts were pinging off the walls like a drunk's haphazard gunshots.

"Yes, Your Honor?"

"I said you may cross-examine." Nasty voice. Judge O'Hara, ex-prosecutor, ex-cop, did not like screwups in his courtroom. Especially if they themselves were ex-prosecutors now prowling the defense side of the aisle. O'Hara glared at Steve from the bench, his imperious eyebrows seeming to frame the Great Seal of the State of California on the wall behind him.

"Excuse me, Your Honor." Steve Conroy stood up, feeling the heat from all the eyes in the courtroom.

The eyes of Judge O'Hara, of course.

Everyone on the jury.

His client.

And his client's extended family, which seemed like the entire population of Guadalajara, all packed into Division 115 of the Van Nuys courthouse.

Officer Charles Siebel was on the stand. The one who'd claimed that Steve's client, an ex-felon, was packing. An ex-felon with a gun could land in the slam for up to three years, depending on priors. Which his client had a boatload of. The one hope Carlos Mendez had of getting his sorry can back on the street, free of the law's embrace, lay in Steve's ability to knock the credibility out of a dedicated veteran of the Los Angeles Police Department.

And doing it with no sleep. Steve had fought the cold sweats all night. Which always made the morning after an adventure in mental gymnastics. His brain would fire off an unending stream of random and contradictory thoughts. He'd have to practically grunt to keep focus. The chemical consequence of recovery.

"Excuse me, Your Honor," Steve said, grabbing for his yellow pages of notes. He trucked the pages to the podium and buttoned his suit coat. It fell open. He buttoned it again. It fell open again. A yellow sheet slipped from the podium. Steve grabbed it in mid-descent, like a Venus flytrap snatching its prey, and slapped it back on the podium in front of him.

He saw a couple of jurors smiling at the show.

Steve cleared his throat. "According to your report, Officer Siebel, you saw my client standing on the corner of Sepulveda and Vanowen, is that correct?"

"Yes." Clipped and authoritative, like the prosecutors trained them to be.

"You were in your vehicle, is that right?"

"Yes."

"Alone?"

"Yes."

"Driving which way?"

"North."

"On what street?"

Officer Siebel and Judge O'Hara sighed at the same time.

Just like a comedy team. The whole courtroom was one big sit-com, Steve playing the incompetent sidekick.

"Sepulveda," Siebel said.

"At what time?"

"Is this cross-examination or skeet shooting?" Judge O'Hara snapped.

Steve clenched his teeth. O'Hara liked to inject himself into the thick of things, showboating for the jury. For some reason, he'd been doing it to Steve throughout the trial.

"If I may, Your Honor, I'm laying a foundation," Steve said.

"Sounds like you're just letting the witness repeat direct testimony."

Why thank you, Judge. I had no idea. How helpful you are! The DA didn't even have to object!

"I'll try it this way," Steve said, turning back to the witness. "Officer Siebel, you were driving north on Sepulveda at 10:32 p.m., correct?"

"That's what happened."

"It's in your report, isn't it?"

"Of course."

Steve went to counsel table and picked up a copy of the police report. As he did, Carlos Mendez, in his jailhouse blues, gave him the look, the one that said, *I hope you know what you're doing.*

Ah yes, the confident client. When was the last time he'd had one of those?

Steve held up the report. "The lighting conditions are not mentioned in your report, are they?"

"I didn't see any need, I was able to see —"

"I'd like an answer to the question I asked, sir."

The deputy DA, Moira Hanson, stood. "Objection. The witness should be allowed to answer."

Steve looked at the DDA, who was about his age, thirty. That's where the resemblance ended. She was short and blond. He was an even six feet with hair as dark as the marks against him. She was new to the office. He hadn't met her when he was prosecuting for the county of Los Angeles.

"Your Honor," he said, "the answer was clearly nonresponsive. As you pointed out so eloquently, this is cross-examination."

O'Hara was not impressed. "Thank you very much for the endorsement, Mr. Conroy. Now if you'll let me rule? Ask your question again, and I direct the witness to answer only the question asked."

A minor victory, Steve knew, but in this trial any bone was welcome.

"Are there any lighting conditions in your report?" Steve asked.

"No," Siebel said.

"You are aware that the corner you mention has dark patches, aren't you?"

"Dark patches?"

"What scientists refer to as illumination absences?"

Officer Siebel squinted at Steve.

"You do know what I'm talking about, surely," Steve said.

Moira Hanson objected again. "No foundation, Your Honor."

"Sustained. In plain English, Mr. Conroy."

That was fine with Steve. Because he'd just made up the term *illumination absences.* All he wanted was the jury to think he had Bill Nye the Science Guy on the defense team. These days, juries were under the spell of the *CSI* effect. They all thought forensic evidence was abundant and could clinch any case in an hour. Prosecutors hated that, because most cases weren't so cut, dried, preserved, and plattered. Steve intended to plant the idea that science was against the DA.

"*Illumination absences* refers to measurable dark spots. There are all sorts of dark spots on that corner, Officer Siebel, where you can't see a thing, right?"

"I don't know what you're talking about. I could see clearly."

Steve turned to the judge. "Why don't we take the jury down there tonight, Your Honor, and we can—"

"Approach the bench," O'Hara ordered. "With the reporter."

Putting on a sheepish look, Steve joined Hanson in front of the judge.

"You know better than to make a motion in front of the jury," O'Hara said.

"He knows, but does it anyway," Hanson added. She was like the smarty in school who dumps extra on the kids who get sent to the principal's office.

"What?" Steve said. "It was just a request."

"I know what you're doing," O'Hara said.

"Representing my client?"

"If this is representation, I'm Britney Spears. You're taking shortcuts. Well, you're not going to get away with it. Not here. And you don't want to tempt me. Another disciplinary strike and you're out."

That was true. Steve had been out of rehab for a year after dealing with a coke addiction and losing his job with the DA's office. Now that he was trying to establish a private practice, no easy task, he did not need the State Bar on his back again. They wouldn't be so forgiving this time.

"And what's that load about this illumination thing?" O'Hara asked. "You better have a foundation for asking that."

"I can find a scientist to back it up."

"You can find a scientist to back up anything," Hanson said.

"I won't allow it," O'Hara said. "I think you're just whistling in the dark, so to speak."

"Representing my client, Your Honor."

"Call me Britney. Go on. But watch every step you take, sir."

Steve didn't have to. He'd gotten what he could out of the witness. All he needed was one juror to think that maybe this officer didn't see what he thought he saw. One juror to hang the thing, and then maybe Moira Hanson would call her boss and say it's not worth a retrial. Let the guy walk.

Sure. And Santa Claus sips Cuba Libres at the North Pole.

TWO

Steve's cross of Officer Siebel was the last order of business on a hot August Friday. Monday they'd all come back for closing arguments, giving Steve a whole weekend to come up with some verbal gold. Which he knew he had to spin to get Carlos Mendez a fair shake.

It would also give him time, he hoped, to get some sleep.

Steve pointed his Ark toward his Canoga Park office. The Ark was what he called his vintage Cadillac, and by vintage he meant *has seen better days*. It dated from the Reagan administration and had been overhauled and repainted and taped together many times over. Steve scored it at a police auction five years earlier. The main advantage was it was big. He could sleep in it if he needed to. Even back then, as he was sucking blow up his snout like a Hoover, Steve suspected he might be homeless someday.

Hadn't happened yet. And with the help of the State Bar's Lawyer Assistance Program, maybe it wouldn't. The LAP was supposed to help lawyers with substance-abuse problems. Steve had managed to keep the monkey off his back for a year. Not that he wasn't close to falling, especially on those nights when he lay in bed staring at the ceiling.

Steve took Sherman Way into Canoga Park, an LA burg in the west end of the San Fernando Valley. It was a venerable town that had hit its stride in 1955, when Rocketdyne, a division of North American Aviation, made its home there. The aerospace industry brought a boomlet of people to the area, and American dreams were born and realized. Rocketdyne engines were used to help put men on the moon in 1969, and sent NASA space shuttles on their appointed rounds.

At its peak during the space race with the Soviets, Rocketdyne employed twenty-two thousand people, and Canoga Park was a great place to live, shop, and open a business. But the realities of economy and urban decline were as inevitable and poisonous as wild oleander.

The aerospace industry dried up. The blocks of apartments that once housed Rocketdyne line workers became homes for Latino immigrants. The Rocketdyne building itself, a dinosaur of 1950s architecture, was used sparingly now, surrounded by fast-food restaurants and big-box electronics stores.

But Canoga Park was going through a rebirth of sorts, with its famous shopping mall on Topanga undergoing a major refurbish. High-end boutiques and a Nordstrom were cornerstones of the new place. Things were looking up, economically speaking.

Steve wanted to see it as a hopeful metaphor of his own career. Once promising, then a descent into the absolute toilet, now ready for a comeback. If he could just land a well-heeled client or two. Maybe a big white-collar CEO type. Right. They always came to the small-time solo operator like him.

The building that housed Steve's office came into view. A two-story corner job, it wasn't on the best part of the main drag. Across the street was a notorious strip mall that drew a lot of Steve's future clients—young thugs. They'd hang out at night in front of the coin laundry, under the red glow of the Chinese restaurant sign. *Pick Up or Dine In,* the sign said. Steve thought they should add a line—*Hang Out.* Because that's all people did over there—mostly unemployed, mostly Latino.

Mostly tired, Steve turned into the outdoor parking lot of his office building.

And almost ran over a chair. What was that all about? True, this wasn't the toniest address in town, but they didn't need junk all over the place. Maybe some of the homeless had—

Steve recognized the chair. One of his own. A secretarial chair with rollers that was rarely used, the main reason being he had no secretary.

At the far end of the lot was a collection of more furniture. Piled up in the corner of the gray cinderblock wall. And all of it from his office.

The jerk had evicted him.

Trembling with rage, Steve braked the Ark, jumped out, and stared at his desk, chairs, credenza, filing cabinets, bookcases. It wasn't everything, but enough for his Serbian landlord to make his point.

He saw himself grabbing a tire iron from the Ark's trunk and breaking some of the building's windows. Street justice. Maybe smash a door or two. Then he saw the tatters of his reputation and called Ashley.

His soon-to-be ex-wife—they had a month left on the mandatory wait—was the only one who might help him. She'd been there in the past. But he also knew that the thin thread that held them together was close to snapping.

"What's wrong, Steve?" That was the first thing out of her mouth.

"Why do you always assume something's wrong?"

"You only call when something's wrong."

"Not so."

"Then what is it?"

"Something's wrong," Steve said.

"Not funny."

"Not trying to be. He evicted me."

"Your apartment?"

"Office."

"Why?"

"Non-payment of rent, of course. But he didn't have to do it this way. I mean, the stuff is all over the parking lot."

"Steve, I'm sorry."

"I was wondering if I could borrow a little."

The pause on the other end was heavy, like a water-soaked blanket.

"Ashley?"

"I just can't."

"Why not?"

"You know why not."

"Oh what, you're going to bring up that enablement stuff?"

"It's not *stuff*. It's for your own good. The counselor even—"

"Don't bring up the counselor, please. I don't exactly have feelings for the guy who is the reason you filed."

"I filed because it was the only thing left for me. For us."

"I'm clean, Ashley. Over a year."

"I'm glad."

"Glad enough to stop this thing and try again?"

Another pause, heavier than the first.

"Ashley?"

"It's not going to happen, Steve. The sooner you accept that, the better it's going to be all around."

"Can't we at least just talk and—"

"No. Is there anything else? I've got a client I have to see."

The finality in her voice was like a hook, deep in fish guts, being ripped out. It almost took Steve's breath away.

He saw a young woman emerge from the back of the office building. She appeared to be looking for someone. He turned his back on her.

"I'm sitting here with half my office out on the street!" Steve said. "I need to get a trailer, get this stuff moved, get some money so I can convince the guy to let me back in. I'm maxed out on the cards, nothing in the bank. Nothing. I haven't even been paid by my client yet, and I'm almost through with the trial."

"Steve—"

"I'm a mess, Ashley, and you're the only one I ever had in my whole life who could put up with me. Can't we just—"

"*We're* a mess," she said. "We're not good for each other."

"I'm just asking"—he looked behind and saw the woman staring at him. She was early twenties, wore her copper-colored hair tightly back. Her black glasses and gray suit gave off a definite professional air. So why was she looking at him?—"for a loan, basically. And one dinner together. Just to talk. No pressure—"

"I can't do it, Steve. I can't forget what it was like. I tried that once and it bit me."

The time he stole a hundred dollars from her purse for a fix. He remembered that clearly. Bad, real bad. "Please—"

"Don't call me again, Steve. We've managed to settle amicably, and I want to keep it that way."

"Ashley, don't—"

She clicked off. Steve dropped his hands to his sides and bowed his head. Eyes closed, he tried to make his brain find a file marked *It'll Be Okay*. But it was gone. Snatched and tossed into the fire pit of lost hopes.

The woman in the parking lot said, "You're not Steve Conroy, are you?"

THREE

He whipped around and faced her. "Who are you?"

"Excuse me?"

"Tell me what you want and why you know my name. And make it fast, because I've got—"

She held up a sheet of paper. "Sienna Ciccone."

"Ciccone?" It sounded familiar. "Ciccone ..."

"Like Madonna."

"Madonna?"

"That was her original last name."

"You a singer?"

"Law student."

Steve shook his head.

"You requested a clerk through DeWitt," she said. "We were supposed to meet?"

Steve held the bridge of his nose. Tried to form a place where all his thoughts could come to rest and keep his head from exploding. "I made a request through DeWitt?"

"It was on the computer. Could have been there from a long time ago."

It very well could have been a long time, and he very well could have forgotten. His memory was Swiss cheese then.

"I'm sorry," he said. "I've got a few things I'm dealing with here."

She nodded and looked at the corner of the parking lot where his office stuff was.

"Yours?" she said.

"Yeah."

"Tell you the truth, I was sort of hoping for a cubicle."

"Look, Ms. Ciccone, I—"

"Sienna. Call me Sienna."

"Things have sort of changed since I put out that request."

"I gathered that."

"I've had a little misunderstanding with my landlord."

"Then we better straighten it out."

31

"We?"

"Did your landlord give you a three-day notice?"

"Uh, no, but I am behind—"

"Let's get your stuff back inside. What's your landlord's number?" She took a cell phone from her hip, flicked it open with her thumb. Steve didn't know whether to be impressed or annoyed. Didn't know if she was full of confidence or just attitude. All he knew for sure was he couldn't pay her.

"I can't hire anybody right now," Steve said.

"I didn't ask to be hired. I asked what your landlord's number was."

"But I—"

A car horn blared. Steve turned, saw he was blocking a Mercedes trying to get in.

"You move your car," Sienna Ciccone said, "while I call the landlord. Number?"

Steve gave it to her, then moved his car. When he got back to Sienna, she was pacing the parking lot, negotiating with a former Serbian policeman, firmly explaining American law to him—"Have you not heard of unlawful detainer, sir?"—and how it would be worth his while to let Steve put his office back together rather than become a respondent—"It's called forcible entry, sir." She also pledged a deposit of rent before Steve could stop her. Not that he would have at that point.

He had no idea what to do. His stuff all over the lot and somebody advocating, actually arguing his case for him. When was the last time anybody had done that? He couldn't recall.

A few minutes later, the building manager unlocked Steve's office door, giving him the evil eye as he did. "We change locks," he said. He was a hairy one. Steve thought he probably had a five o'clock shadow when he was born.

"No worries," Sienna told the manager. "Just give us the key and the authorities won't have to get involved."

The ape handed Sienna the key. Then she helped Steve move the furniture back into his office. All under his admiring eye. She had some muscle on that small frame. Looked like she could pack a punch if she got behind it. There was a little dance in her hazel eyes, but a seriousness too. Like she'd seen plenty of the hard side of life.

It took half an hour to get everything back inside. In the office, sitting with bottles of water — at least the Mad Serb had left Steve's small refrigerator plugged in — he said to Sienna, "Why'd you do all this?"

"You looked like you needed some help," she answered.

"I'll pay you back for the deposit."

"I know."

"But ..."

"Go ahead," she said. "We know each other pretty well now."

"I can't pay you for legal work. I'm sorry. I'd like to be able to pay a clerk for some projects, but that's just not possible right now. You've got pretty eyes."

She blinked. "Whoa. Random."

"I meant it. I wasn't hitting on you." Then what *was* he doing? *Slow down*, he told himself. *You're reacting against Ashley. Don't be a complete idiot.* "So you're at DeWitt?"

"Night program."

"Good for you."

"Nothing noble. I have to work."

"Sorry it can't be me."

"Maybe it will be," she said. "God works in mysterious ways."

"God? I don't think he works at all."

She cocked her head.

Steve said with a smile, "If God existed, would he allow *Deal or No Deal*? I don't think so."

At which point his office phone rang. Steve made a move toward it, but Sienna picked up and said, "Mr. Conroy's office." He liked that, liked her attitude. A little aggressive but without giving offense. Steve watched her eyes as she processed whatever was on the other end. "And what is this regarding? Mr. Conroy is very busy ... Oh? If you'll hold, please."

She covered the mouthpiece and whispered, "I told you God works. You want a chance to make some serious bucks?"

FOUR

An hour later, the woman was gone and Steve was still wondering what had happened.

He'd come back to an office he couldn't get into, with prospects about as promising as a one-legged tap dancer, to find a mysterious but welcome young woman saving his sorry behind.

Not only that, but she'd fielded a call from a prisoner in Fenton named Johnny LaSalle, who had called him with an offer to pay ten thousand dollars.

More than enough to justify a Saturday drive out to Fenton in the morning.

As tantalizing as that possibility was, it was the woman who kept sneaking into his thoughts.

She was obviously sharp. She'd proven that on the fly.

And more than a little good-looking.

Which made him wonder if any woman could love him again, after what he'd done to Ashley, what he'd put her through. He didn't believe in God, but there was some kind of yin and yang thing going on. You mess up over here, you have to pay over there. Flip off a driver on the 101, you're going to get the finger on the 405. It's just a matter of time.

Could somebody trust him again, like Ashley had? More to the point, could he justify that trust?

Not bloody likely. His record was not a good one. And what was the point of hopes after all? You only get them smashed like ants under a boot. The cycle repeats itself. It had ever since he was five years old. He was damaged goods, and there wasn't any God, no warranty from a Creator that guaranteed good working order. He knew that even at five, when he'd prayed and got nothing back but a dead brother.

The cycle, the cycle.

He needed something to get his mind off it.

The monkey was screeching and he knew he'd better call Gincy.

But he wanted to handle it himself, which he knew was wrong. Bad move for recovery. The moment the screeches sound in the background, you call your sponsor.

You don't go play pool. That's a fool's gambit.

So naturally it's the one he took.

His favorite place for a rack was The Cue on Sherman Way, about a mile from his office. It was just past four thirty when he pulled to the curb in front of the place and fed the meter.

It felt good to go in. Here he was among friends. The fellowship of the stick. Here he could shoot around and indulge his fantasy of being a champ at something. Living in a pretend world was a very good thing. When he was snorting, he used to say reality was just an escape for people who can't face drugs. Now that he was clean, the occasional illusion was the ticket. In a pretend world, the shadows couldn't get you.

For a while at least.

He scattered the balls randomly on table six and started making kick shots and cross sides and muttering to his phantom opponent, *I'm the best you've ever seen, Red. Admit it. Up the bet? Sure. Hundred a game?*

He was getting ready to put some hard English on the rock when he heard, "Hey, boy, we don't like hustlers around here."

Steve recognized the voice. Without turning he said, "How's it goin', Norm?"

"You come down here just for me?"

"Right, Norm. We who orbit around you just can't help it."

With face stubble and a wrinkled flannel shirt, Norm Gaylord looked like one of the roving homeless along Topanga. He also looked like what he really was, an Emmy Award–winning TV writer who couldn't get arrested. Steve had met him here at The Cue a few years after Norm's sitcom was cancelled and he was turning to meth to write faster.

Which resulted in the loss of his wife and house. Later, when the cops nabbed him in a buy, he called Steve. Steve got Norm into diversion and out of being prosecuted. Norm was grateful and, like several other clients, still owed Steve money.

"Shouldn't you be in court getting criminals back on the street where they belong?" Norm asked.

"Shouldn't you be writing so you can earn enough to pay me?"

"What is it with you lawyers?" In a high-pitched voice Norm sang, "*Money, money, mo-ney.*"

"You write better than you sing, and I'm not even sure how good you write."

"Thanks, pal."

"How's the job prospects?"

"You want to know or you just blowing methane?"

"Norm, I've got a vested interest in your career now."

"Okay. I got a killer idea. This one's gonna sell. It's called *The Littlest Mayor.* A kid gets elected mayor of a major city."

"And zany hijinks ensue?" Steve said.

"How'd you know?"

"Wild guess."

"This one's got to go. I need it, man."

"You clean?"

"Of course I'm clean!"

"Good."

"You?"

"Yeah," Steve said. Sure. About as clean as a rusty pipe.

"How's the wife?" Norm asked.

Steve shook his head. No verbal requirement here. He'd let Norm in a little closer than most clients. Recognized Norm was a fellow traveler along the troubled road. He'd allowed it to come out that he and Ashley weren't likely to make it. Norm knew all about that too.

"Sorry to hear it," Norm said. "Really, man."

Steve said nothing. He pressed the chalk on his cue a little too hard. Like he wanted to rub some thoughts away.

"So," Norm said, "you want to shoot a ten-game freeze-out?"

Steve put the chalk down with a loud *thwack.* "You kiddin' me? You're betting with what?"

"I'm not gonna lose, so it don't matter."

"Maybe another time. After you've paid me."

"Will you drop that?"

Instead, Steve bent over the cue ball and shot the nine in the corner.

"Very nice shot," Norm said.

"I'll shoot you friendly."

"You buying the beer?"

Steve couldn't help laughing at the audacity, the nerve, the gall. For that reason alone he bought the beers. Norm Gaylord was one of those guys who seemed to be able to charge through life's minefield and somehow come up on the other side wounded, but having everyone else buy his drinks. Steve could use a little of that same luck himself.

Maybe tomorrow would be a new day. If he could make it through the night without scratching the itch, maybe tomorrow would be the beginning of a Steve Conroy upswing.

A ten-thousand-dollar upswing. It was worth a drive.

FIVE

The state prison at Fenton was an hour and a half northeast of Los Angeles. A maximum-security facility, it housed nearly four thousand hard-core felons. A year ago the National Guard had to be called in to put down a riot that left one guard and seven inmates dead.

A racial thing, the news said. Steve knew how true that was. As a deputy district attorney, he'd seen the full racial spectrum pass through the court system and into the jails and prisons. And despite the best efforts and intentions of everyone involved, from the ACLU to the governor of the state, racial separatism was endemic in corrections.

He thought about this on Saturday morning as he drove up Highway 14, got off on the hot flats where he could see the forbidding brown walls, razor wire, and guard towers of Fenton. As far as he knew, he had only one client here. A three-striker named George Clarke who went down for the full term for stealing a CD player. Steve was hoping he wouldn't see Clarke in the attorney room. Clarke hadn't been too thankful for the legal representation he got.

Steve completely agreed with Clarke. Steve was on the candy back then, and it showed. Clarke had a review pending in the appellate court for ineffective assistance of counsel. He was likely to prevail. Then he'd be out for another trial. And Steve's name would get speckled with some more mud.

The price you pay. His last foster father, Harley Rust, used to say that. No free meals in this life. Well, the meal had been served. Plenty of crow. And Steve was still paying.

How long would it last? Who knew? But you had to start someplace, and maybe this would be it. Maybe Sienna Ciccone was some kind of good-luck charm. She's in the office and you get a phone call that has some good money on the other end.

Steve pulled up to the gate and gave his name, driver's license, and bar card to the guard, who checked Steve off a list and told him where to park. He took a spot next to a black SUV, grabbed his briefcase from the backseat. The case had nothing in it but a pad and pen and an apple, but it gave a lawyerly illusion. Steve didn't want to hand his potential new client an instant reason to say, "No thanks, I was actually looking for somebody who seems to know what he's doing."

Steve was buzzed in and escorted through a heavy steel door, then down a yellow corridor to the attorney room of the prison. It was a rectangular chamber containing four heavy desks with aluminum benches. The beige linoleum floor was well scuffed, testimony to the heavy steps of overworked deputies and midlevel lawyers.

The room was empty as Steve entered, except for a deputy sheriff with arms like rolled-up sleeping bags sitting at a special desk with a single, multiline phone. He looked at Steve and made no attempt at conversation. Not that Steve expected any. Here, criminal defense lawyers were considered on the same level as stuff scraped off a farmer's shoe.

Steve sat at one of the tables, opened his briefcase, and pulled out the pad and pen. He wiped a film of sweat off his forehead. At the top of the page he wrote *Johnny LaSalle* and the date. The scratching of the pen seemed all the louder for the silence in the room.

For the next five minutes he jotted random notes, so it looked like he was thinking about the situation.

Actually, he was. Johnny LaSalle was finishing a seven-year stretch for armed robbery. According to the research Steve had done the night before, LaSalle had some sort of white supremacist record. Not much more on that, except that he was allegedly a pretty violent guy. Once beat up a Vietnamese busboy in a bar, sending the kid to the hospital. Was charged with a hate crime. Pretty easy to prove when you're shouting racial slurs as you stomp a guy's head.

The record didn't deter Steve in any way. He knew that when you rep criminals you're not going to get the Vienna Boys' Choir. The most important thing was the criminal defense lawyer's number one rule: Get the fee up front.

A rule he'd forgotten in his representation of Carlos Mendez. But Steve was more than a little desperate at the time. Sort of like now.

Finally the gray interior door opened and a deputy sheriff walked in. Behind him jangled the prisoner.

Johnny LaSalle wore prison whites and had shackled hands and ankles. His hair was cut short. No skinhead. They didn't allow that here. His forearms were covered with dark blue prison tats. Blue eyes in deep sockets made him seem older than he was. The effects of a hard life were inscribed in lines and crags on a face that, in other circumstances, might have been angelic.

The entire effect, from the very start, was electric. Almost mesmerizing. LaSalle had that rare face that could command— *demand*—attention just by showing up. A dangerous kind of face to be around for any length of time.

As he slid onto the opposite bench, LaSalle kept his eyes trained on Steve. Disconcerting to say the least. A typical prisoner's move, Steve knew. Trying to capture the high ground. But even though Steve had seen the move before, it was never as effective as this.

Steve gave him a casual nod. He wanted to make it seem like he could take this case or leave it, even though the thought of a ten-grand retainer kept nibbling at his cerebral cortex, causing twitches.

Steve waited until the deputy attached LaSalle's wrist shackles to the desk and then left through the same door.

"How you doing?" Steve said.

"The scent of hope slips through my fingers," LaSalle said with the hint of a smile.

"Excuse me?"

"The scent of hope."

"Is that Shakespeare or something?"

"Jessica Simpson. You like her music?"

Okay. Weird. Steve had not driven all the way up here to engage in a colloquy about the merits of airhead music. "Mr. LaSalle, you asked to see me."

"Indeed."

"Well, I'm here."

"It's good to see you."

Good to see you? What was that supposed to mean? It felt for a second like the guy wanted to sell a used car or something.

"What can I do for you?" Steve said. "I understand you'll be paroled in a couple of weeks. You need representation on another matter?"

"It's much deeper than that."

"How deep?"

"Real deep, Steve."

Calling him by his first name. A familiarity the prisoner hadn't earned. Cynicism crawled into Steve's gut. This whole thing was starting to feel like a very bad idea.

"I'm not really in a mood to guess what you want," Steve said. "Can you tell me in twenty-five words or less?"

"Easy," LaSalle said. "Let me ask you something first. It's important. I think you'll see why. Do you believe in God?"

The sharp blue eyes, which seemed to have halcyon sources, bore into Steve. He shifted a little on the hard chair.

"I don't see how that has anything to do with anything," Steve said.

"Maybe it does. Maybe it is everything."

"LaSalle, why don't you drop the games? You're starting to hack me off. I can get up and leave, right now."

A corner of LaSalle's mouth went up. "Wait, Steve. Wait. You have to believe in God. Life has no meaning without that. Because if you don't believe in God, you're not gonna believe the rest of it."

Steve looked at his watch. "Suppose I give you five minutes to get to the point?"

"Steve, the heart is deceitful above all things."

"Jessica Simpson again?"

"Jeremiah."

"Jeremiah?"

"In the Bible."

"Look—"

"Do you believe people can change?" LaSalle said. "I need to know that."

"Sometimes," Steve said quietly. He was not exactly Exhibit A in the character-formation department.

"It's harder than you think," LaSalle said. "But it happens. It's a miracle when it does. Do you know about me?"

"Some."

"You know that I used to walk in the darkness?"

"Sounds like a reasonably good summary."

"It's biblical. Listen, the Word of God says if you hate your brother, you walk in the darkness. That's what I used to be like, Steve. I hated. People who weren't my color, I hated. People who were against me, I hated. That's what gave my life meaning. Hate."

"What gives it meaning now?"

"Jesus."

"Okay."

"You don't believe that?"

Steve knew only too well that hard-core prisoners often jump to Jesus as a way to show the parole board what nice little citizens they have become. As soon as they get out, many go back to their merry ways. What Would Jesus Steal?

"Listen," LaSalle said: "'And this is the condemnation, that light is come into the world, and men loved darkness rather than light, because their deeds were evil.' I was in love with my evil, you see? It took a shank to the ribs to get my attention, but God got it. Boy, he dialed me direct."

Steve said nothing.

"It was right here, in the infirmary, where I saw an angel of the Lord. I don't know if I was out when it happened or wide awake. All I know is there was an angel in the room with me and he looked like, I don't know, he looked big and perfect. Scared the living—I was scared, boy, but then he spoke to me. He said, 'Don't be afraid.' Did you know angels say that right out of the box?"

"Never talked to one myself."

"Yeah, they say, 'Don't be afraid,' because man, you will be. But his voice calmed me down and he called me Johnny."

"Had your file, did he?"

LaSalle narrowed his eyes. "This is not something to mock, my man. I'm telling you about a visit from a heavenly being, coming to

me to tell me my life had been given back to me, but I had to follow the living Christ from now on. I was given a choice, don't you
see? And I knew even if I stayed in prison the rest of my life, I was
going to follow Jesus. Right there in that bed I confessed the name
of Jesus to the angel."

"Is that all you confessed?"

"Don't you believe me?"

"Sure." The word didn't sound the least bit convincing, not even
to Steve.

"Then spake Jesus again unto them, saying, I am the light of the
world: he that followeth me shall not walk in darkness, but shall
have the light of life."

Steve placed his palms on the desk for emphasis. "Mr. LaSalle,
let me give you one more shot at this. Why did you call me up
here?"

"To save you."

"To save *me*?"

Johnny LaSalle nodded.

"I don't need saving," Steve said.

"You know you do." LaSalle's eyes burned with an inner fire,
like a prophet or madman or murderer. Maybe he was all three.

Steve put his legal pad back in his briefcase, snapped it shut.

"You do need to be saved," LaSalle said. "I know it."

Steve turned to the desk guard. "I'm through here."

"And now, behold, the hand of the Lord is upon thee, and thou
shalt be blind, not seeing the sun for a season."

The guard picked up the phone and said something.

Steve started to get up.

"Don't go!" LaSalle said.

"Good luck."

The interior door opened and the same deputy returned, looking like he'd just been disturbed from a nap.

Steve was on his feet when LaSalle said, "You won't stay and
talk to your own brother?"

The deputy approached LaSalle.

"Wait a second," Steve said. "What is that supposed to mean?"

"Your brother. He was lost. And now is found."

Steve's chest tightened. The fact that this man would say that, that he knew Steve had a brother at all, needed explanation.

"I'm here for the prisoner," the deputy said.

"I'm not through," Steve said.

"You called it," the desk deputy said. "That's it." He started unlocking Johnny LaSalle's desk cuffs.

LaSalle said nothing, but his face was almost glowing.

"You're one sick puppy," Steve said.

"You just finding that out?" the escort deputy said with a laugh. He pulled LaSalle to his feet. The shackles jangled like loose change.

"Don't believe them, Steve," LaSalle said. "I bless the entire world. I need you." Just before he turned his back he added, "My true name is Robert Conroy. *I am your brother*!"

SIX

The next few moments passed like a slow-motion death scene. The deputy got LaSalle out the door, closed it, and all the while Steve stood mute. Like a statue named *Stupid*.

What had just happened? A prisoner calls him for an interview and knows about his dead brother? Not just that, invokes the name for himself?

That meant this guy had done research, actual research on him. Or had the information fed to him by another. But what sense did that make?

"Have a nice day," the desk deputy said.

Steve was a cocktail of rage and sorrow and dark memories. The butt of a sick joke.

But why would this guy do it? Why go to all that trouble to put the needle in like that?

As Steve stumbled out, all the old memories flooding back, he knew it would be a long drive back to the Valley. He would be thinking of relief all the way, how he used to handle situations like this in the past.

He hit the speed dial as he drove. For his sponsor. Needed him right now.

Gincy answered. "Hey, what's up?"

"You are not going to believe this one," Steve said.

"Try me."

His open invitation to talk, and his promise to listen. That's what he was good at.

Gincy Farguson, his Cocaine Anonymous sponsor, was a former Las Vegas dancer turned body builder and gardening enthusiast. During daylight hours, Gincy installed and serviced home fitness equipment, then volunteered his time helping at-risk youth at a big church in Tarzana.

At forty, Gincy had lines etched in his face that read like a relief map of an improbably hard life. He'd come from a little town in

Georgia, where his father had become the first African American in the county fire department. A father who died in a blaze when Gincy was ten. That was the main reason, Steve decided, that they hit it off. Both were from the brotherhood of the fatherless.

Gincy's big mistake was going for the glamour instead of the gold. "I could have had a job with the fire department myself," he told Steve once. "But I wanted a different kind of light and heat."

Landing in Vegas, Gincy discovered he had been granted two things "by the hand of God." An almost perfect body and the ability to move it. With his movie-star looks—his nickname among the dancers was Denzel—it wasn't long before he landed in the chorus of a Las Vegas revue that went on for seven years.

Which was more than enough time for Gincy to fall into the gaping maw of the high life. As one of the few straight male dancers on the Strip, he had his pick of the female contingent. And because of his natural gregariousness, Gincy got to be a favorite on the party circuit. Cocaine became his drug of choice.

It got so bad he was burning through his salary every month, then having to borrow, and finally having to borrow from the wrong people. Of which there are plenty in Las Vegas.

The debt got too high. One night Gincy was picked up by a couple of thugs and ended up with two broken legs.

No more dancing for Gincy Farguson.

It was while he was in the county hospital that he had what he called a *vision*. When pressed he said it could have been just a very vivid dream, but it didn't matter. It was still as real to him as a live performance of *Chicago*.

In the vision he saw his father walking through flames. But the man wasn't burning. He was actually calm and calling out, "Get out of the fire, Gincy! Get out of the fire!"

When Gincy woke up, he was on the other side of belief. Still in leg casts, he checked himself into the addiction unit of the hospital and began the hard road to sobriety. And faith.

It was fine with Steve, the faith part, as long as Gincy was there when he needed him. Like now.

"I've just been out to the prison at Fenton," Steve said, holding the phone to his left ear and steering with his other hand. "A guy pulled a weird one on me. Claimed to be my brother."

Pause, then Gincy said, "That is weird. Why would he do that?"

"No idea. It threw me. I'm buzzing like a wire."

"All right, all right. Let's get to a meeting."

"I can't right now. I have a closing on Monday. I have to focus."

"You can't if you're feeling this way. Meet me at my place."

"Later. Work first. I just needed to hear your voice. I need you to tell me you'll slap me around if I even think about getting high."

"Are you thinking about it now?"

"Yeah, I am."

"Okay. Listen to me. I am going to slap you. I am going to slap you hard. Right now. *Smack!* Did you feel it?"

"Ouch."

"Good. Now come to my place and—"

"I'll call you later. Maybe you can do that thing you do."

"What thing?"

"Pray."

"Always. But you don't believe it."

"No, but the vibes. Maybe the vibes do something. I'll take it. At this point, I'll take anything."

SEVEN

He got back to his office around one. Blasting a little R.E.M. on the way helped push out thoughts of what had happened at Fenton. Also got his juices flowing, so maybe he could really get ready for the fight on Monday morning. Spin some closing argument gold out of the lousy legal straw he had to work with.

He walked into his office and found it immaculate.

Sienna Ciccone was at the metal filing cabinet, putting some folders away.

"Hi," she said.

Like it was the most understandable thing in the world. "How'd you even get in here?"

"New locks, remember? New keys? I took one."

"Why?"

"You hired me. I wanted to—"

"No," Steve said. "I told you I couldn't hire you, remember? No funds."

"What happened to that ten-thousand-dollar client?"

She wore tan slacks and a casual white blouse. It was more than a little strange to be sharing a small space with a woman again, even if she was just a law student. Suddenly Steve felt shy.

He put his briefcase on the front desk. "Sienna, I appreciate what you've done. But it's Saturday. You shouldn't be—"

"I don't mind."

"Listen. I'm not going to be getting any ten thousand."

"What's up with that?"

"The guy, LaSalle, he just wanted to mess with me."

"Why?"

"I don't know."

"I mean, what'd he say?"

"It was just a big joke."

"Tell me."

"Why should I tell you anything?" Steve's shyness turned to heat. It came on like a flash and he didn't care to cool down. "I didn't ask you to do this, to be here."

"Hey, I thought I helped get you the gig. I thought maybe I'd like to hear about it."

"Well, think again."

She nodded at him, tight lipped, then grabbed her purse and started out.

"Wait a second," Steve said.

"Why?"

"Just hold on." He sighed to gather his thoughts. "I'm sorry. Look, sit down a minute. I guess I owe you an explanation. In addition to the money."

She hesitated, then sat in the chair behind the front desk. Steve took a deep breath. He hadn't told anyone the story in years. He didn't know why he should tell her. Other than that he didn't want her to go.

"When I was a kid my brother got kidnapped. I was five. Two men came in our room and took him."

Her stunned expression didn't need words.

"A couple weeks later they tracked one of the guys. He was some sort of a religious wacko, had a small following. He was living in a shack in the mountains, had Robert with him. That was my brother's name, Robert. When they closed in he set fire to the place rather than get taken. They found two bodies in there, had to ID them by dental records. It was Robert and this guy, a guy named Cole."

"How awful for you."

"The night he was taken, one of the kidnappers told me if I said anything or made a noise, they'd kill Robert. And me. I believed him. But because I didn't say anything, they had plenty of time to get away. My dad never forgave me. He ended up shooting himself."

Sienna looked down.

"So this guy at the prison, LaSalle, finds out about me, has me come all the way out there, and get this, tells me he's my brother."

"Why would he do that?"

"You tell me. Maybe it's a way for some ex-client of mine to get back at me. You know about me?"

"Other than what?"

"You know I was suspended for a cocaine addiction?"

"I didn't know," she said evenly.

"So now you do. And I'm going to sit here today and shake and try to prepare a closing argument. And maybe in my dreams it'll come to me why some slime in state prison wants to jerk me around and say he's my brother."

Sienna leaned forward. "Is it possible he might be your brother?"

"No."

"Wilder things have happened."

"Not this wild. I looked at him. I—" Suddenly he wasn't sure. And he was angry about it. What was this law school irritant doing by suggesting the impossible? "Why don't you run along. I'll get you your money—"

"Maybe we should research this a little—"

"No." Steve slapped the table. "It's just digging up what I want buried."

"But—"

"Just go, will you? Just get out of here."

"Won't you please—"

"Get out. You're … fired." Steve felt like a bad Donald Trump imitation, if there ever could be such a thing.

"I was never hired, sir." Sienna looped her purse over her shoulder and started to leave. She stopped, reached into her purse, and took something out. She tossed it on the glass-topped desk, where it pinged to rest. It was a key.

She left without another word.

Steve picked up the key, looked at it. Then threw it as hard as he could at the far wall. It made a mark, one he could see from all the way across the office. *That's what you're good at, boy. Throwing stuff, making marks on walls and people. Keep it up.*

He saw the face of Johnny LaSalle in his mind and wished he could throw something at it. Make it go away.

EIGHT

Monday morning Steve gave his closing argument in the case of *People v. Carlos Mendez.*

Moira Hanson preceded him, laying out the devastating facts that made Mendez out to be the proverbial toast. Steve had to admit she was good. Poised and professional. A little cold perhaps, but a DDA could get away with that.

Not so the defense lawyer. As Steve got ready to make his argument he kept thinking about the old saying, supposedly uttered by Abraham Lincoln himself. *When the law is against you, argue the facts. When the facts are against you, argue the law. When both are against you, pound the table and shout for justice!*

Facing the jury, Steve thought Honest Abe knew what he was talking about. And as he had no facts or law on his side to speak of, he was going to start pounding the table.

He was simply going to persuade. That was the lawyer's bottom line, after all. You persuaded, you did the best with what you had. As his crim-law prof had said that first year, if you find a nit you pick it. And that was how you "make a noise like a lawyer."

Could he still do it? Could he marshal all his inner resources and put them to work to change minds? For weeks he had kicked the dogs of self-loathing back. They always seemed to bay and snap before and during trial. Now was the final shot, and he told himself to give it everything. Make a noise like a lawyer. At least show the client he was getting his money's worth.

Which, considering Steve hadn't been paid yet, was a lot.

"Ladies and gentlemen, when you took your oath as jurors, you swore to do your duty to see that justice is done. You did not swear to listen only to the prosecutor, or me, or even to the judge alone. You stand in the most important position possible for a citizen in our country. You stand between the awful power of the State and a man who is presumed innocent. That is your role in our system of justice."

51

Steve looked at the jurors for a face to connect with. Number six, a forty-year-old woman who worked for BlueCross insurance, nodded slightly.

"That means you must hold the prosecution to its burden of proof," he said to number seven. "That's a great big burden too. Beyond a reasonable doubt. You know what that's like?"

Steve walked to the prosecutor's table, where Moira Hanson was wearing her best skeptic's expression for the jurors. "It's like there's a great, big boulder sitting here on the prosecution table. Can you see it?" He pantomimed feeling the contours of a gigantic rock.

"It's here, and Ms. Hanson can't just chip away at it, which she tried to do in her summation. No, she can't leave any of it on the table. Not even little pebbles. The rock is still here."

He smiled at the DDA. She glared back. She hadn't been a happy camper when the judge decided to use the traditional jury instructions, called CALJIC. There'd been a revamping of instructions in California, to make them more "user friendly," but some judges were sticking with the tried and true.

Which is what Steve knew best. He turned to the jury once again and said, "And you must also remember that you are the sole judges of the facts. And the testimony. Did you know you don't have to believe a police officer just because he sits in that witness chair? Police make mistakes too. Let's talk about that."

And he did. For half an hour he put the best face on the bad facts that he could. That was his job. Defense lawyer. You don't lie down and die because a prosecutor has a slam dunk.

He finished with, "So remember, ladies and gentlemen, only you represent justice here. Only you. And Mr. Mendez and I know you will do your task well."

This time, more than one head nodded in the jury box. Steve hoped that several members of the Mendez clan, out in the gallery, agreed.

Then it was Moira Hanson's turn to rebut. This would be the last word to the jury from either lawyer. The next step would be instructions on the law from the judge, and then deliberations.

"Do not be fooled by the empty rhetoric of the defense lawyer," she said. "You know, Abraham Lincoln said when the law and the facts are against you, pound on the table and shout for justice."

Steve's face started to burn. He just hoped the jury couldn't see it.

Hanson took just twenty minutes to wrap it all up. In another half hour the judge had given the jury instructions. At 11:57 the judge told the jury to go get lunch and be back by 1:30 to start deliberations.

Steve felt the urge to drink his lunch. He always felt that way at the end of a trial. Last time, in fact, he'd done that very thing and woke up in the parking lot in back of a Safeway.

In the hallway he was surrounded by Mendezes, Carlos's mother taking the lead. She was a fireplug of a woman looking up at him with ever-increasing intensity.

"What happen now?" she said. "What happen now?"

"The jury will come back to deliberate," Steve said.

"How long it take?"

"We just don't know."

"Carlos get out?"

"No, Mrs. Mendez, Carlos is in the lockup."

"When he get out?"

"Um, the jury has to—"

"He get out, right?"

Several Mendez faces looked at Steve expectantly. As if he were Harry Potter and could wave a stick and make everything all right. What he really wanted was an invisibility cloak.

"We have to wait for the jury, so I'll call you when they have a decision," Steve said. "So just try to relax and—"

"No relax! No, no!"

Steve patted her arm and was grateful when a couple of the men took over and led her toward the elevators. But all the while he was thinking it was always true when a jury was out. *No relax.*

NINE

He sought some quiet in the courthouse law library. It was never populated with more than a lawyer or two trying to find that case the judge cited, or the occasional citizen representing himself or trying to find out how to sue his neighbor.

Steve snagged a copy of the *Daily Journal*, the city's leading legal newspaper, and scanned it to pass the time. Made sure his name wasn't in it. *No news is no noose.* Last time he got his name in the paper it was as a disciplinary stat and his career was hanging by the neck from a tree.

On the opinion page there was a column about a couple of horrific gang slayings. It wasn't just drive-bys this time. Two black gang members had been ritually skinned. Their inner works, so to speak, were spread around and their outer casings nailed to a wall.

Steve held in his breakfast. Just when you thought things couldn't get any worse in this world, good old reality comes along and gives you a fresh kick in the teeth. Nice place, the world. That's what cocaine was for, after all. So you could forget you lived here for a while.

Steve went to the editorial cartoon, this one of the US Supreme Court, and was admiring the rendering of Scalia when he sensed someone at his side. He tried to ignore the figure, but when a guy sat down in the chair beside his, Steve gave a quick look.

The guy was looking right at Steve. He wore a black shirt buttoned to the top, but Steve could still see the tentacles of a tattoo above the collar. His hair was blond, cut close to the pate. He had the prison look. Steve had seen enough of that in his career to sense it. Like a bad smell before you see the actual Dumpster.

"Mr. Conroy." Not a question.

"Who are you?"

"I was watching you in there. Not a bad job."

"You a reporter?" Steve asked facetiously.

"In a way," the guy said. "I've got a report for you."

Steve waited as the guy pulled a fat white envelope from his back jeans pocket and laid it on top of the newspaper. As he did, Steve saw some letters tattooed on his left hand, on the webbing between his thumb and forefinger.

"Johnny says go buy yourself a couple of new suits," the guy said. "He wants you to. As a gift."

"Johnny LaSalle?"

"Right."

"My dead brother." In a tone of annoyance.

The guy nodded.

"What's in here?" Steve asked.

"Five large," the guy said. "Another five when Johnny comes home and you come work for him."

Steve's instinct to push the envelope away was overcome by a neon thought blinking, *Ten thousand dollars. Ten thousand dollars.*

Five thousand of which, if the guy was telling the truth, was under Steve's slightly trembling hand. Ten grand could keep more than a few wolves from the door. And a new suit sounded so right just about now. The one Steve was wearing, his best, had elbows you could almost see through.

But he picked up the envelope and tossed it in front of the guy. With a dry throat Steve said, "Not interested."

"No, no," the guy said. "That's yours. Like I said, a gift."

"I don't want any gift from Johnny LaSalle. You can tell him that. Thanks, but no thanks."

"Steve, there is no obligation. Johnny wants to give you a blessing. After all these years."

"And you both can stop calling me Steve. You can tell LaSalle I don't want to hear from him again. Tell him he's a sick man."

Aware that the librarian, a bespectacled man at the front desk, was looking at them with disapproval, Steve lowered his voice. "Is that clear?"

"Please, Steve, this is your brother—"

"Listen." Steve spun in his seat to face him. "There are cops and deputy sheriffs all up and down this building. If you don't leave now I'm going to walk outside and get one of them to explain the law to you."

"So you don't believe Johnny?"

Steve suddenly sensed a security camera on him. In fact, there was. Looking at it only made him more nervous.

This was absurd, something out of a Martin Scorsese movie. People didn't just hand you envelopes with money, let alone somebody representing a guy who was still in prison.

Steve noticed his chair vibrating. And then realized his right leg was twitching.

"Take your money and get out," he said.

"Johnny told me you might react this way. He really is a good judge of character. He's a man of God."

"That's why he's doing time, I guess."

"You do time when bad people are against you."

"Like the police?"

The uninvited guest pulled a folded piece of paper from his shirt pocket. He unfolded it. It was notebook paper, three holes and lines. He put it in front of Steve.

"Johnny wanted you to see this," he said.

Steve looked at it.

> Brother I know I blew you away. I couldn't tell everything at once. I want to tell you face to face when I get out but you don't believe me and I guess I wouldn't either if I was you. Something bad happened back then but not what you think. I didn't die. I'm alive. My real name is Robert Conroy. And just to show you I tried to think of something that only you and I would of known of. That was kind of hard. We're talking 25 years, bro. I don't know how much you remember from that far back but I thought maybe you remember this.
>
> Once upon a time there were two monsters named Arnold and Beebleobble. One was green and one was blue.

Steve's world, inside and out, started spinning. He thought for a second he might pass out. Light was fading and the guy's voice sounded off in the distance.

"The money's yours," he said. "Johnny'll get in touch with you."

He got up and walked out.

TEN

It couldn't be.

It was.

There was no way anybody would know about the monster stories Robert used to tell him. Oh, sure, maybe in a fantasy world of some kind, where coincidences rained like candy drops, this information could have come to a prisoner named Johnny LaSalle.

That was so unlikely.

Suddenly he was back in his old room. With the clown clock on the white chest of drawers and the red ball with the black stars. The way the sheets smelled like Tide and he'd put them up to his nose and breathe in deep.

And Robert, lying on top of the bedsheets, a teller of tales and protector of little brothers. Once, they'd been sitting on the sidewalk one summer day, enriched with two packs of M&Ms and a Mountain Dew from Sipe's Market, courtesy of Mom. Robert wanted to play Nerf football and ran in to get the ball.

Stevie waited on the sidewalk. The day was hot and the Mountain Dew sweet and cold. Sipe's always had the coldest drinks, and it was a good thing the store was so close to home.

A shadow fell across his face and Stevie looked up and saw Cody Messina standing there. The Messinas were a family Stevie wanted to avoid at all costs. They were in some kind of business that involved junk, and their yard was always a stinking mess of rusty parts of things that used to work. Cody was ten, three years older than Robert, and as mean as the Messina's Doberman, Deuce, who was kept on a chain in their backyard but who had enough chain to get to the fence and bare his teeth at whoever walked by.

"Gimme a sip," Cody said.

No way. It wasn't just the principle of the thing, as far as Stevie understood principle. It was the thought of the gross, slobbering lips of Cody Messina on his can of Mountain Dew. There would be no drinking it after that.

Stevie was too scared to say anything. If he said no he'd probably get his jaw unhinged. And if he said yes he knew, even at five, that he'd be giving up too much of his spirit to a common bully.

Sitting cross-legged, he was also not able to get up and run. Even if he did, Cody was big and fast and would catch him as easily as Deuce snatching a tossed tennis ball.

"Gimme it," Cody said.

Stevie didn't move. The Dew was cool in his hands. He tightened his grip on the can.

"I'm gonna pound your head down your neck."

He could do it too. Stevie did not want his head to take that trip. But still he held to the can. He was, in fact, immobile.

Cody started to reach for the can. "Give it!"

Thunk.

Cody's head snapped back. A Mountain Dew, another one, clunked to the sidewalk. Cody slapped his hands on his head, yelping like a wounded puppy.

"Run!"

It was Robert. Stevie rolled right, shot to his feet, took off down Hoover Street. He didn't look back for four blocks. He held onto his Mountain Dew and kept going. When he did finally stop he saw he was alone. No hot pursuit by the hated Cody.

But what about Robert? Had Cody caught him? What would he do to Robert's head?

Stevie ran back, fast, scared that the whole neighborhood would be crawling with Messinas, from the oldest, Red, who drove and smoked and was mean, to the youngest, Danny, only three but who'd just as soon bite you as drool on you.

Any one of that pack could jump out of a bush or trash can. And they could swarm over Robert like cockroaches.

But when Stevie got home there was no one around. No! Carried off! Robert had been captured and was being hauled to the Messinas as fresh meat for Deuce! He'd get his leg chewed off! And it was all Stevie's fault, because he ran away and left Robert for dead!

"Get in here." His mother, standing at the open front door.

"Mom, Robert's in trouble!"

"You both are. Come here now."

Both? Running in, heart thumping, Stevie let out a huge gust of relief. Robert was there. Sitting on the hard wooden punishment chair, his red T-shirt ripped.

"What happened?" Stevie said.

"I bit him," Robert said.

Stevie laughed. The biting Messinas had gotten what they deserved.

"It's not funny," Mom said. "He really hurt that boy. There's going to be hell to pay. Don't think there won't be."

Hell? He could pay that, as long as he still had his head in the same place, on top of his neck.

Yep, Robert could sure throw. He'd nailed Cody Messina with that can of Mountain Dew and changed the course of neighborhood history. No Messina ever bothered them again.

In the law library, the vividness of the memory surprised Steve. It had been a long time since he'd thought about that day, and never so clearly, so emotionally as now.

All because his big brother was still alive.

If Johnny LaSalle was his big brother.

And if he wasn't, how did he know what he knew?

The clerk read the verdict at 4:27 in the afternoon, that same day. The jury had deliberated just two hours.

Carlos Mendez was found guilty of one count under penal code section 12021.

Steve felt his client tense up next to him, as if this was some sort of surprise. There were grumbles from the gallery. The sounds of a family not pleased.

They were sounds only half heard by Steve. He was still dazed by the money and the note he'd been given in the library.

The half awareness was blitzed by Judge O'Hara's voice as he polled the jury, then sent them on their merry way. None of them made eye contact with Steve as they filed out. A few smiled at Moira Hanson.

"Any reason we shouldn't set a date for sentencing?" the judge said.

The defense lawyer's tape player clicked on in Steve's mind. "I move, Your Honor, to set aside the verdict under PC 1181.6."

It was the old insufficiency of evidence section, which gave judges discretion to set aside a jury verdict. The odds of that happening were about the same as the dice coming up thirteen on a Vegas crap table.

"Denied," Judge O'Hara said. "How's August 20?"

Moira Hanson checked her appointment book and said, "That's fine with the People."

Steve didn't check anything but mumbled an okay. He knew he didn't have any appointments coming up. A bottom feeder usually has a calendar as clean and empty as a desert preserve.

As the deputy approached, Mendez looked at Steve with a *now what?* expression.

"There's a sentencing package that needs to be worked up," Steve said. "I'll come see you and we'll talk about it."

"When?"

"I don't know when. Soon."

"Am I getting out?"

Of course not. He was on the way to the slam, do not pass go, do not collect two hundred dollars. Steve said, "I'll do my best."

That didn't inspire any look of confidence on Mendez's face. The same look was on the faces of his family members who jumbled at the rail, chattering in Spanish.

In his own head, Steve's voice sounded far away. He heard himself say something about getting in touch and doing all he could.

ELEVEN

That night Steve had another dance with the demons.

He well knew you never totally get rid of the mind vibe once you've been hooked on blow. You're supposed to call your sponsor the moment you feel the hot claw of craving scratching at your brain. But you've got to decide to do it.

First, you go through a little five rounder with the imps of addiction. You jab at them, but they have punches too. You start to think about driving downtown to the Box, that collection of drug-infested city blocks between 4th and 7th, where a rock can be had for a drive-by and a sawbuck. You think about the night and the easy road to forgetfulness, and you remember how good it feels. Your body starts to vibrate with the remembering.

It's only a second before you make the decision and grab the keys, and once you grab them it's over. You're going all the way, there won't be any turning back.

In a world where your old nightmares come screaming back in the form of a guy who may be your dead brother, not dead anymore but alive, in that world you have a way out. Don't think about things you don't want to think about. Take the quick and easy road and float, get happy, that's all that matters.

Don't grab the keys.

Grab them.

Call Gincy.

Keys.

Once you grab them it's over.

Grab.

Was Robert really alive?

Would it make any difference?

Would it stop the pain?

Or just make it worse? Just dredge up the whole thing again, make it fresh, because there's no going back and revising your history. There's no going back and taking away the horrors. Taking away the memory of when you were fourteen and almost jumped off the cliffs near the Palisades. You were close then, and if it all comes back, might you actually do it?

Was Robert really alive? If he was, and that alone would be enough to blow an unstable mind, could he be saved this time? Given a new chance to live a good life?

Ten thousand dollars. Who cared who was who?

Or remember that first time you chased the dragon? You stopped then and knew it was about Robert. You had that instant insight that you were going to freebase because it was the only way to stop the dreams. And you thought about not going through with it, but then you did.

Make it stop.

Grab.

Steve snatched the keys from his front table and looked at himself in the hall mirror. His hair was sticking out a little. He smoothed it down. The eyes, normally dark brown, seemed almost black, with a rim of fire-engine red around them.

You'll look worse in the morning, pal, but then again maybe you won't wake up. That'd take care of a lot of things.

He jangled the keys and walked out. Down the stairs to the parking area. Jumped in the Ark, his mind already on autopilot. The map in his head was on-screen and would take him to the drug supermarket.

Then the engine wouldn't turn over.

He kept trying and kept getting the grinding in return. Got to where he was screaming at the car to start, cursing at it. Grinding, cursing, screaming. Until his throat got raw.

And then he sat back and started laughing. Hysterically. Steve Conroy was the biggest joke in the world. The butt of a joke, actually. It was enough to keep him laughing all the way back up to his apartment, where he fell back on his sofa, knowing he wouldn't sleep.

TWELVE

Tuesday.

In the morning, Steve had his car towed to a shop and got a loaner. A Camry. After the Ark it felt like he was driving an eyeglass case.

At least he'd managed to stay clean one more night. Nights were the worst. Now, in the light of day, he could pretend he was a lawyer again.

He wanted to be a lawyer. He started out with the plan to be the best. From foster home to college, from college to law school, a great American success story. Going into law, he'd be able to tilt the scales of justice in a way that had been denied him.

In moments of reflection over beer or bourbon, he'd sometimes think he was trying to be Archimedes. Give me a lever and a place to stand and I can move the world. That project alone was enough to keep his mind from the bad things. The yesterdays.

He remembered clearly the day the idea got in his head.

He was ten and his mom was dead and they had a little funeral. His aunt came out from New Jersey, Aunt Kate, the only time in his life Steve ever saw her. She had stringy hair and fat lips. She didn't sit next to Stevie in the chapel. The only one who sat next to him was Mrs. Bloom, who lived two houses down. She was a nice old lady, a widow who his mom used to borrow eggs from.

There weren't more than six or seven others there. His mom was in a casket at the front. Organ music was playing somewhere. It was like in a haunted house movie.

Then a red-faced man with a funny collar came out with this smile on his face. It looked fake. He stood in front of the casket and said, "This was a lady."

He started saying some things about Steve's mom. But he'd never seen this man before in his life.

Then it hit him. For some reason he knew that this guy hadn't ever known his mom at all. That he worked at this place. That he gave speeches about people who were dead. If somebody wanted that kind of thing.

He knew that Aunt Kate had set this up. And he hated her for it.

Then the man stopped talking and invited people to come and view "the dear departed."

What? Get up and look at her?

No.

Yes. Mrs. Bloom took his hand and walked him forward. Behind Aunt Kate, whose wide ride swayed under a blue print dress in a way both sickening and mesmerizing to Stevie.

The waxwork that was supposed to be his mother lay in a white satin hollow. The moment Stevie saw it, a chill that would soon lead to hot tears started swirling in his chest, an iceball behind the sternum.

It couldn't be Mom. She never looked this still. And the grotesque upturn of her mouth was horrifying.

For some odd reason he thought of a flashlight then, how if you put the two batteries in wrong the thing wouldn't light up. No life, no juice. Maybe they'd put his mother in wrong. Maybe if they turned her around in the box there'd be a spark and she'd be alive again.

It was too soon for her to be dead.

He burst out crying. Once the tears started he knew he couldn't turn them off and he pressed them out harder and harder.

Mrs. Bloom put her arms around him. Aunt Kate looked back at him, disgust on her face.

Maybe that was the moment she decided she didn't want anything to do with Stevie. He suspected she was like that anyway.

Stuff happened after that. Mom's possessions went to Aunt Kate. She left the trunk with the pictures, and Stevie raised such a stink he somehow got to keep it. When he went into foster care, they let him bring the trunk.

He would never give that up. They'd have to put him in a casket if they ever wanted to get it.

When he got to his office, he retrieved the envelope with the money, opened it, and spread the bills on his desk.

Fifty crisp Benjamins.

Probably dirty. The fruit of some sort of crime. Maybe even counterfeit.

Or maybe laundered.

If laundered, clean. And if clean, he could spend it.

He decided to drink it over. Pulled out the half-empty bottle of Jim Beam. But as he started to pour, something stopped him. A little voice. Maybe it sounded like Sienna Ciccone. Maybe he wanted it to sound like her. Whatever, he stopped and tried to keep a clear head.

Johnny LaSalle had told him something only his brother would have known. Steve did remember the stories Robert used to tell. Arnold and Beebleobble. Names that would make him cry when he was seven and eight and missing Robert terribly. Knowing he helped put Robert in the house that got burned down.

What about that? Could it really have been another kid in there? But the dental records. What about the records?

Might there have been a mistake?

Or something else. Steve's brain started writing screenplays for Oliver Stone. This would all mean conspiracy.

Data is what he needed now. He put the bills back in the envelope and woke up his computer. Robert had died in Verner, California. Steve googled the coroner's office in the county where Verner was situated. Came up with a number for the county sheriff.

Called. Got a receptionist. A woman.

"I'd like to speak to the coroner's office," Steve said.

"This is it. The sheriff is the county coroner. Would you like his voice mail?"

"Maybe you can help me."

"I'll try." Her voice was young and informal.

"I'm interested in the records of an autopsy from July of 1983."

"I can connect you to Lieutenant Oderkirk. He's the chief deputy coroner."

"Yes. Please."

"One moment."

Steve hefted the envelope of bills as he waited.

"Oderkirk."

"Hi, my name's Steve Conroy. I'm a lawyer in LA."

"Sorry to hear that."

"We're not all bad."

"Kidding. What can I do for you?"

"I'm interested in an autopsy that was done back in 1983. Are those records available?"

"Sure. Back then they'd be on paper, but we're in the process of putting them on microfiche. Is this some official business?"

"For me it is. It was my brother, Robert Conroy."

"Oh." Pause. "Well, let me see what I can come up with. You have the exact date of death?"

"It was July of 1983. That's all I know. In a town called Verner."

"Sure. Mountain town. I can look into it. What was the name again?"

"Robert Conroy."

"All right. You have a fax?"

Steve gave him the number.

"Let me see what I can do," Oderkirk said. "I'll try to get it to you by close of business. If not, then tomorrow."

"Anything you can do. Thanks."

"You bet."

Steve thought about calling Ashley again. This time he wouldn't be asking for money. But he'd be able to tell her about LaSalle and the prison and five thou. She was really the only one he trusted.

But he decided against it. Whenever he called her now, there was part of him hoping she'd say, "Come on home, Steve. All is forgiven." He had to get over that, had to accept the fact his marriage wasn't going to be put back together again.

The door opened and Milos Slbodnik walked in as if he owned the place.

Which he did.

"So," he said. "Here you are." Slbodnik was in his fifties, with a head like an unshaved coconut. He seemed to have hair coming out of every cavity and crevice. His substantial pot belly masked the fact that he was once a wrestling champion—a fact he loved to repeat as often as he demanded rent.

"A knock on the door would be appreciated," Steve said.

"You making good or what?"

"You've got a payment."

"I got a nephew."

"Excuse me?"

"You make threat with law, I got law."

"Mr. S, I just finished a case. I'm due to get paid." Steve shot a quick look at the envelope on his desk. "And I may just have a major new client. Before you file anything, give me at least a week of good time."

The landlord lowered his substantial eyebrows. "One week. And what you are owing is four thousand."

"I got it."

"I hope you got it."

He grunted and left.

THIRTEEN

Steve's fax bleeped at 4:20. The cover page had Oderkirk's name on it. And then a report, which began with a doctor's letterhead.

Walker C. Phillips, M.D.
Pathology
Traynor Memorial Hospital
Verner, Calif.

Re: County Coroner's Case #83–015
Name: Robert Conroy
Age: 7 years
Date of Death: 07-14-83 at 0122
Date of Autopsy: 07-16-83 at 1530
Place of Autopsy: Bruck Mortuary
Witness: Leon Bruck

CAUSE OF DEATH:
    CARDIAC AND RESPIRATORY FAILURE
    due to
    SECOND AND THIRD DEGREE BURNS OVER 85%
        OF BODY

EXTERNAL EXAMINATION
The body is that of a normally developed Cau-
casian juvenile measuring 4 feet 5 inches in
length and weighing approximately 95 pounds.

Steve stopped then, swallowed hard. Saw on the movie screen of his mind the little charred body of his big brother. *If it was Robert.* The report went on for four pages with medical jargon relating to different bodily organs. Steve flipped through them, but stopped for the final paragraph:

A review of the ante-mortem dental records
revealed recent tooth loss at the site noted on
the victim (see exhibit). This information in
addition to routine odontological forensic land-
marks aided in concluding a positive identification of the victim.

So there had been a dental ID. Plus, his mom must have seen the body. Steve couldn't ask her about it now, and she never spoke about it to him while she was alive. She did everything she could to give Steve a normal life. She just wasn't able to dig deep enough.

Steve guessed nobody could have. You're pretty much alone in this world and you're dealt certain cards. Some people pair up aces or get a flush draw. Others get nothing, and draw nothing.

You deal with it.

Right now he had to deal with five thousand and the mystery of Johnny LaSalle. How could he be Robert in light of this autopsy report? If he was, then somebody messed up on the ID of a dead kid's body. The body in Robert's grave would be somebody else. That was too wild to believe.

Stranger things had happened. But if LaSalle really was Robert, would Steve want to get to know him? He was split down the middle, like a crack in a house foundation. If LaSalle was Robert, maybe Steve could root out the dark inner core that had been weighing him down for a quarter century.

On the other hand, the guy was a convicted felon. A bad guy. Would he want to think of Robert this way?

The five thousand, which had a promise of doubling, was helping Steve make the decision. He was a lawyer. He represented bad people all the time. Why couldn't he do the same here? No matter who LaSalle turned out to be, he was a paying customer.

And that sounded pretty good.

FOURTEEN

A week went by. Steve didn't hear from LaSalle or his buddy, but he did spend their money.

He gave Slbodnik another check, one that wouldn't bounce. And bought a new suit. Not an expensive one. Off the rack. But it at least made him feel like he was on the way up again.

There was a DUI that settled on Monday. If it had gone to trial, Steve would have been able to get another fifteen hundred dollars from the client. But he well knew most of the time that things settled. DUIs were a volume business. You could scrape by if you got a lot and pled out most. But this was the only DUI on Steve's plate. He started counting the days when LaSalle would get out and hand him five more grand. At the very least he could have a good long talk about what happened, what kid was burned in that fire. And why LaSalle was contacting him now, after all these years.

Steve spat out a form motion for reduced sentence and credit for time served, to be used in the Mendez sentencing.

On Thursday afternoon he was in his office and got a call.

"Wanted to check in," Sienna said. "I hadn't heard from you."

"What? Was I supposed to call you?"

"I'm checking to see if you're okay."

"Sure I'm okay. Why shouldn't I be okay?" He stopped himself. "Look, sorry, okay? I was sort of on the downslope back there. Now maybe I'm on the upslope. A paying client and everything."

"LaSalle?"

"You've got a good memory."

"It was only a week ago."

"Yeah, LaSalle."

"What's he want?"

"I don't know yet. He's not out."

"You may need some help."

Steve laughed. "You would still consider working with me? After the way I treated you?"

"Let's just say I'm still looking for some work."

"When do you want to start?" He imagined her walking into his office again, saw her at the door. Keep hope alive, Reverend Jackson.

"Anytime," she said.

Go for it. "How about now?"

"Now?"

"How long will it take you to get here?"

An hour, as it turned out. She was dressed in a soft blue blouse with a silver cross necklace, and jeans. She had her hair down. It was long and silky. Made Steve think of a Fourth of July picnic, and the green flecks in her eyes were sparklers.

"Do you know anything about dead bodies in California?" Steve asked.

"It's nice to see you too," she said.

"Come on in." He closed the door behind her. "The law of exhumation. As in, if I want to have a body exhumed, what do I do?"

"You want me to find out?"

"That's what I hired you for, isn't it?"

"Hired?"

"I'll cut you a check right now."

As she typed away at the computer, researching in a California-specific legal database, Steve looked at her silver cross.

"So, are you a Catholic like Madonna?"

She kept her eyes on the screen. "Nobody's a Catholic like Madonna."

"Good point. Catholic?"

"No."

"Fundamentalist? Evangelical?"

"Christian."

"Theocratic government type? Or laid-back, pro-choice type?"

She cast a quick look at Steve. "You want me to research here, or talk about religion?"

"You ever heard of multitasking? Come on, I'm interested."

"You know, don't you, that under California law you can't ask me that question."

"As a basis for employment. I'm just asking as a fellow human being. I still qualify there, don't I?"

She stopped typing. "Okay. You have to file a request with the court and cc the county coroner's office. There's a form with points and authorities. You want me to print it?"

"You're very good," Steve said.

"I'll take that as a yes." She hit the print command and Steve's printer started spitting pages.

"Maybe now would be a good time to formalize our agreement," she said. "How does fifty an hour sound?"

"Expensive."

"I'll take that as a yes too."

"On a per project basis," Steve said. "I don't want you billing me while you're playing golf. You can do that after you pass the bar."

"Done," she said.

He would have paid her twice that. Because he wanted her around. He was liking her. She was smart and attractive. Not surface-level beautiful like some airbrushed model on the cover of *Vogue*. Hers was a more substantial allure.

Like Ashley's. She was an Ashley type, and he was on the rebound.

So what? What was wrong with a rebound? It could be the best thing in the world bouncing your way, and you could miss it, and he had missed so many things already. Years of missing things, feeling things were just out of reach—like a sense of *normalcy*. Big deal. Rebound. Take it. Start majoring in the art of forgetting Ashley.

"It's almost dinnertime," he said. "You have any plans?"

She narrowed her gaze. "It's also not wise for an employer to make a social move."

"You going to sue me?"

"I am going to go home. I'll be available next week."

"For dinner?"

"For research. Thanks for the check. Are you ready for Monday?"

"What's Monday?"

"Mendez sentencing."

"Oh, right. As ready as I'll ever be."

"If you need me, you know the number."

FIFTEEN

Steve almost called her Monday morning. But that would have been a little too obvious.

Carlos Mendez never had a chance of getting a reduced sentence. He did collect some credit for time served in custody. But his home for the next five years was going to be the California Men's Colony north of San Luis Obispo.

News which was not greeted with good cheer by the extended Mendez family.

Mrs. Mendez started in just outside the courtroom doors. "You lying son of a—"

"Excuse me, Mrs. Mendez—"

"Lie, lie, lie!"

"Ma'am, I never lied—"

"You say Carlos come home!"

"Ma'am, I—"

"You say it!"

"No, ma'am, I said there would be an appeal—"

"I no talk to you no more!"

"Ma'am, there's a little matter of the bill. I—"

"Liar!"

She turned her back and walked toward the elevators. The gaggle grumbled and cursed in low tones, words in Spanish that Steve didn't have to understand to know.

Which left him with a dicey proposition. He could try to squeeze the Mendez family for the fee, but that would be a long and probably uncollectible prospect. Or he could just let it rest. He hadn't been officially fired from prepping the appeal, but he wasn't going to do an ounce of work until he got something in the coffers. He guessed she'd cool off and come back for more.

The very picture of wishful thinking.

All he had now was Johnny LaSalle, who had retained him for he didn't know what.

Steve learned in recovery that idleness is opportunity. And his experience a few nights before alerted him to how close he was to a fall. If he was going to continue practicing law, he knew he had to do everything to keep from falling into the powder again.

In his car he had a booklet and looked up a meeting. When he'd been forced into recovery by the State Bar, he at first refused to go to a traditional twelve-step program. They were all based on the "higher power" idea, and he didn't buy that. But that was all he could find in the Valley, so it started as a matter of convenience. What saved him was a good sponsor, and that, he decided, mattered more than what people believed about powers, higher or lower or nonexistent.

The Ark had been repaired by his genius mechanic, Thomas Charles, who could make tin foil run. He drove to the meeting, which was in the fellowship hall of a Methodist church on Winnetka. At the meeting, ten of them sat in the traditional circle. People could share their tales. Steve passed. Just listened. Get through another day, that's the ticket.

His cell vibrated near the end of the meeting. He walked quickly outside and took the call.

"Steve?"

He knew immediately who it was. "LaSalle?"

"Hey, I'm out early," LaSalle said. "How do you like that? Three days off for good behavior."

"Where are you?"

"Reseda. The Wendy's right on the boulevard. You know how long it's been since I've had a really good burger?"

"Wendy's?"

"Hey, compared to where I was. How long 'til you can get here?"

Johnny LaSalle was dressed in jeans and a blue Hawaiian shirt with pineapples and sunsets and swaying palms. He looked rested. Or relieved. He smiled broadly and when Steve got to his table, Johnny threw his arms around him. It was the strangest feeling

Steve could ever remember. Being hugged by a corpse, embraced by a nightmare that had broken into a waking dream.

"We have a lot of catching up to do," Johnny said.

"You're right."

"Can I order you something? It's on me."

Steve shook his head.

"You mind if I finish these?" Johnny LaSalle had some french fries spread out on a wrapper, covered with ketchup. "The fries in the joint are terrible. I think they get them from McDonald's Dumpsters all over the state and microwave them for the inmates."

It was hard for Steve not to smile at the relish with which Johnny consumed the fatty slivers. And it was hard to deny the magnetic rays that came from his presence. He thought of that character Alec Baldwin played in that movie about the real estate salesmen, the one with Jack Lemmon. Baldwin had one scene but practically stole the whole picture.

Steve reminded himself that Baldwin was something like the devil in that scene. Tread carefully.

"What should I call you?" Steve said.

"Johnny's fine. I've been Johnny longer than Robert."

"This is so strange."

"I know, Brother. I know." Johnny picked up three fries at once, downed them, spoke around them. "How about I just tell you what happened?"

"Please," Steve said, noticing how jittery he was. His past was about to come flying in on all cylinders. Could he handle it?

"First," Johnny said, "some of the good things. Remember me teaching you how to throw a baseball?"

Steve thought a moment. "I'm not sure."

"We were at the park near the house. I remember that park. It had two baseball diamonds."

"Right. Raintree Park. It's still there as far as I know."

"And I told you, this I remember, that you had to reach all the way back with the ball. Do you remember me telling you that?"

Steve had no recollection. "I'm sorry. I was just five."

"How about this. Do you remember the Sesame Street character you were afraid of?"

"Sesame Street. Now that I do remember."

"Let me tell you," Johnny said. "It was the two-headed monster. With the horns. You used to hide your face when you saw them."

That was right. That was exactly what Steve did. He never forgot the two-headed monster. You don't forget the things that scare you as a kid. Or the losses you suffer when you're five years old.

Johnny LaSalle had to be Robert. Had to be, or else he was the coolest liar on earth. Steve had seen some pretty cool ones before, but not like this. The echo of doubt was fading, but Steve wasn't ready to stop listening. Still, Johnny's face had changed. A moment before, Steve thought it potentially menacing. Now it seemed soft and open. Even vulnerable.

Quite unexpectedly, tears pushed at Steve's eyes. He bit down and fought them back.

"Hey," Johnny said. He put his hand on Steve's arm.

"Sorry. You just don't know ..."

"I think I do. Listen, Bro, just listen. Life is a veil of tears, as they say. We're part of that. But there's a way out. Let me talk a minute."

I want you to talk, Steve thought. *I want you to talk your way back into my life and talk out all the pain. And talk fast so I don't just burst the dam here.*

"Here's what happened," Johnny said. "The guy who took me was named Cole."

"Clinton Cole," Steve said. "I looked up the story when I was a teenager."

"Then you know a lot of it."

"Not really."

Johnny said, "Here's how it went down. Cole was a guy who thought he was a demon. A chief demon of Satan. And it was his job to raise up apprentice demons. That meant little boys. Like me. He found me because he knew our father, did some construction with him. He decided I was going to be one of his boys."

"Why didn't he take both of us?"

Johnny shrugged. "I never got to ask. He wrapped me up and the next thing I knew I was in this place in the mountains, a real dive of a shack. Terrible."

Steve swallowed hard. "Did he ..."

Closing his eyes, Johnny nodded. "Yeah. Thank the good Lord above it never happened to you, Steve. It didn't, did it?"

"No."

"Well, somewhere along in there, I got rescued. By some guys who knew about Cole, knew what a bad guy he was. Some people might have called these guys a gang of some sort, but they were like family to me. A man named Eldon LaSalle took me in. Do you know that name?"

"I don't think so."

"All right. I'll tell you more about him later. One step at a time."

"Why didn't this man bring you back to us?"

"It's complicated. I don't remember a lot from that time. I just know Cole had done a real number on me. Steve, I was really screwed up. Eldon LaSalle treated me like his own son. But he could only do so much. I got into trouble. No excuses. That's just the way it was."

As he spoke, Steve noticed him looking this way and that, never keeping his eyes locked on Steve for any length of time. Steve knew that's how long-term prisoners act. In the slam they have to constantly be looking around in order to survive.

He could scarcely imagine what Johnny—Robert—had been through to this point in his life.

"I remembered you," Johnny said. "But by the time I was fifteen, sixteen, I was into my own deal and I didn't think about the past. But then things changed."

Steve said, "Whose body was that in the fire? And how did they make it an ID on you? I have the autopsy report and it says—"

"You have the autopsy report? How'd you get that?"

"I asked. The deputy coroner faxed it to me. It used dental records to make a positive ID on Robert Conroy."

Johnny frowned. "I've never seen that. I don't even know who it was in that shack. The kid I mean. The man was Cole. And good riddance."

He looked down and was silent for a long moment. Then he looked at Steve. "I've paid my debt to society. At least that's what they tell me. But this time I'm not going back. I want to turn my life completely around. It started inside when I found the Lord. How much do you know about my record?"

"Some."

"I was into an Aryan thing. Thugs. That's what we were. Pretty heavy into it. But Jesus broke through all that."

Steve said nothing.

Johnny said, "Do you know the story of Paul and the road to Damascus?"

"Some kind of light, right?"

"Blinded him. Got his attention. That's what happened to me in that prison infirmary. Only I didn't go blind. For the first time in my life, I could see. Saw all the bad stuff I'd done, saw that I was going to die soon if I didn't get my life together. No, that's not what I mean. I mean I couldn't get my own life together so it had to be from God. From Jesus. And I got on my knees and prayed. And I got saved, man. I got saved."

"That's great," Steve said.

"You're not a believer then."

"It shows?"

"I can hear it in your voice. Or not hear it, as the case may be. Well, let me tell you, you've got to come to the Lord, Brother. It's the only way."

"Let's keep it on you for now. What are your plans?"

"That's where you come in. I want you to be my lawyer."

"Hopefully you won't need a lawyer anymore."

Johnny shook his head. "They won't give up. The feds. They hate us. And the lawyer I had before this was a lying sack of"—he grimaced—"was just no good. I landed in prison because of him. I have never had a lawyer I could really trust. Who would bleed for me if he had to, and who I would bleed for. Until I got saved, I never would have thought this way. But now I do. That's why I came to you after all these years, Steve. Family. That's what it's all about."

Steve took a breath, trying to process the whole thing. For a moment he felt like Jimmy Stewart in that Christmas movie, getting a chance to go back after jumping off a bridge. But that was a movie and this was a Wendy's in Reseda.

"Rob—Johnny, I'd like to help, but federal's a major deal—"

"Say you will. Just say it."

"You need somebody who specializes—"

"There's more to it. I don't just want you to be my lawyer. I want somebody who can guide me on the outside, help me get on the right track. But most of all ..." He paused, then took a deep breath. "Most of all I want you to be my brother again. For the rest of our lives."

Steve couldn't speak for a long moment. It was like the moment was frozen in time, yet rushing by like a bullet train. And he had to grab on now. If he didn't, it would pass, and with it the last chance to make everything right again.

"Of course I'll help you, Johnny."

With a relieved grin, Johnny said, "I was hoping for that. Knowing I have you to count on will make all the difference in the world."

He put his hand out. Steve shook it. A sealed deal.

And then Steve couldn't hold back any longer. The tears came. His body shook and he put his head in his hands.

He felt Johnny's hand on his back. "Hey, it's all okay," Johnny said. "It's all okay."

Dear God, he wanted that. He wanted it to be more than that.

He wanted his brother back, and now here he was and the tears would not stop.

SIXTEEN

Steve didn't turn the lights on when he got back to his apartment. He felt if he did he might shatter the delicate, glassy hope he'd allowed to form on his unsteady insides.

Once, when he and Ashley knew they were heading toward the end but had not yet formulated the words, Steve suggested a trip to Napa. Ashley loved the wine country, and Steve thought a last-ditch trip together might mend at least the edges of the fabric of their marriage. Ashley almost didn't go. But he persuaded her, and all the way up on the plane, and in the rental car, he chose his words so carefully lest he ruin what he knew was his final chance.

The trip went well, better than expected. At one of the wineries Ashley remarked how much she liked the logo—a centaur holding a cluster of grapes. When she went to the restroom, Steve bought two expensive wine glasses with the logo in gold and had the clerk hold on to the box. When they left, he told Ashley he'd be right out, and he got the box and held it behind him as he went to the car.

She smiled at him.

He presented the glasses to her as a gift, and she was pleased. She kissed him, a warm kiss like they hadn't done in months. It could happen, it could heal. He allowed himself to believe it.

Then, just a week later, it was all bad again. The coke did it. It always did. After an argument one night, Steve went to the kitchen, to the sink to throw water on his face. He was careless, his hand hit one of the wine glasses with the centaur logo. Ashley had put them out, but they never got around to pouring the wine.

The glass shattered on the counter.

The shattering sound hit him in the gut like a cannon blast. His insides were like the shards of glass, strewn, irreparable.

It had been so over-the-top symbolic he almost laughed.

Then he heard mewing.

Steve took a small bowl of milk down to the courtyard of the Sheridan Arms Apartments to feed Nick Nolte.

Nick Nolte was a scruffy, homeless cat. Steve had started feeding him a few months back and couldn't get rid of him. Not that he'd tried. Nick's fur was matted and wild and stuck out at odd angles. Steve decided he looked like that mug shot of Nick Nolte when he got arrested for DUI some years back.

Thus, the name.

Nick met Steve at the bench just inside the apartment building gates. He seemed to have a lot of bad stuff in his background too.

Steve supposed that's why he and the cat got along.

"What's up, Nick?" He put the bowl down and let the cat go to it.

"Hey, you'll never guess," Steve said. "I met my long-lost brother today. Can you even believe that? I haven't told you the whole story, but you wouldn't believe it anyway."

Nick Nolte was concentrating on the milk.

"I mean, you guys have nine lives, right? So maybe it isn't such a big deal to you. But, pal, this is a big deal for me. Let me try to explain it to you. You got it easy. You chase mice and squirrels, and then you eat. You don't have to think. We have to think. That's the breaks of evolution, Nick. Sorry about that. If it was up to me you'd be the owner of a convenience store. Or a psychiatrist. You'd be a good psychiatrist, Nick. You listen and don't talk much. And you roll with the punches."

Right now, he was rolling with the milk. Steve could hear the *womp* of a stereo system blasting 50 Cent. No doubt the gangsta wannabe in number seven. He was a white kid, maybe twenty-two, with the fake swagger of the middle-class pretender. The less Steve saw of him, the better.

"So all of sudden, today, I feel like there might be a reason to keep getting up in the morning. I'm still in shock. You got to understand, Nick, I've been living with this thing in my gut for twenty-five years. That's a long time. Can you please explain to me the complex I've got?"

Nick lapped with rhythmic indifference.

"Maybe I'm cat-atonic. Maybe I'm feline fine."

No response.

"This is quality material here, what's up with you?"

"Quit feeding that devil cat."

Mrs. Edna Mae Stanky was standing behind the bench. Steve hadn't heard her wheel up. She was on oxygen and had a tank on wheels and plastic tubes up her nose. At somewhere north of seventy years, she spent her days and evenings patrolling the grounds, looking for something to complain about. Steve knew this to be true, because he'd been Stankied on numerous occasions.

"You keep feeding 'im," Mrs. Stanky said, "he'll keep coming back."

"I'll make sure he behaves, Mrs. Stanky. How you feeling tonight?"

"He's got disease, you can tell by lookin' at 'im. We got kids who play down here."

"Nick is as gentle as a ... he won't hurt anybody."

"Nick? Who's Nick?"

"The cat."

"I need some Afrin. Would you run to the Rite Aid and get me some Afrin?"

Steve knew she also patrolled the grounds looking for people to run errands for her, people who weren't her immediate family, her immediate family being those who largely stayed away. It struck Steve then that Mrs. Stanky and Nick the cat had a little more in common than she realized.

"Sure, Mrs. Stanky. I'll pop right over."

"And quit feeding that devil cat."

Nick looked up from the bowl, singularly unconcerned.

"And I'm going to get somebody to turn off that devil music."

Steve waited until the old woman wheeled off, then gave Nick a quick pat. "Hey, I've got a job. I'm a nasal spray delivery man. Aren't you proud?"

Nick turned his backside to Steve and started off toward another end of the courtyard. For a moment Steve envied him. Eat, drink, and be furry. Wander the earth without memory. Rely on the kindness of strangers.

Then he heard, "Mr. Conroy?"

Two men in suits had entered the courtyard from the front. They looked like government types. One was tall, with thinning, sandy-blond hair. The smaller one was well on the way to male-pattern baldness and didn't look happy about it. He didn't look happy about anything.

"Do I know you?" Steve said, not standing up.

The tall one took the lead. He was about forty and whipped out a leatherette case, flipped it open. Showed a credential.

"My name's Issler, and this is Weingarten. Mind if we talk?"

"What did you just flash?" Steve said.

"We're investigators for the US Attorneys Office."

"FBI?"

"Special Task Force. Can we—"

"You guys come to my house?"

"Apartment, isn't it?" Issler said.

"What's this about?" It had to be about Johnny, but this was too soon.

"Maybe we could go inside," Issler said.

"Maybe not," Steve said.

Issler looked at Weingarten, who looked even unhappier now.

Issler said, "Look, we don't want to conduct business out here, do we?"

"Tell me why I'm listening to you," Steve said. "Then I'll tell you whether we'll keep talking."

"It's about Johnny LaSalle, sir. I believe you saw him today."

"Whoa. You were surveilling me?"

"If you don't mind, Mr. Conroy, not out here."

"What kind of procedure is this?"

"Please, sir—"

"I have an office." Steve got to his feet. "You want to see me, call my receptionist and make an appointment."

"You don't have a receptionist," Weingarten said.

"I want to know why you were surveilling me. I want to know why you seem to know about my office. And what's your interest in Johnny LaSalle?"

"Are you his attorney?" Issler said.

"Why don't you tell me. You seem to know everything else."

"This is really not very efficient for us. Can we please step into your apartment?"

"Me and William Pitt say no."

"Excuse me?"

"William Pitt. They don't teach you guys about William Pitt at Quantico?"

Issler said nothing. Weingarten was unhappy again.

"William Pitt," Steve explained, "stood up on the floor of parliament and said, 'The poorest man may, in his cottage, bid defiance to all the forces of the Crown.'"

"What is that supposed to mean?" Weingarten said.

"It's the basis of the Fourth Amendment," Steve said. "And it means unless you have a warrant, I don't have to let you in. I don't have to talk to you. And our little interview is over."

"Shame," Issler said. "We wanted to help you."

"Sure you did."

"We'll be back," Weingarten said.

"Better have a judge's approval," Steve said.

Issler nodded. "We will."

They turned their backsides to Steve. Just like Nick, he thought. But these cats had sharp teeth. Johnny LaSalle was involved in something federal, and the US Attorneys Office didn't waste any time putting a tail on him.

There was something Johnny LaSalle had not shared with his brother, but his brother was going to find out.

SEVENTEEN

As he drove to Rite Aid, Steve wondered if the two agents were following him. He even wondered if they were watching him buy Afrin, pay for it, drive back. A hot sense of paranoia settled over him, like a flu.

He'd only been involved with feds once before and hated every part of the experience. Especially their sense of entitlement, their unspoken expectation that all should bow before their mighty authority. But they still put their pants on one leg at a time, unless Quantico was teaching them new tricks.

So having a couple of agents show up at his *sanctum sanctorum* was not his idea of a great way to finish the night.

Mrs. Stanky was waiting for him at her open door, arms folding over her oxygen tubes. "What took you so long?" she said.

"I'm sorry, Mrs. Stanky. I had something come up."

"You mean those men? Who were they?"

"Oh, just some gentlemen with questions."

"Questions? What kind of questions?"

"Mrs. Stanky, let's get you sitting down." Steve had done this several times before. The excitable old woman, a former grade-school teacher, needed to keep her blood pressure down.

He took her arm and guided her into the apartment, which smelled of hard-boiled eggs and walnuts. She resisted only slightly.

"I have a right to know what's been going on outside my door," she insisted. "Were they police?"

"No, not police. Now why don't—"

"FBI?"

"You're a curious one, aren't you?"

"What did they have questions about?"

"Feeding stray cats. I guess you were right to make a federal case out of it."

"You're not making sense."

"Not the first time," Steve said. He got her settled on the brown sofa with red throw pillows, then opened the Afrin spray for her, putting the bottle on the coffee table.

"There," Steve said. "You need anything else?"

"How come you have the FBI after you? What have you been doing?"

Resigned to his fate, Steve said. "Now don't you worry. You know I'm a lawyer, right? It's just a business call. I may be able to help those gentlemen on a case." *Or not.*

"Why did a nice young man like you become a lawyer?"

"Oh, well, I guess it's the only profession that would have me."

"You could have been something respectable."

"Like a teacher maybe?"

"That's right. Molding the young. Setting an example. Instead of trying to bend the rules."

Steve cleared his throat. "I better get back. Are you all right?"

"Turn on the TV for me, will you?"

"Sure." Steve looked for a remote, found the tail end of it sticking out from under one of the throw pillows. He clicked the tube on.

"Anything you want to watch?" he asked.

"See if you can find a *Matlock*. I haven't seen *Matlock* in a long time."

"Uh, I'm not sure I can do that."

"Can you find anything close?"

He did the best he could, which was an old *Law & Order*. That seemed to satisfy Mrs. Stanky.

He thought about his mother just then. She'd been a TV watcher near the end. Couldn't do much else as the cancer ate away at her. But whenever he would visit her at hospice, after school, she'd always want him to read to her.

Her favorite was Dickens. Steve read her *David Copperfield*. She'd smile and close her eyes and drift off to sleep. Maybe dreaming of Peggotty and Barkis, whom she loved. "Barkis is willin'" made her laugh.

The last time he'd read to her, the night she died, her eyes never opened. He was reading the part where Aunt Betsey faces down the Murdstones. A good scene to end on, he thought. He cried for three hours after he left, before Mr. Casey, his first foster father, told him to shut up or he'd do the job himself.

So a little *Law & Order* to comfort an old woman hooked up to a tank. Not much, but maybe not so bad when you got right down to it.

She asked if he'd like to stay and watch. He waited until Jerry Orbach started grilling a witness. Always good, that Orbach. At the commercial Steve patted Mrs. Stanky's hand and said, "I think they can win this one without me."

Mrs. Stanky smiled, and that was a good note on which to let himself out the door.

EIGHTEEN

The next day Steve drove three hours to Verner to see Johnny in his new habitat. The terms of Johnny's parole had him working a job there. All the way out Steve kept thinking of two things—Johnny's professed conversion, and the two government types who had their eyes on him.

The religious angle was especially strange.

There was no God. Steve had figured that out when he prayed harder than anything in his life for God to bring Robert back. Prayed and promised that he would stop lying forever if God would do that for him. Prayed the way his mom had shown him when he was three. On his knees with his hands folded.

He remembered saying, *Dear God Dear God please please please.*

Over and over, through tears.

Please bring Robert back please please Dear God.

But God didn't bring Robert back, so there was no God. It was simple. Simple as the alphabet and 2 + 2.

He had never found any reason to reconsider this conclusion. Not through the foster-care years, the high school football years, the college days, or at law school. God didn't help him an ounce when his first foster father beat the living crud out of him.

Most of his reasoning, though, had to do with Robert.

So what was he to do with this appearance—*resurrection?*—of his brother? Maybe fate just had a sense of humor.

All Steve knew about Johnny's parole so far was that it allowed him to live and work within a sixty-mile radius of Verner. He had to report to his parole officer once a week and, of course, was subject to both random drug testing and warrantless searches.

None of this seemed to bother Johnny as he met Steve outside a rustic home in the foothills. Verner was one of the oldest towns in California, off Highway 40. Steve had been there once before, on his way to Las Vegas. It was named for Samuel Verner, a cattleman from Colorado who came to the state in the gold-rush days. He established a ranch and started selling beef to miners and business owners. Made a bundle.

Now the place was a mix of old, new, and touristy. It had a museum of Shoshone and Paiute history. Boasted good fishing and a tri-county fair. The kind of place where a young family could live the slow life, or a parolee get a fresh start. With mountains close by, it was a postcard setting much of the time.

"Welcome, little bro," Johnny said outside the modest clapboard house. It was off a dirt road, surrounded by plenty of property on either side. Had wooden steps and posts and a front porch with a swing. Without the obvious need for a paint job, it could have been a home out of a Norman Rockwell.

Johnny put his arm around Steve and walked him toward the house. "Any trouble finding the place?"

"MapQuest."

"Man! That's the trouble. No privacy anymore. Government looking over your shoulder all the time. This isn't the America we grew up in."

"Whose house is this?"

"The old man's."

"Your—"

"The guy who raised me. Eldon LaSalle. You know the name, I'm sure. Didn't you put it together with mine?"

Even after the second mention, Steve still couldn't connect the name to anything.

They went up the steps and into the house.

Johnny said, "This is just a little place some of us use when we need to. A little home away from home."

"Oh yeah? Where's home?"

"Later, Steve. One step at a time."

The inside smelled of beer and cigars. Like a Saturday-night poker game. On a sofa in the living room sat the guy who'd given Steve the five thousand dollars in the law library. He stood up.

"Hey, Neal, here's my baby brother," Johnny said.

Neal shook Steve's hand. "Good to see you again."

"Likewise."

The room was small with several chairs scattered around. Reminded Steve a little of recovery meetings. On the mantel above a stone fireplace hung a wooden cross.

"This is where we hold some meetings," Johnny said. "Helping guys get back on their feet. Like me."

"Yeah?"

"We get some pretty messed-up people in here. We may not be what most people think of when it comes to a church, but God isn't finished with us yet."

"Hey, doesn't the Bible say, 'Judge not'?"

"Right on! We'll make you a believer yet."

Don't knock yourself out on that one, Steve thought. "Do you consider yourselves a church?" he asked.

"Of course."

"What sort?"

"Independent. The only kind the Bible ever talks about."

"No denomination?"

"Name me a denomination in the Bible."

"I'm not really up on—"

"Go on. Try."

"Baptist?"

"Not there."

"What about John the Baptist?"

Johnny laughed and Neal joined him.

"I like you, Steve. We're going to get along fine, like brothers should."

Johnny took Steve out to the backyard. The grass was patchy and there was no fence. Pine and birch all around. A nice-looking, peaceful place, Steve thought. Not like city life. But not a place he thought he could ever live. He liked the beat of the city. He'd go crazy here.

Steve heard a growl and turned. A dog with a big black head and eyes blacker than death was tied to a stake in the ground. Checking Steve out.

"That's Ezekiel," Johnny said. "After the prophet. He's a Presa Canario. Good-looking, huh?"

"He thinks I look like lunch," Steve said, feeling some wetness under his arms. He once had to defend a man who owned a pit bull, one that had mauled an eight-year-old girl. It was not pretty what the dog did to her. It wasn't pretty what the judge did to the owner, either.

This dog was bigger than a pit bull. Scarier.

"Don't you worry about Zeke," Johnny said. "We trained 'im. He's gentle as a kitten. Unless he thinks one of us is in trouble, of course. Then he's got a whole Old Testament thing going on."

They sat at a redwood table in the sun. Neal made up tuna-fish sandwiches and brought out a big bag of Lay's potato chips. Neal drank a Coors and Johnny a Coke. To keep from getting sloppy, Steve followed Johnny's lead.

Johnny noticed. "I like it that you're watching yourself."

"How's that?" Steve said.

"Alcohol. It's the root of so many problems. I gave it up myself. Neal's on the way. Right, Neal?"

There was a snap of authority in Johnny's voice. Neal nodded obediently.

"You staying off the 'caine?" Johnny said to Steve.

"You know about that?" Steve said.

Johnny smiled. "I know all about you."

"What, you had somebody looking into me or something?"

"You're not mad, are you?"

"I don't know—"

Johnny put his hand up. "It was all part of finding you, Steve. I didn't know if you ever wanted to see me again, and I had to try to figure that out. So Neal here did some Internet searching and found out about that disciplinary thing. I'm only asking because I want to help you any way I can."

"How can you help me?"

"By showing the deliverance of the Lord Jesus Christ, and the freedom we have in him."

"Why don't we start with me just being your lawyer?" Steve said.

"Let's talk about why you don't believe in God—"

"Johnny, I believe in the law and in getting things done. And I believe everybody is free to believe the way they want. If religion brings you peace, great."

"What about the truth?"

"I'm all for that too."

"Jesus Christ is the Way, the Truth, and the Life."

Steve took a bite of his sandwich to buy time. He didn't want this to turn into a high-pressure religious sales job. He washed the bite down with Coke and said, "What's the nature of the work you want me to do for you?"

"Set us up as a church under the laws of the State of California," Johnny said. "I want to do it up right. I've decided to go into the ministry."

"He's got the anointing," Neal said.

"What's that?" Steve said.

"God has set me apart," Johnny said. "That's the way he used to do it. Anointing with oil. Making people holy. Now it's done by the Holy Ghost. I didn't ask for it, Steve. It just happened."

"In prison?"

"That's right. Best thing that ever happened to me. Do you know the story of Joseph in the Bible?"

"Jesus' dad?"

"No, way back. Joseph, son of Jacob. Jacob favored him and Joseph's brothers got bent about that, faked his death, sold him into slavery."

"Okay."

"Joseph ends up in prison, but God is with him, right? God eventually makes it so Joseph is head dude in Egypt, right behind Pharaoh. There's a famine, Joseph got Egypt to save up food, then Joseph's brothers come down there looking for food, and that's how God gets Jacob's family down to Egypt and saves them. See, Joseph says it was all God's plan."

"Prison was God's plan? I should use that with my clients."

Neal laughed.

"So what do you say, Steve? You can be part of God's plan too."

Steve wasn't sure about that. "Setting up a church shouldn't be too hard to do. The law is pretty liberal when it comes to legitimate religious organizations."

"That's your job, then. Make us legit. Neal's got another five thousand for you. And there will be more, Steve. I can see you being like an in-house counsel. What would you say to that?"

"You making an offer?"

"Suppose I did? Suppose it meant a steady income?"

Steve cleared his throat and looked at Ezekiel the dog. He was staring at Steve like he wanted to get to know him. Or his ankle.

"First," Steve said, "I have a question. Last night a couple of feds came to see me at my apartment. They knew we were talking at Wendy's. Maybe they had me or you under surveillance. I'm guessing you, because you're the one who would be easy to watch on parole."

Johnny shot a look at Neal, who shrugged. "Isn't that what I've been saying?"

"What exactly is it about? You said they're after you for something. What is it?"

"They just don't leave you alone! They don't think a guy can change. A guy does his time, and they're waiting when he gets out! Can you do anything about this, Steve?"

"I have to know what it's about first."

"It's nothing but a fishing expedition. They've been in our face for years. I just want to serve the Lord, and this is what they give me. Steve, can you do anything to stop the harassment?"

"Well, your parole status is High Services. That's a break." In California, a parolee with a record like Johnny's would usually be classified as High Control. That designation had the most restrictions. Johnny must have been a model prisoner.

"You do have a search condition," Steve said. "They can work with the local departments and search you or drug test you without probable cause."

"This is worse than North Korea!"

"What is the local situation here? You have run-ins with the sheriff or anything?"

Johnny and Neal exchanged looks. "Mott? He's been around forever. He doesn't hassle us. No need. We keep to ourselves."

"As long as you're not doing anything wrong—"

"Who says we're doing anything wrong?"

"Nobody—"

"Then don't put it that way."

Silence. A little wind blew through the pines. Johnny put on an easy smile.

"Do what you can to get me legitimized," he said. "I'm going to have a ministry and we're going to need a good lawyer. There's guys in the flock who still have some legal troubles. Maybe you can help them too. And as an organization, I'll need somebody I can trust, really trust. That's why I've come to you, Steve. God has given you to me."

Ezekiel barked. Loud. Startling Steve. Someone was coming out the back door.

NINETEEN

He was someone out of the biker outlaw hall of fame.

He had a hacksaw face and arms forged, no doubt, in a prison yard. If he wanted to advertise his ex-felon status, Steve thought he couldn't have done it any better. A lot of exes, who could no longer vote and knew they'd never get very far in society, let it be known they didn't give a rip. This guy was one of them, from his sleeveless T-shirt to the jeans and boots.

Johnny didn't seem all that happy to see him.

"This your brother?" the guy said.

"What are you doing here, Rennie?" Johnny said.

"I gotta have a reason to come over?"

Rennie met Steve's eyes with a cold steel gaze. It could have been Cody Messina, all grown up and worse than ever. For a long moment he looked Steve up and down. If he was a member in good standing of Johnny's "church," Steve was going to have to say something about the social customs being taught.

"Hey, OK, Rennie," Johnny said, "this is my brother Steve."

Rennie didn't offer his hand.

"Hi," Steve said.

A simple nod from Rennie, who then looked at Neal with an expression Steve couldn't quite read, but didn't fall on the friendly side of the ledger. There were tense crosscurrents all over the place. Ezekiel watched, ready to spring any second, like he expected fresh meat.

Rennie said nothing more, then turned and walked over to the dog. The dog started jumping around. Rennie knelt and put the dog's head in his hands. The dog started licking Rennie's face.

"Friendly sort," Steve said, quietly so Rennie wouldn't hear.

"Rennie's a work in progress," Johnny said.

Rennie got up and walked back into the house, the dog barking.

"Zeke!" Johnny shouted. "Shut up!"

The chastened dog did as he was told. Johnny, who seemed to have unchallenged authority over people, apparently had the same over the animal world.

Johnny said, "God. He's just amazing. You're here. We're together. This is just awesome. Now I got a question for you, little bro."

Steve waited.

"What happened to you after I got kidnapped? I mean, what was your life like?"

"Not a real smooth ride," Steve said.

"Can you tell me about it?"

"I don't know. Our dad killed himself. Did you know about that?"

Johnny nodded slowly. "You remember much about him?"

Steve shook his head. "Mom didn't talk about him much. Once she said something about his being no good and I was better off. But I don't think she ever got over losing you. She died when I was ten. Bad cancer. Did you know about that?"

Johnny shook his head. "Must have been tough on you. What happened to you after that?"

"Went into the foster-care system. Woo-hoo."

"No relatives?"

"Back east, Mom had a sister."

"I never knew that."

"Aunt Kate was her name. Not one of the good people. She didn't want me. I went through a couple of foster homes, ended up with a couple named Rust. They were good to me, but by that time I was ..."

"Go ahead."

"Nah," I said.

"Drugs?"

Steve shrugged. "I got through school. I was pretty good at it, despite all the other stuff."

"You got through law school," Johnny said. "That's something."

"It wasn't the best school. Not your Ivy League. But yeah, I got through and passed the bar and everything, and did okay. Worked for the DA's office for a couple of years before I had my problem."

"The coke thing?"

Steve nodded.

"Never got married?" Johnny asked.

"Oh, that's another great mark on my record. My divorce is almost final."

"Yeah? Who was she?"

"A lawyer. Like me. Met her in law school, as a matter of fact." Steve paused to catch a glimpse of the memories flashing around in his head.

"Whose idea was it? The divorce, I mean."

"I drove her to it, no doubt about that."

"Kids?"

"No. Probably a good thing."

Johnny put his hand on Steve's arm. "Then this is a new start, Steve. Your new family. You and me. It's God's plan."

Steve didn't know whose plan it was, but it did feel like Johnny was extending the thinnest of reeds. If Steve grabbed it, it could keep him from being carried downriver, toward the falls.

Steve grabbed. "I want to get to know you again," he said.

"Same here, Bro. And now we have all the time in the world."

TWENTY

"Good news," Steve said on the phone as he drove through Verner. "I've got a client for sure."

"Mr. LaSalle?"

"The same. And here is something that will interest you. He wants to form a church."

Pause. "What kind of church?"

"A Christian church of some kind. That's why I'm calling you. I figure you can help me figure out all that religious stuff."

"Stuff?"

"Yeah. My brother wants to be a minister. He's a convicted felon. I don't know anything about people going into the ministry, if there's a license requirement and all that. You seem to be an expert on these matters."

"Hardly."

"So when can we start?"

"I have classes today."

"Tomorrow then. Noon. My office. We'll do lunch."

"Do lunch? Are you a lawyer or a movie producer?"

Steve didn't care at this point. All he knew was he wanted to see her again.

That she was religious didn't seem to be an obstacle. The same way it wasn't an obstacle between him and Johnny. People were people, right? They all had the same junk inside; some dealt with it one way, some another.

Some did drugs, then got off drugs, then thought about doing drugs again.

Some used religion as a drug. The opiate of the masses.

Big deal. Of all the places to be born into, the world was about the worst, and everybody was on the same boat. You had to snag whoever came by who seemed like a halfway decent person and see if you could keep each other warm.

Once, Ashley had kept him warm, and he liked her warmth. But it was gone now and that was that. Sienna Ciccone was here now, and that was also that.

Steve drove leisurely, taking in the environment. Verner had an actual downtown, with rows of shops. Boutiques, hardware, shoes, antiques, books. The place hadn't been Wal-Marted yet, though it did have the obligatory Starbucks. He stopped in and treated himself to a Mocha Frap. It was a long drive back to LA.

He walked around a little. Verner had a nice-looking Mexican grill and a Carl's Jr. A bowling alley and a two-screen theater. Brad Pitt's latest, along with some teen horror flick, the kind that inevitably featured the latest TV hotties making their big-screen debuts in an entirely forgettable waste of celluloid. The posters always featured the ample bosom of the latest eye candy, who would soon enough occupy the same dustbin of cultural irrelevancy as Paris Hilton.

All in all, it seemed like a perfect place for his brother to start his re-entry into society. Not a big city with concentrated temptations. But not so small that you couldn't find some things to do. Steve thought he might even take up bowling and roll a few with Johnny.

What if he even moved out here sometime? Could be the right kind of place for him to start over again too. Him and Johnny, same place again.

Still, he wasn't quite sure what to make of his brother and the company he kept. Steve had defended a lot of cons, and the odds of their staying out of trouble after they got sprung were pretty low. Johnny seemed determined. He wasn't so sure about that guy Rennie.

Rennie no doubt had trouble tattooed on his chest.

Steve got back to the Ark and drove toward the highway. At the edge of town he saw a brown brick building and a six-point star sign that said Sheriff. He paused, then turned left into the outdoor parking lot. He'd come all this way. Why not bunch up on the tasks?

Inside, it had a revamped look. Fresh coat of beige paint on the walls, clean brown carpeting, a Western painting on the wall—a couple of cowpunchers beneath an orange sunset. Behind the reception desk, a woman of about fifty worked a keyboard. She got up when she saw Steve standing there.

He took out one of his attorney cards and handed it to her. "Stephen Conroy. I talked to a Lieutenant Oderkirk."

She looked up from the card, her face ashen. "You haven't heard?"

"Heard what?"

"Terrible. An accident. Four days ago."

Steve couldn't find a word.

"He was driving," the woman said. "At night. We don't know exactly. He went off the road." She looked down.

"Is he hurt bad?"

"He died," she said.

A jolt ripped through Steve. "I'm sorry."

"We are too. He was a good man. Had a wife and two daughters."

"He was helping me."

She said nothing.

"Is the sheriff in?" he asked.

She shook her head. "I don't expect him back today. I think he's at the mortuary, in fact. The funeral's on Saturday."

"Which mortuary would that be?"

"There's only one. Bruck. It's over on Hazleton."

Bruck sounded familiar. Then he remembered it was the mortuary where Robert's autopsy was performed.

"How do I get there?" he asked.

TWENTY-ONE

An older man, maybe seventy-five, greeted Steve in the softly lit reception area of the Bruck Mortuary. Scarlet velvet curtains with gold brocade hung over an inner doorway. A large chandelier issued muted light. The room had an abundance of ferns that may or may not have been real. It wouldn't matter to the stiffs, Steve mused.

"Good afternoon, sir," the gentleman said. He wore a gray suit, white shirt, red tie. His white hair was wispy, like a bird's nest. The nameplate on his desk said Edward Hendrickson.

"I was sent over here from the sheriff's station. I was told the sheriff was here."

"He's in with Mr. Bruck," Hendrickson said. "Would you like to wait?"

"It's about Lieutenant Oderkirk," Steve said.

"Oh. Yes. I see." It didn't seem like he saw, but he picked up the phone and pressed a button. Into the receiver he said, "Excuse me, Mr. Bruck, but a gentleman is here regarding Lieutenant Oderkirk. No, I didn't get his name." He looked at Steve.

"Conroy."

"Conroy," Hendrickson repeated. Then, "Thank you." He hung up the phone. "Mr. Bruck will be right with you."

"Thanks," Steve said. "Would that be the original Mr. Bruck?"

"Oh no. It's third generation. William. This was all started by his grandfather."

"And the sheriff. What's his name again?"

"Mott, sir. Owen Mott."

"How long's he been sheriff?"

"Long time. Fifteen years at least."

The velvet curtains flapped and a guy about Steve's age stepped in. He wore an open-collared shirt and a black coat and slacks. New breed of mortician, Steve thought. More hip. Make the bereaved think their dear departed has all the latest, whatever that might be in this business.

"Hi, I'm Bill Bruck." He offered his hand. He was a head shorter than Steve, with thick black hair gelled flat. "Mr. Hendrickson says you're here about Larry Oderkirk."

"In a way." Steve handed him one of his cards.

"Lawyer?"

"That's right."

"Were you representing Larry for something?"

"No."

"Friend of the family?"

"Not exactly."

He frowned. "How can I help you?"

"I was actually hoping to talk to the sheriff."

"Oh." Bruck made little squeezing motions with his fingers, like he was holding a little rubber ball. "Well, we're going over some details right now. I wonder if you can arrange an appointment."

"Thing is, I'm heading back to LA. I had some business with Lieutenant Oderkirk and I thought I could ask the sheriff about it."

A uniform stepped through the curtains. "What sort of business was that?"

He was tall and thin, with a salt-and-pepper moustache and tortoiseshell glasses. He wore a sheriff's star on his chest. The pants of his uniform were stuffed inside black cowboy boots.

"Sheriff Mott?" Steve said.

"Who's asking?"

"My name's Steve Conroy. I spoke to Lieutenant Oderkirk recently."

Bruck handed Steve's card to the sheriff, who gave it a quick once-over. "Uh-huh. What about?"

"He was helping me locate an autopsy record."

Mott looked at Bruck, who kept working the phantom super ball.

"And I guess that autopsy was done right here, back in 1983," Steve said.

"Before I was elected," Sheriff Mott said.

"My dad was running the business then," Bruck said.

No one offered anything else, so Steve said, "Maybe you could help me, Sheriff. If I want to locate the full record of the case, can I get that at your office?"

"We're in a transition period at the moment," Mott said. "A lot of the old records are in San Bernardino being transferred to micro-fiche. So I'm afraid now is about the worst time to ask."

"You must have some sort of index, a centralized record."

"What is the nature of your interest, Mr. Conroy?"

"The victim was my brother."

Mott nodded. "I see. Let me suggest this. Call our office on Monday and have Sandra fax you an official request form. Fill that out and fax it back to us. We'll see what we can do."

Steve glanced at Hendrickson, the man behind the desk. He was looking down at what appeared to be nothing.

To Bruck Steve said, "Do you keep records of autopsies?"

Mott answered. "I'd rather you go through the proper channels, Mr. Conroy. That way we can make sure it's all done right. Is that the only reason you drove out here from"—he looked at the card again—"Canoga Park?"

"I had some other business."

"Oh? What was that?"

"Legal matter."

Mott waited for Steve to add something. He didn't.

"If that's all," Mott said, "then I'll be sure—"

"One more thing," Steve said. "What were the circumstances of Lieutenant Oderkirk's death?"

"And your reason for that information is what?"

"Just curious."

"Curious just isn't enough, Mr. Conroy. As a lawyer, I'm sure you understand."

Steve heard something that sounded like a ticking clock. It was the old guy at the front desk. He was tapping a pencil on the edge. When he saw Steve looking at him, he stopped. An embarrassed silence descended from the dark crimson ceiling.

"Well," Mott said, "I think we all have things to do. Nice meeting you, Mr. Conroy."

TWENTY-TWO

A haze had drifted up against the mountains as Steve pulled out of the parking lot. Made things fuzzy. He thought about Oderkirk's death. A thin layer of uncertainty shrouded that too.

Maybe it was all coincidence. Or maybe Johnny's God had planned it out.

Some planner. If he was so all-powerful, why'd he make everything such a mess? You don't do it that way if you're God.

Time for a little clearing of the air. Steve had the autopsy report in his briefcase in the car. It was four fifteen. He'd come this far and spent this much time. Maybe one more stop.

Traynor Memorial Hospital.

Steve got directions at an ARCO station. The hospital was tucked up against the foothills. A three-story, sage-green structure with tinted windows. Just inside the front doors, two elderly women sat at a reception desk. They were dressed in blue smocks with yellow tags identifying them as volunteers. One of them had sleet-colored hair done up in curls. The other had dyed hers a shade of red that did not exist in nature.

They looked surprised and delighted when Steve came in, as if he were the Pony Express riding into the fort.

They fought for the first word. Curls said, "May I help—" at the same time Red said, "Who are you here to—"

They stopped and looked at each other, half-annoyed, half-amused, then back at Steve.

And spoke over each other again.

"Let me help you out," Steve said. "I'm looking for a doctor, a certain—"

"Are you hurt?" Curls said.

"Our emergency entrance is around to the side," Red said.

"No, I—"

"Oh, but we just had a shooting," Curls said.

"A colored man," Red added.

"Black, Liv. They don't like to be called *colored*."

105

"I always forget." Red shook her head.

Steve said, "I'm trying to locate a certain doctor—"

"We don't do referrals here," Curls said. "But if you—"

Red jumped in. "We have a medical building just down the block if you'll—"

"He didn't ask for a medical building," Curls snapped.

"I know that, but if he's looking for a doctor that would be the place to start."

"Not any doctor," Steve said. "A specific doctor, named Walker C. Phillips."

A silence fell upon the volunteers. Neither seemed eager to tackle that one.

"Is he still practicing?" Steve said.

Red leaned forward and whispered, "Lost his license to practice."

"Terrible tragedy," Curls said, shaking her head.

"He drank," Red added, and gave a tippling motion with her hand.

"When was this?" Steve asked.

"Oh, it's been, what, ten years, at least," Curls said. "His wife left him, you know."

"Ah, no, I did not know that."

The two women nodded.

"Can you tell me, is he still around?"

"Oh, he moved," Red said. "To Tehachapi."

"I thought it was Temecula," Curls said.

"No, Tehachapi."

"He moved where the prison is."

"That's Tehachapi."

"No, it's Temecula."

"Oh, no. I have a granddaughter in Temecula."

"That doesn't mean—"

"I would have remembered."

"Excuse me," Steve said. "Maybe there's someone here at the hospital who would know for sure?"

That seemed like a delightful suggestion to the ladies, who fought over the phone. Curls won and punched in a number and took about five minutes to formulate the question, and finally listened. She started to frown. Then seemed almost angry.

She replaced the phone. "Apparently he moved to Tehachapi."

Red smiled without saying a word.

Curls quickly added, "But he may have moved *from* Temecula."

"Thank you, ladies," Steve said. "You've been very helpful."

"That's our job," Curls said.

"It's not really a *job*," Red said.

Steve walked quickly for the doors, hearing Curls as he did. "I think you'd do much better if you did consider it a job."

As he was driving back to LA, Steve got a call from Ashley.

"This is a surprise," he said. He noted, with consternation, that his heart was kicking up. With longing. He wanted to be over that reaction. Now.

"I've been meaning to call you," she said.

"Uh-huh."

"Are you all right?"

"I'm fine. I'm driving and everything."

"Steve—"

"Sorry."

She paused. "You have some things in the garage. I was just wondering what you planned to do with all of it."

"Is it in the way?"

"Well, sort of."

"Is it a health hazard?"

"Steve, I'm not a storage service."

"No, you're the one who filed for divorce and forced me out of the—"

"I didn't force anything."

"And now you're ragging my face about a few things in the garage? Come on, I live in an apartment."

"We can't just leave it like this. I own the house now—"

"You will, when I get my share."

"—and I can't have a portion of my garage filled with your things."

"At least give me a chance to get a house of my own."

"How likely is that?"

"Thank you."

"I mean, are you going to rent?"

"No, I had my eye on the Getty Villa overlooking the ocean."

"Steve, I'm serious. I'm going to be working at home tomorrow, so if you'd like—"

"What great timing you have."

"Excuse me?"

"I don't know, today was a great day. I haven't told you, have I?"

"Told me what?"

Steve started and stopped a couple of times. His eyes felt hot.

"Steve?"

"I'm here. Listen. Robert. He's not dead."

There was a long pause. "Your brother?"

"Yeah."

"How could it be?"

"I can't go into the whole thing. But it was a whole scheme, and the boy who died was misidentified as Robert. He's alive. He's been in prison, but he contacted me. I've just been out to see him. It's—" He fought back tears. "I don't know, it's been a lot."

"I'm sorry, Steve. I didn't know."

"I know you didn't."

"That's just so ... unbelievable. How did he find you?"

"I don't really want to talk about it right now. I'll move my stuff. Just give me time."

"Sure, sure. I'm really—"

He snapped the phone shut. It was almost dark now and the city was still an hour away. Move his stuff. It reminded him of that scene in *Moonstruck* when the college professor gets water thrown at him by one of his young female students. He tells the waiter to clear the table and remove all evidence of her and bring him a tall glass of vodka.

Ashley sure wanted all evidence of Steve removed. He knew they were finished, but as long as he had some things in the garage, well, maybe he had a shot. Yeah, and maybe there were barbequed ribs on the moon.

But then there was Sienna. Why had she come into his life at this particular time? Maybe getting his brother back and a new woman in his life was a twist of the old wheel of fortune. Coming up his way for a change.

That was something to cling to. They call that *hope*, he guessed. Or maybe delusion.

He stopped at The Cue and ran a couple of racks. Drank a pitcher but kept it to one and got back to the apartment without incident.

That would be a fine thing to show his new clients, a DUI charge. What an idiot, what a stupid idiot he was.

As he approached the apartment building he saw the telltale flash of red light and spotty gatherings of people on the street. The urban distress code. And the ambulance was right in front of his place.

Which kept him from getting into the driveway. So he double-parked and got out, blinking to try to clear his beer goggles.

He was sufficiently successful to spot the manager, Mr. Jong Choi, standing on the front grass with his arms across his chest and a cigarette smoldering in one hand.

"Who?" Steve asked.

"Six," he said.

Six was Mrs. Stanky. "What happened?"

Choi shrugged. He was slight of build and smoked incessantly. "She trouble, alway trouble."

"You're a fount of information."

"Huh?"

Steve turned away and looked to the ambulance. It was clear the paramedics were inside the complex. He made a beeline for number six.

The door was open. The white gangsta wannabe kid from number seven was standing outside with a couple of his wannabe friends. A little something happening in their pointless world.

Two paramedics were standing over Mrs. Stanky, who was on the sofa.

"She okay?" Steve said.

One of the medics turned around. "You are?"

"Neighbor. Upstairs."

"Who is that?" Mrs. Stanky's voice chimed.

"It's me, Mrs. Stanky. Steve from upstairs."

"Steve?"

"Right here."

"Don't go."

To the medic he said, "Can you tell me what happened here?"

"We think she kinked her hose," he said. "No oxygen. Passed out."

"How'd you get the call?"

The medic shrugged. "I think somebody called it in."

"I did." Mr. Wannabe was in the doorway. "She wasn't complaining about the music. I looked in and saw her on the floor."

So Mrs. Stanky's disposition had saved her, by its very absence. Steve thought there was a certain poeticism in that.

"Good work, dude," Steve said.

Wannabe looked disgusted at being called *dude*. But a little proud too.

The medics finished their business and decided Mrs. Stanky could stay as is, provided someone sat with her for a while.

So Steve watched another episode of *Law & Order*, this time all the way through. By the time the jury got the case handed to them, Mrs. Stanky seemed her old self. Which meant lodging some complaints with Steve.

Satisfied she was good as new—or at least as good as she'd been—Steve went outside, where he was met by Nick Nolte, looking for a dish.

The routine seemed like a good thing. Verner, California, was starting to feel a bit strange.

TWENTY-THREE

Steve went to see Ashley the next day.

They'd bought a house together in Altadena, a nice little town about twenty minutes from downtown LA. It was community property, and as part of the divorce settlement Ashley kept the place. That just about covered the debts Steve had left on the marriage.

Maybe his friends and drug connections wouldn't have believed it, but Steve really wanted the marriage to work out. Even though he probably married Ashley for the wrong reasons. He wanted an emotional savior, and nobody was up for that job.

They met first year of law school. Steve was still managing to get pretty good grades even while toking and drinking at night. One day Ashley sat next to him in contracts and said, "You're such a jerk."

He looked at her through sore eyes. "Good morning to you too."

"You're one of the smartest guys in here," she said, "and you're wasted all the time."

He started to throw some attitude. She batted it back like Mike Piazza. So they compromised and went for coffee, where he found out she was the daughter of a judge, a champion high school swimmer, and a birdwatcher. When he asked if she'd ever seen a blue-footed booby she laughed. That got him a dinner.

By the end of the term they were in love. To celebrate the end of finals, Steve took Ashley to a carnival near the school. Just for laughs. They'd been studying hard for so long they almost forgot what laughs were like.

But that night the laughs came in buckets, and on the Ferris wheel he asked her to marry him. She answered with an immediate yes and a kiss that jumped to the top of the all-time-best-kiss list.

Her dad was less than thrilled with Steve, who could tell the old man sensed something a little off about him. Ashley protested, chalking up Steve's lesser qualities to boyish eccentricity. Because of her, Steve stopped with the weed. Built up enough trust that she married him after graduation.

She went to a firm in Beverly Hills, Steve to the DA's office downtown. For two years it was a pretty good marriage. Everything was cool until Steve defended a drug dealer from the west side, a middle-class kid whose parents got him out on bail.

He'd managed to keep the guilt over Robert hidden from Ashley and his employer, the county of Los Angeles. But the deep things eventually bubble up, like the hot stuff in the La Brea Tar Pits. Instead of admitting it to Ashley and getting help, he took an 8-ball of coke from his young client, free of charge. Not the cheap stuff, either.

Which is what started the downfall. Ashley hung in there. Steve knew she lasted longer than most women would have. But damage was done to the foundation, the cornerstones of trust and loyalty. He lied to her and put his habit above everything else.

And so he couldn't blame her for finally calling it quits. She was better off without him. Most people were, even his clients.

Ashley met him at the front door, looking great. Brown hair and emerald eyes. Lean and athletic as always.

He wanted to hug her but she preferred a handshake.

"I'm sorry about yesterday," she said.

"Me too."

"That's just amazing news, finding your brother."

"Yeah. Can I come in?"

"If you wouldn't mind just going on into the garage, I have some work to do in the study," she said.

"You don't have to worry about me. I'm not going to lose it." The last time he was actually inside this house, he broke some furniture and threw a bookend through a window.

"I think it would just be better," Ashley said.

Steve went around the side of the house, the once familiar now alien and shadowed, and into the garage. It was obvious where his stuff was. The disordered pile in the back corner. The rest of the place was Ashley all over. Rows of color-coded boxes, perfectly stacked like LEGOs, with her notations on the side in a neat, even hand.

His things, what had remained when he moved out, were in brown boxes, a couple of garbage bags with twist ties, and his mom's old trunk. It was the one thing his dad made for her, his mom told Steve once. And it was where she kept the old family photos.

Steve hadn't looked at those in years. When he'd gone into foster care, the trunk was the one thing he insisted on dragging along with him, as if it were his last link to normalcy. There were pictures of Robert and Steve in that trunk, a photographic lifeline. Paper-thin slices of the past, linked like a fragile chain, one that might be able to pull him out of a dark hole someday.

When Ashley and he got the house, he put the trunk out here in the garage but had not looked inside it since.

Now he did.

There were three photo albums, some envelopes, and several loose pictures scattered around. Also, his mom's old high school yearbooks. He opened one. All those black-and-white pictures of faculty and kids. His mom was a sophomore, Carla Rigney. She had her head turned slightly, wore glasses, and half smiled. She seemed uncertain about her future but trying to put a brave look on things. She wasn't one of the babes. You could tell the babes, with their eye makeup and blond hair and I-dated-the-quarterback expressions.

His mom's picture also showed up in a couple of the clubs. Something called Knowledge Bowl, which looked like all the geeky smart kids. She was one of two girls among ten boys. She was also in Ecology Club and Student Store Workers. In that last picture her dark hair framed a round face and came to rest in flip curls below her shoulders. She was looking straight into the camera, as if ready to sell you a notebook.

The inside front cover didn't have a lot of signatures. One said, *Carla, we haven't known each other real well but you are a real sincere person and I wish you a lot of luck. Have a great summer and a beautiful life. Patty.*

Steve guessed Patty didn't wish hard enough.

He put the yearbook back on top of the other two, then picked up a handful of the loose photos. A lot of baby pictures of Robert.

There was one of Robert in a Superman suit, maybe when he was four. Steve was on his lap smiling, the little brother, and Robert had his arm around him, as if holding him up. But Robert's look was uncertain, like he was afraid he might drop the little one. Steve could see Johnny in Robert's face. A definite resemblance.

Another one showed them a little older. Robert a full head taller than Steve, with his arm over Steve's shoulder. They were out in the backyard covered with dirt. Steve remembered the moment. They'd just built a fort. Used wood and cardboard and leafy branches for camouflage. Steve could still see the inside of that fort, the sunlight streaming through the gaps, the smell of the dirt.

The feeling of security, inside with his brother.

Steve went through about two dozen more of the loose pictures. One of the last reached out and gripped his throat. It was Robert in his train pjs. The ones he'd been wearing the night he was taken. He was eating a bowl of cereal. Looking up at the camera like he'd been disturbed, as if their mother, taking the picture, was interrupting his life. A life that would soon become a nightmare.

Closing his eyes, Steve fought back tears.

"Is everything all right?"

He didn't turn to face Ashley. "No," he said. "I mean, I'll be okay. Would you mind"—he tossed the photos in the trunk and closed it—"if I took this with me today and came back for the rest?"

"The trunk?"

"Yeah. I can fit it in the backseat. I'll take a couple of the bags too. Maybe I can borrow a truck for the other stuff."

"Sure, Steve. Just as long as you get it taken care of."

"I said I would."

Ashley said nothing. The feeling was familiar. Many times in their marriage he'd lose it over some small thing. She wouldn't dignify him with a response. He'd put her down for saying nothing, and she'd ask him why he always wanted to fight. He wouldn't say anything at that point. How could he explain that fighting was just another way to distract him from the void? He couldn't because he didn't have the words then. Most of the time he was high anyway.

Ashley helped him get the trunk in his car. He drove back to his office and got a dolly from the storage room and wheeled the trunk into his office.

And then sat there. Looking at it. Wishing the contents would fly out on their own and spread before him, showing him what his life was supposed to look like now and forever.

TWENTY-FOUR

On Thursday Steve took Sienna to his favorite rib shack in Los Angeles. He offered to drive, but she wanted to meet him there. Still keeping a professional distance. *Well,* Steve thought, *nothing like Willie's ribs to break that down. We'll see just how long she lasts.*

Willie A's Kansas City Barbeque was the proverbial hole-in-the-wall on Sepulveda. Its meat melted off the bone, drawing a clientele from all over the city. The proprietor always piled on the extras for Steve, because he once got Willie's son off on a robbery charge. Willie Anderson's kid was in the wrong place at the wrong time with the wrong people. But he was no gangbanger, and Steve actually convinced a jury of that fact. It may have been his greatest performance as a criminal defense lawyer, and Willie A did not forget.

So he, all three hundred pounds of him, would come out in his sauce-stained whites to say hi whenever Steve dropped by for a meal. Today was no different. Steve introduced Willie to Sienna.

"She's a pretty one," Willie said, smiling.

"She's a law student," Steve said. "Working for me."

"Oh, that's too bad," Willie said to Sienna. "With what he tips, I can't imagine what he pays his help."

"If he pays," Sienna said.

Willie let out one of his characteristic laughs. Steve always thought it sounded like a goose in a cement mixer. Sienna did a classic double take before laughing herself.

The magic was working. "Here's what we want," Steve said. "And make it special."

"Do I ever do any less?" Willie said.

"No—"

"Did Roberto Clemente ever give half a swing at the plate?"

"No, Willie."

"Magic going to the hoop?"

"No, Willie."

"L. T. going to the end zone?"

Sienna said, "He could make a great closing argument."

"Don't encourage him," Steve said. "Now listen, bring on a whole slab of baby backs, whole loaf of bread, beans and slaw, a root beer for me. And for the lady?"

"Diet Coke," Sienna said.

Willie nodded and wiped his hands on a cloth. "I'll get Annie to bring it around. You folks have a nice lunch on me."

"Willie—"

"No, I insist. You brought me a nice new customer. Relax and enjoy the magic."

"It's a secret combination of pepper, molasses, and attitude," Steve said.

"Attitude is everything," Willie said. "Even for lawyers."

"Especially for lawyers," Steve said.

Willie bowed and rumbled back toward the kitchen.

"What a cool guy," Sienna said.

"Willie's good people. But enough about him. I want to know all about you."

"Not much to know," she said.

"Come on, you know all about me."

"Right."

"What a charming employer I am. Generous."

"Humble."

"Hey, I read a whole book on being humble. I know more about the subject than anybody."

She laughed.

"So," he said, "you got a boyfriend?"

Before Sienna could say a word, Annie was plopping drinks on the table. "Root beer for you, Steve," she said. "The lady has the Diet Coke."

"How you doing, Annie?"

"Better'n most, not as good as some." Annie was about sixty, half Willie's size, with platinum blond hair piled high. "This your girl?"

"I'm about to find out," Steve said.

"Can I stay and listen?"

"Go get us some bread, Annie."

"Yes, boss." Off she went.

"Now, back to business," Steve said.

"We were discussing business?" Sienna said.

"Sure. The boyfriend part."

"Isn't that rather personal?"

"Of course."

"Then why'd you ask?"

"Because," Steve said, "attitude is everything."

"Attitude is less than nothing."

"So. Boyfriend?"

"Mr. Conroy—"

"Steve."

"Mr. Conroy. We need to get some things straight."

"Uh-oh."

"Business is business. I don't want this to get personal."

"What's the harm?"

"Have you ever considered that under the law this could very easily turn into harassment?"

"You really don't think that."

She looked him in the eye without a flinch. "The afternoon is young."

"Come on, Sienna."

"Mr. Conroy—"

"Steve!"

She placed both hands on the table. "No. Listen, please. I am a law student and you've hired me to do some work and that's it."

"Why so sure?"

"I'd rather not—"

"Please. Tell me. I can take it. If I unhired you and then asked you out, why not?"

She sighed. "I just think—we have a basic difference in how we look at things."

"Why, because you believe in God?"

"Kind of important, don't you think?"

"People get together all the time that don't see eye to eye on that."

"And it doesn't work out."

"Sometimes it does."

She shook her head and looked away. Steve thought, *Back off. Let it go.*

He said, "Look, there's the idea of God. If it helps people—"

"I'm not comfortable talking about this right now."

"Okay, right. I've got a great idea." He waited until she met his eyes again. "Let's make world news and agree to disagree."

"With one proviso," she said. "We don't go out."

Steve threw up his hands. "I surrender."

"Okay."

"But if you ever change your mind, I'm just a phone call away."

She rebuked him with her eyes.

"Business then," Steve said quickly. "Johnny LaSalle, it turns out, really is my brother."

Sienna froze with her drink in the air. "You're kidding."

"Knew things only my brother would know. It's a whole long story. But here's the deal. He has turned his life around. I have the chance to help him now. It's like a . . ."

"A God thing?"

It sounded sensible, the way she said it. Possible even. "Whatever it is, I want to get back some of the life we lost together. Will you help me do that?"

"Of course," Sienna said. "Legal and aboveboard."

Their food arrived and Steve forgot about the law and concentrated on the ribs. And how he could not stop thinking about Sienna Ciccone as a woman he was very much attracted to.

TWENTY-FIVE

After tasking Sienna to do a memo on church incorporation, Steve drove back to his office. As soon as he turned into the parking lot, a Lincoln pulled in behind him. He didn't think much of it until he saw the two feds stepping out to greet him.

"Don't you guys have real work to do?" Steve said.

"You're our work, Mr. Conroy," Issler said. "We love what we do."

"So you're saying you love me?"

"We'd love to see you mess up," Weingarten said, "just once. Because we'll be right there to—"

"That's enough," Issler said.

"Good cop, bad cop?" Steve asked.

"Both bad," Issler said, "as far as you're concerned. Or I should say, your client?"

"You both know I'm not going to say anything about my client, so why bother? If you have something to charge him with, then do it. Otherwise, there's a corner on Topanga Canyon Boulevard where you can catch some speeders."

Weingarten smiled and removed a document from his coat pocket. It was folded in thirds. Steve knew what it was before he opened it.

"Unbelievable," Steve said.

"If you'll just show us to your office," Issler said.

"Sorry, not going to do it. Not until I read this whole thing. You do understand I have every right to read it, don't you?"

"You can read it while we conduct the search."

"Eat my briefs," Steve said, not caring if they cuffed him. They had just handed him a search warrant. Some rubber-stamp judge had approved a search of his office. That meant one of these guys had sworn under oath that there was probable cause to believe evidence of a crime was somewhere present behind Steve's door. As that was a complete crock, veins started throbbing in Steve's temples.

The face of the warrant described his office under *Premises To Be Searched* and then —

ITEMS TO BE SEARCHED

A. Records, documents, receipts, and materials which reflect identities of and/or connection with named individuals (see Exhibit 1); and/or which reflect connection to an ongoing criminal enterprise, including but not limited to money laundering, racketeering, and extortion.

B. As used above, the terms records, documents, programs, applications or materials includes records, documents, programs, applications or materials created, modified, or stored in any form.

Flipping to the attached exhibit, Steve saw the names John LaSalle, aka Johnny LaSalle, aka *Silk*; Eldon LaSalle, aka *Chief*; Casey Renfro, aka *Rennie*; Neal Cullen; William Reagan; Axel LaFontaine, Don Stead, Michael Dietz ...

And so on. Translation: the federal government was trying to make out a criminal conspiracy and include Steve in it.

Cold sweat tickled his armpits. This was no longer a little dance in the tulips. This was hard time stuff.

Or persecution of his brother and himself.

He let them in. But he watched carefully as they poked around. And poke they did. Two hours' worth. Steve thought early on that the agents knew they'd find nothing. They just liked their work when it came to defense lawyers. You didn't often get a chance to mess up a law office.

At one point Issler went to Steve's trunk.

"Don't touch anything in there," Steve said.

Issler looked inside.

"It's just family photos. Keep your hands off."

"I'll decide — "

"I don't want your greasy fingerprints on anything in there."

"Easy."

Steve whipped out his cell phone and took a picture of Issler looking in the trunk.

"What're you doing?" he said.

"Making a record in case I need to tell a judge where you were looking. This is a business office, and you are only authorized to search where records would reasonably—"

"Yeah, yeah." Issler closed the trunk. "I don't think there's anything in there. See, I'm not out to make life miserable for you."

Weingarten, on the other hand, didn't seem to have any such hesitation. In fact, he looked to be having a lot of fun going through Steve's computer records. It was a Gateway desktop Steve had since forever, and was stuffed with all sorts of things not relevant to the practice of law. Weingarten lingered there, typing away. At one point he said, "Got hooked on the blow, did you?"

"Get out of my journal," Steve snapped. For a while he'd kept a journal, spilling his guts on the page about cocaine, depression, fear, and loathing. That's the only place he would have recorded something like that.

"That stuff'll mess you up," Weingarten said.

Steve cursed at him. Weingarten's face tightened. Issler stepped in and said, "Just do a word search for names and let's get out of here."

Weingarten gave Steve the cold stare and he gave it right back. Steve knew he would probably live to regret it, but there it was. He didn't give a rip.

"You've been retained by Johnny LaSalle," Issler said. "Is that right?"

"You know it's right."

"All I know is what you told me."

"Then you know."

"How were you paid?"

"Excuse me?"

"Do you not understand the question? To be retained means you have been paid. How did Mr. Johnny LaSalle transfer money to you?"

"That's privileged information."

"No," Issler said. "It's not."

"Where did you go to law school, Agent Issler?"

"If we find out that you were paid, let's say, in cash, and banked it, and that the cash can be traced to a criminal conspiracy, then you can bet we'll be a lot more intrusive than we have been today."

"A lot more," Weingarten said.

"Why don't you guys just lay it on the line?" Steve said. "Why don't you tell me exactly what you think you've got here?"

"As if you didn't know," Weingarten said.

"Then it won't hurt you to tell me, will it?"

"What do you know about Eldon LaSalle?" Issler said.

"He's the father of my client."

"Anything else?"

"He's probably got some background. So? Doesn't show my client's involved in a conspiracy."

Issler said to Weingarten, "Go get the book."

"You really think?" Weingarten said.

"Why not? Might as well let the counselor here know what's really going on."

"What book?" Steve said.

Weingarten left and Issler didn't say anything until he got back and handed something to Steve. It was more of a pamphlet than a book. It had a plain white cover with black script on the front. *Booth Speaks* was the title. By Eldon LaSalle Jr.

"That's right," Issler said. "Eldon LaSalle's a writer. Or was. This is his best seller."

Weingarten snorted. Steve thumbed the pages. It was done in Courier font, as if it had been typed, then published. Or rather, self-published. A crude-looking thing.

"You want to tell me what this is supposed to be?" Steve said.

"Just read it yourself," Issler said. "We have several copies."

"And if I read it—"

"Just call me and tell me what you think. Maybe you'll want to talk about it with your client."

TWENTY-SIX

After they left and Steve cooled off, he thumbed through the short book, then went back to the first page. *I, John Wilkes Booth, do write my last will, testament, and confession.*

He gathered from the opening pages that this was supposed to be what Booth wrote during his attempt to evade capture after shooting Lincoln. Steve's recollection from high school history was that Booth was on the run with a co-conspirator for almost two weeks. Then he was cornered in a barn and killed by federal troops. Steve was no expert on the buying habits of book readers, but the subject didn't seem like one destined for best-seller status.

It soon became clear what this book really was. Skimming the pages, Steve came across several troubling passages.

> I am a hunted man because I love my country and know what is best for it. Because I have a divine insight and had the courage to act, the lovers of darkness, and darkies, seek my neck. Having killed a tyrant, I am now trying to get back to the bosom of my people. But a broken leg has hampered me. Let me make my confession before I die!
>
> This country was formed for the white, not for the black man! And looking upon African slavery from the same standpoint held by those noble framers of our Constitution, I for one have ever considered it one of the greatest blessings (both for themselves and us) that God ever bestowed upon a favored nation.
>
> The darkies cannot fend for themselves. We have given them a better life upon our shores. We have taken them from Africa and given them civilization. If they go free, they die!

A racist's creed. Not worth the staples that held it together. More of the same through the rest of the short book. It didn't have much ... what was the term, literary depth? Mostly long-winded reflections on the superiority of the white race.

Steve flipped to the last page.

> So ends all. For my country I have given up all that makes life sweet and holy, brought misery upon my family, and am sure there is no pardon in Heaven for me, since man condemns me so. I have only heard of what has been done (except what I did myself), and it fills me with horror. God, try and forgive me, and bless my mother. Tonight I will once more try the river with the intent to cross. Though I have a greater desire and almost a mind to return to Washington, and in a measure clear my name, which I feel I can do. I do not repent of the blow I struck. I may before my God, but not to man. I think I have done well. Though I am abandoned, with the curse of Cain upon me, when, if the world knew my heart, that one blow would have made me great, though I did desire no greatness. Tonight I try to escape these bloodhounds once more. Who, who can read his fate? God's will be done. I have too great a soul to die like a criminal. Oh, may He, may He spare me that, and let me die bravely. I bless the entire world. I have never hated or wronged anyone. This last was not a wrong, unless God deems it so, and it's with Him to damn or bless me.

For a long time Steve sat there trying to figure out what this meant for the one who really mattered, his brother. How much of this drool would Johnny agree with? Something else was bothering him about this book. He couldn't quite figure out what. It was like a distant voice echoing through a forest, where you can't quite make out the words.

Could a son entirely escape a father's influence? And just how much influence did Eldon LaSalle have over his son?

Who was this man?

Steve went to the computer and Googled. There was a Wikipedia entry on him, with a boxed text above it stating, "The neutrality of this article is disputed. Please see the discussion on the talk page."

Eldon Longtree LaSalle was born on August 12, 1930, in Montgomery, Alabama. His father, Homer L. LaSalle, was born in Richmond, Virginia, in 1893. His mother, Margaret Watts, was born in Christiansburg, Virginia, in 1912. Both of LaSalle's parents had a rich ancestry tied to the "Old South."

LaSalle was a brilliant student from an early age, but appears to have had trouble in high school. He allegedly beat another boy almost to death over an insult. The result was his expulsion from school. His father enrolled him in military school in 1946. After graduation he received a scholarship to attend Duke University. He graduated with a degree in mathematics in 1952.

Later that same year he married a cousin, Patricia Farrell. The marriage ended in divorce in 1960.

Sometime during the early 1960s, LaSalle became associated with Frederic Cleveland Hayes and his American Nationalist Party. Hayes, an early collaborator with George Lincoln Rockwell's American Nazi Party, broke ranks with Rockwell in 1961. LaSalle was arrested numerous times in the next several years, most notably for violence in opposition to Martin Luther King, Jr.'s march on Selma, Alabama, in 1965. Shortly after his release, LaSalle went into seclusion and began formulating a religious view he dubbed "Eugenotheism." The philosophy was an eclectic amalgam of Christian, Manichean, and scientific thought.

In essence, LaSalle began to teach that God is an all-encompassing power of light opposed by an equally strong power of darkness. The universe is thus a battleground between the two, and the forces of light must continue to progress, in an evolutionary sense, toward perfection. To LaSalle that meant purging the population of racial and mental impurities.

In 1970 he established a church in California, with himself as the head. He ran afoul of the IRS, which asserted that the church was little more than a tax dodge. LaSalle made millions in donations which, according to the IRS, he used primarily to fund a lavish lifestyle. After a ten-year legal battle, LaSalle was convicted of tax evasion and sentenced to eight years in prison. The conviction was later overturned by the Ninth Circuit Court of Appeals. It was while he was serving part of his sentence that LaSalle wrote a small book, *Booth Speaks*, which became popular among white-supremacist groups.

LaSalle has kept a low profile in recent years. He has been accused at various times of leading a cult, a Christian militia, and a polygamous sect. None of these charges appears to have been substantiated.

A blood-warm disquiet snarled around Steve's stomach. He had never been one for guilt by association, but this was a little too close to home.

There was still something extra bothering him about the book *Booth Speaks*. He looked at it again, read the last page one more time. That's when it hit him.

I bless the entire world.

Somebody else had said that to him. His brother, the first time he saw him in prison.

TWENTY-SEVEN

Gincy arrived at Steve's apartment at six, half an hour after Steve called him. The monkey was whispering again, telling Steve what a prize jerk he was for trusting a con named Johnny LaSalle with a father like Eldon.

Didn't help to argue, to scream inside that Johnny could be innocent in all this, could be a victim himself.

The monkey did not care for fine points, and when it turned to screeching, Steve called Gincy, because if he didn't he knew he'd fall big-time.

He wanted Gincy there, not just on the phone. Something about Gincy's disposition always calmed the beast.

"Let's get out of here," Steve said as soon as Gincy walked in. "Let's drive, go see a movie or something."

"Got a better idea," Gincy said, flashing his famous smile.

"What?"

"Trust me."

Gincy he could trust. They piled into Gincy's red and white MINI Cooper. Gincy's weightlifter arms seemed bigger than the car. He popped in a U2 CD and said, "So what's going on in that lawyer head tonight?"

"I got a new client," Steve said.

"Oh yeah?"

"Only this one's a little different. It's my brother."

"Your brother? I thought—"

"It's him. The one who we all thought died."

"Wow. How'd you find him?"

"He found me." Steve told him the story, and about Eldon LaSalle and *Booth Speaks*. Gincy took it all in without comment.

When Steve was finished, Gincy said, "One day you think all those guys'll have dried up and blown away. Then you find out there's enough people who still think this way that you want to get yourself a gun and get ready for when they come for you."

He paused. Bono filled the space for a minute.

"I remember a Klan rally when I was a kid," Gincy said. "Right in our town. A town where my daddy was on the fire department. I remember him telling me to stay in the house. I remember him getting down the shotgun. And I remember his face. He wasn't scared. He was disgusted."

"So what do I do about my brother?"

"You talked to him about it yet?"

"No."

"Then you talk to him. You be up-front."

"And if I find out he's just as bad as his old man?"

"Maybe you're the one who can get him turned around. Maybe that's why this has all happened. God works like that."

"Not exactly great work, if you ask me."

Gincy finally pulled into a lot at the park by his own apartment. Steve was greeted by the multicolored lights and giddy screams of—

"A carnival?" Steve said.

"Hey," Gincy said, "Cotton candy is the single most underutilized antidepressant in America. Let's go get ourselves some pink happiness and walk around."

"*Carnival?*" Steve put his head back on the seat. "Oh man."

"What?"

"I asked Ashley to marry me at a carnival. Shall I just shoot myself now?"

"Oh man, I didn't know!"

"Why should you? You have a shotgun in the trunk, I hope?"

"Will you knock it off?"

"A .22? Anything will do."

"Shut your pie hole, Dilbert." Gincy sometimes called him the name of the well-known comic strip character to jolt him out of complacency.

Then Gincy was out of the MINI Cooper and on his way toward the lights.

Steve paused, then decided walking was preferable to car sitting. He caught up with Gincy at the entrance.

"Is this great or what?" Gincy said, waving his arms at the attractions.

Steve said, "What makes you so happy all the time?"

"I have my reasons, and—"

"Well, cut it out."

"Cut out being happy?"

"Don't you realize there's only a certain amount of happiness in the world?"

"Huh?"

"Yeah. The amount of happiness is constant and has to stay in balance. So every time you smile, somewhere in the world a unicorn's getting punched in the face."

"No such thing as unicorns."

"Oh? Maybe you've made them extinct with all that gladness."

"Let's get some cotton candy, boy." Gincy clapped Steve on the shoulder. Hard. The slap made a popping sound. They did get their pink confections, then walked the carnival. Kids were everywhere, playing games and riding rides and hanging onto balloons and whining at their parents. Real Americana. Something Steve and Gincy had both missed.

They were near the Ferris wheel. It was stopped, and a couple of kids at the top looked down, screaming.

Gincy faced Steve. "Is there anything else you want to tell me before we venture on?"

Steve looked at the ground.

"Steve, what's going on?"

"I met a girl," Steve said.

"Whoa."

"She works for me."

"And you want it to be more than that, huh?"

Steve said nothing. He felt like screaming, like the kids on the Ferris wheel.

"Who is she?" Gincy asked.

"Law student from DeWitt. There's something else about her."

"Now what?"

"She's pretty religious."

"She's pretty and religious?"

"Okay, yeah."

Gincy started laughing. He rocked back and let it go. "I love it!"

"What's so funny?"

"God has a sense of humor, maestro. I mean, here you are, Mr. Hardcore Atheist, Mr. I-Can-Do-It-All-Myself, Mr. There's-No-Higher-Power, and God hooks you up with a religious chick."

"Don't get all giddy about it. She wants to keep it strictly business."

"But you don't?"

"I don't know, I—"

"Oh man! Look at that."

He pointed to that sledgehammer attraction. "Remember those cartoons where the guy knocks the bell off, he hits it so hard? That's your stress level, dude."

"It's not that bad."

"Your divorce final?" Gincy asked.

"Almost. And Ashley wants me to move my stuff from the house."

Gincy got his serious sponsor look. "You been going to meetings?"

"Here and there."

He put a hand on Steve's shoulder. "Anything else you want to tell me? Aliens landing in your apartment maybe?"

"Isn't that enough for one night?"

"You got it." Gincy made a hunk of cotton candy disappear. "You're under a lot of stress. Maybe more than when you got hooked on blow. It's all coming back."

They moved on, past the milk-bottle pyramid and ping-pong-ball-in-the-cup game.

"So what's your advice, sponsor of mine?" Steve said.

"My only advice is the same as always. Give up."

"Excuse me?"

"Give up. Quit trying to do everything on your own. Go to God. That's how—"

"Not tonight, man." Steve tossed the rest of his cotton candy into a trash can. "I've had to look out for myself for twenty years."

"And what's come of that?"

What Steve didn't need right now was another one of Gincy's higher-power lectures. They were near one end of the carnival now. At a ride called the Zipper. Gincy turned to Steve, his eyes reflecting the red, blues, and greens of the carnival lights.

"You ever been on that?" Gincy pointed at the Zipper.

"What? No. I hate those rides." The Zipper went around in a fast, tight oval, almost like a small Ferris wheel. But as it did, each individual car—more like cages—spun around too. "If I got on that thing I'd color the inside pink."

"You afraid?"

"I just don't like 'em," Steve said.

"You have to take a risk in this life, bub. It looks scary to you, but it'll take you to a whole new level. And faith is the same way."

"I'm fine where I am, feet on the ground."

"I don't think you are."

"When did you get a license to practice psychotherapy?"

"The day I met you, man. Wait here. And think about what I just told you."

Gincy licked the last of the cotton candy from the paper, tossed it into a can, then handed a ticket to the guy running the Zipper.

TWENTY-EIGHT

"The big question," Sienna said, "is whether the church should incorporate as a 501(c)(3) or not. The main advantage is that it's easier for people to give tax-deductible gifts. But there's a theological question."

She'd arrived at Steve's office at two minutes before three on Friday afternoon. Looking good in gray business casual. He poured them a couple of Diet Cokes from the little refrigerator, then sat at his desk. Her printed memo was in front of him. He'd read about half of it. The point was, she was here.

"We have to bring theology into it?" Steve said.

"Hello. Church."

"Excuse me. What's the issue?"

"Does the church want to be tied up with the government? In a way, the whole idea of Christianity was against the government. It refused to bow down to Caesar."

"What about the whole rendering unto Caesar thing?"

"What about it? There's a difference between obeying the law and getting your church tangled up in the government."

"So what's the alternative?"

"You just declare yourself a church."

"You know what?"

"What?"

"You're pretty when you get theological."

Her eyes narrowed. "You're going to have to stop that."

"Can I help myself?"

"Yes."

"All right," Steve said. "Here's what I'm thinking, Sienna. Seriously. I'm having a hard time with this setup."

She sat back and sipped her Coke, waiting for him to explain.

"It's like this," Steve said. "I think they want a church so they can launder money."

"What gave you that idea?"

133

"It's Eldon LaSalle's background. He got in trouble with the IRS before. And let's face it, my brother is an ex-con."

"You don't believe people can change in prison?"

"I haven't seen it."

"You've seen your brother. Don't you believe him?"

"I haven't had enough time to believe him."

"Are you his lawyer?"

"I'm somebody's lawyer. I just got a big fat retainer."

"So there you are."

"Where am I?"

"Hired. Count your blessings."

"You see?" Steve said. "You had to bring theology into it again."

She shook her head. "You can be a very annoying person when you put your mind to it."

"That's what the judges all say."

When Sienna smiled, Steve counted it as a small but significant victory. Maybe he could wear her down. Like global warming on the ice caps.

"There is another problem," he said.

"And that is?"

"The old man, Eldon, is a rank racist."

She cocked her head but didn't say anything.

"Yeah. He wrote this crazy book about John Wilkes Booth and the goodness of slavery and don't mix the races. I guess he's still got a lot of followers. Maybe even my loving brother."

"Have you talked to him about it?"

"Haven't had a chance. I'm driving out there tomorrow. What do you think I should say?"

Sienna shrugged. "Be honest. Do you think you can't represent them?"

"It's a lot of money."

"That's not what I asked."

"You're a clever little vixen. You want to get me to open up."

"Answer the question."

"I'm, like, a criminal defense lawyer, okay?"

"And what do the canons of ethics say about representing people you loathe?"

"You just took ethics, didn't you?"

"Answer the question."

"Okay, professor! Yes, I am obligated to provide representation to people unless I cannot perform my duties due to conscience."

"Hmm, I don't know."

"What don't you know?"

"You said you were a criminal defense lawyer. Ergo, no conscience."

She smiled super sweetly, and Steve wanted to give her a noogie. He wanted to kiss her. He wanted to take her home with him. He wanted to run away so he wouldn't ruin her.

He wanted to run to something that would finally pull him up, not down.

Johnny. He was the way. He had to be. The way to get rid of the past forever and the way to secure his professional future. Be a lawyer, for his own flesh and blood.

"Are you okay?" Sienna said.

"What?"

"You drifted for a minute."

"Drifted," he said. "That's the right word."

TWENTY-NINE

Hercules Auto Body was located on the east end of Verner, just before the main road hangs a hard right and heads toward the mountains. Steve arrived a little after eleven on a hot Monday and parked the Ark just inside the chain-link and razor-wire fence.

A Wyoming-sized man in dirty coveralls emerged from the office, turning slightly sideways to get out. He wore aviator shades and his mess of dark—or dirty—hair was pulled back in a pony-tail. A beard of like color and equal hygienic chaos covered most of his face.

"Whoa," the man said, eyeing the Ark. "She's a classic, she is."

Steve nodded. "She's a gas guzzler, she is, but nice and wide."

"Like me." The man smiled. Yellow teeth peeked through the beard. "What's wrong with her?"

"Nothing a little Turtle Wax won't fix. I came to see Johnny."

The yellow teeth disappeared behind a clamped mouth. "You his PO?"

"No. His brother."

Wyoming gave Steve a once-over. "You look a little more respectable."

"Is he around?"

"He's working."

"Can you tell him I'm here? I'll wait—"

"I don't run a messenger service."

"You can't just tell him?"

Wyoming didn't say anything, or move. The smell of grease and hand cleanser wafted off him.

"Look, this isn't a prison," Steve said. "You're doing him a great favor hiring him on. I want to make sure he keeps the job and does good work. I'm as interested in seeing him return to society as you are."

"I don't give a rat's patoot about society," Wyoming said. "I got a business to run and I don't need any distractions. Now if you—"

"Steve!"

Johnny, smiling broadly and wiping his hands on a red rag, was coming across the yard.

"Problem solved," Steve said.

Wyoming didn't look convinced. Before he could say a word, Johnny piped, "I'll take my break now, if you don't mind, Russ."

"I do mind," Russ said.

"I got it coming. I take it now, we get it out of the way, am I right?"

"You ain't calling any shots."

"And that's why I'm just asking," Johnny said. "Your word goes."

"Ten minutes," Russ said. "No more." Then he headed back to his lair.

When the office door closed, Johnny said, "So what do you think? I'm a working stiff again."

"Great boss."

"Ah, he needs to get over himself. He didn't want to hire me at first."

"So why did he?"

"I think he saw it was in his best interest, know what I mean?" Johnny smiled.

"No, I don't know what you mean."

"I mean, little brother, it's good business to do a little favor for the LaSalle family from time to time."

"Hey, what a coincidence."

"Huh?"

"The LaSalle family. That's what I wanted to talk to you about."

Johnny worked the red bandanna in his hands again, then used it to wipe his forehead. "What about it?"

"You tell me."

He studied Steve. Then he smiled and wiggled a finger in Steve's face. "You've been doing a little digging, haven't you?"

"I guess somebody had to. Why don't you tell me about *Booth Speaks*?"

Johnny shook his head slowly. "Don't be like all the rest, Steve."

"Why don't you answer—"

"You're my lawyer."

"You don't hold out on your lawyer. That's not a good way to start."

"How much time have we had? Have you given me a chance?"

That was true. Steve didn't like the slight hurt in Johnny's eyes.

"Okay, Johnny. But I need to know what's up with that stuff. If we're going to set up a church, I have to have all the info."

"All right," Johnny said. "But not right out here. Come on." He turned, and Steve followed him around the side of the garage. There were a couple of big white buckets there, turned over. Johnny sat on one, Steve took the other. The sun beat against the white wall, casting off heat.

Johnny said, "Do we still have a right to free speech in this country?"

"Of course," Steve said.

"I'm not so sure. Race is one example. You can't talk about race unless it's along politically correct lines. Eldon just wants to be able to say what he thinks."

"Like he wants to ship blacks back to Africa?"

"First of all, Steve, that's what a lot of the blacks themselves were saying back in the sixties. Eldon just agreed with 'em. They were burning down cities then. Killing cops. Rioting in the streets."

"*They?*"

"Blacks."

"That is classic bigotry."

"You think this country is better off with all the 'la-la and let's hold hands'? You think we got racial harmony? Go to any college, and what do you see? The blacks with the blacks, Latinos with Latinos. Come on. And in the joint it's a lot worse. It all breaks down that way eventually."

"But you can't have a country that way."

"We don't have a country now! And that's all Eldon is saying."

"What are *you* saying?" Steve asked. "That's the important thing."

Johnny paused a long moment before answering. "I'm also a work in progress, Steve."

Steve folded his arms across his chest. "When I came and saw you in prison that first time, you said, 'I bless the world.' Remember?"

"I bless the entire world," Johnny said. "That's the last thing John Wilkes Booth wrote."

"So you're cool with what your father wrote?"

"He read that to me as a kid, like a bedtime story. That stuff stays with you."

"Is it with you now?"

"Does it matter so much to you?"

Steve thought about it. "It does."

"Then do me a favor." Johnny touched Steve's arm. "Walk with me a little. Work with me. And in the process, make some good money. What's wrong with that?"

Nothing he could think of at the moment.

"Make a leap of faith," Johnny said.

Faith. He thought of Gincy then, and the Zipper. Only this thing Steve was experiencing wasn't faith in God, but in Johnny LaSalle. It had to be faith. What else could it be? Johnny was his brother because Steve wanted to believe it.

In a way, this whole thing would be like the opposite of kicking an addiction—one day at a time.

"I think it's time for you to meet the old man," Johnny said.

"Eldon?"

"Eldon."

"Yeah, I guess." Steve's nerves took a jolt. The prospect of meeting the great patriarch made him feel like the Scarecrow granted audience with the mighty Oz.

"You drive up around three," Johnny said. "I'll show you around Beth-El."

"Beth-El?"

"That's what we call our compound in the mountains."

"Compound? It sounds like Superman should be living there," Steve said.

Johnny smiled. "What makes you think he doesn't?"

THIRTY

First Johnny had to finish his workday, and Steve had to wonder what sort of world he was getting involved with. *Involved* wasn't the right word. On the one hand he was a lawyer doing a job. He needed the job. He needed the client and the money. By working for Johnny, he wasn't endorsing anything Johnny believed. If Steve were a doctor and Johnny came in for treatment, Steve would have to help him. When he defended a criminal he was bound by the canons of ethics to defend the person with zeal. Doing so wasn't the same as endorsing the crime.

He walked away from the shop, toward town, figuring to get a Subway sandwich or something, when Neal ran up from behind.

"Hey," Neal said.

Steve turned.

"You're starting to get the picture, right?" Neal said.

"What are you talking about?"

"Johnny. He's a prophet, you know."

"Prophet?"

"Yes. Someone who gets direct revelation from God. That means you have to listen to him."

The poor guy. He had that look in his eyes, the gullible-follower look. Steve knew that in prison culture there are two kinds of people, and only two. Those who rule and those who get stomped. The stomped only feel protected when they're hooked up with the strongest ruler. If they find him, they can become loyal to the point of giving up their minds. That's what Neal smelled like to Steve.

They're dangerous, these types, because if you cross the ruler, you cross them.

He was in front of Steve now and didn't move.

"Is that all?" Steve said.

"You don't believe."

"I'm going to get a sandwich. You want one?"

"You have to listen to me. If you don't, you could miss out."

Steve slapped Neal's shoulder. "Thanks anyway, man, I—"

"He had a prophecy about you."

Dead seriousness in Neal's face. Steve waited.

"Johnny said you would come. He said you would bring deliverance."

"Johnny said that?"

Neal nodded.

"What did he mean, deliverance? From what?" Steve said.

"I don't know. But you're here, aren't you?"

"I'm here because you gave me ten thousand dollars."

"No, you're not. You're here because God meant you to be here. He made you to be here."

"How did you get here, Neal?"

He didn't answer.

"I mean, how did you meet Johnny LaSalle, get hooked up with him?"

Still didn't answer. Which ticked Steve off. "You meet him in prison?"

"It's not important."

"Let me decide that."

"I'm not important. The only thing that matters is Johnny. He's got the anointing and you've got to help him. Don't mess up. If you do, it'll be bad."

"Let me ask you something. I'm sure Johnny won't mind you telling me about your organization."

"What's the question?"

"I did some reading up on Eldon LaSalle."

"So?"

"He's quite a controversial figure."

"All great men are."

"He's been tied to things like the so-called Christian militia movement."

Neal smiled and shook his head. "Man, that is such a crock. You know what the problem is? People don't know how to think for themselves. They basically buy into all the lies the government tells them, or TV tells them. It'd be funny if wasn't so sad."

"But why would people even say that if there wasn't some basis?"

"Look, man, there's been people trying to peg us for something ever since the Master put stakes down here."

"Master?"

"Enlightened Masters are rare, and Eldon LaSalle is one of them."

"What's an Enlightened Master do, Neal?"

"Enlightens, fool. He has been given the true Word."

"Who gave him the true Word?"

"God. Who do you think?"

"How do you know it was God who gave him the true Word?"

"You have to be around him to find out. Once you meet him, you'll know. You won't even question it. And once you know, man, you'll never be the same."

That's what I'm afraid of.

"And Johnny," Steve said. "You say he has some appointment?"

"*Anointing.* He's going to carry on after the Master is gone. It's like Jesus and his apostles."

"There were twelve of them, weren't there?"

"Johnny don't need nobody else." Neal put his finger on Steve's chest. "You best remember that. You can't stay the same. You stay the same and you die. You got to get in the fight. There's good and evil and light and darkness, and if you don't line up on the right side . . ." He didn't finish the sentence, but made a fist.

Then he turned and walked back toward the shop. Steve wondered if he'd just been threatened. Or merely confronted by a guy who had pretty much given up his own personhood to a "prophet."

It was now two thirty in the afternoon. Soon it would be time for a friendly visit with Eldon LaSalle.

Steve's stomach did a few half gainers thinking about it.

Steve munched a six-inch turkey breast sub in the corner of a small Subway shop on Main Street. It didn't go down without a fight. He didn't feel much like eating, tried not to think about the strangeness of it all, but there wasn't any way to avoid it. Prophecies about Steve Conroy, the deliverer? It sounded like something out of *Ghostbusters*. Maybe he'd tell Johnny he was the Key Master and be done with it.

What if his brother was certifiable? Lost in delusion? What then? Would it be better if he'd never heard from Johnny in the first place?

There was a mussed-up newspaper on an adjoining table. The *Verner Herald*. Steve gave it a quick look, trying to get more of a sense of the place. Small-town stuff. A book fair coming up at the local library. A man named Howard Lochner had landed a twenty-five pound rainbow trout in a local mountain lake. Almost a record, they said.

The door swung open and a bit of LA walked in. Two black kids wearing basketball jerseys. One was the purple and gold of the Lakers. The other was a New Jersey Net. Neither one was exactly Verner attire.

Steve watched them, but not as hard as the manager of the store, a short man with a comb-over who perspired from the forehead. He kept his eye on them as they took their time looking at the menu and cracking a joke only they were in on.

A funny kind of tourist, Steve thought.

He went back to the paper. Exciting stuff. Green Valley Elementary was starting in a week. The president of the PTA, Kitty Bates-Rooney, was looking forward to an "awesome year" because of "the most dedicated teachers in the county, who are already at work preparing for the kids."

And then she mentioned how everyone was rallying behind Joyce Oderkirk at this "very difficult time."

Joyce Oderkirk.

Steve pushed the last of his sandwich in his mouth and washed it down with now watery Pepsi. He asked the skinny kid at the cash register the way to Green Valley Elementary. He had to ask again because the kid kept taking glances at the two new customers.

But he finally gave Steve the information in a voice that cracked twice.

THIRTY-ONE

"My name's Conroy. I wonder if I might speak with Joyce Oderkirk?"

The woman gave Steve a suspicious look. "Are you a reporter or something?"

"No."

"What then?"

"I'm a lawyer."

Wariness dug deeper into her eyes. "You know she's suffered a terrible loss, don't you?"

"I do. I knew her husband."

"I'm sorry. It's awful. Two little girls. I don't know how Joyce does it, but she's here and she's—" The woman stopped as if she'd just revealed a state secret.

"Please," Steve said. "I think she'll want to see me. If you could tell her I'm here."

"What's it about?"

"If you don't mind, ma'am, that's personal. But important."

She shrugged, but her shoulders fought it. She told Steve to wait and went to an inner office. He looked at a framed picture of Dr. Martin Luther King, Jr., speaking at the famous Washington rally. The "I have a dream" speech. He wondered if Johnny LaSalle went to school here, if he looked at this same picture, if his elementary mind was molded more for racism by his father than inclusion by his teachers.

The woman returned and, tight-lipped, said, "She said she would see you. Room twelve."

Steve found the room at the end of a row, near the chain-link fence typical of the penitentiary look favored by California elementary schools. Even in Verner. The blue door under a rusty 12 was open.

Poking his head in, Steve saw a woman sitting at an old-fashioned wooden desk on the other side of the room. "Mrs. Oderkirk?"

She looked up. "Yes. Come in."

The room was done up in fourth- or fifth-grade style. Steve couldn't really tell the difference. Pictures of all the presidents lined the wall like a ring of imperial heads. Except one was missing. Steve glanced at the vacant spot as he offered his hand to Joyce Oderkirk. She took it without standing up.

"One of your presidents is missing," Steve said.

"Oh," Joyce Oderkirk said. "Yes."

"Let me guess," Steve said. "I used to know them." He took a step to the left and saw that it was the one after Millard Fillmore and before James Buchanan. "Oh man," he said. "This is going to be tough."

Joyce Oderkirk said nothing. She was about thirty, with black hair and light almond skin, maybe Mediterranean blood in her background. Pretty.

"I'll guess Harrison," Steve said.

Glumly, Joyce Oderkirk shook her head. "Pierce."

"You lost Franklin Pierce?"

"Brenda said you were a friend of Larry's."

"Not a friend exactly."

Joyce frowned. "She said you were in business together?"

"Let me explain," Steve said. "I had called him to help me locate an autopsy record. When I came out here to see him, I found out he'd been killed."

"That's not what you told Brenda. I thought you were a friend—"

"I'm sorry for the misunderstanding."

"There was no misunderstanding." She glared. "You purposely ... who are you?"

"My name is Steve Conroy. I'm a lawyer. I'm—"

She stood up. "I don't want to talk to you." She looked frightened, like Steve might be wearing a wire or carrying plutonium.

"I'm not here on a legal matter," Steve said. "I just wanted to see how you were doing."

"Why?"

How to explain the coincidence of her husband's dying at the same time he was being retained by a brother with nefarious connections? How to phrase a remark that wouldn't deepen her grief, but would prompt her to give him a word worth having?

He thought about leaving the poor woman alone. She didn't need to think foul play was involved. Thought about it, then stayed.

"I just wanted to know, that's all," Steve said. "Larry seemed like a nice guy, and ... well, that's all."

She paused, considered, then sat back down, folded her hands on the desk like one of her students might. "I'm sorry. It's just been so hard."

"I understand."

"There wasn't a better-liked man in this whole community." She started to tear up, but fought the breakdown like someone who'd been doing nothing else for the last couple of weeks. "He was not reckless. I just can't imagine he'd drive off the road like that, unless something caused it."

"Maybe an oncoming car."

She shook her head. "That was my first thought. I went to the exact spot it happened. I looked up and down that stretch of road and I didn't see skid marks of any kind. I can't imagine there wouldn't have been some marks."

"Could be something was in the road. A deer maybe."

Mrs. Oderkirk actually smiled a little, looking at her hands. "It's funny you should say that. There was one thing Larry always told me, something he said his father taught him. About animals in the road. He said you just have to hit them. You just have to, if you can't stop, otherwise you could swerve and hit another car. And as much as we love animals, Larry said, we have to love people more."

Now she was crying softly. "I never could follow his advice. Even if it was a little squirrel." She pulled open a drawer and withdrew a tissue, dabbed her eyes.

Steve gave her a moment. "Mrs. Oderkirk, you mentioned that Larry was well liked. I can see that, having just talked to him on the phone. He seemed that kind of person."

"He was."

"Can you think, though, of anyone who might have had something against him? He was a deputy sheriff, after all. Maybe somebody he arrested one time?"

"I suppose that's possible. Anything's possible." She met his eyes directly. Hers were brown and dark. "You don't suppose?"

"Can I ask, does the name Eldon LaSalle mean anything to you?"

Her wet eyes widened. "Of course it does. Not in a good way."

"Why's that?"

"He doesn't exactly reflect well on the community."

"Might Larry have had some dealings with him? Maybe a run-in with him or one of his followers?"

She shook her head. "He never mentioned anything like that. That crowd pretty much keeps to itself. Owen ... Sheriff Mott, he seems to have found a way to keep things in order."

"Where do these followers hang out?"

"I don't know, I don't think about them."

"You haven't heard anything?"

"Why are you asking me these questions?" she snapped. "What's your business here?"

"I have a client who lives here."

"Who?"

"I can't really say."

Cogs turned in her head. "Do you have something to do with the LaSalles?"

Steve said nothing.

"You're trying to get information from me." She got to her feet again. "Get out, please."

"I assure you—"

"I've said all I'm going to say."

"Mrs. Oderkirk—"

"Please leave."

"Can I at least leave you my card?"

"No."

Steve put one down on her desk anyway. "Thank you for your time," he said, and walked out.

THIRTY-TWO

Sheriff Owen Mott was leaning on his cruiser just outside the school's front gate.

"I guess you like it here," he said. He still wore his pants tucked inside his boots. For some reason Steve found this comical, but he kept himself from laughing.

"It's all right," Steve said. "A little small for my tastes."

"But you keep coming back. Is it the food?"

"The Mickey D's in town is reputed to be one of the best."

From the look on Mott's face, Steve knew jokes were not his thing. "What were you doing talking to Joyce?"

"Did the woman in the office call you or something?"

"We have a close-knit community, Mr. Conlon."

"Conroy."

"And if some lawyer from LA comes all the way back here to hassle a widow, then—"

"I wasn't hassling her."

"She just lost her husband."

"I wanted to ask her some questions is all. When she asked me to leave, I did. Go on in and talk to her."

"I asked you this before, Mr. Conlon. What is the nature of your business here in Verner?"

"And I told you that I'm a lawyer, and that's all I need to say. This isn't Alabama in the thirties, after all."

Mott didn't crack a smile. "It could be," he said. "You're working with the LaSalles, aren't you?"

"Sheriff, I don't have to tell you that."

"You don't have to. It was a rhetorical question. You know, the kind you already—"

"I know what a rhetorical question is."

"And I know you're in with the LaSalles. The kid's on parole, the old man is doing who knows what, and they pretend it's for the glory of God."

"Maybe it is. Didn't Jesus hang out with sinners?"

"Didn't have much good to say about lawyers, though."

"Is there anything else?"

"Just the story of Zeke and the draw."

"Excuse me?"

"There's a tombstone in a graveyard somewhere that says, 'Here lies a man named Zeke, the second fastest draw in Cripple Creek.'"

So now he was the funny one. But Steve didn't even try to force a smile.

"What I mean, Mr. Conlon, is that you're free to do your business here, but stick to your clients. Don't try to get cute."

Steve looked at Mott's boots and knew this sheriff had been reading a little too much Louis L'Amour.

"I don't do cute," Steve said as he got into the Ark. As he drove off he looked in the mirror and saw Mott watching him. Steve gave him a little wave.

Small-town attitude. He couldn't help feeling this was going to be more of a problem than he'd anticipated. He half thought about heading right out of town, back to LA, calling Johnny later and saying, Thanks but no thanks. The pleasure of meeting your old man will just have to wait, Bro. Good luck with the rest of your life.

But that life was wrapped up in his now. For better or worse, he couldn't bring himself to just walk away.

He paused at the intersection where a green sign with white letters indicated the Verner Pass Highway. The road pointed up into the mountains.

The LaSalle compound was up there. What had Johnny called it? Beth-El. Whatever that meant.

Steve made the turn.

THIRTY-THREE

Beth-El's entrance appeared a few hundred heavily wooded yards from the highway. The private road was well marked with No Trespassing signs and ended at a huge black iron gate. On either side of the gate was an eight-foot wall, covered with ivy. It might have been the entrance to Yale or Harvard. But it was so out of place in these mountains, where wooden A-frames and ersatz log cabins were the more common design.

To Steve, Beth-El seemed the sort of enclave an eccentric with a lot of money and strong opinions could hole up in without worrying about someone sneaking in one night with a gun and a grudge.

Steve got out of his Caddy and pressed the button on a call box by the gate. A voice asked who it was and Steve told him and the voice said to wait.

Leaning against the Ark, Steve listened to the sounds of the woods and the wind in the trees. He wondered why he felt so nervous. He'd been around great wealth before, from the outside looking in, of course. He'd once prosecuted a rich Hollywood agent who was into forcing sex with his female clients. The guy had all the monuments of power and money, including a huge house in Pacific Palisades with a killer view of the Pacific Ocean.

Now all he had was a view of the exercise yard at the CMC in San Luis Obispo.

Money and land were the hard currency of California, unless you ended up doing hard time in the slam. Like Johnny had. And now it was Steve's job to keep him out forever, and maybe do the same for Eldon LaSalle.

Steve heard the crunch of steps approaching. Through the iron bars he saw the big guy he'd met at Johnny's place. Rennie. That was it. He was dressed in a tight, slate-colored T-shirt that gave him the look of an industrial press, like the one that crushed Arnold Schwarzenegger in *The Terminator*.

Without a word, Rennie opened a box and entered something on a keypad.

The iron gate slowly swung open.

Rennie said, "Drive up to the house." An order.

Steve got in the Ark, drove in, and saw in his mirror the iron gate swinging closed. Like prison gates.

The asphalt drive was cracked with age and covered with pine needles. It twisted for a quarter mile through a healthy blanket of trees. The place was enormous, like some sort of game preserve. Eldon LaSalle was, at the very least, a land baron. He'd done pretty well with tax dodges and bad racist fiction.

Steve took a couple more curves, then hit a straightaway into a clearing. And saw a mansion. No, mansions were too small. It was a *manor*. Or a fortress, one made of stone and redwood and gables with copper cornices. Paul Bunyan–sized steps led up to an expansive porch, and what looked like the door of a European cathedral. Only this door had horns of some kind prominently displayed.

Steve pulled the Ark to a stop in front of the steps and looked up and saw Johnny there. For a moment the horns on the door framed Johnny's head.

"Welcome, little brother!" Johnny called. "Come on up."

As Steve got out of his car, he noticed a couple of men off to the side, dressed in jeans and blue work shirts and military haircuts. They were just looking at him. The new arrival.

"What do you think of the place?" Johnny said.

Steve started up the steps. "Impressive."

"Impressive? You ain't seen nothin' yet. Come in and check it out."

Johnny pushed the door open and motioned Steve inside.

The first thing Steve saw was a moose head mounted on the wall. A big one, with cold glass eyes staring. If this were Disneyland, it might have blinked a couple of times and started talking. Welcome to Mooseland, kids!

The interior design was like a 1920s hunting lodge, a place William Randolph Hearst might have built for his buddies weekending for a little elk bagging. Everything was wood and rustic, with ornaments and furniture and fabrics that all seemed to come from antler-bearing beasts.

The doorways were all extra wide, as if trucks backed through them regularly.

"You a hunter, Steve?" Johnny said, leading him down a long dim hallway.

"Never took it up," Steve said.

"Boy, you don't know what you're missing. There's nothing like the hunt."

"Do you hunt for your food here?"

"Food and sport. You know, in the joint, there were two things I wanted right away when I got out. And the second thing was to go hunting."

He winked at Steve.

"Third day I was back," Johnny said, "me and Eldon went out with bows and I bagged me a big old buck. That's getting down to it, don't you think?"

"Down to what?"

"The elements. The essentials. Man against nature and all that."

"Like *Moby Dick*."

"Whatever." He opened an oak door at the end of the hall. "Come in and meet the old man."

Steve hesitated, half expecting flames to shoot out of the room. *I am Oz!*

Indeed, the most prominent feature in the room was the fireplace. It was the first thing Steve saw. It could hardly be avoided. It was maybe six feet high, with an ornate mantel of white stone. In the stone was a bas-relief Steve couldn't quite make out. It looked intense, like the fire crackling in the fireplace.

Another in a seemingly unending collection of huge antlers hung above the mantel. There were two further sets of antlers on the far wall, just above a solid oak bookcase packed with neat, leather-bound volumes. A leather wingback chair faced the bookshelf. Steve saw the top of a head in the chair, and smoke swirling up from in front of it.

"Pop," Johnny said, "here he is."

The head did not move.

The chair did. With a *whirring* that sounded just like a—
Wheelchair.

Eldon LaSalle was in the biggest, plushest wheelchair Steve had ever seen. A control panel with joystick—they did call them joysticks, didn't they?—took up the right arm of the chair.

Eldon LaSalle wheeled forward.

He was dressed in a red flannel shirt and black suspenders. He might have been a farmer, or a mortician on his day off. In his mouth a black briar pipe smoldered, the smoke framing his head like a halo of haze. His face was long and equine, his ears too big for the head. Gray, owlish eyes peered at Steve through the pipe smoke, the kind of eyes that miss nothing. Steve guessed him to be in his late seventies.

He put his hand out. Steve met him halfway, right in front of the roaring fire. He took LaSalle's hand. It was bony but strong and seemingly covered with leather, just like the chair. When he tried to let go, LaSalle kept the grip. He still had his pipe in his mouth. Steve could smell the blend now. It was a deep woodland smoke, something fit for a wizard.

"I've heard a great deal about you," Eldon said in a deep, resonant voice. Almost too much voice for the thin body.

"Good, I hope," Steve said.

"There is none good, but God alone."

All this while gripping Steve's hand and staring straight into his eyes. Steve felt like the cobra looking at the charmer.

Finally Eldon let go of Steve's hand, removed his pipe, and smiled a mouthful of yellow teeth. On his lap was a red, leather-bound book. He held it up. "Plato," he said. "You know Plato?"

"Not personally," Steve said.

"He got as close to God as one can get without knowing Jesus Christ. Quite an accomplishment." He held the book out to Johnny, who took it and walked it to the bookshelf.

"I'm happy to welcome you, my son," Eldon said. "For that is what you are. A brother to Johnny."

Steve swallowed, nodded.

"And what do you think of my home?"

"Quaint. A little vacation getaway."

"Far from it. This is Beth-El. The House of God. 'And God said unto Jacob, Arise, go up to Beth-el, and dwell there: and make there an altar unto God.' Do you know your Bible?"

"Um, not really."

"Ah, the riches that await you."

Steve smiled weakly, and looked again at the bas-relief on the fireplace. He could see it clearly now. Some figures in ancient garb, with serious faces and raised arms, loomed over a pathetic-looking man on the ground. He cowered, about to receive something very unpleasant.

"Do you like it?" Eldon LaSalle asked.

"Gets your attention," Steve said.

"I had it commissioned. It is the stoning of Achan."

Steve tried not to look overly befuddled.

Eldon paused, then waved a spectral hand at the artwork. "A division of Joshua's army was defeated by the city of Ai. Joshua rent his garments, for he thought the Lord was with him. But Achan, the son of Carmi, the son of Zabdi, the son of Zerah, of the tribe of Judah, took of the accursed things. A trespass before the Lord."

Steve had no idea what Eldon LaSalle was talking about. He looked to the side, at Johnny, who smiled with a go-with-the-flow look.

Eldon continued. "So Joshua, and all Israel with him, took Achan and the accursed things, and his sons and his daughters and his oxen and asses and sheep, and his tent, and all that he had, took them to the valley of Achor. And all Israel stoned him with stones, and burned them with fire."

"Ouch," Steve said.

"Exactly," Eldon said. "The commands of the Lord are serious things, but he is a God of mercy and love when you obey him. When you don't hurt your own tribe, when you're on the right side." Eldon placed his hand on Steve's shoulder. "Glad to have you on our side, Son."

Johnny said, "We finally got a lawyer we can trust, Pop."

"Indeed." Eldon LaSalle's owl eyes probed Steve's. Steve felt like he was being searched and warned at the same time. And wondered if there was a stone pile on the grounds somewhere.

"There is nothing worse than a lawyer you can't trust," LaSalle said. "But I'm sure you know that. And now it is time to break bread together. Enjoy the earth's bounty, Son."

THIRTY-FOUR

The dining hall was like something out of the old *Knights of the Round Table* movie. Dim lighting in the windowless chamber was provided by two wrought-iron chandeliers hanging from the high-beamed ceiling. A dark wood table ran nearly the whole length of the hall. As Steve walked in, twenty or so men were standing behind large wooden chairs.

Silent.

Most of them had a similar look. Short hair and work clothes. The arms with prison tats. The look of the ex- or soon-to-be con.

His new family?

Johnny led Steve to one of the empty chairs and left him there. Steve assumed the silent stance. When in Rome. When in the house of God.

He looked at the guy directly across from him. The guy stared back aggressively. Like if Steve went for the potatoes au gratin too soon he'd get his hand slapped.

He scanned the rest of the assembly, saw Rennie about halfway down, looking at him. Neal was next to Rennie. Johnny had gone to the other end of the table to the chair by the head. The only empty chair now.

A few minutes ticked by. Some of the guys at the table had their eyes closed. Praying? Or wishing the food was there?

Then Eldon LaSalle appeared at the far end. Steve hadn't heard any door open. It was almost like the old man had materialized through the wall. The wingback wheelchair hummed to the head of the table. He paused, then raised his hands.

At that, everybody bowed heads. Steve didn't. Until he saw Eldon looking straight at him. Steve closed his eyes.

Eldon's voice rose like a down-home preacher's. "'The LORD is my light and my salvation; whom shall I fear? The LORD is the strength of my life; of whom shall I be afraid? When the wicked, even mine enemies and my foes, came upon me to eat up my flesh, they stumbled and fell.'"

Eat up my flesh? Steve thought. Bring on dinner.

" 'Though an host should encamp against me, my heart shall not fear: though war should rise against me, in this will I be confident. One thing have I desired of the LORD, that will I seek after; that I may dwell in the house of the LORD all the days of my life.' "

If we ever get to dinner.

" 'For in the time of trouble he shall hide me in his pavilion: in the secret of his tabernacle shall he hide me; he shall set me up upon a rock. Arise, O LORD; save me, O my God: for thou hast smitten all mine enemies upon the cheek bone; thou hast broken the teeth of the ungodly.' Amen."

A hail of voices answered, "Amen."

Everyone sat.

Steve did too, in front of a table setting of pewter and silver.

Then the entertainment began.

A line of women, seven of them, varying in age, in simple, long cotton dresses, entered with platters and bowls of food, and dishes and pitchers. They began to serve and the men began to talk. The guy to Steve's right said, "So whattaya think, uh?"

He wore a buzz cut and scowl. Steve said, "What are we having?"

"Venison, hunted down by the ladies themselves."

"They hunt?"

"With the best."

"Is that legal?" Steve asked. "I mean, it isn't hunting season, is it?"

The guy gave Steve a half smile and a wink.

"Ah," Steve said. "So what do they hunt with?"

"Rifle or bow. Taught by the Master himself."

"Master?"

"Mr. LaSalle."

"Is that what you call him? The Master?"

"That's what he is, so that's what you call him. So you're Johnny's brother."

"That's right."

"You have a special privilege, my friend. Special. To be allowed in here."

A woman, maybe in her early thirties, came by with a pitcher and poured libation into Steve's and Buzz Cut's cups—chalices, actually. The woman kept her eyes down, except for a brief look at Steve.

For a quick moment he thought she was ... pleading with him.

Then, just as quickly, she looked away.

And moved down the table, serving.

Steve turned to Buzz Cut and said, "Can I ask you about the women?"

"Thought you might be interested," Buzz Cut said. "Hands off. They belong to the Master."

"Belong?"

"You know what I mean."

"I'm not sure I do."

Buzz Cut leaned a little closer. "We get our fish in town. Plenty to go around. You'll see. Right now, just take it easy and don't ask too many questions. You'll catch on."

He caught on to the food, at least. It was meaty, hot, abundant. He was trying to figure out how this gathering could be legally positioned as a church. In some ways this was like a Catholic monastery. Not that he was expert in that. But didn't they eat venison in cloisters and down casks of ale? Wasn't that what Friar Tuck did before joining the merry men?

Maybe Robin Hood could have made a claim he was running a church.

All Steve knew was that the First Amendment was pretty broad these days. From Scientology to Santeria, there was a smorgasbord of religion for all tastes. America was the HomeTown Buffet of spirituality.

But LaSalle's group was claiming to be part of the Christian tradition, so he'd have to watch carefully. He knew that any religion needed to operate consistent with its own charters. Eldon LaSalle was for the separation of the races. That was going to be a dicey item for the church bylaws.

The pinging of a utensil against a cup brought all conversation to a halt. Eldon LaSalle had called for order.

"We have a special guest with us tonight," he announced. "Steve Conroy, Johnny's long-lost brother, a renowned legal mind, has joined us tonight. Let's welcome him."

The group applauded as heads turned his way. Steve gave an embarrassed half wave.

"Steve and Johnny were separated as children, but now by God's grace are brought together again," Eldon LaSalle continued. He leaned forward. "It was my desire that the relationship between Johnny and Steve remain a secret. But that wasn't done."

He paused, and Steve caught a glimpse of Johnny's face. It was tight, and it seemed clear to Steve he'd just been rebuked by the patriarch.

"And so it is absolutely imperative that this news does not spread. Is that clear to every one of you?"

Heads nodded.

" 'If ye endure chastening, God dealeth with you as with sons; for what son is he whom the father chasteneth not?' "

Whatever that means, Steve thought. Though he had to admit the combination of King James English and LaSalle's deep voice was effective.

Only Johnny seemed to be stewing.

But one thing these people knew how to do was eat, so that's what he did. He did note the passive faces of the women as they served. That would be another item to look into. If this was a polygamy thing—women *belonging* to Eldon?—he'd have a whole new area for Sienna to research.

After the dessert, a robust serving of cookies-'n'-cream ice cream—Buzz Cut said it was the Master's favorite—the table was officially dismissed by LaSalle. The men got up and started filtering out.

Johnny left without saying anything further to Steve. Or anyone else that Steve saw. Steve was about to follow Johnny out when Eldon said, "Steve, would you join me in the library, please?"

THIRTY-FIVE

In the library, Eldon indicated a large chair for Steve, facing the fire. The flames cast a flickering glow on the wall of books. Achan still warded off his fate on the bas-relief.

Eldon positioned his chair across from Steve and next to a pipe carousel on a small table. He removed a pipe, packed it, and took a wooden match and lit up.

"Quite a collection you've got here," Steve said.

"All the people are here of their own volition," Eldon said.

"I meant the books. On the wall."

"Ah." He hissed a couple of puffs. "You are certainly correct about that. And I have read every one in here, some several times. The great books, the timeless ones. The men who move the world are those who have made the most of the life of the mind. Would you agree?"

"Sure, I suppose."

"No supposition about it. Books have been my education and my solace and have enabled me to understand the ebb and flow of history, without which we would all be subject to brute force."

Steve thought he was waiting for a response, and Steve had no idea what to say. So he offered, "How is that?"

Eldon puffed a few times. "History is but a fragment of biology, Steve. That's the first lesson you must learn. It is the key to understanding everything we do here."

Which is what Steve wanted to hear about. He looked into the fire and listened.

Eldon said, "Biology is about competition. Darwin was right about that much. Competition is not just the life of trade. It is the trade of life. Cooperation between groups may keep the peace for a time, but only until resources—material or spiritual or psychological—become scarce. Then survival is a matter of who eats whom first."

Steve nodded. He could agree that not getting eaten first was a good thing.

"Every group," Eldon continued, "be it a community or race or nation, has an ethos centered on partisanship and pride, acquisitiveness and aggression. In such an environment, selection is bound to take place. On a national level, there are wars. Within nations, there are groups that seek to dominate. And one of the factors that plays a role in all this is race. Would you agree?"

Steve measured his words carefully. "That's the reason we have laws. To keep people from killing each other."

"Which happens despite the law. We cannot depend on man-made institutions to save us when the enemy comes calling."

"Who is the enemy?"

"Anyone who is against us."

That might be a pretty large group, Steve thought. And it might include the federal government. "Could I ask you something completely personal?"

"Of course, Son."

"How did Johnny come to live with you?"

Eldon, his face half in shadow from the firelight, nodded slowly. "Our Lord said, 'Suffer the little children to come unto me.' When I heard about the terrible thing that was done to your brother, I couldn't sit back and do nothing. Johnny became my son as surely as if he had come from my own loins."

"Why didn't you try to get Johnny back to our mother?" Steve asked.

"I considered that. I even had some of my people look into it. But in prayer the Lord told me that this boy needed one thing above all else. A father. A real father. Yours had, in despair, taken his own life. That's a terrible thing to inflict on a child."

He had that right. In spades.

"May I ask another question?" Steve said.

"Certainly."

"We were told that my brother died in a fire. There was a body found, a little boy Robert's age. An autopsy was performed by a doctor named Phillips. Walker Phillips."

Removing the pipe from his mouth, Eldon said, "Phillips. He was a fool. But God uses fools, and used him for a greater good."

"How so?"

Eldon put his head back against the chair. "Your brother was kidnapped by a loathsome creature named Clinton Cole. Cole had a cabin in these mountains. Do you know what kind of a man Cole was?"

"A pedophile?"

Eldon nodded. "Evil. I found out what he'd done and dispatched some of my people to get Johnny out of there. Not long after that, Cole was killed in a fire. No one knows if he set it himself or someone else did. But they found in the fire not only Cole, but the body of a child. Connections were made. The authorities assumed the child was that of Robert Conroy, your brother. Phillips confirmed that in his autopsy. That was the hand of God, you see?"

"But you could have cleared everything up. You could have brought Johnny back to us. Why didn't you?"

For nearly a minute Eldon LaSalle did not speak. The crackling of the fire filled the space, popping like the random thoughts in Steve's mind. And he was feeling the desire again. He tried to picture Gincy in the room, pointing at him, telling him to calm down.

Finally Eldon spoke, just above a whisper. "I want you to prepare yourself, Son. I hoped I wouldn't have to tell you this."

"Please tell me."

"Your father. He was a friend of Clinton Cole. He shared Cole's ... interests."

Steve's throat clenched. Short breaths squeezed through.

"Steve, I don't pretend to have acted properly at all times. But I was not going to let your brother go back to that. Time went on, and when your father killed himself, it seemed to me a sign from God. I am sorry for your mother. And for you. I want you to believe that I was always acting in what I thought was the best interest of your brother. Will you believe me, Son?"

Believe this? *This?*

Could he? He didn't know.

"You're not a praying man, are you?" Eldon asked.

"No," Steve managed to say.

"Not a believing man?"

"There are some things I believe in."

"Would love to hear them."

"Recovery. I believe in recovery. And, as imperfect as it is, the justice system."

"Those are good things to believe in. Tell me, do you think I deserve justice?"

"Everybody does."

"Do you think people deserve a chance to recover from their past sins?"

How could Steve argue otherwise, now that he'd put his high-sounding philosophy out on the table? "Sure."

"Then I must know, Son. Do you have any hesitation about coming to work for us? To be our trusted adviser in all things legal?"

"I'm not saying no at this point. I just—"

"Would a sixty-thousand-dollar retainer help make up your mind?"

Steve's stomach almost jumped out of his body, megaphone attached, shouting, Take the money!

"Is that not enough?" LaSalle said. "How about seventy?"

"I think," Steve said, "that sounds very fair."

"And for that we will expect top-notch work, agreed?"

"Top."

Eldon stuck his hand out and Steve took it with some reservation. But not enough reservation to turn down seventy grand.

"Good," Eldon said. "This is very good. This is the will of God, that you're here with us. Here, you can begin to heal."

Johnny walked Steve out to his car. A half moon hung in the sky. The cold night air bit.

"You sure you won't stay?" Johnny said.

"I think I'll drive back." He needed to get back to his own place. His small apartment and a scruffy cat. He needed to think this all through.

"Got lots of room."

"Thanks anyway."

"It's been quite a night, hasn't it?"

"You could say that."

"You were in the library a long time with Eldon."

"He told me. Everything."

Johnny stopped on the gravel drive, looked at the ground.

"Why is he in a wheelchair?" Steve asked.

"Happened about ten years ago. One of the women rebelled. Got a gun and shot him."

"Whoa. What happened to her?"

"We went through the system. She was arrested, tried, and convicted."

"How long did she get?"

"Forever. She died in prison."

"What?"

"That happens sometimes."

Hardly ever in prisons for women, Steve knew. But things were tough all over.

Johnny said, "I know the whole thing. When I got nabbed, must have been hard on you, on our mother."

Steve said nothing.

Suddenly Johnny held him in an embrace. "You're home now."

Steve felt the warmth and strength of Johnny LaSalle, and for one moment in the night it was life and redemption. A starting over and a healing. A grip of one last hope. Steve threw his arms around Johnny and pulled hard, as if to squeeze the last of his doubts away.

To allow himself to be home.

THIRTY-SIX

Tuesday, Steve met Sienna just outside the entrance to DeWitt Law School. The school was tucked in near an old residential area about three miles from downtown Los Angeles. It was not one of the prestigious ivory towers attached to a university. But for almost seventy years it had catered to students who usually had to work their way through. It was known for its four-year night program.

"You didn't have to drive all the way down here," Sienna said, meeting him in the lobby.

"You're a struggling law student," Steve said. "You can't afford the gas to come out to my office all the time."

"How do you know I can't afford it?"

"You have a rich father or something?"

"No. But you don't know that."

"There's a lot I don't know about you, Ms. Ciccone. But we're going to take care of that right now."

They walked around the corner to the street behind the law school. The brick building was from the early thirties and was, at one time, a Presbyterian church. Steve had used the library a few times and read a pamphlet on the history of the place. It was fitting, Steve thought, that Sienna Ciccone would have chosen this place to study law. A little religious heritage to go with her own.

A strip of grass along the south side of the school held a couple of red iron benches. They sat. Sienna was dressed in Levi's and a navy blue sweatshirt with the school emblem on it. Steve caught a whiff of her hair. It smelled like morning.

"I need more help on this LaSalle thing," Steve said. "I need to know just how much they can get away with and still be legit under California law."

"What do you mean get away with?"

"Regarding views on race. Can they claim that according to their religion, they are not to be bound by things like equal protection and antidiscrimination laws? Can you do me a memo on that?"

"Sure."

"I'll pay. I can pay now."

"That's a good thing."

"There's more." He paused. "I don't know if you want to hear about the personal angle."

"If you want to tell me."

He did. He wanted to tell her and have her understand him, and then he wanted her to put her arms around him and kiss him and tell him all would be well.

So he gave her the story all the way up to the troubling revelations of Eldon LaSalle. He spoke evenly, wanting her to assess all the information for herself. When he was finished, he felt more vulnerable than he had in many years.

She looked off for a long moment. Then said, "That's an unbelievable story. How does it make you feel?"

"I don't think I know yet. I don't know if I completely believe it all."

"No? You think he's lying to you?"

"Or maybe he's got selective memory. I know one way to find out, though. There's a doctor named Phillips who may still be around. I want to see if I can track him down. He was there. He did the autopsy on the boy who was burned. He can corroborate what Eldon LaSalle told me. Or not."

"Do you know where he is?"

"I have a lead. I'll follow it up."

Sienna looked at her watch. "I have a class."

"There's another reason I drove down here."

"Yes?"

"I just wanted to see you."

When she hesitated in her answer, Steve felt like a sliding door had been left open, only slightly, with the curtains lifted by the breeze. Maybe he could sneak in after all.

"Mr. Conroy, I thought I made it plain—"

"It's because I'm not religious like you, is that it?"

"This is not getting us—"

"Or do you have an *other*? And I don't care if you sue me or run away screaming, I really want to know."

She smiled and shook her head. The door slid a little farther open. "You don't give up, do you?"

"Let me put it to you this way. You ever heard of Satchel Paige?"

"Baseball player?"

"And philosopher. He once said, 'Don't look back, something may be gaining on you.' "

"Profound."

"Yeah, it is. It's how I've lived my life. If I look back, I'm cooked. I've got to keep moving forward, and I will. So let me make my case."

"What case?"

"The case about taking you out to dinner, with no strings attached, just to get to know each other a little better."

Sienna looked at the sky. A heavenly appeal? Or a signal of frustration at the end of her rope?

"All right," she said. "Dinner. One time."

"Tomorrow night?"

"You do move forward, don't you?"

Driving back to the Valley, Steve had to make a case on himself.

Okay, boy, you've got your foot in the door. Keep it out of your mouth. Clean up your act. Maybe this is just what you need, a little inspiration. Motivation. A good woman.

She is good. Too good for you. Who are you, pal? She's got something. What have you got? You're a day-to-day guy, afraid to look back. Maybe you shouldn't do this thing. Maybe you'll drag her down instead of her dragging you up.

You'll get to know her and like her and maybe she'll like you, and then you'll fall and get high and ruin everything.

Bad idea, the whole thing. Call her back and call it off.

Steve flipped his phone open just as he merged onto the 101. Then he snapped it shut.

Life was risk. Life was the Zipper, Gincy said.

Go for it.

THIRTY-SEVEN

Steve stopped off at the Starbucks on Victory near the Warner Center. As he thought, Norm was there, laptop open, fingers flying, eyes wild with a desperate search for inspiration.

"Hey, Norm," Steve said.

The writer looked up, startled. "Don't do that!"

"What?"

"I'm in flow here."

"I need to talk to you, Norm."

"I'm working here!"

"Can I get you a refill?"

Norm's eyes flashed to the venti cup on the round table. He rubbed the stubble on his chin with his right hand, then nodded. "Okay," he said. "Straight drip."

Steve took the cup and got in line. He bought a tall drip and got a refill for Norm, then took them back to the table, pulling up a chair.

Norm took a slug of coffee, then said, "What are you doing here?"

"I thought maybe we could finally settle that account," Steve said.

"Oh, man! Don't hit me now. Give me some time, will you?"

"Norm, we can work it out another way."

"What way is that?"

"Your brother works for the DMV, right?"

Norm narrowed his gaze. "What are you asking?"

"I need an address."

"Can't do that."

"Of course you can. You did it before."

He cocked his head. "Now you're not gonna bring that up, are you?"

"Don't you remember me keeping that out of the public record? The prosecutor was going to present that evidence to the judge, that you used your brother to get that dealer's address. I kept that from happening, my friend."

Norm shook his head. "Man, you guys are like elephants. You never forget what you can use against somebody."

"I'm not against you. I'm asking you for a favor. Do this favor for me and we'll call our account all square."

"All?"

"Interested?"

"Do you realize what you're asking me?"

"Yes."

"Do you realize the trouble my brother could get in?"

"Yes. You in or out?"

"In."

"Good." Steve took out a pen and wrote the name *Dr. Walker C. Phillips* on the back of a brown Starbucks napkin. "Here's a clue. Temecula or Tehachapi."

"That's a clue?"

"He may be in one of those two places."

Norm ran his hand over his face, his chin, the back of his head. "All right! Fine! But I don't want any nickel-and-diming after this, are we clear?"

"Clear, Norm. You'll be doing a big favor for society."

"Yeah, right. If I sell this series, then I'll be doing a favor."

Steve nodded. "You're exactly right, Norm. We need a television show about a boy who becomes mayor. World peace to follow."

"You know," Norm said, "if I didn't know lawyers better, I'd say you were making fun of me."

THIRTY-EIGHT

Wednesday morning, Steve ordered a dozen red roses to be delivered to Sienna Ciccone at her apartment on Vermont. Might as well go all the way. It could be his one and only shot.

He went down to the bench in the courtyard of the apartment building and fed Nick Nolte a small bowl of milk. Mrs. Stanky yelled at him from her ground-floor apartment window. She didn't want that cat around. Steve smiled and waved, like someone who spoke English as a second language.

The boy from number ten, on the other side of the courtyard, was pedaling his tricycle around the perimeter, going for a land speed record. His name was Ramon and he lived with his mother. His mother was gone a lot. Ramon was too young to be left alone. Steve checked the apartment every now and then. Ramon was usually glad to see him, unless cartoons were on TV.

Then he heard: "Hey, what up?"

It was the guy from number seven, the little gangsta. He was smiling stupidly at Steve, his eyes with the red rims of the newly high. Short, maybe five seven in his socks, he wore an oversized jacket and low-riding jeans that bunched up over his white Converse sneaks.

Steve nodded, then looked back at Nick. He was in no mood for a conversation with Number Seven, which suddenly struck him as a perfect name for a rapper. Numba Sev'n.

Just shoot me now, Steve thought.

"Lissen up, we got to talk." Numba sat on the bench.

"Who invited you to sit down?" Steve said.

Numba's stupid smile melted into attitude. "What up with you?"

"Why don't you quit pretending you're from Compton? You have something to say, say it and then move along."

"Oh man, you are trippin'."

"Don't say *trippin'*."

"Don't tell me how to talk, dog."

"Don't say *dog*."

"You don't even know what I want."

"Whatever it is, I'm not buying."

"Don't know about that." His smile came back. "I can take care of you."

"Excuse me?"

Numba looked around, then whispered, "Set you up. Get you what you need."

A skin-tightening jolt hit the back of Steve's neck. "You have no idea what I need."

"I do, my friend."

"I'm not your friend."

Numba wrinkled his nose and made a sniffing sound.

Steve jumped off the bench. His foot hit the dish of milk. Nick Nolte jumped a foot in the air.

Grabbing two handfuls of Numba's jacket, Steve pulled the kid to his feet. "Who told you?"

"Get your hands—"

"*Who?*"

The gangsta in training tried to shake loose, but Steve was able to keep hold. "I don't have to tell you nothin'."

"Stop that right now!" Mrs. Stanky yelled from the window.

The distraction got Steve to loosen his grip enough for Numba to jerk free. He stepped back, bumped into the bench, recovered, and pointed at Steve. Didn't say anything. Just tried to screw his face into a menacing expression.

Then he turned his back and went off toward his apartment.

"That was a very bad thing to do!" Mrs. Stanky said.

Steve picked Nick Nolte up by the back of the neck, walked to Mrs. Stanky's window. Before he could say anything Nick put his paws out and clawed the screen. Mrs. Stanky yelped and took a step away from the window.

"Get him away from here!" she said.

Steve pulled Nick Nolte to his chest, where the cat relaxed. "Don't get excited, Mrs. Stanky. Breathe easy."

"Don't tell me how to breathe!"

That wasn't all he wanted to tell her. He walked away before he lost it completely.

He'd cooled off by five o'clock. All seemed quiet for once on the apartment grounds. Nobody screaming at him or getting in his face. He was getting tired of the flotsam and jetsam of society floating into the Valley, into his very apartment building.

He missed the Altadena house. It was a place with a lawn, his own place. He and Ashley hadn't been too unhappy together, had they?

Yeah, they had, thanks to him.

With the LaSalle money, if it kept up, maybe he could put a down payment on another house, or at least a condo. He had to get out of the Sheridan Arms before he went nuts. So maybe there were some unresolved questions about Eldon LaSalle, so what? How much did you ever know about any client?

Traffic was heavy through the Cahuenga Pass and past Hollywood, but Steve managed to get to Sienna's apartment a little before six.

She was waiting outside, talking on her cell phone. She saw him and gestured she'd be just a moment.

Giving Steve time to appreciate her all over again. He knew he was on major rebound. He knew he was doing this to cover the pain of the breakup with Ashley. And he knew he didn't care.

THIRTY-NINE

"How about a nice pinot?" Steve said.

"I think I'll pass," Sienna said.

"Religious scruples?"

"I have a feeling I need to keep a clear head tonight."

They were seated in a booth at Bistro Michel, always Steve's secret weapon. Whenever he needed some credits in Ashley's ledger, he brought her here. Until he burned through most of their accounts to fund his habit.

Steve said, "Then I will keep a clear head too." When the waiter, one of the old-world gentleman types, arrived, Steve closed the wine list. "Two of your finest colas, my good man. A Pepsi '98 if you have it."

The waiter frowned. Then nodded and left.

"Tough room," Steve said.

"Not with the right material," Sienna said.

"You are definitely the right material."

"Oh, please."

"Come on! That was a very slick line."

Sienna said, "I would rather not have this be a night of slick lines, all right?"

"Check." Steve wanted to stab himself with the butter knife. Instead, he asked, "How about this. What kind of law do you want to practice?"

"I'm not really sure. What's it like being a solo?"

"Not easy. You have scramble. You have to market. And you have to stay off drugs. Think you can stay off drugs?"

She smiled. "I'll try real hard."

"You also end up hacking off a lot of people. Like the feds. So do you want to help me take on the feds?"

She looked confused. "How?"

"Maybe you can help me with a 1983 action." Section 1983 of the United States Code was the statute authorizing civil rights violations against federal officials.

"On what basis?" Sienna said. "They have immunity."

"Qualified immunity," Steve corrected. "Your job would be to find a way around that."

"You have any ideas how?"

"Yes," Steve said, leaning forward with his elbows on the table. "Write a lengthy brief on my sophistication and charm."

"I think I can handle that in a memo."

"Ouch." His cell vibrated. He checked the number. "I have to take this," he said to Sienna, then flipped it open.

Norm Gaylord said, "Okay, I got it."

"Hang on." Steve took a pen and scrap of paper from his coat pocket. "Give it to me."

Norm read off an address in Tehachapi. "So is that it? I'm free of you, right?"

"As if you really want to be," Steve said.

"I really want to be."

"If it checks out, then yeah."

"And what if it doesn't?"

"I know what Starbucks you like. Thanks."

Steve clicked off. "Sorry. Where were we?"

"Memos?"

"Right. I have another one for you. Suppose I found out something about Eldon LaSalle that's criminal. Do I have to cooperate with the authorities?"

She thought a moment. "What about lawyer-client confidentiality?"

"You tell me, law student. Pretend this is the bar exam."

"Please, I don't need that stress just yet."

"What would you say?"

She paused, thought. "Attorney-client privilege. What is told to you in your capacity as a lawyer is protected."

"Unless it refers to a crime yet to be committed."

Sienna nodded thoughtfully. "That would be correct, but I believe you would have to show knowledge of actual intent."

"I can't remember," Steve said. "I'm a criminal defense lawyer. It's been so long since I've thought about ethics."

"I don't believe it."

"Okay, I'm tired of talking about myself. What do *you* think of me?"

She laughed and shook her head. "Incorrigible."

Sienna had duck. She'd never had duck before, and the waiter insisted she try it. Steve had the old reliable New York steak. When in doubt, go for the cow.

"It's very good," Sienna said. "But I feel like I'm eating poor Daffy or something. He was my favorite cartoon character growing up."

"And where was that?" Steve asked.

"I bounced around. My dad was an airline mechanic. Had jobs in Seattle, Detroit, Louisville. That's where I finished high school."

"How'd you end up out here?"

"I came out to go to UC Irvine. I was a theater major."

"No joke? You wanted to be an actress?"

"For a while. I wanted to be the next Julia Roberts, but my lips weren't big enough."

"You never heard of collagen?"

"Of course, but then I wasn't pretty enough, either."

"I don't think that's your problem at all."

She stuck her fork in some duck and held it there, looking at him. "You're smooth, I will give you that."

Steve said nothing.

"Did I say something?" she said.

Yeah, she had. But how could he tell her that Ashley had used the exact same words on *their* first time out? He'd been turning on the old charm and Ashley wasn't buying it and offered that he was *smooth*. Like she knew his every thought. It was a little strange having that same impression with Sienna Ciccone.

"Sorry, I zoned," Steve said. "After you decided you weren't going to be Julia Roberts, what did you do?"

"Decided I wanted to be Ashley Judd in *High Crimes*."

"Never saw that one."

"Your basic intelligent female lawyer solves everything."

Steve nodded. "And then you got married?"

"Excuse me?"

"Sorry, I mean your fiancé. The guy you met at church but it didn't work out."

"You're fishing?"

"Yeah, I'm asking about your love life here."

She shook her head, looked down at her food. Poked an asparagus spear, then poked it again. "I'm not ready to have this conversation."

"Hey, I didn't mean to offend. It's just, I think in the interest of full disclosure—ack, I can't help sounding like a lawyer."

"I'd rather we talk about something else."

"You've been hurt."

Putting her fork down, Sienna gave him the serious eye. "I don't want to discuss this. Maybe this was a bad idea."

Door sliding closed. "No, a good one. We can talk business. Or movies. Or TV shows. Or law or court or law school. Whatever it takes to keep you on my side."

"I work for you, don't I? I guess I owe you the same zeal you'd owe a client."

"Have you tried the zeal here? It's great."

"Bad puns, however, are a form of harassment."

And Steve decided it was love. He didn't need it. It wouldn't end well that he could see. He couldn't be good for her. He'd make a stupid move too soon and it would be over. He'd lose not just a companion but a sharp legal assistant.

When he took her home she requested he drop her at the curb. He told her the city was a jungle but he could tell she knew he wanted to kiss her. It was not going to be.

If only he could buy into some kind of faith. Take that ride Gincy talked about. Make the jump.

But when she closed the door of the car and started toward her apartment building, it felt, more than anything else, like the fade-out in a very sad movie. The kind where the guy doesn't get the girl after all.

FORTY

It was almost nine thirty when Steve got back to Canoga Park. He decided to stop at the office to get his CEB handbook on criminal procedure. He could work at the apartment tomorrow and needed to bone up on a few matters.

He parked in back and saw a couple of lighted windows in the building. One of them belonged to a CPA who seemed to live here, or else lived to work. Steve wasn't sure of the other one. But there were three cars in the lot, including his. He knew the CPA drove a blue Chevy. The other car was a sleek silver Porsche. Whoever it belonged to should know you don't park a car like that here, at night.

Whoever it was would probably find that out soon enough.

Steve was almost to the back door when someone materialized out of the darkness, spiking Steve's heart into overdrive.

The man was Latino, thickset. In the dim light Steve saw *vida loca* eyes. Steve had seen those more than enough defending juvi gangbangers.

"Let's go inside," he said to Steve, jerking his head toward the building.

"What?"

"Inside. Now."

"Look, I'll give you a card and you can call and—"

Catlike, the guy whipped out a switchblade and clicked it open.

"Whoa." Steve instinctively put his hands up in the universal gesture of *no problem.*

"Let's go," the man said.

"You got it," Steve punched in the after-hours code and the door clicked open. "I usually prefer prospective clients offer a retainer."

"Just go."

Steve took the stairs to the second floor, wondering the whole way if he was going to get a blade in his back. But none came. Yet.

Steve unlocked his office door, reminding himself to talk to Slbodnik about installing security cameras. The guy actually put the point in Steve's back.

"Easy, man," the guy said.

Steve did not intend to be anything *but* easy. He flicked on the lights. And gasped.

The office was a disaster area. Papers and files and plants and phones all over the floor. The credenza under the window was turned over on its back, like a dead animal with four legs in the air and guts spilled out. The metal filing cabinet was a shell, all the drawers out of it.

"Man, you got to take better care of this place," the guy said.

Steve turned around. The knife caught his shirt. He heard it tear. "Did you do this?"

The guy held the knife up. "Don't make any moves, man. Sit down."

"I want to know—"

The intruder put the knife under Steve's chin. "Sit."

"Sure." Steve threw his keys on the reception desk, which was now completely bare. All the contents, including the little plant that was dying anyway, were on the floor in front of it. Even the glass top was off. Steve saw one half of the broken glass on the floor.

Why the glass? That was just mean.

"Sit!"

Steve sat in the swivel chair.

The guy gave a quick look around. "You got security in here?"

"Of course."

"Where?" He pointed the knife toward Steve.

"My landlord," Steve said. "He's got guns. He waits for people with knives who mess up offices and then he starts shooting."

"Funny, man. You stay in that chair." He shook his head. "Somebody don't like you."

"And you know who it is."

"I don't like you. But I didn't do this."

"So what? You going to rob me?" Steve said. "I haven't got much to steal. As you can see."

The guy nodded. "No, you just steal life."

Steve fought to keep his voice from vibrating around in his throat. "What do you want then?"

"Carlos, man. You gave him up."

"Carlos? Mendez?"

"You got another Carlos doing hard time?"

"Carlos is serving his sentence, yes."

"You didn't get him off like you said."

"I never said that."

"You said something like that."

"Only an idiot lawyer would say that. You can't guarantee what a judge or a jury is going to do. I never tell somebody I can get him off. I just do the best I can."

"I don't think you do."

"All right, you want to get to the point?" Steve wished he hadn't said *point*.

"Yeah, I got a point. How long it take you to be a lawyer?"

"What do you mean, like school?"

"Yeah. Like school."

"Three years law school."

"You think I could go? I wanna be a lawyer."

"That right?"

He took a step closer to Steve. "That's right. You think I can do it? You think I got the brain?"

"Sure, a bright young man like you, ambitious."

The guy smiled. "I think you talking smack to me, baby."

"Me? Talk smack? I thought you wanted some career counseling."

"See, if a scumbag like you can be a lawyer, anybody can, right?"

Steve swallowed. "Is this a great country or what?"

The guy nodded, then held up the knife again. Steve was sure this time he'd use it.

He wondered if he could get a kick in. But a guy with a knife looking you in the eye pretty much has the drop. He decided to do nothing.

The guy thrust the knife into the desk, leaving it sticking out.

Steve looked at the knife. The guy stood there, almost daring him to take it. Steve said, "That's going to leave a mark."

"Okay, lawyer baby, I came to check out what you doing for Carlos."

"What I'm doing for him?"

"Getting him out of prison. What's wrong with you? You forget about Carlos? Eh? You blow the trial and then you just forget him? That it?"

"I did the trial, yeah. And I didn't get paid for it. But I did it anyway. I did what I could. You know, if Carlos hadn't been carrying he—"

"It don't matter about that." The guy took hold of the knife handle, wiggled back and forth to remove it, then stuck it in the desk again.

"Come on." Steve sounded feeble, even to himself.

"So you still got some work to do."

"I wasn't paid, okay? My part is over. They have legal aid, you can get an appellate lawyer."

"We want you, man. We want you to help."

"Who's *we*?"

"Carlos. And me. Ain't you listening?" He did the knife thing again. Removed it. New hole in the desk. "He's my cousin, dude. He's family. We are not happy."

"If I did such a lousy job," Steve said, "how come he wants me to be his lawyer?"

"No, you don't got to be his lawyer. Carlos, he's gonna represent himself."

"Okay then."

"But you got all sorts of things you can help him with, right? You got a computer. You got books. And you got time. You got time to help Carlos."

"I can't help Carlos."

"You going to." The guy took the knife out. "See, Carlos says, you help him. That's the way you pay him off."

Steve started to get up. The guy pointed the blade. Steve settled back down. Next thing the guy sprang forward, put his left hand on

Steve's neck. Put the point of the knife on Steve's bone, just below the left eye.

"You going to listen now, or you going to get this in your brain, huh? Tell me you listening."

"You've got my attention."

"That's good. Carlos'll tell you what he needs. You don't go to no cops, yeah? 'Cause I know where you live, man. I know where you work. Got that good?"

"Sure."

He pressed the knife into Steve's skin, enough for a puncture. Enough to draw blood. Maybe death was preferable to all this. What good was he as a lawyer or person? It had all caught up with him. Robert coming back was a curse, not a blessing. The other side held nothing. Sienna and Gincy were saps to believe it did.

"Okay, man. I think you got it. I really do. I think you got a lot of problems on your hands, you know? But you help out Carlos and you can stay walking around, yeah? And maybe you get your act together, man."

Finally, the guy withdrew the knife. Folded it back in the handle. "You got a card?"

Steve put his hand on his cheek, wiped, saw the blood on his fingers. "You cut me and you want my card?"

"Got to know how to get in touch."

Steve heard some words forming in his head, words that might get him killed.

But the guy said, "Wait." He bent to the floor and picked up a card, which was one of several scattered on the floor. "Got it." He slipped it in the back pocket of his jeans. "Later, man."

For a long time after he left Steve sat, staring. He felt an actual paralysis. Something stank, even more than the usual stink of his life. Smell over smell covered this one.

He wouldn't put it past the mad Serb to do this. But he was all paid up on the rent. Slobo should be happy with his money.

Somebody had to have picked the lock in this low-security building. A squirrel could get in without a problem. But how and when? It was true this office didn't have the highest traffic in the hallways. The tenants kept to themselves. There were a number of unoccupied offices too. It wouldn't have been too hard for somebody with intent to get in here.

Or somebody with authority. The feds? Not exactly the rule of law if that was the case.

What if it was random? His office was picked by a pro looking for a score.

His head was pounding now and rational thought was not to be had.

He got up and walked around, surveying the damage.

His interior office was trashed. All the bookshelves down.

And his computer gone.

Gone. Stolen, taken, everything in it.

Black's Law Dictionary was open at his feet. He reached down, picked up the cinder block–sized volume, and threw it against the wall. Grunted as he did.

Then it was book after book. Against the wall. Let them be damaged. Books and walls, who cared? It was all a farce, this office, this facade of respectability.

He kicked more books, started kicking them into a pile in the middle of the office.

Burn it down, he thought. Let's have a fire. Why not? A nice going-away present for the landlord.

Burn everything including—

The trunk. Had the guy messed up the trunk?

Steve went to it, opened it. The papers and photos were stirred around, but nothing seemed to be missing.

On top of it all was the photo of Robert in his train pajamas. Eating cereal.

Steve closed his eyes and let his breathing return to normal. His brother needed him. In some way he wasn't quite sure of, but there it was.

At that moment, Steve made his decision.

FORTY-ONE

Gincy came an hour later, in answer to Steve's call.

"You want to tell me why this happened?" Gincy asked as he perused the devastation that was Steve's office.

"No," Steve said. "I want you to help me pack it all so I can get out."

"Out where?"

"I have no idea. I'm tired of this building, I'm tired of paying for space here. Maybe I'll move out to Verner and be closer to my meal ticket."

"You're just a little upset."

"You figured that out, did you?"

"Sarcasm won't help."

"As if it won't."

"Funny."

"Just help me get this stuff packed, will you?"

"What's the rush?"

"I just had a guy in here with a very sharp knife threatening to do an unlicensed lobotomy."

"What?"

"Yeah, and he looked serious."

Gincy frowned. "You sure he wasn't just a repo man?"

"Will you help me clean up or not?"

"Did you report this to the police?"

"You go ahead if you want to."

"Anything missing?"

"Only my computer."

"What?"

"And my Dodger bobble-head doll."

"Did you have it backed up?"

"How do you back up a Dodger bobble-head doll?"

Gincy's mouth hung open. "Steve, this is serious."

"I'm seriously getting out of here. I have a backup somewhere. I'll be fine. But I've had it with this place."

"What about your books?"

"Let's burn 'em."

"How about you don't make any major decisions right now, huh?" Gincy started picking up some of the papers on the floor. "We'll deal with the big picture later."

"The big picture is no better than the little picture. It's all out of focus."

Four bags and three boxes later, the floor was clean. Gincy wouldn't leave until Steve promised not to make a move without thinking about it overnight.

Back at the apartment, Steve fed Nick Nolte in the courtyard, then called Johnny LaSalle.

"You want me?" Steve said. "You got me."

"What's up?"

"How would you like it if I opened an office in Verner?"

"Yeah? Great. Why not?"

"I'm thinking about it."

"What got you thinking?"

"City life."

"That's all?"

"When the cousin of your recently imprisoned client comes around with a knife and a threat, you get motivated." That, and a trashed office. An ex-wife who is really ex now. And a woman you're crazy about who isn't returning the feeling.

"Come on up then," Johnny said. "It's win-win!"

FORTY-TWO

Move fast. Make the cut sharp and quick. Don't look back. Something may be gaining on you.

Steve gave his notice to Jong Choi and said he could have the measly sticks of furniture that were in the apartment—unless he wanted them moved. Choi said he'd be happy to try to sell them and keep the proceeds, if Steve would move them to the parking garage.

Deal.

Then Steve called Ashley.

"Hey, it's your favorite lawyer."

"Steve, why—"

"Sorry to call, really—"

"What is it?"

"I need a favor."

"Steve—"

"Please."

"What is it?"

"You know that garage of ours—yours?"

"Yes?"

"Can I impose for a bit longer? Before I completely clean out my stuff?"

"Steve—"

"I feel terrible asking, but I'm leaving LA."

"You're what?"

"Getting out. Packing my bags."

"But why?"

"You really want to know?"

"I don't know. Do I?"

"It doesn't have to do with anything bad. I mean, that I've done. I just don't see any future here anymore. I've got my brother as a client. I figured I'd move out there. To Verner."

"Verner? What kind of practice can you set up out there?"

"They commit crimes in Verner. They also have church issues."

"Church?"

"My brother. He's wanting to be a minister."

"I still can't believe you found your brother."

"He found me."

"And he's religious now?"

"Let's just say I'm giving him the benefit of the doubt. He has some issues to work out, and I'm going to help him."

"Do you know anybody else out there?"

"No."

"What about support?"

"I'll find a group."

"Please do."

"So I need to leave some stuff behind. Just temporarily. Until I get settled."

"What is it exactly that you want to put in the garage?"

"My office," he said.

"Your *office?*"

"Somebody came in and sacked the place. A client's cousin threatened me with a knife. In general, not a good week. I have some bags and boxes and I promise as soon as I get the space in Verner, I'll be back and clean it all out. I'll even pay you."

"You don't have to pay me a thing, Steve. As long as it's not long-term."

"Yeah," Steve said, "sort of like our marriage."

"Steve—"

"Sorry. Thank you, Ashley. I'll be right over. I promise I won't let you down again."

Steve punched in the next speed dial.

"Hi, Sienna."

"Oh, hi, Mr. Conroy."

"You studying?"

"Con Law. First Amendment. Separation of church and state."

"What have you found out?"

"It's not in the Constitution."

"The First Amendment?" Steve asked.

"No, separation of church and state. The whole area has been a mess since 1947."

"*Everson v. Board of Education.*"

"Hey, you remembered." She sounded impressed. Steve liked that sound.

"Some of it stuck," he said. "I used to think the law was pretty cool."

"And you don't now?"

"Let's just say I have a much more realistic view of things. But don't let that keep you from being high-minded. That's one of the things I love about you, your—"

"Mr. Conroy—"

"So you still want to work for me?"

Pause. "Well, yes," she said.

"Even if I'm not an LA lawyer?"

"What are you?"

"A man without a city. I'm moving out. Taking my show on the road. To Verner."

"You're going to live there?"

"You don't sound too thrilled."

"No, I—"

"I'm flattered, don't get me wrong."

Silence.

"I didn't hear a hearty *amen*," Steve said. "Could it be you'll miss me or something?"

"I wish you well," she said.

"Hey, I didn't say we'd stop working together. They have phones now, and computers, and cars, the latest thing. They take you wherever—"

"Why would you want me to keep working with you?"

"I'm still going to need help. We don't have to be in proximity to do it, although being in close proximity might not be such a bad idea."

"Mr. Conroy—"

"Call me Steve now, please, and didn't you have a good time the other night?"

"Yes, but—"

"No buts. Let's just leave it at that. Okay?"

"Okay. Mr.—Steve, can I ask you something?"

"Yes."

"It's about your brother."

"What about him?"

"Considering his background, and considering the Eldon LaSalle connection, I wonder how much you can trust what's going on out there."

"I've thought about that. I know I may not be getting an angel here. But like you said, I can't—wait a second. Did you just show some concern for my well-being?"

"Don't you think being so close will make the situation more, what's the word, precarious?"

"Maybe I'll get a cat."

"Do you have any idea what living in a small town is like?"

"Do you?"

"I've lived in some small towns. There aren't a whole lot of secrets. Your life is going to be an open book."

"Well," Steve said, "it's been a pretty lousy book so far. A new chapter would be nice."

"Take care," she said. "I mean it."

"I'm glad somebody does," he said.

PART 2

FORTY-THREE

The new landlady, Mrs. Opal Little, had owned the building on Glade Street in Verner for forty-seven years. Originally it was the house her husband, Warner, built with his own hands and kept adding to, until it became a sprawling, eclectic residence that used to attract tourists. When Warner died in '92, Mrs. Little moved to a smaller house with her daughter and turned the house into commercial rental. This was about the same time Verner was discovered by the baby boomers and experienced an influx of professionals.

The Little building had six main units, three on the bottom and three upstairs. The corner upstairs was recently vacated by a chiropractor named Wilson who had decided to give up his practice, buy a sailboat, and circumnavigate the globe.

"Seems silly to me," Mrs. Little said, showing Steve the office. "What's he going to do when he gets back?"

"Maybe he won't ever come back," Steve said. "Maybe he'll end up cracking bones in Madagascar."

"You're a lawyer, you say?"

"That's right."

"We have too many of 'em right now, but I don't go around telling people what to do. All I want to know is if you have enough work to pay your rent."

"I've got a big client here in town already."

"And who might that be?"

"Well, that's sort of confidential."

"Oh my, of course. Where do you live?"

"Well, I haven't quite got a place yet. I thought I'd move to the office first, get the lay of the land so to speak, and take it one step at a time."

"You mean you're going to sleep here, in this office?"

"I might. Any rules against that?"

"And what might you do for a shower and shave?"

"Good question. Is there a health club in town?"

She thought a moment. "You're not married then?"

"Divorced."

"Shame. Divorce is such a shame."

"Maybe sometimes it's the best thing."

"Not according to the Good Book," Mrs. Little said. "I'm not one to meddle, but do you go to church?"

"Not as a rule," Steve said.

"Not even on Easter?"

Steve shook his head.

"That'd be a good thing for you to remedy," she said.

"Maybe it would be."

"All right. I've got a little add-on bathroom, shower, and kitchenette just off the garage. Warner put it there in case of emergencies."

"What emergencies?"

"He never explained that. Anyway, I'll let you use it until you find a place of your own."

"That's very nice of you, Mrs. Little. Oh, one more thing. Any rules against cats?"

"Cats? Here?"

"One cat. A very decent, well-groomed ... decent cat. I had one back home named Nick Nolte. I thought—"

"Like the movie actor?"

"That's right."

"I don't care for him. I like that Bruce Willis."

"That settles it. I'll name the cat Willis. That way I can say, 'What you mewin' 'bout, Willis?'"

"I don't understand what you just said."

"I think it's best that way."

"All right. I'll allow you one cat, but I'm going to up the deposit. If I have to do extra cleaning around here, well ..."

"Sold, Mrs. Little. Happy to be part of the family."

Part of the family. He'd never really had one. His brother ripped away, his father killing himself, his mother never the same after that. Foster care in California, that was a pitiful substitute for family.

Now he was here in Verner and was going to be part of a family again, only this one wasn't exactly the Brady Bunch. This was Eldon LaSalle and his religious ideas. Eldon LaSalle and his own little world.

But Johnny was here, and that thread was enough to keep Steve hoping that his past could get stitched up.

Maybe Eldon LaSalle wasn't all that much of an issue. A bigot to be sure, but he was getting old. He couldn't last forever, and Steve could work on Johnny to do things nice and legal.

He could save his brother.

That was it. That was the reason he was here. He couldn't save his brother before, when he was taken. Now he could. If he played it just right, he could get his brother back for real.

Get himself back too.

At two in the afternoon he decided to walk into the middle of town and find himself a real, authentic Verner lunch establishment. Something with atmosphere and plain good eating.

He found it on the main drag.

Chip's Cafeteria was a relic of a bygone era. It had a sixties look. Certainly the carpet seemed to have absorbed forty years of gravy and mashed peas and chocolate milk. The music over the system predated the looks. It was organ music, happily playing songs of the fifties.

Steve found out why as he entered. A display case offered several CDs, featuring a portly gentleman with curly white hair and a black moustache. He was sitting at an organ and smiling. *Chip's Favorites* was the title of the CD.

He had wandered into a Verner celebrity hangout. Where he felt like he should be wearing polyester.

The average age of the munchers seemed to be about eighty. He wondered if Curls and Red ate here. And argued over what kind of Jell-O was being served.

Steve was about to approach the tray station when he looked right. At a table by the front window, nattily dressed and reading a newspaper, was Edward Hendrickson.

Steve slalomed through the tables of octogenarians.

"Mr. Hendrickson?"

The old man looked up with a smile. "Why yes—" He stopped with a look of recognition.

"Steve Conroy's my name. I met you at the Bruck Mortuary."

"I remember." Guarded.

"Great. How's business? People dying to get in?"

Hendrickson looked puzzled. "Excuse me?"

"I have a friend, he's a writer. When he dies he's leaving his body to science fiction."

Stone face. "May I ask what you're doing here?"

"I heard the meatloaf was terrific."

"It is, but that still doesn't explain—"

"May I?" Steve pulled out a chair and sat down.

"If you'd like to inquire about our services," Hendrickson said, "I would ask you to come to the office during—"

"No, I'm not planning on dying just yet," Steve said. "And I hope I'm not there when it happens."

Hendrickson blinked.

"You're a long-time resident of this place," Steve said.

"Yes."

"Must know a lot of people, some of the old stories."

"What old stories are you interested in? Do you mind?" Hendrickson indicated his plate. It had half a filet of sole on it, with some pearl onions and broccoli off to the side.

"Please," Steve said.

Hendrickson took a bite. "Now. What stories?"

"I'm interested in finding out about a doctor, Phillips. You know him?"

Hendrickson stopped midchew. "Phillips?"

"Walker Phillips. I was told you knew him pretty well."

"Who told you that?"

"Does it make a difference?"

"Yes, I knew Dr. Phillips, but he moved away."

"I'm more interested in an autopsy he did back in 1983. Do you remember me coming and asking about that?"

Hendrickson took the napkin out of his lap and wiped his mouth. His hand was shaking. Like Parkinson's. Or raw nerves.

"I don't know anything about those days," he said.

"But you did say you knew Dr. Phillips. I was wondering—"

"He was a doctor in town. That's all."

"Mr. Hendrickson, if I told you that this was very important—"

"I thought Sheriff Mott made it clear to you that there are channels. I suggest you take them."

"Mott is a brick wall, and I think you know that."

"Young man, I know I want to finish my lunch. That is all I have to say."

"Something happened back there and you know about it."

"That's all I am going to say to you, sir. Please leave."

His voice had risen above the organ music, and Steve was aware of several looks coming from even the hard of hearing.

Steve stood. "That autopsy was performed on my brother. At least that's what they told us. But I think it was someone else. I want to know what happened. I need to know what happened."

"It is best," Hendrickson said, "to let the dead bury the dead."

"I've heard that," Steve said, "but I have no idea what that means, unless you're Dracula."

FORTY-FOUR

The next afternoon, Steve pulled into Ashley's driveway with a rented trailer attached to the Ark.

Ashley opened the garage door from inside the house.

"You could have kept your stuff here longer," she said.

"I got lucky and found an office right away. Thanks anyway."

"Can I help you load?"

"No, I'll do it myself. I've put you out enough."

"Really, I– –"

"I'll tell you when I'm done."

It took him a little more than an hour to get everything packed right. Then he was ready to do it, really do it. In Verner he'd be able to start afresh and be a small-town lawyer. He had a client with some deep pockets and he could build an actual practice. He wouldn't have to scrape for misdemeanor assignments or conflict cases.

Maybe he could become what he never was in Canoga Park—a respected member of the community.

Steve said good-bye to Ashley at the front door. For a fleeting moment she seemed to show the slightest wisp of sadness. Or maybe it was just his imagination bucking for a promotion.

"So this is really it?" Ashley said. "You're making a clean break?"

"Clean," he said.

"I really hope it works out for you."

"You never know. I might actually not muck this one up."

"You're a good lawyer, Steve. Don't forget that. Don't let anything get in the way of that."

Steve smiled. "You're the great lawyer in the fam … the best one I know."

Ashley looked at the ground.

"So anyway," he said, "I guess we won't be seeing each other again."

"Steve—"

"No, it's best that way. Time for me to leave you alone."

"We know where to find each other," Ashley said.

"At the corner of Bedlam and Squalor?"

"Drive safely, will you?"

"Hey, the Ark is—"

The sound of tires squealing into the driveway stopped him. A silver Lexus convertible.

Steve turned back to Ashley. "The Ark is not that car."

In that car was a perfectly coiffed guy of about forty, who emerged with the strut and bearing of the Los Angeles superlawyer. Steve knew the look. It was as unmistakable as the downtown skyline.

The new arrival took off his shades as he approached, folded them, and held them in his left hand. He wore a white shirt with blue stripes and patterned blue tie.

"Steve," Ashley said, "this is Ben Knight."

Knight stuck out a hand and Steve caught a whiff of cologne. Steve shook the hand. Knight put the vice grip on it.

"How ya doin'?" he said.

"Great." Not.

"That your Caddy? It's a classic."

"I could fit your car in my trunk."

"No doubt." To Ashley, Knight said, "I'm early. Can I pour us a drink?"

"Sure," Ashley said.

Knight slapped Steve on the shoulder, the old frat-boy pat. "Nice to meet you finally." He gave Ashley a kiss on the mouth and walked inside like he owned the place.

"Congratulations," Steve said.

"We just started going out," Ashley said.

"Oh? How many times? I don't usually do the kiss-and-I'll-fix-us-a-drink 'til the fifth date."

"Steve—"

"Are you up to fix-me-a-sandwich-and-take-off-your-clothes?"

"Don't act this way."

"Who's he a partner with?"

"How do you know he's a lawyer?"

"He almost tripped over his ego on the way in."

"That's not fair. You don't know him. He's a genuinely nice guy."

"Unlike your former husband, right?"

"I'm not going to do this. We can be nice to each other, can't we? You've said you're changed, and I'm happy for you, and I hope you'll meet someone who will make you happy too."

"Let's all be happy."

"Yes."

"Yeah. Well." He didn't know whether to shake her hand or give her a noncommittal hug or let her make the first move. They stood like topiary hedges, swaying a little in the breeze but fixed to the ground.

"Later," Steve said finally. He walked past the Lexus with the black leather interior and out to his Ark with the coffee-stain interior and drove away.

FORTY-FIVE

After a Taco Bell dinner, Steve made a last stop at The Cue. A farewell to the old place. Bye to the ex-wife, bye to the pool hall. Bye to life as he knew it.

Only not bye to the thought of Ashley and Superlawyer thrashing around. It hadn't taken her long. One thing about Ashley, she knew how to get the right things in life. He had been her only glitch, apparently.

Steve thought about it for only two seconds, then ordered a pitcher of Bud. He rented a rack and set up at the table in the back. He didn't bother with a glass. Just drank from the pitcher and shot pool.

The balls on the table were the scattered remnants of his life. He made up a game. The harder he hit them, the better it would be. Every pocketed ball would kill a voice in his head.

Only the voices just seemed to get louder.

So he ordered another pitcher.

Somewhere along there a guy asked him if he wanted a game. Steve said sure and tried to roll the balls without rolling on the floor. Shots faded into other shots. The Cue got cut out with a saw and put on a slow-moving roller coaster. The green felt of the table got fuzzier. Time moved too fast or didn't move at all.

And then, out of nowhere, this voice came into his ear. "A hundred you owe me," it said.

"Mh?" Steve looked for the source and saw a guy who looked familiar, only he was moving back and forth in front of him, sometimes looking like two guys, twins, and big. He had a smell too, like sweat, like body odor. Or maybe, Steve thought, that's me.

"A hundred," the voice said. "We played for a hundred."

"Hunnerd?"

"Yeah. Pay up."

Pay up. That got his attention. "I din'n play for no hunnerd."

"Yeah you did, and you pay me now."

"Don' got no hunnerd, why don' I buy you a beer?"

The guy threw his cue on the table—Steve heard the sound of it, like thunder—then grabbed a hunk of Steve's shirt and started dragging him toward the rear exit. The movement wasn't a good thing for a stomach full of Taco Bell and beer and Steve thought he was going to lose it. Either way, he wasn't in any condition to resist.

In a few seconds he was out in the back lot, then pushed up against the wall.

"Now you pay," the guy said. He put his hand on Steve's head and smashed it against the bricks.

Lights out.

Then swirls of light, and voices, and Steve feeling he was on his back and he knew he was inside The Cue again and a couple of guys were tending to him. And he smelled like ... oh no, all over himself.

"You deserved it," Gincy was saying.

Steve was lying on his sofa, head feeling like it was part of an Abe Lincoln rail-splitting contest. The guys at The Cue had made the call for him, and Gincy, loyal Gincy, had gathered him up.

Cleaned him up. Undressed him and threw his vomit-stained shirt and pants in the washer downstairs. Stuck him in the shower and gave him some oversized pajamas and made him lie down.

"I know," Steve said. "What was I thinking?"

"You weren't thinking, that's the point. How much money did you have with you?"

"Huh? I don't know."

"He emptied you. At least he left your wallet and credit cards."

"He cleaned me?"

"I put a couple of twenties in there for you, to tide you over."

"Gincy, you didn't have to. I've got some money in the bank."

"Did you gamble with this guy?"

"I guess."

"You were tanked up! What were you thinking?"

"I was thinking about my frat brothers."

"What?"

"My fraternity in college. Tappa Kegga Brew."

"Very funny."

Steve sat up. Abe put an axe through his head. He closed his eyes and groaned.

"Easy there, big fella," Gincy said.

Steve rubbed his eyes, then his temples. The axe stayed in, chunked down through his brain and behind his eyes, and hit the water.

Steve cried into his hands. Couldn't stop.

He felt Gincy next to him, then an arm around his shoulder, squeezing hard.

Steve fought to speak. "What ... am I ... gonna do?"

"Just be here," Gincy said. "That's all for now. That's enough."

For one night, it was. Gincy sat with him until Steve was cried out and finally fell asleep on the sofa.

Dreamless.

FORTY-SIX

Steve woke up at 4:00 a.m. and decided to slip out of town right then. Like an outlaw getting sprung from jail, wanting to leave under cover of darkness.

His head felt like Rocky Balboa's punching bag. He made some coffee and left a note for Gincy, and got on the road.

It was a peaceful drive, actually. Seeing the sun come up as he approached the mountains was a good sign.

He got to his new office before most of Verner was awake. The labor of moving his stuff in helped clear his head. At eight he unhitched the trailer and drove to a real ham-and-eggs place and ate his fill.

So here he was. It was Saturday, and he was already weaving himself into the fabric of small-town life. Invigorated, he wanted to do something, get going. And then it occurred to him there was a call he needed to make.

The house wasn't much to look at. Could have used a coat of paint. About twenty years ago. The yard was dirt and yellowing grass with a couple of old lawn chairs, bleached by the sun, sitting in the middle. But what was there to view from here? The front yards of some other houses were equally run-down.

Not a great place for a medical doctor to retire. As Steve knocked on the front door, covered by a screen, he wondered if this could really be the right place.

It was late morning in Tehachapi, a high-desert town known primarily for its prison.

He knocked again. The guy who answered was not a medical-looking man. He wore a white T-shirt stretched out by an ample gut. Looked about forty, with brown hair worn long and stringy.

"Yeah?" he said through the screen.

"My name's Steve Conroy. I'm looking for a Dr. Walker Phillips."

"Why?"

Not *who*. *Why*. Steve had hit pay dirt. "I have an urgent need for some information from an old autopsy he did. It involves a family member. My brother."

Long pause. Then a shake of the head. "I don't think so."

"Does he live here?"

"No."

"But you know him."

"So?"

"It's really important. I'm a lawyer, and I've come all this way—"

"Look, all I know is Dr. Phillips used to live here. I don't know where he is now. He hasn't been around for, oh, a year."

"A year?"

"Give or take."

"Any idea where he went?"

The guy shook his head. "He said something about back east, but that's all I know."

And all Steve knew was the feeling that this guy was not telling the truth. He took out his wallet, the one with Gincy's twin twenties in it. "If it'll help you remember," Steve said, "I can make this a financial transaction."

The door, which he'd almost shut, opened again. "What're you saying?"

"How's twenty bucks sound?"

"Insulting."

"Forty?"

"No way."

Steve shrugged and did the walk-away routine. He was two steps from the door when the guy said, "Okay."

Back Steve came, fishing the bills out of his wallet. The guy opened the screen door and put his hand out.

"Information first," Steve said.

"Out back," he said.

"He lives here?"

The guy snatched the bills out of Steve's hand. "Listen, he's an old man who's drinking himself to death, right? He's got some sort of income and he pays me rent and just asks to be left alone. Every

now and then I run some errand for him. I get him his food and his
liquor. He doesn't do anybody any dirt. He's quiet. So don't go getting him all upset, okay?"

"Thanks."

Steve went around the side of the house and walked down the
driveway. The place was a small duplex. The back portion looked
even more worn than the front. A small, square dwelling. Looked
like it might have been the garage at one time. A place for an old
car, not a dying old doctor.

He knocked on the door. Waited. The gray sky over the desert
was rippling like an ocean of sludge. Probably a storm coming.

No answer so he knocked again. Waited again.

He put his ear to the door and listened. Didn't hear anything.
He looked back at the main house and saw the T-shirt guy watching
him from a back window.

Figuring he'd paid for the privilege, Steve tried the door.

It opened.

Dark inside, and stale. But there was enough light that Steve
could make out a couple of items. Like the chair in the middle of
the room with a body in it. And a TV in the corner that was on
some NASCAR race, but with the sound off.

"Dr. Phillips?" Steve couldn't clearly see the man's face or eyes.
The odor of hard liquor hit his nose. "Dr. Phillips?"

A grunt, and the head rolled along the back of the chair. Steve's
eyes were adjusting and could make out a gaunt man. A gone man.

Steve looked around and found a lamp, turned it on. The interior
was late-American mess. Empty glasses in various places, including
the floor. A pair of scuffed black shoes by the door. The curtains
on the windows had orange boats and green palm trees on them,
as if to try to fool the occupant into a sense of tropical well-being.
A stack of *National Geographics* leaned precariously against a half-
empty bookcase under one of the windows.

The man in the chair snorted. He was wearing wrinkled khaki
pants, brown socks, and a light-yellow short-sleeved shirt with the
top two buttons undone. A tuft of pathetic white hair coiled from

his chest. On the coffee table in front of him was a nearly empty bottle of Ancient Age.

"Who is it?" the man said, lifting his head finally and looking at Steve. The man blinked his rheumy eyes a few times.

"You're Dr. Phillips?"

"Who are you?"

"Someone who needs to talk to you."

"Who let you in here?"

"The door was open."

Phillips rubbed his eyes with his hands, then looked for the bottle, as if to reassure himself it was still there.

"Can I buy you a cup of coffee?" Steve asked.

"What are you doing in here?"

"If you'll let me explain—"

"I don't want to talk to anyone." He waved a bony arm. He tried to sit up and, tiring of the effort, slumped back in his chair.

"I have to talk to you, sir, I'm sorry. I won't be long. Just give me a minute and tell me what you can and I'll leave."

A wisp of suspicion blew across his face. "Who are you? Who told you where to find me?"

"My name's Conroy. I have to ask you something about an autopsy you performed."

"I don't do that anymore."

"This was back in '83. It was a boy who died in a fire. His name was Robert Conroy. At least, that's what it said on the report. I have to know what—"

He swore.

"—you remember about that case. I'm sure it sticks out in your mind. That's not something that happens every day."

The eyes widened a little, the red in them the color of fresh blood. "Who *are* you? I demand you tell me."

"Robert Conroy was my brother. According to the autopsy report, which bears your signature, you made an identification by dental records. Do you recall that?"

He said nothing.

"Does the name Larry Oderkirk mean anything to you?" Steve said.

He looked to be drifting away.

"How about Owen Mott? Or Eldon LaSalle?" Steve said.

"Give me a drink. I need a drink." He found the strength to sit up. He reached out for the bottle of whisky. Steve snatched it away.

"You don't need any more of this," Steve said.

"Give that to me."

"After you talk. Then you can get as drunk as you want."

"How dare you? Give me that bottle."

"Talk."

When Phillips saw Steve wasn't going to give him the liquor, he seemed to shrink. He buried his head in his hands, and his shoulders started to shake. Like the quake of the ground before oil gushes, Steve thought. He was hoping the doctor would gush the story he had obviously tried to hide for years.

"All right, all right," Steve said. He left the man to cry a little, went into the bathroom, and looked for some tissue. Finding nothing but an old towel, he opted for a wad of toilet paper instead. The bathroom was not the cleanest he'd ever seen. The smell almost made him gag. He poured the rest of the whisky down the drain and left the bottle on the sink.

He came back to the doctor, who was in the same position, and put a gentle hand on his shoulder. "It's all right," Steve said, knowing it wasn't. He pushed the toilet paper into Phillips's hands. The doctor used it to dab his eyes.

His breathing started to normalize. "I never thought," he said.

"Take it easy. Just tell me from the top what happened."

"I was a good doctor," he said to his hands, now open in his lap. "A very good doctor."

"I'm sure you were."

"You don't know. Anything."

"Why don't you tell me?" If he wanted to lay out his life story, Steve wouldn't mind. As long as he got to the important stuff.

But the doctor said nothing, seeming to drift back into a fog.

"Doctor," Steve said, "do you know Edward Hendrickson?"

That blasted him out of the fog, and his wide eyes were the headlights. "Ed. You talked to Ed?"

"Yes."

"Oh no." His head slumped.

"Easy."

"I need to clean up." He touched his chest with both hands. "I'm a mess."

"I don't care."

"I care. Get me up."

Steve took hold of one of his skinny arms and lifted him. What was left of him anyway.

"Where's the bottle?" he said.

"Look, let's get some food and coffee in you. My car's out front."

"I feel sick."

Great.

"Sit," Phillips said. "Wait." He trundled toward the bathroom.

As Steve waited he almost said a prayer. He thought that the good doctor was what he, Steve Conroy, could very easily become if he ever lost it to blow again. He appreciated the warning.

He wanted to get out of this hole as soon as he could. Breathe some air. Maybe drop the doc off at the nearest hospital and say, Here, do something.

There was a car crash on the TV. No sound, just a flaming car and people running around. They were trying to get a guy out before he burned up.

Steve heard a door slam.

He turned around and saw the only two interior doors—one to the bathroom, one to what must be the bedroom—wide open. The doctor certainly hadn't gone out the front door.

Then it hit him. What he'd heard was a gunshot.

He ran to the bathroom.

Phillips was there, his frail body motionless, blood oozing out of the back of his head.

There'd be no doctor for Phillips. There'd be nothing, ever again.

FORTY-SEVEN

The detective looked about twelve years old. "You just found him there?" he said.

Steve was surprised the cop's voice didn't crack. "I heard the shot, yeah," Steve said. "He wasn't going anywhere."

Nearly an hour had gone by since Steve had called 9 – 1 – 1. Now the local homicide team was on the job. They were in front of the doctor's hovel, and Steve could hear the landlord screaming from inside his house. A few epithets and a couple of threats. Toward him.

"Now why is he so upset?" the detective, named Ross, asked.

"Why don't you ask him?" Steve said.

"I'm asking you, if you don't mind."

"I do mind. I told you what happened. I told you twice."

"I'm still not getting why you came to see Dr. Phillips."

"Toothache."

"He was a medical doctor."

"I misread the ad."

Ross heaved breath. He had ruddy cheeks and blue eyes. He could have been serving hamburgers at the In-N-Out. "You're not helping yourself here. You think being an LA lawyer is going to do you any good, you got another—"

"I don't have to help myself. I don't have to answer your questions, either. I had a personal matter to discuss with Dr. Phillips and I want it to remain personal. All I can tell you is that I came here, I started to talk things over with him, and he went in the back and shot himself."

"You must have upset him."

"He was already upset. The man was a drunk."

"Drunks don't always shoot themselves."

"This one did."

"And you have no idea why?"

208

"There are a million reasons for people to cash in. I'm sure if you dig around you'll find out whatever you need to know. It was a suicide, not a homicide, all right? There's nothing criminal here."

"That's what I have to find out."

"I'm telling you. There's only two people who know what happened in there, and one of them's dead. The other one is right here and he's telling you what happened. All right? Are we done here?"

"Mr. Conroy, you seem a little anxious to leave."

"Yeah, I'm anxious. Like Al Sharpton at a Klan rally."

"Excuse me?"

"Al Sharpton? Klan?"

"Sure."

"I can tell you're a real fan of stand-up." Steve handed the man his card. "I'll be happy to do up a formal statement and sign it under penalty of perjury. I'll fax it to your office. Okay?"

"I may have some more questions for you."

"I always like to help the local constabulary."

"Excuse me?"

"Constabulary? It means 'cops'."

The detective's face flushed like a fourth grader who just got reamed by the teacher. "I could hold you as a material witness, you know."

"That would just make both of us crabby. I prefer that you be crabby and I go home. How's that?"

"You'll be hearing from me."

"Looking forward to it."

FORTY-EIGHT

On the drive back to Verner, Steve considered whether to tell Johnny about finding Dr. Phillips. His big brother would definitely want to know, but then he'd also want to know what Steve was doing snooping around in the past.

And he'd have to say he didn't know exactly why. That he had these suspicions taking up residence in his brain. Formless doubts hovering around like the bad stink you get from an alley after the rain. It brings up the trash you might otherwise have missed.

Besides, what he did on his own time was his own business. Yes, he was working for the LaSalles, but he had not signed an exclusivity contract with them. He also didn't want to get anywhere near "belonging" to them. Like that guy said about the women of Beth-El.

That was more than a little strange.

At four in the afternoon, he drove to Beth-El for a client meeting with the LaSalles. His bread and butter now. Yes, the butter smelled rancid if you were to judge by the past. Maybe his being here was going to be a good thing for Eldon LaSalle. And Johnny. Maybe he'd be able to guide them along a way that was not completely nutty.

And make a nice, tidy, ongoing sum.

Yes, it could all work out very nicely. Except that driving into the Beth-El compound reminded Steve of *The Godfather* movies. The men standing around trying to look attitudinal were just like the mafia soldiers who were always around to protect the don.

Yep, religion was certainly a force for good. At least it was keeping these guys off the streets.

Steve met with Johnny and Eldon LaSalle in another room of the compound. It had the same hunting décor, but was set up like a conference room. The table in the middle looked like the cross section of a giant redwood. Glass was fitted over the top, shaped to fit the natural shape of the cut. Impressive.

And like every other room in the house, this one had a large, active fireplace.

"It looks as if there is not going to be any impediment for your official designation as a church," Steve said. "The free-exercise clause is a wide protection these days."

Eldon LaSalle nodded. "In principle," he said. "But what about views that society deems out of the mainstream? Such as that the Bible teaches racial purity, which it does. What's to stop the politically correct machinery of government sticking its nose in our business?"

"The Supreme Court," Steve said. "Back in 1993 there was a case involving Santeria. A city in Florida passed an ordinance that targeted a Santeria church because they have this little practice they call animal sacrifice. The court said, No way, Jose. In almost exactly those words. They said this was a sincere religious belief that was targeted by the city. Now, you don't sacrifice animals, do you?"

Johnny smiled. "Only for food, dude."

"So," Steve said, "this *practice* is protected. It follows that *beliefs* are even more protected, and expression of those beliefs also gets the benefit of free speech. As long as you're not inciting violence, you can believe whatever you want, teach it, promulgate it. You can be a church that does this. And the state can't touch you."

Eldon LaSalle leaned back in his regal wheelchair and smiled. "Well done."

Johnny winked at Steve.

Steve felt gratified and sick at the same time. He liked being a lawyer. He didn't like what Eldon LaSalle was all about.

But he kept reminding himself that this was no different than representing defendants who were guilty. Sienna would have approved.

Sienna.

He wondered what she was doing now. Wondered if she ever gave him a passing thought.

Then told himself not to think about her anymore, which made the thought all the stronger.

Eldon LaSalle backed away from the table a bit and positioned his chair between the fireplace and Steve.

"Son," Eldon said, "I can't tell you how glad I am to have you with us. To have you on our side. To have you working with Johnny."

"Thank you," Steve said.

"Do you know what I love about fire?" Eldon said.

Steve waited for the answer.

"It is both an instrument of wrath and an instrument of cleansing. Have you ever been near a forest fire, Steve?"

"Nope. Nearest was looking up at the wildfires in LA County, but I was in the flatland."

"Son, you don't ever want to be caught anywhere near such a thing. The sound is almost as bad as the heat. It's like hell coming up from the earth to visit for a while. And that's what God's wrath is like, Steve. It is going to be just like that for the wicked when the Lord returns to judge the nations. When he sends his angels to gather up the wheat and the chaff, and he throws the chaff into the unquenchable fire where the worm dieth not."

Steve swallowed. "Worms, huh?"

"Do you have any idea what it would be like to be eaten by worms for eternity?"

"Like having *Wild Hogs* on an endless loop?"

Eldon LaSalle did not smile. Steve looked at Johnny. He gave Steve a half smile. It was better than nothing.

Eldon said, "The Lord's judgment is nothing to be made light of, Son. For 'when the people complained, it displeased the LORD: and the LORD heard it; and his anger was kindled; and the fire of the LORD burnt among them, and consumed them that were in the uttermost parts of the camp.'"

"Bummer," Steve said.

"Our camp is somewhat the same, Steve. It's an instrument of the Lord. And that's why we'd like you to consider yourself more than just a lawyer for us, more than just someone who is being paid. We want you to think of yourself as part of a family. A big family.

You see, I know what it's like to need family and not have it. I know what you've gone through."

Steve sensed Eldon was on a preacherlike roll and said nothing.

"And as part of the family," Eldon said, "I'd like to think we're all on the same page, so to speak. Do you know what I'm talking about here?"

Without knowing the specifics, Steve certainly sensed the gist. He felt one of those mountain fogs starting to descend, or maybe an avalanche, covering the landscape.

"Do you?" Eldon repeated.

"Maybe." Steve cleared his throat. "You have a view of things that is rather well known. And controversial."

Eldon waved his hand. "I've been lied about for many years. That's why I stopped talking to the press. They never report what you say. They never make an effort to truly understand. They are tools of the corporations and the government. They have no interest in the truth. Do you have an interest in the truth, Steve?"

"Of course."

"Think about your answer."

Johnny, sitting on Steve's other side, added, "Think real hard, Steve."

Pressed between the rock of Eldon and the hard place of Johnny, Steve swallowed and said, "Yeah. Of course I do."

"Then do you believe in good and evil?" Eldon asked.

"Well, yeah."

"How? Tell me, how do you determine what is good and what is evil?" Eldon took a pipe from the carousel on the conference table and opened up the tobacco jar.

Steve did not want to get into this. He had better things to do than talk philosophy with a former associate of white supremacist groups. Yes, that had been in the past, but that sort of poison never leaves a system. Steve had come across many neo-Nazis over the years, and even the ones who "reformed" never completely gave up their views. It was like the fat drippings on a barbeque. Scrape all you want, the residue remains.

What he really wanted to know was what Johnny thought of all this. How much was Johnny invested in the warped views of his stepfather?

"I think everybody pretty much knows what's good and evil," Steve said.

"I disagree, Son." Eldon lit his pipe. "Unless people have a common frame of reference, they can't distinguish good from evil. You have to start with a source, and that source is God. God is the one who created good and evil to begin with."

"Okay," Steve said.

"Now wouldn't you agree if God says something is evil, then it is?"

"I'll go along with that."

"And if he says something is good, then it is good?"

"Pure logic."

"All right then." Eldon sucked his pipe a couple of times, issuing smoke. "All I want to know is if you will make an attempt to understand my views."

"Mr. LaSalle, I'm not a religious guy. I don't mind if anyone else is. I'm good with that."

"I don't think you are."

"Excuse me?"

"I sense your disapproval."

The old face of Eldon LaSalle took on the impression of a Halloween mask. Steve looked quickly at Johnny. Johnny was looking down.

"It's not up to me to approve or disapprove," Steve said. "Just to make sure you stay within the law."

"I want more than that, Steve. I want you to *see*. Will you at least keep an open mind?"

"Open mind? I can do that."

"Good. And a good job on rendering an opinion." Eldon LaSalle smiled. "You're one of us now. Don't ever forget that. I want you to come to our Bible study tonight. I think you'll find it most edifying."

"I don't know, I thought—"

"I really would appreciate it if you'd come."

The Eldon LaSalle eyes bore into him.

"Well, you know," Steve said. "I wouldn't miss it."

"What the heck was that all about?" Steve asked Johnny out on the driveway.

"What do you mean?" Johnny said.

"I don't like being told what to do."

"Who's telling you?"

"Who do you think? He orders me to a Bible study."

Johnny patted Steve's arm. "I think it's a good idea."

"I think I'm being set up," Steve said. "I think you and Eldon want me to start thinking like you."

"Is that such a bad thing? To try to convince you that what we're doing is something that's right?"

"I find it hard to believe that your God would be a racist."

"You don't think everybody's racist to some degree?"

"No."

"You were never in the joint. You find out real quick it's all about race. It's how God wired us—"

"Come on."

"Can you honestly say that mixing the races has given us any good thing?"

"I don't want to get into that," Steve said. He looked at the sky the way a prisoner might out in the yard. "Johnny, I need to know. How much of this do you actually buy into?"

"Why do you need to know that?"

"Because that's why I'm here! That's the only reason. It's *you*. It's you I want to be with and know and help and be around for. I don't care about all this. It's you I care about."

"Steve—"

"You're my brother. We're the same blood, but are we the same at all? Or is it too late? Has it been too long, too many turns by each of us?"

"No, don't say that." Johnny looked Steve straight in the eye. "Trust me, will you? Stick with me. There's more going on."

"More?"

"This is just between you and me, okay?"

"What is?"

"What I'm about to say."

"All right."

"There is more going on here than you know. But the thing you want, you and me together, it will happen. If you can just trust me and wait, it will happen."

"What will happen?"

"Just be patient. Get to know us, get to know the town. Settle in. One step at a time, huh?"

Just like recovery. Well, what else did he have? He'd made the break, he was in with one foot if not two.

"Okay, Robert. Johnny."

Johnny said, "That's the ticket, my brother. Tonight. Here. Seven o'clock. Just come on in and see what we do. I guarantee you won't be bored."

Of that Steve was certain. It was the one certain thing about this whole deal.

FORTY-NINE

The Bible study gathered in the largest room of the compound, bigger even than the dining hall. Steve was amazed that Beth-El seemed to grow larger each time he visited.

Tonight he was with an assemblage of LaSalleites, maybe twenty in number. Not your average Sunday school class.

A friendly bunch, though. They greeted Steve warmly, pumped his hand, gave him a brother-of-Johnny welcome.

One of them was Rennie, the muscled guy Steve had seen at Johnny's place. He was convinced the guy loved to put serious hurt on people for the sheer fun of it.

Now, at least, Rennie had a smile. With one gold tooth in the front.

He squeezed Steve's hand harder than necessary. "How you doing?"

"Better than most," Steve said. "Not as good as some." From this distance he could see more clearly the tats on Rennie's arms and neck. Prominent on the left side, just under the ear, were the letters *FTW*.

Which had a particular connotation, depending on one's view of the world. Steve must have been staring because Rennie said, "For the Word."

"Excuse me?"

"That's what it stands for now. The Word. The Word of God. That's what it's all about."

Steve remembered Neal's muttered warning that last time, about Rennie ending up killing someone someday. WWJK? Who would Jesus kill?

He did not want to be here.

He wanted to be with Sienna. He wanted to be sitting across from her in a local bistro, just talking. He didn't care what she said. Just hearing her voice would have been enough.

The women who had served dinner also laid out refreshments for the Bible study. These included a large platter of deli meats, with bread and condiments on the side, and a washtub of ice for beer and soft drinks.

No, not like any Sunday school he'd ever heard of. Wasn't there supposed to be a flannel board with Bible characters?

Beer?

Johnny offered Steve a Coors. Steve went for a Pepsi instead. Then Johnny introduced him around. Steve shook hands with Axel LaFontaine, a friendly sort in a Hawaiian shirt who had done time at Soledad.

Don Stead was a dog lover who had once been in prison for shooting cows. "Target practice," he said.

Mike Dietz was a fast-talking, guitar-playing ex-con from Fresno.

All regular guys with one thing in common—loyalty to an old man who preached the gospel of racial segregation and white superiority.

The sooner this thing was over, the better Steve was going to like it.

A little after seven, the big door opened and Eldon LaSalle drove his thronelike wheelchair into the room. Steve wondered how fast that baby could go if he cranked it up.

On his lap was a big black book with gilt edging. A Bible. Everyone took Eldon's entrance as a cue to find a seat.

Steve sat near the back, next to a guy named Bill Reagan. Did time for grand theft auto.

Eldon LaSalle wheeled to the front of the assembly, smoking his ever-present pipe. The room was silent as he slowly opened the Bible and took a few studious pulls on his tobacco as he turned the pages.

Then he looked up.

"The Word of the Lord," LaSalle said, then put his eyes back on the Bible and began to read. "'And Noah began to be an husbandman, and he planted a vineyard: And he drank of the wine, and was drunken; and he was uncovered within his tent. And Ham, the father of Canaan, saw the nakedness of his father, and told his two brethren without: And Shem and Japheth took a garment, and laid it upon both their shoulders, and went backward, and covered the nakedness of their father; and their faces were backward, and they saw not their father's nakedness. And Noah awoke from his wine, and knew what his younger son had done unto him. And he said, Cursed be Canaan; a servant of servants shall he be unto his brethren. And he said, Blessed be the LORD God of Shem; and Canaan shall be his servant. God shall enlarge Japheth, and he shall dwell in the tents of Shem; and Canaan shall be his servant.' "

The words came out in the rich honey tones of a baseball announcer. Steve could see immediately how LaSalle might hold a crowd in rapt attention. He would have made one great trial lawyer too.

Instead, he had chosen the life of a nut. But a powerful nut, not easy to crack.

"Yea," Eldon said, not reading now but looking at his congregation. "Ham did have his own mother, as the word of the Lord tells us in Leviticus twenty and eleven. And the product of that union was Canaan, the cursed one. His was a perverted, animal race. And lest they become enticing unto the line of Shem, God did remove their white skin and cause blackness to come upon them."

Steve looked around the room, wondering if anybody at all would at least ask a question. Like, How can anyone believe this?

No one did.

"Cursed too shall be those who mix their seed with the accursed ones, the mud people. A sentence of death shall be upon their heads."

Some in the group nodded their heads.

"It is pleasing unto the Lord to have a pure race in covenant with him, and that race can only be the white race, without any of the blood of Ham running through. The boil that holds such blood must be lanced and cauterized with fire. For the hour is coming, and now is, when a great beast shall do battle with the church, a beast of black and brown skin, and yellow eye."

Steve murmured, "Oh, brother."

A little too loudly. He got a frown from Bill Reagan. The LaSalleites were vigilant.

And, Steve shuddered to think, completely sold out to the man in the wheelchair.

The sermon continued. Steve tuned it out. He was more interested in scanning the faces of the men who were listening.

Especially Johnny's. But the expression was blank and unreadable.

Something moved in the back of the room. Steve turned and saw one of the women. He recognized her as the one who had briefly made eye contact with him in the dining hall. She was thin, with brown hair worn short and plain, and was holding what looked like a jar of pickles.

She placed this carefully on the table that held refreshments. She looked nervous. Then she turned back the way she came.

"Stop!" The voice of Eldon LaSalle thundered as if from the clouds.

The woman froze in place, head down.

In the dead silence that followed, the only sound was the ominous whirring of Eldon's motorized chair heading straight for the woman.

Steve watched, fascinated. The poor woman looked like a dog who knew its master approached with a rolled-up newspaper. The other men in the room watched silently, some with amused looks.

Like they'd seen this before. They knew what was coming.

The old man stopped in front of the woman and waited. She didn't move, didn't look up.

Then Eldon slowly reached out and stroked her hair. And again.

"You were wrong, weren't you?" he said.

The woman nodded.

"It comes from not being careful, doesn't it?"

Another nod.

"From a lack of total commitment."

Nod.

Steve tried to figure out what was so wrong about bringing a jar of pickles into a meeting.

"You have had this trouble before," Eldon said.

The woman's head did not move.

Until Eldon slapped the side of it.

The smack gave Steve a jolt. He squirmed in his chair, then felt a hand on his arm. It was Bill Reagan. He shook his head at Steve, a clear warning not to interfere.

"Now," Eldon said to the woman, "this is not going to happen again, is it?"

Slow shake of her head.

"That's right. Now, down on the floor and look at my shoes."

Steve looked around at the faces watching.

The woman sank to her knees, staring down at the feet of the great Eldon LaSalle.

He sat looking at her for a painfully extended moment.

No one said anything.

Then Steve heard a small sound, like the beep of a child's bicycle horn. A sob. The woman had obviously been trying to hold it in. Her body jerked.

"That's enough," Eldon said softly, reaching down to stroke her hair. "Enough now. No need for that. I am here."

Another cry burst out of her, louder this time, followed by another.

"No no," Eldon commanded. "I said none of that."

Too late. She was sobbing uncontrollably now.

Eldon looked around the room, at last making eye contact with Steve and holding the gaze. He may even have smiled, but Steve could not be sure.

The woman was sucking in air, trying to stop crying.

"Turn that noise into something useful," Eldon said. "Scream it out. Scream out the sin."

That suggestion brought a couple of muted guffaws from the mob. Steve noticed goose flesh on his arms even though the room was warm.

"Be a good girl, and give us a scream," Eldon said.

But she wasn't a good girl, apparently, and was not able to stop crying.

Eldon LaSalle shook his head at the sight, a *whatever shall I do?* gesture.

"Come on now, bark it out, all out, for me," Eldon said. "And all will be well."

Laughter from the assemblage rippled through the room.

"Bark like a dog, girl," Eldon said.

When she didn't he slapped her again.

Steve lurched out of his chair and said, "Hold it!"

In the next moment, several things happened simultaneously. Eldon looked up as if he'd been shot in the rear end with a BB gun. Heads around the room turned to look at the crazy man.

Bill Reagan's hand gripped Steve's arm like a trap.

With a quick jerk, Steve yanked free and almost ran to the spot where the woman was on the floor.

He'd better think fast and talk even faster. "As your legal counsel," he said, "I've got to advise you to cease and desist at this time."

Before Eldon could say anything—not that he looked like he would, preferring instead the hard stare of the truly ticked off—Steve leaned over and put his hand under the woman's right arm. He pulled. She came up halfway so she was on her knees.

Her surprised face, streaked with tears, looked at him. Confusion and fear merged in her eyes. He tried to help her to her feet, but she pulled her arm away and shook her head.

Steve heard Johnny say, "Steve, back off, you can't—" then stop when Eldon raised his hand. Silence filled the room. Even the girl had stopped crying, probably shocked out of it by Steve's butting in.

The goose bumps on Steve's arms came back, pebble sized.

Steve cleared his throat. "As your lawyer, in advising you on your status as a church and all the benefits that go with it, I have to tell you that this sort of practice would not be viewed with favor in a court of law."

Eldon's face did not move, though the crags in his face deepened. Like there were little daggers hidden there waiting to be pulled out and inserted variously in Steve's body.

"So," Steve continued, "it doesn't make legal sense to set yourself up for charges of abuse. No sense at all. The costs and benefits"—*and what am I doing trying to convince this crazy old man of costs and benefits? What am I doing here at all?*—"weigh convincingly in keeping the practices of the church in line with community standards."

A long pause gave no sign that Eldon LaSalle cared about what Steve was saying. Steve raised his eyebrows to communicate that he was finished.

"Is that all?" Eldon said.

"That's pretty much it," Steve said, hoping the woman would get up and get out.

But she didn't move. Eldon looked at her and said, "My dear, do you feel abused?"

The woman's eyes darted to Steve for one quick look. Then she shook her head.

"Are you sure about that?" Eldon said. "Because my lawyer here needs to know. He needs to hear it from you."

The woman shook her head again.

"So you don't feel abused?" Eldon said.

Another shake.

"You see?" Eldon said to Steve. "Do you know now that your assumptions are based upon lack of knowledge?"

Right. A woman scared out of her gourd, surrounded by neo-Nazi hominids, is going to offer a contradiction? Steve thought about reminding Eldon and everyone else that the fact of abuse does not rely on the opinion of the victim.

"It looks bad," Steve said. "Why don't we have a meeting about it and—"

"There will be no meeting," Eldon said. "This is not something to be decided by committee. This is a matter of the eternal Word of God."

"Sir, with all due respect, making a woman grovel and bark like a dog doesn't sound godly to me."

"You are a pagan," Eldon said. "You do not understand the things of God. That's why you're here."

"I thought I was here to be your lawyer."

"We are more interested in souls. Eternal souls, pure and undefiled, white as snow before God."

Steve said, "Sure. Sounds great. Now why don't you let her off the hook this time? Isn't there something about mercy in the Bible? Then you and I can sit down and you can straighten me out to your heart's content."

Which, Steve suddenly realized, might include something like what this woman had just gone through.

Eldon stared into Steve's eyes, and this time Steve did not flinch. He looked right back into those dark orbs, wondering how many people had fallen under their curse.

Finally, Eldon LaSalle spoke. "There is much you don't understand yet, Steven. And I don't wish to take up any more of our time with it." To the girl on the floor he said, "Go."

With a couple of large blinks, the woman slowly got to her feet. She looked around at the crowd once, then turned and scampered from the room. The big wooden door slammed behind her.

"Well," said Eldon, "let's not let this little setback interfere with our devotion to God. Let's get back to our seats, eh?"

A quiet search for seats began. Steve didn't move.

"You too," Eldon said.

Steve said, "I think I need to get back to the office."

"That would not be advisable," Eldon said.

"Well," Steve said, "I've never been very good about following advice. Later."

He turned and walked from the room.

Johnny caught up with Steve at the front steps outside the house.

"Steve, man, what is up with you?"

"Me?" Steve turned to him, faced him fully. "What is up with the whole crazy program here? When do you all start howling at the moon?"

"Don't be a jerk."

"What do you call making a girl scream at some shoes? What is wrong with you people?"

"If you'll shut your hole for more than a second maybe you can get it."

"I don't want to get it."

"You need to get it. Don't you believe in freedom of religion?"

"Religion, yeah. Not abuse."

"She wants it that way."

"Oh right, the way a dog wants to be whacked."

"No, the way a repentant sinner wants to be disciplined."

"Okay, you're going to have to explain that one."

"Exactly what I've been trying to do. Now listen, will you?"

"Go for it." As if Johnny could make any sense out of it.

"She was a whore," Johnny said. "And an addict. We found her on the streets when she was sixteen, man, hooked on the Kokomo. And you know what that's like."

Steve said nothing.

"We found her and brought her here to clean her up and save her life. And her soul. Look at me."

Steve looked at him, seeing the outlines of his face in the dark. His eyes seemed to burn. "She asked to stay here, to be helped to stay clean."

Steve did not know if he could believe him. And he had to know. "Johnny, I've got to ask you a question."

A slight flinching in the eyes, then: "Go ahead."

"How much of this is just an act?"

"Act?"

"To please Eldon. How much does he control you?"

"You got it all wrong."

"Do I? He's the divine master of everything up here. He butters your bread, and if he tells you to jam it, you do. Isn't that right?"

Johnny didn't answer.

"You're better than this," Steve said. "You don't need to carry water for Eldon LaSalle."

"I don't carry for anybody."

"That's what I'm talking about. I know he raised you up and all that and you're probably connected to him in a way that's hard to break."

"You don't know what you're talking about."

"Then why don't you tell me."

Johnny grabbed Steve's shoulders. "Listen to me, Steve. Listen carefully. There's gonna be changes coming down. You don't even have any idea. But you will. Soon. If you'll just stick with me. You're part of me. We're part of each other. I'm your guardian angel. Just trust me. Things are going to be happening. And when they do I'm gonna need somebody I can trust without question. That's you, my brother. Tell me it's you."

Steve couldn't. Not then. But he couldn't pull away completely. He'd come too far with his only brother. "I don't know what to tell you right now."

"Then just frost for a while. That's all. You're still getting your Verner legs. When you get them all the way, you'll be ready to dance."

FIFTY

Bible study, my shorts, Steve thought the next morning.

He'd spent a restless night on the sofa in his office. He knew why. Weirdness did that to you. What he'd seen at Beth-El last night was weirdness on wheels. Literally.

He sat up and flicked the switch on the Mr. Coffee machine he'd set up before trying to sleep. But he knew it would take more than a couple cups of joe to clear the cobwebs of disquiet from his mind.

He had no professional prospects at all, other than the LaSalles. He'd jumped at the money and the chance to start over.

Had he sold his soul?

Metaphorically speaking, of course.

And what would happen to him if he tried to get it back?

He poured himself the first cup of the morning, sat looking out the window of his office. He had a wonderful view of the parking lot.

He felt alone and lost. Like he'd been plucked out of Los Angeles by a huge, cosmic kidnapper and placed here, in an alien world, where his only link to sanity was a brother who was too connected to a certifiable old man.

Or was there another link?

He grabbed his phone and speed dialed Sienna Ciccone.

"Mr. Conroy," she answered, surprised.

"Is this a bad time? I know it's early. You're not in church or anything, are you?"

"Actually, I was just doing some Real Property reading."

"How exciting. When you get to the doctrine of incorporeal hereditaments let me know."

"Is there something I can—"

"Can we just talk?" he said.

"Um. Sure. Is there a legal issue you'd—"

"I've got an issue, but it's not legal."

"I don't understand."

"I have to decide what to do."

"About what?"

"About staying here."

"In Verner?"

"Yeah."

"But you just got there."

"Can I tell you what happened last night?"

"Yes, sure."

"I went to a Bible study."

"You did?"

"You sound shocked."

"Surprised, maybe."

"It was up at Beth-El, the mini fortress where Eldon LaSalle rules his little world. It was bizarre."

He gave her the whole account, all the way up to the woman forced to her knees in front of the Master.

When he was finished, he asked, "Does that sound like any Christianity you are familiar with?"

Pause. "There is a thin line to be sure. A line between free exercise and criminal activity."

"How about between free exercise and common decency?"

"What's not decent in one person's eyes may be decent in another's."

Steve took a deep breath. "I don't know what to do."

"Maybe you should walk away."

"Walk away?"

"Maybe it's just too close to the edge. You could chalk it up to experience and come back to LA."

She wanted him to come back.

Or not.

"But there's Johnny," Steve said. "If I did that, I'd be leaving him up there. Part of me thinks I'm supposed to get him out."

"Out?"

"Yeah. Out of that life. I couldn't save him when I was five. Maybe I can now. Maybe that's what my whole life is supposed to come down to."

It was the first time that thought had come to him so clearly.

"That's a pretty heavy burden to put on yourself," Sienna said.

"Why don't you come up for a visit?" Steve said.

"Excuse me?"

"To Verner. Come on up. I'll show you my new office. I'll ..." He paused, looked out at the parking lot that held only one car, his. "I just would like to see you, that's all."

After a moment, Sienna said, "Mr. Conroy, I don't think ..."

"I know. I just gave it a shot, you know?"

A beep. His call waiting.

"I've another call here," he said. "Sorry I took up your time."

"No, it's not that—"

"Later," he said, then hit the talk button.

It was Johnny.

"You feeling any better today, my brother?" he said.

Steve said, "Don't really know yet."

"Give it time. Remember what I told you. You know what you need? You need some work, to get in the game."

"Game?"

"You're a lawyer, right?"

"I used to think so."

"You know the criminal law, am I right?"

"To a degree that's kept me in cheap suits."

"Then I got some work for you to do. Think you can find your way to the county jail?"

FIFTY-ONE

The county jail in downtown Verner was connected to the court-house and run by the sheriff's department. It was a two-story, cream-colored design, able to hold a relative few, considering the size of the town. If there was ever a riot, Steve thought, the place wouldn't be able to accommodate more than a hockey team's worth.

Right now, though, it held one LaSalleite named Neal Cullen. The place was quiet, it being Sunday, so only the weekend staff was around. Steve showed his bar card at the counter and said he was representing Cullen. They gave him the booking sheet. He gave it a scan as he was led by a dark-haired female deputy to the attorney room. There were four stations, all of which were empty at the moment. No crime wave in Verner. But the day was young.

Another deputy, a robust man of linebacker size, brought in Neal, dressed in blues, hands shackled in front of him. He took a place opposite a one-foot partition. Smiling.

"Hey, Steve," Neal said brightly. "What up?"

"What do you mean what up? You're in jail, that's what up. You're going to be charged with felony assault."

"Don't worry about it."

The linebacker deputy grunted and moved to the other side of the room. Technically he wasn't supposed to listen, and anything Neal said was privileged. Still, Steve kept his voice low. "I'm not the one who needs to worry," he said. "Felony assault is not a minor thing. It's no misdemeanor."

"Steve, I'm going to walk out of here. I got a witness."

"A witness?"

"Rennie."

"How convenient."

"Huh?"

Steve opened his briefcase and took out a yellow legal pad and pen. "Why don't you just tell me what happened, from the beginning."

"Sure, Steve. Here's how it went down. Me and Rennie, we went down to shoot some pool at Vic's. You can ask Vic. Vic Cook, owns the place. We shoot there almost every Saturday night. You shoot pool, Steve?"

"So you're telling me you went to shoot pool after your Bible study, is that it?"

"Yeah, nothing about not shooting pool in the Bible, right?"

"Go on."

"So we played till about eleven, eleven thirty."

"Any drinking?"

"Oh, a beer or two."

"How many is a beer or two?"

Neal said, "You're a great lawyer, Steve. That's why I'm glad you're on our side."

"So how many?"

"You want a real number?"

"I like real numbers, Neal."

"Okay." Neal closed his eyes and started touching his thumb with his other fingers, counting. "I had maybe five or six. Rennie about the same."

"Any shots?"

"Man, you *are* good. Okay, I had a couple JDs. I don't think Rennie did."

"When did you start drinking?"

"How many questions you gonna ask me?"

"As many as I think I need to cover your sorry—never mind, just answer me."

"Steve, are you trying to say you think I was too jacked up to know what I was doing?"

"I'm asking you what the DA'll ask you."

"How should I answer?"

"Excuse me?"

"What answer'll do me the most good?"

"Neal, just for today, let's play a little game called Truth. I'm your lawyer, you tell me the truth, the whole truth, and nothing but. Then you let me take that little ball of info and bounce it around. Now, concentrate real hard. When did you start drinking and when did you stop?"

"Oh man, this is so not worth it. Let me get to the good part."

"There's a good part?"

Neal smiled. "Yeah, where I opened up a can of whoop on that mud."

"The what?"

"The mud baby."

"You mean an African American?"

"That's your word, not mine."

"You better learn it."

"Why should I?"

Steve rubbed his eyes.

"What's wrong?" Neal said.

"I've got another word for you, *hate*. As in *hate crime*. You even aware of that?"

"Come on, me? I don't hate anybody. Against my religion."

"Right, the religion of the barking dog and John Wilkes Booth. You know how that's going to look to a jury?"

Neal shook his head. "That's what I'm talkin' about. This ain't going to no jury. You got to hear my story. Can I tell you or not? I'm telling you what I drank has nothing to do with anything."

"All right, get it over with."

"No, listen. Me and Rennie, we play until eleven, eleven thirty. Then we walk out and think maybe of stopping at The Pipe for another drink."

"Oh, this is getting better and better."

"So we're walking down Arroyo and guess what I find out? I'm holding a cue in my hand."

"A pool cue?"

"Yeah! I walked right out of Vic's with it." Neal laughed. "I mean, I didn't even know I had it."

"Sure."

"No, really. I was playing so long it just kind of became a part of me, I guess. So I say to Rennie, let's go back and return it."

"Rennie, he didn't even mention to you that you were out on the street holding a pool cue?"

"Hey, you're right. Why didn't he say anything?" Neal laughed again. "That Rennie."

"Barrel of laughs."

"So we turn around to go back and that's when the guy steps out of the parking lot."

"The victim?"

"He's no victim."

"Neal, look around. This thing here is called a jail cell. As of right now, you are called a perp."

"Not gonna last. Rennie saw the whole thing."

"Oh yeah, I forgot about good ol' Rennie being right there. So what happened?"

"This mud comes at me with a chain."

"Just like that?"

"Yeah, can you believe it?"

Steve stifled his response.

Neal continued, "It's a good thing I had that cue in my hand."

"Lucky."

"You got that right."

"Any reason why this guy should come at you with a chain?"

"None! That's the whole thing, Steve. Except that he probably wanted to rob me."

"You and Rennie."

"Yeah."

"Rennie's a pretty big guy."

"Yeah."

"This guy with the chain, he was alone?"

"Yeah."

"How big was this guy?"

"I don't know, about my size maybe."

"You're not that big, Neal."

"It's not the size of the dog in the fight, it's the—"

"I know, I know. I'm just saying it seems odd, doesn't it, that a guy your size would come after you and Rennie both? Alone?"

"I can only tell you what happened, Steve. You wouldn't want me to start making stuff up, would you?"

The snort that issued from Steve's nose was completely involuntary. But not surprising. "Go on then."

"So I jump to the side and he comes down with the chain on the ground. Sparks and everything. And as quick as a cat, I swing the pool cue at him and get him on the back of the head. He tries to get up and by this time I'm sure he wants me dead, so I make sure he stays down."

"How bad is he?"

"I didn't stick around to find out."

"You left the scene?"

"I walked away at a good pace."

"And then where?"

"To The Pipe."

"Just went to the bar as if nothing happened? Didn't call the sheriff?"

"Why should I bother the sheriff? I took care of my own business."

"How did you get arrested?"

"Oh yeah. Darn pool cue. It broke up. I guess they figured somebody from Vic's did this, and went and asked about me. But that's the whole story, Steve. When can I get out?"

"When somebody posts your bail."

"When will that be?"

"Monday. You get to spend the weekend in this little home away from home."

"Oh man! I was hoping to watch the game today."

"What game?"

"Any game!" And Neal laughed again, like a jolly circus clown. That's how Steve left him.

FIFTY-TWO

He'd had too many lying clients to take any of what Neal said at face value. And that's what he needed now, face time. With the "witness" to the whole thing.

In truth, Steve did not want to be within twenty yards of Rennie at any given moment. Menace came off him like onion fumes. Get too close and your eyes would water.

Especially when he had an acetylene torch in his hand as he did now, in the open garage of the house where Steve had first set eyes on him. Steve wondered if Ezekiel the monster dog was chained up in the backyard. He didn't care to find out.

Johnny had his face stuck under the hood of a Lincoln. Rennie saw Steve first and didn't bother to ease the flame. He held it at his side like a gun.

"Your brother's here," Rennie said.

Johnny pulled out from the engine, looking none too pleased. Then he smiled. "Hey, Bro. How's Neal doing?"

Steve didn't enter the garage, as if going inside would take him into a dimension he'd rather avoid. "He's cooling for the weekend. I need to talk to Rennie here."

Rennie didn't move, the hot flame still gushing.

Johnny said, "We're doing a thing right now, trying to fix this—"

"I'm doing a thing too," Steve said. "Like I said, I need to talk to Rennie. I'll wait at the end of the driveway." Without waiting for an answer, Steve turned and walked to the road. He leaned against his car and looked at the mountainside. A touch of flame from Rennie's torch, and the whole thing could go up.

A few minutes later Rennie joined him. "Make it fast." At least he'd left the torch in the garage.

"You had quite a night last night," Steve said.

"Neal tell you about it?"

"Yeah."

"What did he tell you?"

"I'd rather hear it from you."

"Why?"

"Humor me."

"I don't have time for this—"

"Make time," Steve said. "Because if you get on the witness stand and lie, it could turn out to be very bad."

"Who said anything about lying?"

"What happened last night?"

"A mud tried to mess up Neal, but Neal was too quick for him."

"Where were you?"

"Around."

"Why didn't you try to help Neal?"

"He didn't need my help. He was doing fine."

"Uh-huh. What did this kid do to make you think he was attacking?"

"He had a chain in his hand, dude. What's that tell you?"

"Maybe he was fixing a bike."

Rennie's eyes narrowed. "You know what I think? I think you don't really believe me."

Steve said nothing.

"Now why is that?" Rennie said. "I thought you worked for the family."

"You sound like Michael Corleone."

"Who?"

"The godfather."

"You got it wrong, friend. Eldon LaSalle is the godfather."

"Then I don't have it wrong at all."

Pulling himself up to his full height, half a head taller than Steve, Rennie said, "You tell me to my face that I'm lying."

"I'm not going to tell you a thing."

"You just did."

"What's your head made of? Foam? I'm just listening right now, because you may have to tell this story under oath. And a jury isn't going to be impressed with your natural charm."

For a moment Rennie looked like he wanted to wrap his massive hands around Steve's throat and make like a two-year-old with a squeeze toy. Steve managed to keep his gaze steady, though not without effort.

"You got what happened," Rennie finally said. "We were walking down the street minding our own business when this gangbanger comes out and—"

"Whoa, wait a minute. What do you mean *gangbanger?*"

Rennie took in a snort of air. "Well, what else?"

"Is there gang activity in Verner? Is that what you're telling me?"

"They come up from LA, genius. When the heat's on. They try to blend in."

"Now you sound like Joe McCarthy."

"Who? What do you keep dropping these names for?"

"Why don't you crack a book sometime?"

"You want me to crack something? I'll be happy to."

And he looked about to do it too. Then Johnny's voice piped in from behind Rennie. "You boys get it all straightened out?"

Rennie leaned away from Steve and said nothing, waiting for Steve to give the word.

"Oh sure," Steve said. "I think we understand each other."

Rennie turned and walked toward the garage.

"I don't much like that guy," Steve said to his brother. "He's not getting the whole Christian thing."

"Relax. You're doing a good job. We're taking care of you."

"What exactly does that mean, Johnny? Taking care of me how?"

Johnny smiled and put a hand on Steve's shoulder. "Every which way. Just have a little faith in me, huh?"

FIFTY-THREE

Steve wondered about faith all the way to the hospital. What did he actually have faith in? Anything?

Even himself?

It was good, yes, to be going through the motions of being a real lawyer again. But the case stank to high heaven.

If there was a heaven.

Curls and Red greeted him at the front desk. Didn't they ever take a day off?

"Well, hello there," Curls said.

"Nice to see you," Red said.

"I'm here about a kid who came in last night, got severely beaten. I'm a lawyer. You know what I'm talking about?"

"We know several lawyers," Red said.

"I mean about the kid who was beaten," Steve said.

Curls looked at Red and Red at Curls, as if they knew exactly what it was all about.

"If you will wait just a moment," Red said.

"I'll do it," said Curls.

Red had the phone in her hand. "I'm doing it right now."

Curls looked at Steve. "She always wants to do it."

"Do what?" Steve said.

"A young man is here," Red said into the phone. "A lawyer. Yes. He's inquiring." Red listened. She put her hand on the mouthpiece and whispered, "What is the nature of your request?"

"I'm representing the suspect," Steve said.

"Oh my," Curls said.

Red returned to the phone. "He says he is representing the suspect." Red's eyes grew wide. "I'll tell him." She hung up the phone. "Mr. Meyer will be right down."

"Meyer?"

"He's the DA," Curls said.

"I was going to tell him," Red said.

"I'm perfectly capable," Curls said.

238

"I'll wait over here." Steve shot to one of the blue chairs on the other side of the reception area. Sat and picked up a *Time* magazine. Only four months old. He read a story about the presidential campaign, about a candidate who was no longer a candidate.

"You repping Cullen?"

Steve looked up at a short and doughy guy of about forty, with springy black hair and a fuzzy moustache. He wore a rumpled brown suit with a loosened tie. In his black-rimmed glasses he reminded Steve of a young version of that film critic on TV, what was his name, Shalit?

"That's right," Steve said.

"Mal Meyer." He stuck out his hand. Steve stood up and shook it.

"You working on Sunday?" Steve said.

"Same as you apparently. Come on over let's talk about it what do you say?" Meyer talked without any pause between words. He motioned Steve to follow him down the corridor and looked over his shoulder as he walked. "So you came down to do what?"

"Talk to the victim."

"Did you think I would let you do that?"

"Why not? I'm interested in the facts."

"So am I. But that doesn't mean I'm going to let you talk to the vic."

"Are you charging my client?"

The little dynamo turned. "Oh you can bet your ever-loving we're charging him and I'll be there first thing Monday morning my friend."

"Slow down a second."

"What's that?"

"Have you done any investigating?"

"Yeah I investigated the vic's face is what I investigated and I'll tell you something right now there's no way this isn't a felony assault under Penal Code 245 my friend."

"So there's no way I can convince you not to file right away?" Steve said.

"No way my friend."

"Can I ask you something, Mr. Meyer?"

"Shoot."

"Do you call everybody *my friend*?"

"It's a way I have of talking sort of breaks the ice and makes it all informal if you prefer to do business that way and that's the way I prefer to do business."

"Here is how I prefer to do business: I. Like. To. Know. The. Facts. First."

With each enunciation, Mal Meyer blinked as if to count the wasted seconds.

"Got the facts all the facts I need," Meyer said.

"You don't have a witness. I do."

Meyer smiled. At least it looked that way under the moustache. "You're talking about another one of those Eldonites up in the mountains aren't you? You're new around here right?"

"Maybe."

"What do you know about the Eldonites?"

"Some."

"We been dealing with that ilk for as long as I can remember and I grew up here just over the county line. I know all about 'em and if you're going to get involved you better get involved with your eyes open."

"Thanks, Meyer, but I think I can make my own decisions regarding my professional life." Oh no, he couldn't, but he was not going to let some deputy DA know that. "But facts are stubborn things, as one president used to say, and the fact is you don't have a witness and I do."

"Who said I don't have a witness?" Meyer pushed his glasses up with his middle finger, a gesture that looked both smug and insulting.

"Who?" Steve asked.

"Not so fast not so fast. We'll do discovery at the right time."

"I thought you wanted to do business informally, my friend. What happened to that?"

"You think I'm going to show you my hole cards when I don't have to? Don't you watch the poker channel?"

Meyer knew his cards, all right. The discovery statute in California only required the prosecutor to disclose witnesses thirty days before trial. And no case had yet come down requiring the ID of wits before a preliminary hearing.

"Then I guess," Steve said, "we're not really friends after all."

"See you tomorrow," Meyer said and blew by Steve back toward the elevators.

FIFTY-FOUR

He called Sienna from his car. "Me again," he said. "You still studying?"

"Not right at this moment."

"Good. You ready to go to work?"

"Mr. Conroy—"

"I'll put a check in the mail. I've got an arraignment coming up. One of the LaSalleites. Only there's a little problem."

"And what's that?"

"He may be guilty as sin."

"This is a shock to you?"

"Of course not. But in this case the chief witness is a lying son—he's not telling the truth, let's put it that way."

"Who is it?"

"A big hulk of a guy. An enforcer type."

"How do you know he's lying?"

"Sienna, Saran Wrap couldn't be more transparent. Now, Ms. Law Student, Ms. Ethics Advisory Board, what do you do when you have a lying witness, and he's your only one?"

She paused only a moment. "You cannot suborn perjury, of course."

"Right. But what if I don't know it's perjury? What if I just suspect it because the guy's face is a ten-foot *Liar!* sign in blinking lights?"

"Then it's a real problem."

"You're so helpful."

"So what are you going to do?"

"Wait for you to come out here and join me, and the two of us—"

"I don't think so. No, really, what?"

Steve thought a minute. "Will you do a memo for me?"

"On what?"

"On what my obligations are to talk to law enforcement. What do I need to know, and what do I have to reveal? Find that out for me, will you?"

"All right."

"And ... just thanks for being there. It means a lot."

More, in fact, than he could say.

As he drove back to his office, he wondered why he hadn't chosen to be a rock guitarist. Maybe because he couldn't play the guitar, but beyond that. Maybe music would have been a better career choice. He could have burned up all his angst onstage. Could have done the whole rage thing. Trashed hotel rooms. Died young and become a legend.

Why not? Who remembered you when you were finally planted?

Keep up the cheery thoughts, Steve.

His cell vibrated. An 818 area code.

"Steve, it's Moira Hanson."

"Moira? What's up?"

"Sorry to bother you on Sunday, but I thought you should know."

"Know what?"

"Have you heard about Mendez?"

"What, has he been released? Tunnel out?"

Pause. "I guess you haven't. You won't have to file those appellate briefs after all."

"What are you talking about?"

"He's dead."

"What?"

"Got a toothbrush shoved through his eye."

Steve squeezed his phone.

"Thought you'd like to know," Moira said.

"Thanks, Moira. I appreciate your taking the time."

"No prob. Maybe I'll see you in court sometime."

"I don't know. I'm not in LA anymore."

"Where are you?"

"Verner. It's where I am right now, as a matter of fact."

"Sweet. I've been there. Sleepy little town. No trouble."

"If only that were true, Moira."

Pause. "You okay?" she said.

"I didn't know you cared."

"You were always up front with me," she said. "Take care."

After clicking off, Steve tried to stay calm. But his body wouldn't have it. His body was taking in all the information of the last twelve hours and wasn't handling it so well. With a dry mouth coming on, Steve quickly hit Gincy's speed dial.

"Hey, boy," Gincy said.

"Talk to me," Steve said.

"You feeling it?"

"I'm feeling it."

"Can you get to a meeting?"

"I don't know."

Gincy said, "Call the central office or get on the Net and find out if there's a meeting."

"I don't know."

"You have the book?"

"Not with me. I don't want it with me. I want blow."

"Where you going to get it?"

"Good point. Maybe bourbon."

"Look man, you know the drill. Get in bed right now and pull the covers over your head. Nothing today. Just today. You can do all the blow you want tomorrow."

The old joke of recovery. Pretend you can do it tomorrow. Then when tomorrow becomes today, you say the same thing. Always tomorrow and tomorrow and tomorrow.

"Gincy, you're a good egg."

"Tell me you're going to get to bed."

"I don't know."

"Tell me you'll get on your knees and say the prayer."

"I'll do it Frank Costanza style. Serenity now!"

"The prayer works better."

"Serenity now!"

"I heard you the first time."

"Dude, I feel like there's all these plates spinning and I'm supposed to keep them spinning, but I can't see them all."

"Keep talking. Get it out of your head."

Steve pulled in at the back of his office building. He had been given one parking space by Mrs. Little, the one by the old wooden fence that was falling apart, that separated her property from a family-owned shoe store called The Cobbler.

"I'll be okay," Steve said.

"Don't try and do it on your own."

"I know, I know."

"Steve, go to God. Don't wait."

"I'm sitting in my car next to a shoe store. How about some other time?"

"How about now?"

"Thanks for being there, Gincy."

FIFTY-FIVE

No, Steve thought, it would never be time for him. That train was out of the station. Too many missed stops. If God wanted to drop in, he'd had plenty of time to do it.

Steve trudged up to his office. It was looking like a real workspace. He promised himself he'd start looking for an apartment at the beginning of next week. Something small until he got established.

For now, this was home. He hooked up his MP3 to a set of small speakers and started the jazz library going. Then took off his shoes and sat down at his new laptop. He started a file on Neal Cullen and began a preliminary trial notebook. Even though most cases settled, he tried always to be ready to stand in front of a jury.

He hadn't done so well the last few years at that. Now was the time to get his mojo back.

It wouldn't be easy with Rennie as his chief wit. He wrote down Rennie's version of the events. Tried to imagine Rennie saying any of these things on the stand. The picture was not a pretty one.

At least it was work, and it felt good.

Around five, Steve went out for Chinese. There was a little place called The Golden Dragon a few blocks from the office. He had beef and broccoli, and slippery shrimp. Brown rice and tea. His fortune cookie told him that life with a smile was better than gold with a frown.

He didn't think that was much of a fortune, let alone smart. He'd take the gold and the frown and work it all out later.

After dinner he walked the town a little. Checked out the offering at the Sheffield Dinner Theater. They were putting on *Guys and Dolls*, and the head shots of the cast looked a little silly. Nathan Detroit was being played by a kid too young for a fedora, but would have been right at home under a paper Fatburger hat.

It was fully dark when he got back to the office. He went around to the rear stairs. A lone orange lightbulb on the side of the building cast a sunset glow.

Right on a guy sitting on the stairs. A black guy, wearing a hoodie and black jeans and big red basketball shoes. Sitting in such a way that no one could get by.

"Excuse me," Steve said.

"Hey, lawyer man," the guy said.

"You need a lawyer?" Steve said. "You in some kind of trouble?"

"Uh-uh. You are."

Steve looked at him. He seemed to be in his early twenties. Though he could just be young-looking. "What kind of trouble am I supposed to be in?"

The guy stood up, pulled a piece from under his hoodie, and pointed it at Steve's face.

"I don't believe this," Steve said.

"Believe *what*?"

"Guy waiting for me outside my office at night with a weapon. Man, I get that back in LA. Why don't you just shoot me now?"

"You crazy?"

"A little bit."

"Man, you are." The guy seemed almost amused. "Let's go."

"Go where?"

"Your car, man."

"What?"

"Now."

Steve decided he did not want to get shot. He did not want to go to his car, either. But if it was just a matter of money, the guy could have whatever he wanted. Even the Ark at this point.

He walked to his car, the guy behind him.

"Get in," the guy said.

"What?"

"Get in your car. We're goin' driving."

"You don't have to do this," Steve said. "If you want money, I can get you some money."

"Just get in now."

Steve unlocked the door and got behind the wheel, leaving the door open. The guy reached around and unlocked the back door. He got in behind Steve. "Drive out to the highway," he said.

Steve started the Ark and backed out of the lot. Taking it slow. When they got outside the town line, the guy decided to talk again.

"Now you listen," he said. "You the lawyer gonna defend that guy?"

"What guy?"

"You know what I'm talkin' 'bout."

"Then why don't you tell me what you want."

"Damien didn't go after that guy."

"Who says?"

"I says."

"Were you there?"

"I seen the whole thing go down."

"Oh yeah?"

"That's right."

"You want to tell me what happened?" Steve kept the car going at a steady pace. One pothole and maybe he'd get a hole of his own, in his head.

"All you need to know is I seen it and Damien didn't do nothin'."

"Are you prepared to take the stand in court and swear to what happened?"

"I ain't takin' no stand."

"Then what do you want from me?"

"You make sure your guy goes down."

"Me? I'm his lawyer."

"You gonna lay down," the guy said.

"What, you mean throw the trial?"

"Yeah."

"Sure, that'd look real good."

"You know how to work it. You do it all a-time."

"Why would I want to?"

The guy said, "Pull over."

They were near a field, which in the night only looked like a huge sea of black. Not a bad place to leave a body. But if the guy had wanted to kill Steve, why bother convincing him to take a dive on a trial?

He stopped the car on the shoulder of the road. The headlights shot out down the highway and died in the dark.

"Do I have your attention now?" the guy said. His voice seemed to change. It was more . . . deliberate.

"You definitely have my attention," Steve said.

"Good. You just keep your eyes forward and listen. You are into things you do not know anything about. You are being used."

Definitely a voice change. The manner too. Steve said, "Who are—"

"Shut up. I said listen. Do you know what's been happening in LA, the big news on the street?"

Steve tried to think of something. Couldn't. He waited.

"There's been some gang killings. Not just killings. Executions. Not just executions. Messages. Bodies skinned. Skins hung out."

"Yeah, yeah," Steve said. "I read something on that. Some psycho."

"Not just any psycho. The happy psychos up at Beth-El."

Steve chilled. "Can you prove that?"

"The investigation is ongoing."

"Whose investigation? Are you a fed?"

"Listen, these guys want the gangs in LA to start blaming some Aryan for these things and then go for broke, start taking out a few white people at random. Then it'll be open season. That's the profile."

Hearing the sound of his own breathing, Steve said, "I want to know who you are and why you're telling me this. I want you to tell me why I should believe you."

"I don't have to tell you anything. This is just a warning. You need to get out of there. And you need to tell us what you know."

"You don't give me ID. You come at me with a gun. What are you playing here?"

"Not playing, Mr. Conroy."

"Then make it official. For all I know you could be some shill for the sheriff."

"Look straight ahead, Mr. Conroy."

Steve did. This whack job could still be a shooter. He heard the back door open.

"What you're asking of me is unethical," Steve said. "I have not observed any criminal activity, and as the attorney for the LaSalles I'm telling you that unless and until you have probable cause you don't have any standing with me. Whoever you're working for, if you are working for somebody, this won't be — "

He stopped, having the distinct impression he was now alone. He turned. Saw nothing but the night.

This is one crazy town.

FIFTY-SIX

Monday morning, entering the courtroom for Neal Cullen's felony arraignment, Steve felt like he was sleepwalking. He should have been alert and ready, prepped to do what he'd done so many times before.

But this was not like before. Everything—his client, his case, his whole life now—was encased in a block of industrial-strength strangeness. Night visitors with guns and old men in chairs, preaching racial purity.

And not just a lying client, but a lying chief witness too.

He tried to look semicoherent as he walked through the swinging gate. A row of chairs just inside the bar held a couple of lawyers who gave Steve the eye. These were no doubt local defense counsel waiting to plead their clients. Steve nodded at them.

One, a barrel-bellied bald man in a gray suit, looked away without acknowledging him. The other, a younger version of the bald man, had a little more hair and the gut wasn't as pronounced. They had to be a father-son team. The younger said to Steve, "How you doing?"

Just great! Life's a plate of jelly donuts and this town is the filling, oh yes!

"Fine, thanks," Steve said and approached the clerk. He was around thirty-five, the serious type. Steve gave him his card. "I'm representing Cullen."

The clerk took the card and looked at his day sheet. Put a check mark next to a name, presumably Neal's.

"I assume he's in the holding tank?" Steve said.

"The bailiff'll show you the way," the clerk said.

The bailiff, a female sheriff's deputy with the attitude of a disgruntled Dairy Queen manager, led Steve past the jury box and through a door in the back of the courtroom. The hallway in back was painted pea green. A holding cell to the right held three men. One of them was Neal Cullen, who was sitting on the bench, whistling. When he saw Steve he came to the bars, a huge smile on his face.

"You don't look like a man with too many problems," Steve said.

"Don't ya know it," Neal said. "You are the guy who's gonna get me out of this with no problem."

"To be honest with you, it doesn't look quite that simple."

"Huh?"

"All I am saying is that in this wonderful criminal justice system of ours, anything can happen. Now listen, this morning you have one job and one job only. That is to keep your mouth shut until I tell you to talk. I will tell you to talk when the judge asks how you plead. When the judge asks how you plead you will say, 'Not guilty.' Are you with me so far?"

"All the way, man, down the line."

"The judge'll set bail and I assume somebody will post it for you, or arrange a bond."

"Johnny'll take care of all that."

"Of course he will. Now when you get out, I don't want you wandering around town, *capisce*?"

"Yeah, whatever. No problem!"

So far, everything Steve said was according to the playbook. He'd given the same advice, in different forms, many times over the years.

Why, then, were the words sticking in his throat?

Neal crooked his finger and motioned Steve forward. Then he whispered, "You need another witness?"

"Oh. You have another witness for me?"

"If you need one. If you're feeling nervous."

"Uh-huh. Is there a store in town? Witnesses-R-Us?"

Neal laughed. "You're funny, man."

"Yeah, I am. I'll be here all week. Tip your waiter on the way out."

When he got back to the courtroom, Steve noticed several LaSalleites sitting in the gallery. He recognized them from the Bible study.

Most prominent was Rennie, in the middle of the group, looking at Steve. Like he was hoping Steve would accuse him of lying again. Like he would love to rearrange the LA lawyer's facial bones.

And this was his star witness. Wonderful. The jelly just kept getting sweeter.

Johnny was conspicuously absent.

Mal Meyer had come to the prosecutor's table, studying a file. He looked up briefly, nodded at Steve, went back to his work.

Steve took a chair near the bar and waited.

A few minutes later, the back door opened and the judge walked in. The bailiff told everyone to stand, announced the judge, called the room to order, and everyone sat again. A normal start to another normal day in the great criminal justice system of California.

Right. And Steve was the next American Idol.

The nameplate in front of the judge read *Hon. Robert Lozano*. He was thin with wispy salt-and-pepper hair cut short. Steve guessed him to be in his midfifties. He looked tired. Not physically, just tired of sitting in a lousy arraignment court. He plopped in his chair like he was serving a sentence, not handing them out. Did not bode well. Just enter a plea and get out. That would be the ticket.

The judge dealt with the rotund lawyers first. They had their client, an equally rotund truck driver, plead no contest to driving under the influence. The judge ordered the client into an alcohol program and suspended his license for six months. That seemed to please everybody except the client.

Then it was time for Steve's case. The judge called it. The bailiff brought Neal in from the lockup and had him stand in the jury box.

Neal smiled at the gallery.

The judge asked if the attorneys were ready. Mal Meyer announced ready for the DA. Steve stated his appearance for the record and said he would waive the reading of the complaint and the statement of rights and that his client was ready to plead.

"Not so fast," the judge said. "I want it made perfectly clear here that your client, knowing his background, is certain about what he's doing."

"I've advised my client," Steve said.

"I'll speak to the client directly," Judge Lozano said. He turned to Neal. "Mr. Cullen, do you understand that you have the right to hear about your rights as a citizen and the details of the complaint against you?"

"Sure," Neal said.

"Are you satisfied with your legal representation?"

Steve said, "Wait a second, Your Honor, with all due respect—"

"Save it, Mr. Conrad."

"Conroy."

"This is my courtroom and we do things a little differently than you might be used to. Just relax." To Neal he said, "Are you absolutely sure about your counsel?"

Neal said, "Absolutely, sir. I got no issues or problems with that."

"Because I don't want to hear you coming back later and claiming ineffective assistance."

Steve bristled. The judge was insulting him without knowing one thing about him. Or did he? Maybe the judge knew about Steve's little problem with coke and wanted to make sure Neal knew about it too.

"I'm happy," Neal said.

Too happy. Steve turned and looked at the gallery again. Homed in on Rennie's face. Rennie was smiling too.

Steve's stomach turned on a spit. "Your Honor," he said, "may I have just a moment to confer with my client?"

"You want to talk to Mr. Cullen before he pleads?"

"Oh yeah," Steve said. "I really, really do."

Judge Lozano's eyebrows went up, then down. "I'll call another case. Make it short, Mr. Conrad."

Steve nodded and walked to the jury box. Neal sat in a chair. Steve took the one next to him.

"I told the judge I was happy," Neal said. "I mean it."

"You're happy," Steve said. "Rennie's happy. Everybody's happy around here. One big happy family, right?"

"Right. There a problemo?"

"For you, maybe. I just want you to know that I'm not going to put your buddy Rennie on the stand."

Neal's cheeks twitched. "What're you talking about?"

"You heard me. I am not going to put you or your lying friend on the stand. I am not going to suborn perjury. So my advice is we work out a deal with the DA right now, so you can plead to—"

"Wait a second!"

Judge Lozano said, "Mr. Conrad, keep quiet over there."

"Apologies, Your Honor," Steve said.

Neal leaned in with a loud whisper. "I ain't pleading to nothin'."

"You want to go to trial, is that it?"

"Yeah. With Rennie. He saw the whole thing."

"Rennie is not going to testify."

"Yeah, he is. You're not calling this one. You'll do what you're told."

"I will? You telling me how I'm going to do a trial?"

"That's right. You work for us. You do what we tell you to do. And if you don't ..."

"If I don't *what?*"

"You just do what you're told." Neal folded his arms across his chest and leaned back. Conversation over.

Steve shook his head. He should have seen this coming. All the way from on high, from the eagle perch of Eldon LaSalle.

He got up and walked back to his counsel table. As he did he felt another look from Rennie impale itself in his back. Then heard Judge Lozano call his name.

"I'd like to approach the bench," Steve said.

"Is that really necessary, Mr. Conrad?" Judge Lozano said.

"The name is Conroy, Your Honor, and yes, it is necessary."

Mal Meyer joined Steve at the judge's bench.

"I want to withdraw from the case," Steve said.

"You what?" the judge said.

Mal Meyer blinked behind his thick glasses.

"I have good cause to withdraw," Steve said.

"Let's hear it."

"I can't give that to you."

The judge said, "You're going to have to."

"I'm sure Your Honor is aware of *Aceves v. Superior Court*."

"Go on," Lozano said.

"A lawyer is not required to reveal anything that would violate any ethical duty. That's what I'm representing to this court."

The judge looked at Meyer as if for help.

Meyer said, "That's correct, Your Honor."

With a frustrated sigh, Lozano said, "Well, this is not exactly a good start for you here in Verner, Mr. *Conroy*. Not good at all. What *can* you tell me?"

"Nothing, unfortunately."

"Does this have anything to do with a conflict of interest?"

"I can't say."

"Perjury?"

"I can't say."

"Both? Never mind." The judge slapped a palm on the bench. "Let's go back on the record." He waited for Steve and Meyer to return to their respective places.

Neal Cullen sat smugly in the jury box.

"Mr. Cullen," the judge said, "your attorney has decided to turn down the distinct honor of representing you."

The smugness melted from Neal's face.

"Do you understand?" the judge said.

"No," Neal said.

"Your attorney, Mr. Conroy, is withdrawing from defending you."

Neal shot a look at Steve, who started packing his briefcase. But not without hearing some murmurings in the courtroom.

"So here's what I'm going to do, Mr. Cullen—"

"He can't do that!" Neal said.

"He just did, sir."

"Hey! Steve! What the—"

"Mr. Cullen! Listen carefully. We are going to continue this arraignment so you can consult with an attorney. I'm also going to set a bail amount so you can get out and find one."

"But I got an attorney!"

"*Had*, Mr. Cullen."

"Steve!"

But Steve was already out of the gate and headed for the door.

FIFTY-SEVEN

A hand grabbed his shoulder as he started down the courthouse steps.

Rennie spun him around and said, "What was that stunt?"

"No stunt," Steve said.

"Explain it to me."

"No," Steve said. He could feel incipient rage dripping off Rennie, like sweat from a bull.

"Your ice is getting thin," Rennie said.

"Where'd you get that? Buford's Book of Insults?"

"You are in this up to your neck."

"What page is that on?"

"Shut up."

Steve turned and took the steps two at a time.

"Johnny's gonna be in touch with you," Rennie called after him. "Bet on that."

He didn't have long to wait. He was back in his office when Johnny called, a little past ten. "You in your office?"

"I'm right here," Steve said.

"Then you stay there."

Johnny arrived fifteen minutes after the call. Didn't bother knocking before he came in.

"You want to tell me what you're doing?" Johnny said. He was not in a smiling, good-brother mood.

Not that Steve expected it. He was sitting at his desk and offered Johnny a chair. Johnny didn't move.

"I'm not repping Cullen," Steve said. "That's all."

"Why not?"

"Because he and that goof Rennie are the worst liars I've ever seen."

"Come on."

"And I've seen some pretty bad ones."

"Yeah?"

Steve just stared at him. Until he got it.

"Oh," Johnny said, "you're calling me a liar now. Is that it?"

"What else am I supposed to think?" Steve stood, walked around his desk. "When have you been up front with me?"

"I never lied to you."

"Really? How about just holding back the truth, the whole truth, and nothing but the truth, so help you God?"

"Back off, Steve."

He realized he was almost literally in Johnny's face.

Johnny said, "Didn't I tell you to be patient? Didn't I tell you to trust me and wait? Why didn't you come to me before pulling this?"

"Wouldn't have made a difference."

"How do you know? You don't even know how much you don't know, do you?"

"You want to run that by me again?"

"Haven't I been looking out for you?"

"Have you?"

Johnny slapped his sides. "See that? See how you're talking? I haven't even told you about that little problem you had with a former client."

"What former client?"

"The former client who won't be sending around people to bother you anymore."

Steve went cold. Mendez.

He sat on the edge of his desk. Light-headed. "How?"

"You don't think we know guys in the joint? Steve, look at me."

Steve turned away.

"If you would've just waited, Steve. There's so much I want you to know, but at the right time."

"The time is now, Johnny. Otherwise, I'm outta here."

"Come on—"

Now Steve faced him again. "I mean it. No more hiding. I want to know exactly why you tracked me down and pulled me in."

"I told you. The feds are breathing down our necks."

"Why?"

"Why do they do anything? Because they can."

"Maybe they care about ritual murder."

"What?"

"Do you know anything about gang murders in LA? Where certain gang members were treated like bananas?"

"What's that mean?"

"Skins removed."

Johnny's face stayed impassive. "Steve, who have you been talking to?"

"Why don't you answer my question first?"

"What are you doing this for? Isn't the money good enough? Have I done you wrong in any way?"

"I don't know what you've done, that's the problem."

"It doesn't have to be a problem."

But it was. And the bigger problem was located at Beth-El, sitting in a wheelchair, working Johnny like a puppet master. This couldn't end well.

"Johnny, listen to me. You think about this. Come to LA. Walk out of this whole thing, come out and we'll get a place together and I'll help get you a job. We'll start all over again."

"Are you nuts?"

"Why not?"

"I'll just be another ex-con in LA. What I've got here is what I've waited my whole life to get. There's a lot of money that's going to be made, Steve, and you'll have a big share."

"Money made how? Not from church offerings. What enterprises have you got going that I don't know about?"

"This is where I have to ask you to trust me again, Steve."

"That's not good enough anymore."

"It has to be," Johnny said.

Steve shook his head. "Come with me, Johnny. Please."

"Are you leaving?"

"Yes." At that moment, he decided. He had to get out. Even if it meant losing his brother again.

Johnny didn't speak for a long time. He walked to Steve's window, looked out.

"Do me one favor," Johnny said. "Just one. Think about it for one night. Talk to me again in the morning. Will you do that much for me, Steve?"

"It won't make any difference."

Johnny turned around. "It might. That's all I'm asking."

Well, he wasn't going to be leaving in the next ten minutes anyway.

"All right," Steve said. "One night. But I can't promise I'll change my mind."

Johnny smiled. "That's my brother. You'll see. It'll be better tomorrow." He paused, then nodded and went out the door.

Better tomorrow? Not likely. Not better, ever.

Steve loosened his tie, unbuttoned the top button of his shirt, and fell on the sofa. He closed his eyes and tried to imagine that everything was normal again. That he was a good lawyer at last and didn't have recurring hunger for drugs or liquor.

And had a brother he could trust.

At some point he dozed off.

When he awoke he wanted to see Sienna. Right away. And Gincy. And Nick Nolte. He missed his cat. Was anybody feeding it?

He could go find out right now. Why not? He had no pressing engagements. Not now. All he had was four walls closing in.

Sure. He'd drive to his old building and say hello to Mrs. Stanky and go to the drugstore for her. He'd buy some milk and feed Nick and unload his troubles.

He'd call Gincy and Sienna. Maybe have dinner with her. Maybe she'd be glad to this time.

Whatever happened, the drive itself would do him good. Get him out on the road and feeling that sense of motion.

And not let anything gain on him.

He grabbed his keys.

FIFTY-EIGHT

He was outside of town a half mile or so when he saw the lights—the colored, flashing bar of a law-enforcement vehicle.

What, had he been speeding?

No. The Ark was incapable of speeding, except in a hospital zone. Which this wasn't.

It was a sheriff's car, and it closed in. Steve pulled to the shoulder and came to a stop. In his side-view mirror he watched as the sheriff's car parked behind him, about twenty yards back. A uniform got out and, with a familiar swagger, approached.

Owen Mott.

Who must have followed him. Who must have been waiting for him to leave his office.

He saw another deputy get out of the car on the other side. Two? Approaching him like he was a freaking fugitive or something.

Steve put his window down and waited.

Mott stepped to his window, removed his sunglasses, and said, "Where you headed?"

"Hi, Sheriff," Steve said.

"Asked you a question."

"Was I speeding?"

"One more time. Where were you planning to go?"

Okay, Mott was after something. *Play it very cool.* "I was heading back to Los Angeles, maybe look up some friends."

"Don't you have any friends here?"

"I'm still the new kid in town."

"That you are," Mott said. "Mind stepping out for a moment?"

Hard to stay cool now. "Can I ask why?"

"I'd just like to have you step out."

The other deputy, a younger version of Mott, with sunglasses on, stood on the passenger side of the Ark. To Mott, Steve said, "Sheriff, you know as well as I do there has to be some reasonable suspicion before you can stop a car or detain a driver. So far you haven't indicated anything of the sort."

"Taillight," Mott said quickly.

"What?"

"Busted taillight. That's why I stopped you."

Steve had heard that one before. *Busted taillight* was a catchall if a cop really wanted to stop you and ask some questions.

"I'll be sure to have somebody check out the taillight, Sheriff," Steve said. "If you want to write it up—"

"Out of the car." Sheriff Mott pulled his gun, held it at his side.

"Whoa, what is this?"

Mott put the gun to Steve's head. "Out now or they're gonna have to wash up the interior a bit."

Steve got out.

Mott said, "Now you put your hands on top of your head."

"What?"

"Do it."

Steve complied.

"Now walk to the other side of the car and get down on the ground for me."

"Wait a sec—"

"Did you hear what I said?"

"Why don't you just tell me what you want and we can clear this—"

"I told you what I want," Mott said. "I want you on the ground. I want you there now. You know I mean it."

Steve walked around the front of the Ark, dropped to his knees, then face. He spread-eagled himself on the hot shoulder of the road.

"Resisting an officer in his duties," Mott said. "That's cause for detention. Frank, search the car."

"This is bogus," Steve said.

"You have any weapons in the car?" Mott said.

"No."

"Contraband?"

"No."

"Keep your face down and arms out," Mott said.

Steve breathed dirt.

Somebody had put out a false report on him. That had to be it. Somebody with a grudge. Neal Cullen maybe? Rennie?

Johnny?

"Uh-oh." The voice of the deputy.

"What've you got, Frank?" Mott said.

"Take a look."

What could it possibly be? An old Arby's bag? Loose change? Steve had nothing in the Ark but mess.

"My oh my," Mott said.

My oh my *what?* Steve couldn't help himself. He lifted his head and looked back.

Then something slammed into his back. Like a knee. All breath left him.

His arms were pulled back. Two clicks. He'd just been handcuffed.

Wheezing for air, he was pulled up to his knees. The two lawmen got hands under his arms and yanked him to his feet.

Mott held something up to Steve's face. He tried to focus. It was a baggy, rolled up, the size of a maple bar. Full of white powder.

Steve opened his mouth. No sound but a sucking for breath. Mott pushed him toward the sheriff's car. Steve stumbled toward it, wondering if he'd black out.

And if he did, if he'd ever wake up.

Mott opened the rear door of the sheriff's car and pushed Steve in. He banged his head on the edge of the roof, then fell across the seat, still gasping.

Mott slammed the door.

FIFTY-NINE

The smell of vomit came from his cellmate, a fat guy passed out in the corner, breakfast all over the front of his shirt.

Steve thought it fitting. His life wasn't worth what was on the guy's shirt, and stank just as bad.

Rogue sheriff and partner plant coke in Steve's car. That would be it for the law career. License yanked. You're through now. Sorry, no parting gifts, but thanks for playing.

He'd requested his phone call an hour ago. They'd taken his cell phone and everything else. No one had come back for him. Violation of rights! Sure! And the only witness was snoring in the corner, not out of his stupor yet.

As soon as they let him, he'd get Sienna on the phone and start the ball rolling on hiring a lawyer. He'd have to hock everything to do it, but he needed somebody aggressive, somebody like Cutler, who'd defended John Gotti. A down-and-dirty New Yorker, a bare-knuckle brawler. Get him up to this one-horse burg and chew some rear, because without someone like that, he was dead.

What was Mott after?

It had something to do with Oderkirk's death. Or maybe just the fact that Steve was associating with the LaSalles and Mott didn't like the cut of his jib.

Steve sat on the aluminum bench attached to the wall and knew not even a Bruce Cutler would do him any good. They'd seen to that. Two law-enforcement officers, one former coke-addict lawyer.

His word against theirs.

He didn't need Cutler, he needed Houdini. He'd even settle for Penn & Teller.

The door to the cell unit opened. The young deputy, the one who'd arrested him with Mott, was standing there. Letting in Johnny LaSalle.

"Ten minutes," the deputy said, then slammed the door shut.

"Johnny—"

"Well, this is a fine howdy-do," Johnny said. "I should be in there and you should be out here."

Steve gripped the bars, just like in the movies. "What are you doing here?"

"I'm here to get you out, Steve. To take you home."

"Bail?"

"They're gonna release you OR."

"How'd you manage that?"

"Remember I asked you to trust me, Steve? You can, you know."

"Do you know why I'm in here?"

Johnny nodded.

"Do you know it's all a setup?" Steve said.

"Trust me, Steve. I know. But it's all right now. I'm here for you."

In Johnny's Jeep, heading toward Beth-El, Johnny said, "Mott has done this before. We know all about it. And that's what's going to get you out of this."

Steve breathed in the fresh air, trying to get the cell smell out of his body. "What do you mean, get out of it?"

"Dropped."

"How?"

"I'm gonna make him an offer he can't refuse." Johnny tipped his head back and laughed.

"What do you have over Mott?"

"Why do you think he's where he is? Why do you think he keeps getting re-elected?"

"He's in your pocket?"

"Not without some wriggling, but yeah."

"Why is he going after me then?"

"He's a guy who only understands one thing, and that's power. Who holds it, who can get it back. Maybe he thinks doing this to you is a way to get some power back on his end. But I'm not going to let him do that, Steve. Not to you."

SIXTY

Steve entered the large room where the infamous Bible study had been held, Johnny right behind him. There were several LaSalleites present, some of whom gave Steve a smile and even a slap on the back. Like it was a homecoming.

Which was not what he wanted. He hadn't changed his mind about pulling out.

But those plans were on permanent hold. Johnny held Steve's immediate fate in his hands. Johnny—

"Make yourself at home," Johnny said.

—held his fate—

Johnny turned then and walked to the other side of the room. Where Neal Cullen was standing. Hadn't taken long for Cullen to get bailed out. He smiled at Steve and waved.

No way, could it really be? Could Johnny have been the one to set this up? Had Mott planted coke in his car, so he would be forced to stay?

Johnny was whispering to Cullen. The men in the room had formed an informal circle around Steve.

The big door opened and he heard the familiar whirring of Eldon LaSalle's wheelchair. Steve turned, and the men split like the Red Sea as Eldon wheeled through them, right up to Steve.

The old man stopped, looked at Steve, shook his head.

Johnny came over. "He's okay, Eldon. He's with us now." To Steve, Johnny said, "You are with us, right?"

"You planned this, didn't you?" Steve said.

"Planned?" Johnny said, with an oh-so-innocent look in his eyes.

"Enough," Eldon LaSalle said. Then, wonder of wonders, he pushed himself to his feet and stood eye-to-eye with Steve. The sight unleashed cold ripples through Steve's chest.

"Do you renounce Satan?" Eldon LaSalle said.

"Excuse me?"

"You are in the grip of the enemy, Son. Do you renounce him?"

Oh, this is nice, oh yes. Terrific. "Sure," Steve said. "Why not? I've got nothing else to do."

Then Eldon LaSalle slapped him with the back of his bony right hand. Little white lights sparked behind Steve's eyes. He shook his head. And before he could do anything else, his arms were pinned behind him. Hard.

"What are you doing?" Steve said. "You crazy—"

LaSalle slapped him again. "Quiet! You will renounce Satan now!"

Steve struggled in the arms that held him. The grip was iron. "Johnny, what is this?"

"You answer to me," Eldon said.

The thought repelled Steve as much as the stench of the drunk in his jail cell. "I suppose you want me to get down and beg like a dog too," he said.

"If I say you should, then yes."

Steve stared into the dull, dark eyes of the old man. "Eldon, if I was a dog the only thing I'd do for you is lift my leg."

LaSalle's head snapped back, almost like he'd been slapped himself. Then he gave Steve another whack across the face, this one with extra mustard.

Then he said, " 'And whosoever was not found written in the book of life was cast into the lake of fire.' "

"I'll tell you what you can do with your lake of fire, you can take it and—"

"Hang on a second!" Johnny said.

Eldon shot him a rebuking look. Johnny didn't back down. "I've got it all worked out," Johnny said. "Steve knows we can take care of his legal problem. He knows he owes us his loyalty. Right, Steve?"

"I don't owe you or this motorized nutbag anything. And if I—"

"Steve, please," Johnny said. "Calm down and tell me you'll work this out with me. That you'll stay."

Steve thought about it for two seconds. "I'll take my chances on the outside."

"Steve—"

"Forget it, Johnny. I'd rather flip burgers than work for you or this withered old whack."

LaSalle hit Steve once more.

Steve's head rang. He was blind for a moment. Then he exploded by jerking his right arm free.

Without a thought he plowed his fist into Eldon LaSalle's face. It landed with a smack against skin and cheekbone.

LaSalle went down like loose change.

For a moment there was a stunned silence, a calm before the cracking of thunder.

Then they were all over Steve, throwing him to the ground, punching the side of his head, his back. They went at him like kids at a piñata.

This is it, he thought. Lights out.

Then they were being pulled off him. He heard Johnny shouting, "Hold off! Get him to his feet!"

Hands grabbed his hair and shoulders and shirt and yanked him upright.

Two other LaSalleites were helping the old man into his chair.

For a moment Steve felt sorry for Eldon LaSalle. The feeling passed. This was a guy who needed to be off the earth for good.

No one spoke as LaSalle breathed in and out, in and out, running a scrawny hand over his left cheek.

Then he looked at Steve and said, "Take him out."

The ones who had Steve's arms almost pulled them out of the sockets. Steve tried to resist movement, but there was no chance.

He saw the smiling faces watching. He shouted, "If there's a hell, that's where you're going!"

They shot him out to the corridor, opened what looked like a large closet, shoved him in, and slammed the door.

Into complete darkness. Steve felt for the door handle, and of course it was locked.

He remembered being afraid of the dark. Remembered the night terrors, and when Robert was put in his room so he wouldn't be scared.

So much for that. Johnny LaSalle was a brother no longer. He may have had Steve's blood in him, but in truth he was the spawn of Eldon LaSalle.

Steve heard something scurrying near his feet. He put his back against the door and didn't move.

Okay. Okay. If there was any real justice, any real God, he wouldn't let these things be done in his name. He would send down so much lightning, he would light up Eldon LaSalle like a Christmas tree, then let him burn and take the ashes and dump them in an Andy Gump chemical toilet along with the remains of Johnny LaSalle, and then he'd take care of the house and burn this whole mountain clean.

That's what he would do if he were around, but he doesn't seem to be around and what are they going to do with you now?

They can't let you go. They can't just let you walk out knowing what you know. They are going to take care of business is what they are going to do, and you are the business, and just how much longer are they going to keep me in here and where's that rat? If it was a rat. If it wasn't something else and … night terrors are preferable to this. I'll take the night terrors again.

SIXTY-ONE

The door opened. Dim light shot in, enough that he could make out three shadowy figures. Arms reached in for him, pulled him out. Turned him around. Yanked his arm behind him again — fresh burn in the shoulders — then they taped his wrists.

And his mouth.

They pushed him forward, out to the large foyer. Animal heads on the walls fixed dead eyes on him.

One of the men stepped to the front door ahead of him. It was Rennie. He opened the door and the other two pushed Steve outside, then down the steps into the fading sunlight, down to the crunch of gravel on the driveway.

Somebody started a car and drove toward them.

For some reason Steve turned his head back toward the house.

And saw, in the front bay window, two people looking at him.

His scream, under the tape, came out only as a muffled cry.

Johnny was watching him from that window, his arm around Sienna Ciccone.

PART 3

SIXTY-TWO

Snow.

White snow surrounding, cold yet not cold. Should be freezing. Should be dead.

Am dead. This is death. This is what death is like. Pain lingers. That's the body.

I have left the body and all that remains is snow.

Not wet. Not cold. This can't be snow.

Am I floating? Am I moving?

Snow melting away. Bright, white world fading and hard ground forming under him. Shooting hot pain through his body now, the body not dead.

He had come back, or never left.

But he was not dead.

His right shoulder was a fireball and he opened his eyes.

He was in a box. A coffin? He was alive in a coffin? Buried alive. They'd made a mistake.

He moved his head, saw upside down images. Trees. A snatch of blue sky. Something looming in the distance. A mountain.

He was in the mountains. He was upside down in the mountains.

His hands were bound behind him. And his mouth.

He remembered that part. He remembered being bound.

What had happened? He had been bound and put in a car. In the back of a car.

Wait, there was something else. Like the fading images of a bad dream. He was awake, but the dream was fresh enough to remember.

Sienna.

Sienna had been there. With Johnny.

His mind snapped into a new place, a mix of rage and confusion and pain.

Eldon LaSalle. Renounce Satan. Discipline.

If this was how they treated their lawyers, they had another thing—

Don't get funny now, Son ... they wanted to kill you ... your loving brother Johnny wanted you dead, and Sienna was there all the time.

He forced himself to think back. To go back to seeing Sienna and Johnny in the window.

Check.

He cried out, a muffled cry.

Check.

The back of a car. What kind of car? Didn't matter. The tires crunched on the gravel.

Check.

How long had they driven? Where? He didn't think it was too long or too far. He had the feeling they were going up.

And then ... a drop. Yes. He remembered a drop.

It went black after that.

Sienna. Sienna.

That was the kicker, the most nightmarish element in the whole thing.

Figure it out, he told himself. *Split up the possibilities, like you do when you try a case.*

Either Sienna was at the house of her own free will, or she was not.

Either she had known Johnny all along and did not tell him, or she had not.

Either she was a traitor on the order of Judas Iscariot, or she was a pawn of the LaSalles.

Now, what was the evidence?

Was she the greatest liar he had ever seen? The coldest, most calculating woman he had ever encountered?

Her look at the window was expressionless, but the way Johnny had his arm around her seemed intimate, not coercive.

Still, she could have been a kidnap victim. If so, he was to blame, because he had hired her as his legal assistant. But why would they take her and not tell him? If they had kidnapped her they would use it against him.

But they had said nothing.

Had to get himself free. The tape chafed and it was tight, but if he worked it, maybe he could get loose. Had to try. No other option.

Was anything broken? The pain in the shoulder was the worst, but that could be a strain. A consequence of ... what? How did he get upside down?

The car must have gone over or something. Over from the highway. He must have blacked out.

He remembered a time, clearly, when he and Robert had gone to a lake with his parents, maybe it was Arrowhead, and they had bunked together. Steve had the upper, and sometime during the night he fell out of it. He must have been three years old. But nothing happened. He wasn't hurt, and it was because he was so relaxed.

Steve wondered if that's what happened to him now. Maybe blacking out had been the thing that saved him.

His left leg was throbbing. He managed to curl himself into a position where he could see his leg. Pants torn, dried blood. Fresh blood. That could not be good.

What time was it? How long would he last like this? If somebody didn't find him, somebody other than one of Eldon LaSalle's minions, what chance did he have?

He worked his hands but the tape held strong.

For a moment, surprising himself, he thought about throwing out one of those desperation prayers, the kind where atheists lost at sea suddenly find their voices and raise them to heaven.

He thought about it, then decided he must have just done it.

But you are the one who has to get out now, bud. Nobody's gonna come flying down from the sky to open the door for you.

Where was the driver?

Neal. Neal had been driving the car.

So where was Neal?

Steve rolled to his right and pushed his knees under him. Pain in the left leg was like a hot spoon digging around in his thigh. He was on his stomach now. He brought his knees up again and slowly got to a kneeling position. The back of the seats was to his left.

He put his head underneath the de facto partition. Which put him face-to-face with Neal Cullen. A dead Neal Cullen. His erstwhile assassin.

What a great client he had turned out to be.

SIXTY-THREE

Steve stared at him.

Neal stared back, his eyes wide with dead shock.

Above Neal's left temple was a hole the size of a quarter, with blood caked all around it.

Who? What was going on?

All Steve knew was that he was alive, and that's all he knew. He had to get out now, because now he had a purpose. He almost prayed again, this time for revenge. He flashed to a painting he'd seen once at the Getty in LA. It showed a figure of an angel with a torch and another with a sword. They were about to put the hurt on a guy running away after murdering a figure, all white, his blood drained out of him. The title was something like *Justice and Divine Vengeance*. Yes, he would like to be in the angel business and put a flaming sword to all the LaSalleites.

Right. First he'd have to find his way to the road. He had no idea how far from the road he was. All he knew was that it was up, and up was not a great proposition.

But what if they were coming for him? Where *was* he? How far from the compound? From town?

He worked his hands again, the tape again, but nothing. He was almost helpless.

Then heard something crunch. And again.

Someone coming. There was someone, or several, coming toward the car.

LaSalleites.

Closer. The steps were closer now. Then stopped. Right outside the car.

Then a tapping.

"Are you alive?" a woman's voice said.

A woman?

So how was he supposed to answer with tape on his mouth?

He wiggled.

"Hold on," the voice said.

Hold on to what? Who are you? Just get me out.

"I'm going to break the glass," she said.

No, don't break the—

A cracking sound. Another. He couldn't see what was happening, it was behind him. But then he heard the sound of a reluctant car door being pulled open like a sardine can.

"I've almost got it," the voice said. "There. Oh, I'm so sorry. I didn't mean for this to happen."

He felt her hands on his, working the tape, ripping it off his wrists, the last pull taking some nice chunks of hair with it.

But his arms were free. He tore the strip off his mouth.

He felt like the Tin Man. He felt like saying *oil can.*

She helped him get out from the wreck and into the dropping shadows. He stood and almost fell. His left leg again.

The woman caught him and held him up.

He looked in her face. "It's you." The last time he had seen her, she was on her knees in front of Eldon LaSalle, being shamed.

She nodded. "Are you hurt bad?"

"I don't know. My leg. I think it's bleeding."

She bent down and looked at his leg. "Don't move," she said.

"I'm not going anywhere."

She was wearing one of those plain cotton dresses. Now she tore a large strip from it and used it to start binding his leg.

"What's your name?"

"Rahab," she said. "She was a prostitute. In the Bible."

"Oh, that's just great. Who put that handle on you?"

"My father did. When he gave me to Master."

"Gave you?"

"I was thirteen." She kept working, expertly splitting the strip and tying it off. "Before that my name was Bethany."

"Johnny said you were a street junkie. That they brought you in to clean you up."

Bethany stood up and looked at him. Her face was weathered. "I was given. For Master's use."

"That is just crazy," Steve said.

"I belong to him."

"Then maybe I'd better ask you what you're doing out here with me. And whether you had anything to do with this stiff here. Somebody got him with a clean shot to the head."

Bethany looked down. "I was unlucky, I guess."

"You?"

"I shot him. But I was aiming for the tires."

"What the heck did you use?"

"A rifle. I stole it."

"Where is it?"

"I buried it up on the ridge."

"You buried a rifle?"

"Yes."

"It's too bad because—" Steve grabbed his leg as a fresh shot of pain snaked up to his midsection. "I've got to tell you, Bethany, I'm not in real great shape here. If you were trying to kill me too, you almost did it."

"I wasn't trying to kill you. I was trying to save you. But now it looks like both of us are dead."

"What do you mean by that?"

"They will find us eventually."

"I'm not ready to die yet. I have some revenge I want to take care of."

"It won't work. They are too strong."

"Will you help me?"

"I must. I have broken away and that is punishable by death."

"My leg is pretty bad. I've lost some blood. I need to get medical attention. But I can't move. If you have any bright ideas, now would be the time."

"I do have an idea," Bethany said. "But you must try to walk with me."

"I don't know if I can."

"They will be coming soon to find us."

"In that case," Steve said, "I can."

SIXTY-FOUR

She was strong. The years of working in the fields around the compound must have done it. She was like a true slave, a field hand, with no rights but plenty of lean muscle. She supported Steve with one arm as they made their way up the hillside.

Mercifully, the highway was only about fifty yards away. It felt like a couple of football fields to Steve. But they made it, finally standing on the shoulder of the mountain road.

It was getting dark. "Now what?" Steve asked.

"Quickly," Bethany said. "We have to get across."

"And then what?"

"Come along."

His left leg almost totally useless now, Steve managed to limp halfway across the road with her left arm around his waist. He paused in the middle. "How far do we have to go?"

"A little way."

"Are you sure?"

"Come on."

"Wait. Just a sec—" He heard the sound of an oncoming car.

"Quickly!" Bethany pulled him forward. He almost fell. They were on a curve, so the noise came from around a bend. Which one he didn't know. How far away he had no idea. He hopped along to keep up with his improbable protector.

"We have to get down," Bethany said.

Down in what?

The car was louder now. His brain calculated thirty, maybe twenty seconds until it came to where they stood on a small shoulder before more mountain.

"Here!" Bethany pulled at him, and he fell forward on top of her, as she sat like a human pillow on the ground. She rolled and he went with her, so they to were face-to-face on their sides.

"Keep still," Bethany whispered.

He wasn't exactly going anywhere.

The car came around from the direction behind Bethany. A good thing, as the curve of the road extended away from them in a horseshoe.

Hopefully the driver would keep his eyes on the road.

The car slowed, almost cutting the engine.

They've seen us.

Bethany had her hand on the side of his head and pressed down.

The car slowed even more.

The car gunned and moved on.

It had only slowed for a treacherous turn.

"Come on." Bethany helped him to his feet. "It's not far."

"What's not far?"

"It."

It was not much more than a glorified lean-to some two hundred yards into the woods, just big enough for them both. If Bethany hadn't told him what it was he would have missed it. It was camouflaged by brush.

"I have some water," Bethany said. "I can wash your leg."

"Not exactly the Mayo Clinic," Steve said. "But I'll take it. How did you happen—"

"Inside. Quickly."

He was able to stretch out completely on top of an old sleeping bag. Bethany took up a flashlight and illumined the inside. Steve saw another rolled-up bag and a couple of plastic gallon jugs of water. Three brown shopping bags hugged the lean-to wall.

Bethany set the flashlight on the ground, reached into one of the bags. "Can you rip your pant leg?" she said.

"I'll give it a shot."

"Here." Her hand reached to him. In it was a knife. With a six-inch blade.

"My my," Steve said.

"Go on."

Steve didn't give it a second thought. She was his rescuer, his nurse. And she had a knife. He'd do what she said.

He cut the pant leg open. Cold air hit the wound. He couldn't see it clearly but felt that some blood still flowed.

Bethany reached into one of the paper bags and came out with something, looked like a wadded shirt. She opened one of the jugs of water and doused the material. She began washing the leg.

It was scraping work, but Steve took it gratefully. If nothing else this would buy him some time. Now the only little task was getting to a real doctor.

And after that, getting stitched up and figuring out how to bring the LaSalles into flaming death.

"Does it hurt?" Bethany asked as she swiped the leg some more.

"It's numbing up," Steve said.

"We just need to make it through the night."

"Sounds like a country song."

"Huh?"

"Country song. You like country songs?"

"We don't have those."

"Ah. Eldon doesn't like 'em, I suppose."

Bethany said nothing.

"They have the best titles," Steve said. "Like, 'You Stole My Wife, You Dirty Horse Thief.'"

In the dimness Bethany smiled.

"And, 'If Your Phone Ain't Ringin', It's Me.'"

Bethany laughed.

"That's the ticket," Steve said.

She grew silent. Then began to cry, softly at first.

Steve made himself sit up. She was kneeling at his side. He put his arms around her and pulled her to him, held her against his chest.

"I'm scared," she said.

"I know."

SIXTY-FIVE

She was calm a few minutes later and said, "Jericho told me about this place. He was one of us, but he had a rebellious spirit. He liked me. He was forbidden to talk to me but he found ways. He was out of Soledad prison."

"Big surprise," Steve said.

"He made this place and told me about it. He said if I ever wanted to run away with him we could hide here. Once he took me here in secret. I liked him."

"Is that where you got the knife?"

"Everything in here was what he brought. But he got arrested again. And was killed in jail."

"That seems very convenient."

"Huh?"

"LaSalle has a way of dealing with people he doesn't like. Now maybe you can explain to me how you happened to be shooting at a car with me in it?"

"I heard them talking about you. The men all speak freely around the women. No one has ever resisted them or betrayed them. But ever since I have been here I have played this little game in my mind. It helps me to get through bad days. We all have to learn how to use rifles. The Master—I keep calling him that—has told us that they may come someday to try to take us, and we must all be ready to fight. Everyone does what he says. His word is law. He has told everyone he is the prophet of God, just like Muhammad for the Muslims."

"And people actually believe that?"

"I did. I didn't think my father would give me to anyone but the prophet of God."

"Did you ever try to get away before?"

"To what? That life is all I know. He was good to me."

"Yeah, I saw how good."

"Before that. The last few years have been hard on him."

"I'm all broken up about that."

"You never knew him the way I did."

"Then why are you running out on him?"

"I don't know exactly. I just knew I couldn't let you die."

Steve reached out and took her hand. "Bethany, thank you."

She nodded slowly.

"I need to ask you some questions," Steve said.

"You need to rest."

"Questions first. Do you know about me?"

"I know that you are Johnny's brother."

"How much do you know about Johnny?"

"Much."

"Do you know a woman named Sienna?"

Bethany nodded. "Johnny's woman."

"That's what I want to hear about." Steve shifted on the bedroll. Wood creaked underneath him. Or maybe it was his own bones. "Tell me everything you know about her."

"I know that she helped on Johnny's parole petition when he was in prison. Over a year ago. She is a law student and was volunteering."

"She met Johnny while he was in prison?"

"Yes. Johnny brought her to Beth-El."

Steve shook his head. "She's the best liar I've ever seen. She'll be a great trial lawyer. I just don't see how ..."

"You know Johnny."

"I thought I did."

"He has power like his father."

"Power to use people?"

"He has used me. He has a way. He can get people to do things."

Steve touched her arm. "I can't even begin to imagine what you must have been through."

"You're right, Mr. Conroy. You can't."

"You can call me Steve if you like."

"All right."

"And now we need to figure out how we're going to get out of here."

"God will show us the way."

"How can you believe in God after what they did to you?"

She blinked at him, almost as if she didn't understand the question. "I have always believed in God, even before I believed in Eldon LaSalle. That will not change."

"I guess I don't quite get it," Steve said.

"I saw an angel when I was a girl."

Steve said nothing.

"You don't believe me?" Bethany asked.

"Oh sure, I believe you think you did. I once thought I saw Santa's sleigh."

Bethany giggled. It was at once girlish and charming.

"Yeah," Steve said. "My brother, he was Robert then, was telling me how Santa comes at Christmas and lands on your roof and comes down the chimney and all that. It was Christmas Eve and I got so excited I couldn't get to sleep. Just before I dropped off I looked out my window over at my neighbor's house, and there it was, Santa's sleigh, the moonlight behind it. I can still see it."

"What did you do?"

"I woke up my brother and tried to show him, but it was gone. Robert said Santa moves fast, and told me to go back to sleep."

"But you didn't really see it, did you?"

"I thought I did."

"I know I did."

"Sure."

"I was four years old and I had to have a heart operation. The valve in my heart had a hole in it. I remember them putting me to sleep. The doctor and the nurses were there. I was scared. But then I saw two angels. They were all in white and their faces were bright. And they had noses."

"Noses?"

"That's something I remembered. I told my mommy about the noses. She believed me. She was the only one to believe me. She died a year later. But I saw them."

"You were a little girl under anesthesia."

"I saw them!"

"All right. Who am I to say any different? I saw an angel too."

"You did?" She sounded four years old again.

"It was you," Steve said.

SIXTY-SIX

Steve woke up in the gray of dawn. He didn't know where he was. His mind struggled for a few seconds, trying to figure it out. Recent memories were compressed, like big files on a hard drive. Then they started to open and he remembered.

His leg. He touched it where Bethany had applied a dressing. A big section of it was numb.

Bethany. She was not next to him. The sleeping bag was empty. He tried to move. Every part of his body screamed.

Voices. He heard voices coming from the distance. A conversation. Bethany was talking to someone. A man. Only snatches of words. The man's voice first.

... can make it back ... sure to tell him ... nice to me ...

Bethany: *... I be nice to you?*

The man laughed. ... *cool ... ol' Zeke ... nobody'll know...*

Bethany: *... not here ... let's go back ...*

... not going back ...

Then silence and the sound of steps coming his way.

A dog barked.

Zeke. Ezekiel.

One of the LaSalleites had brought the dog out and found them. Somehow. And he was a few yards away from seeing Steve.

Steve looked around the dismal quarters and saw the knife he'd used to cut his pants.

Grabbed it and listened.

The footsteps stopped right outside the lean-to.

"We should not do this," Bethany said. "Master will not like it."

"Master isn't gonna know about it, is he?" Familiar voice.

Rennie.

"He will find out," Bethany said. Pleading. Protecting him, Steve thought.

The dog kept barking.

"Shut up, Zeke!" Rennie said. Then softly, "I can make it right for you. You don't worry about a thing. You were a bad girl to run

288

off like that. You're lucky I'm the one that found you. You be nice to ol' Rennie and I'll make it right."

"Don't do this."

The dog barked louder, crazy loud. He must have been tied up to a tree or something and was going nuts.

"Zeke!" Rennie shouted. "Shut it!"

The dog kept it up.

"I'm gonna have to slap that dog," Rennie said. "Now you don't want to end up like that lawyer, do you? They're never gonna find his body. You, you got a chance. Zeke!"

More barking.

"Now you get yourself inside there," Rennie said to Bethany. "Now. I'll be right back."

Pause.

"Now," he said.

Steve saw Bethany get to her knees and back slowly inside. She was blocking the view if Rennie should have a look. But he didn't. "Zeke, now you just relax, boy ..." His voice drifted as he moved away from the lean-to.

Steve put his hand on Bethany's arm, indicating that she not move. Paused. Then he whispered, "Stay on your knees facing out. When he sticks his head in, can you pull his head down?"

"I don't know," she whispered back.

"Try. You have to. You have one shot. I'm going to get him with this." He held up the knife.

Bethany stared at it.

"Got it?" Steve said.

"Yes."

"You'll do fine. Get a good grip. I only need a second."

"Have you done this before?"

"No, but I don't intend to miss. Wait. Quiet."

Steps were approaching again, crunching dirt and twigs.

"How you doin', darlin'?" Rennie said.

Bethany was silent.

"I said how you doin'?"

"I'm all right," Bethany said.

Another step outside.

Steve held the knife with the blade up. He was going to go for the neck. His body felt coiled and ready, the adrenaline taking away the pain.

Another outside step.

Then ... nothing.

For a long moment all movement in the world seemed to stop.

A growl.

Not a dog, Steve thought immediately. A man.

A man who grabbed Steve's ankles and pulled.

Steve's face ate dirt.

Rennie had come up on him from the other opening.

In breaking his fall, Steve opened his right hand. And dropped the knife.

He felt the surging strength of Rennie and the fresh fire in his leg. The iron-trap hands that had his ankles let go so Steve was spread out on his face like a bearskin rug.

A foot to his side kicked all the air out of his lungs. White sparklers lit up behind his eyes. The sound of his gasping melted into the renewed barking of the massive Zeke.

"Now look at that," Rennie said. "You never know what you're gonna find out here. Where's Neal?"

Steve rolled slowly onto his back, unable to speak.

Rennie gave another kick, this one just enough to get his attention. "I asked you where Neal was."

"I shot him." Bethany's voice.

Steve saw Rennie turn toward the lean-to.

"You did?" Rennie said, almost admiringly. "Now how did you do that, little thing? You got a weapon in there?"

With one swift move Rennie shot a powerful kick to the lean-to. It cracked. He used his hands to pull at the plywood and cast it away, exposing the sleeping bags.

The knife. He'll see the knife.

Steve couldn't move.

"What'd you use there, Rahab?" Rennie kicked at the exposed bags and the dirt. "Where's the weapon?"

"I don't have it anymore."

"Uh-huh. Like I'm supposed to buy that?"

The dog was so crazed now Steve was sure it would uproot whatever it was tethered to. Surer still that Rennie was about to kill him. And Bethany.

He tried to roll onto his stomach so he could prop himself up.

Rennie wasn't paying any attention to him. He approached Bethany, who stood with her hands at her sides.

She's got it. She's got the knife and she's going to use it.

"Sweetheart, you are in a very big world of hurt right now," Rennie said. "You're gonna need me. You're gonna be nice to me. Now you tell me what you used to shoot poor Neal. Rifle?"

"Yes," Bethany said.

"Sweet. How far away were you, honey? Was he moving?"

"Yes."

"And where is he now?"

"He went over."

"Over? He—" Rennie looked Steve's way. "How'd he get out?"

Bethany didn't answer.

"Where's the rifle, honey?"

"I buried it."

"You buried a rifle? Now why would you go and do a stupid thing like that? Don't you know a gopher might find it and shoot his eye out?"

He laughed. Ezekiel barked like there was no breakfast and no tomorrow.

"I'm gonna give you one chance to tell me where that rifle's at. Then you and me and the lawyer there are gonna go find it together. Then I'll decide what to do with the two of you. Maybe I better just take you back. That'd look good, wouldn't it? Maybe they can mount the lawyer's head on the wall, right next to the moose. Huh?"

Laughing again. Enjoying drawing it out.

Steve's view of Bethany was obscured by Rennie standing in front of her. He was too big. Even if she got a shot at him with the knife, she might not be able to do much damage. At best a distraction.

Rennie gave him a quick glance, making sure he was still down. When he looked back at Bethany, Steve tensed his legs.

"I didn't hear you," Rennie said.

"Over there."

Rennie turned his head slightly to the left.

That's when Bethany struck.

Steve heard her scream and saw Rennie clutch forward, like he'd been hit in the stomach.

Steve pushed to his feet and drove forward with everything he had. Which wasn't much.

Rennie screamed. Then straightened up.

Steve took him from behind, jumping on his back and throwing a stranglehold around him. Steve could feel the back muscles of the big man, rock hard.

Rennie spun once. Steve hung on like a man holding a lamppost in a typhoon. The dog was going berserk. Rennie grabbed Steve's arm with his left hand. With his right he struck back with a fist. It landed on top of Steve's head like a dropped brick.

Steve pushed his head down, to the left side of Rennie's neck.

Where was Bethany? Where was the knife? Everything was whirling, Rennie grunting, dog barking, Steve feeling like he couldn't hold on much longer. A riot of confusion. He thought he might black out.

Rennie struck again with his fist. Weaker this time.

Then he put both hands on Steve's arm, pulling and scratching at it.

Rennie spun once more. Steve hung on. He'd managed to get his good leg, his right, wrapped around Rennie's body.

Rennie dropped to one knee. Then the other.

Steve had a good lock and knew Rennie couldn't breathe. Rennie's hands slipped off Steve's arm. He flailed back wildly at Steve.

Zeke the dog had moved from barking to something worse, a sound Steven thought he'd never heard before. *What hell must sound like.*

Rennie's arms dropped.

So did Rennie. Flat, face down.

Motionless.

Steve held on just to make sure.

Then he heard a guttural sound, a choking sound. Only it wasn't from Rennie. It came from the dog.

SIXTY-SEVEN

Steve looked up and saw the strain on Ezekiel's face as his legs pushed against the leather leash.

Which snapped loose from its mooring.

Snarling death charged his way like a bullet train.

There would be no way out. In the three seconds it took for Ezekiel to span the distance, Steve could only get to his knees and think *momentum*. He could buy a few precious seconds using the madness of the dog, the crazy instinctive charge.

When Ezekiel pushed off into the air, a canine missile, teeth bared, saliva slapping the sides of his mouth, Steve swung his right arm. At the same time he fell right. His fist landed on the dog's jaw, deflecting him.

Ezekiel thudded on the ground behind him. It would take him two seconds to regroup.

Steve twisted around, anticipating the jaws of death.

If only he had the knife.

The dog charged.

Steve put his hands out.

Ezekiel leaped.

Steve rolled left, hearing something crack, rolled over twice, and came up ready again for a strike.

Which didn't come.

Steve heard a wail of pain from the dog, and Steve saw the wet red stain on the side of the animal. Ezekiel lay on his side, moving his legs but going nowhere.

He yelped and yelped.

Steve was aware of someone behind him. Bethany, holding a rifle, walking toward him.

"That time I hit what I was aiming at," she said.

Ezekiel cried out in pain and confusion.

Bethany walked up to the dog. "He's suffering," she said, then put the barrel to the dog's head and fired.

"Hated to do that," Bethany said.

Steve didn't know weapons, but the one she held looked like a state-of-the-art hunter's piece. He considered the two dead bodies and felt sorry for the dog. Ezekiel was just doing what dogs do, especially when they've been trained to kill. He was a victim of circumstances. He had no will of his own.

Then Steve considered Rennie and found himself wondering what lethal mix had been poured into the guy to produce such human waste.

Steve heard a strong buzz and thought it sounded like a bee. The mother of all bees looking for human flesh. A mutant, nuclear bee with a stinger the size of a nail.

Another buzz. Close. And then he knew it was a phone. Rennie's cell phone.

Somebody trying to get in touch with the dead man.

The phone was in Rennie's front pants pocket. Steve waited until the buzzing stopped, then flipped the cell open. Saw a number for a missed call. Also saw a low-battery warning. He punched 4-1-1.

"What are you doing?" Bethany asked.

"Got to move fast," he said. He followed the prompts and asked for Verner, for the district attorney's office, and accepted a straight connection. Got the office's voice directory that gave him several options. He took 0 for reception.

A woman answered.

"I need to speak to Mal Meyer," Steve said.

"Just a moment ... Mr. Meyer isn't in, would you like his voice mail?"

"No. This is an emergency. For Mr. Meyer and for me. My name's Conroy and I'm defense counsel on one of his cases. I need to speak to him now."

"I believe he's in court."

"Does he have a pager?"

"Yes, but—"

"Listen carefully, please. The case we're on is Cullen. You need to tell him that Cullen is dead. He's been shot. And his defense counsel needs to speak to Mal right away."

"Oh my."

"Did this cell number come through on your screen?"

"Yes."

"Can you page him immediately and give him that message? Have him call me?"

"I can try right now. If you hold, I can put him on with you."

"I'll hold. I don't have much battery left, so if you can hurry."

"Please hold."

He looked at Bethany, admiring her strength. What must it have taken for her to get out of that situation? What would become of her now, even if they managed to survive this ordeal?

"We need to hide these bodies," Bethany said.

"That would be a good idea," Steve said.

"I'll do it."

And she did. As Steve waited on Mal Meyer, she went about her work as if she were cleaning up a yard. She dragged Rennie's body to where the floor of the lean-to had been. Then did the same with the dog. Then started reconstructing the lean-to.

The woman came on the line. "Mr. Conroy? I'm going to connect you."

A click, then, "This is Meyer."

"Steve Conroy."

"I got that. What's this about, Cullen?"

"Listen, I don't know how much time I have on this thing. I'll explain everything to you, but you have to come get me. I'm on Verner Pass Highway, I don't know how far, but it's got to be close to the LaSalle place. I just killed one of them. But I've got a bum leg—"

"Hold it. Killed? Killed who?"

"I'll tell you when you get here."

"Me? If you're hurt we'll get an ambulance—"

"No. Listen. This thing is breaking down around both of us. I don't want anybody in Verner to know about this. I need to get to a doctor. I need to get to one in another town. I need you to take me there."

"I'm due in court in ten minutes."

"Whatever you're doing, believe me it's not more important than this. You have to trust me on this one. There's going to be a hunting party out for me and the woman who helped me."

"Woman?"

"Can you get out here?"

"Just take a—"

Silence.

Steve looked at the LCD. "You're kidding me." The juice was gone.

"Is he coming?" Bethany said.

"He didn't sound excited about it. He may alert the sheriff."

"Is that bad?"

"That's bad."

"What do we do?"

"We need to move," Steve said. "Do you know a place we can hole up and still keep an eye on the highway?"

"Yes."

"Do you still believe in God?" he asked.

"Yes," she said.

"Then pray. We can use all the help we can get."

SIXTY-EIGHT

His leg was practically no use now. He dragged it behind him like a sack of wet laundry. He followed Bethany, who went before him like a scout. She carried the rifle with her. She said she had three rounds left. The morning was just getting underway, and he was on the run with a woman with a rifle.

What's next on the agenda?

"Here," Bethany said.

She'd found a jut of gray rock. It provided a sort of prow over which they could see the highway below. It was a sharp drop of about twenty feet to the road.

Better, it gave them a view of where they'd come and a place to hide. Like some old cowboy movie.

Bethany went before him, up the rocks, and helped him. It was easier than he expected that way. He wouldn't mind having Bethany around in any sort of a pinch. She was doing the job.

Once ensconced in the rocks, Steve allowed himself a moment of rest.

"Now?" Bethany said.

"We wait," Steve said. "If something doesn't happen in the next twenty minutes or so, we take a chance and flag a car."

"I don't think that would be good," she said. "They will be looking."

"I don't see any other choice. Keep praying."

She closed her eyes. It was so childlike. He hoped she really had some connection to the supernatural going on. Anything at this point.

A car approached. Steve looked over the rocks in time to see a red pickup zip by. Several more cars, in both directions, passed during the ensuing minutes.

None slowed. No one looked like Mal Meyer.

"I think we're going to have to chance it," Steve said. "Let's try to catch one going toward Verner. If anyone from Beth-El was coming they'd be headed the other way."

"We don't look too good."

"We're going to look even worse if we don't get somewhere safe. You up for this?"

"I'll do what we have to do."

"You could start by leaving the rifle. That may not invite too many stops."

Bethany smiled. It seemed like a relief to her.

He heard the sound of a car horn. A laying-it-on-thick blast. Somebody angry. He looked over the rocks and saw a blue Mercedes burn past the curve, doing about fifty. Five seconds later a black Saturn came into view, going way too slow for the flow.

The driver's side window was down and Steve saw the anxious face of Mal Meyer, scanning the hillside.

"Stand up and wave," Steve said.

SIXTY-NINE

Meyer knew of a hospital in the next county, about a twenty-minute drive, he said. That way they could buy a little time before deciding what to do in Verner.

At least part of Bethany's prayer had been answered. Steve was in a Saturn with a prosecutor, a captive audience.

"Now," Meyer said, "tell me what this is about."

"You're going to be a star, Mal," Steve said. "Are you ready for the TV cameras?"

"I have a face for radio," Meyer said. "What's this about killing a man? That's a little fact that interests me."

"He's one of the guys from Beth-El. They decided to put me on the cooling rack. But I got out."

"How?"

"That's going to take a little more time. What I need to tell you right now is that you have the chance to bring down Eldon LaSalle and his whole little empire."

Meyer's mental gears clicked around. "Nothing would make me happier, but he's been around a long time and has his act together, at least legally."

"Does that include hits on lawyers?"

"How can you prove this?"

"Bethany will testify to it. That's conspiracy to commit murder. She'll also testify to ritual abuse carried on up there."

"Abuse of who?"

"Her. And the other women LaSalle keeps there."

"Is this your only witness?"

"Me too."

"You were their lawyer, weren't you?"

"I was, until they tried to kill me. I consider that a breach of the attorney-client relationship."

"Still, they may be able to keep any statements you make about them out of a trial. You got anything else?"

"You've got probable cause to search the place. You can get a team together and go up and look for evidence of conspiracy. You can bring in a bunch of them and start with the questioning."

"On what charge?"

"Weapons. Bethany here will tell you about the weapons. She doesn't think there's a permit to be had for any of them."

Mal Meyer took a contemplative breath. "I can get a warrant, but I need it to be as specific as possible. If we're going after the big fish, we need a big net."

"Then there's one other man you need to talk to. His name's Hendrickson. He works at Bruck's Mortuary. I have a feeling he knows a lot more than he's willing to tell. You feel up to pulling a bluff?"

"What kind of bluff?"

"Like on *Law & Order*. You know, where the cops say they have a witness against some guy and offer him a deal if he talks now."

"I never watched that show."

"You should. You'll be inspired by Sam Waterston."

Meyer said, "Keep going."

Steve put his head back on the seat. "You mind if we wait until I get this thing looked at? I'm feeling a little beat up at the moment."

"He's been fantastic," Bethany said.

Steve shook his head. "She's the fantastic one. Just wait till you hear the whole thing."

"I'm busting at the seams," Meyer said.

The hospital was bigger than the one in Verner, as was this whole town. There was even a five-story Hyatt within shouting distance. Probably a place for the serious skiers, hunters, and fishermen to hang their collective hats on their way to various points of interest.

They patched Steve up in Emergency. He escaped infection, but not a zipper-like line of sutures. They pumped something into his veins. They fitted him for crutches and sent him out at 12:35 p.m.

Mal Meyer and Bethany were in the waiting area, talking. Or rather it was Bethany talking and Meyer jotting notes.

Meyer stood when Steve came in. "She's spinning quite a tale," he said. "I want to question this guy Hendrickson too. I want enough to go to a grand jury."

"How about the feds?" Steve asked.

"I can try to bring in ATF."

"The feds are already on this. There's two agents in LA, Issler and Weingarten. You had contact?"

"No."

"They're working this thing somehow. But before you talk to them, get to Hendrickson. But do it on the QT. Think you can?"

"QT?"

"Don't you ever watch old movies?"

"No time for that."

"It means on the lowdown," Steve said. "No fanfare. Not yet. Mott is involved."

"Mott! You got proof of that?"

"Oh, I got proof. But you just ask Mr. Hendrickson to come in. Tell him not to say anything to anyone, under threat of indictment."

"What indictment?"

"Make something up. Just bring him in."

At which Mal Meyer smiled like a mischievous kid. "You LA guys really do march to a different beat."

SEVENTY

They got back to the DA's office around three. Meyer took his Saturn into the private below-ground lot, the same place the sheriff's bus would drop prisoners off for court. There was a private elevator for law and court personnel. Meyer guided Steve and Bethany up to the fifth floor, which was relatively devoid of activity. Like a guy leading prison escapees, Meyer led Bethany and Steve to a small conference room halfway down a corridor.

Only a woman carrying a stack of files saw them. She nodded at Meyer like there was nothing amiss. Just another day at the office.

Meyer locked the conference room door from the inside. "You'll be able to kick back here," he said to Steve.

Kick back? "What are you going to do?"

"Persuade. I want to get that Hendrickson in here if I can. And I want to get a full account. Oh yeah, and those federal agents. Names again?"

"Issler and Weingarten," Steve said. "You can just tell them a Mr. Conroy referred them."

Meyer jotted it down on the little pad he carried. "I'll have one of the clerks look in on you. Take care of anything you need. You'll be okay?"

"Just get her a rifle," Steve said.

Meyer looked at him, shook his head. Left.

"Now what happens?" Bethany asked.

"We are in the jaws of the system now," Steve said. "We wait. But you can do a little more of that praying if you want."

"What should I pray for?"

Steve thought a moment. "That Eldon LaSalle and his band of merry men get ripped off the face of the earth."

"Even Johnny?"

"Yeah," Steve said. "Even Johnny."

"I don't know if this matters," Bethany said. "But I don't think Johnny wanted to have you ... you know, taken care of."

"Why would you say that?"

She shrugged. "I don't think he and his father were getting along. Just little things I saw, that's all."

"It's too late to make any difference. Johnny made his choice a long time ago. Now he's got to live with it. Or die with it."

The clerk, a paralegal named Arty who looked like Adam Sandler, did as promised, and brought coffee and bottled water and a bag of Milano cookies. Bethany said she'd never had a Milano and ate almost the whole bag.

It was good to watch her do that. Like she was a little girl again, before innocence was lost to Eldon LaSalle.

At 4:35 Meyer stuck his head through the conference room door. "You all set?" he asked.

"Set for what?" Steve said.

"He's here. I'm bringing him in."

Meyer closed the door. Five minutes later it opened again. Meyer walked in with Edward Hendrickson.

"What is this?" Hendrickson said, looking at Steve.

"You know Mr. Conroy?" Meyer asked.

The old gentlemanly face reddened. "I do not feel I need to be here."

"Please sit down, sir," Meyer said. "Like I said, I would much rather talk informally here than get a subpoena. But that's entirely up to you."

"What is he here for? What am I supposed to have done?"

"I found Doc Phillips," Steve said.

Hendrickson gasped as if he'd had a lung punctured. For a moment Steve thought it was a heart attack. Hendrickson put a hand to his chest and fell into the hard government chair that Meyer held for him.

"Can I get you some water?" Meyer asked.

Hendrickson shook his head, took a moment to steady his breathing. He kept his eyes on the table when he said, "Did Walker tell you anything?"

"He told me enough," Steve said. "Your name came up." He decided not to reveal exactly how Hendrickson's name had come up, as he had been the one to raise it. Nor the little detail of the doctor's blowing himself away. Maybe that news hadn't reached Hendrickson's ears yet. Steve could mention it for shock value later if he needed to.

"Where is Walker now?" Hendrickson asked.

"Tehachapi," Steve said. "Still very much in Tehachapi. I think he's very attached to the place."

"Is he drinking?"

"Not anymore."

"That's good," Hendrickson said. "Perhaps he's found a measure of redemption."

"Why haven't you said anything about the autopsy in '83?" Steve asked. "Why have you kept it secret for so long?" This required assumptions, but he was on a roll.

"It was for old Mr. Bruck's sake," Hendrickson said. "He saved my life. I wanted to save his."

Meyer pulled out a chair now and sat. He removed a handheld tape recorder from his inside jacket pocket. Steve thought it might be too early for that. Might scare Hendrickson off.

"I'd like to tape your statement," Meyer said. "I'll have it transcribed and you can correct anything you want and sign it later. Okay?"

Hendrickson hung on the question for a beat, like a man on a tightrope steadying himself. His eyes seemed to recede, drifting off to a distant memory.

Then he started to talk.

SEVENTY-ONE

"I was an alcoholic when I came to Verner. Came back from Korea and settled in San Berdoo, wife and baby waiting for me. Drank myself into a divorce. Couldn't hold a job. Bruck was my sergeant. We kept in touch, he told me to come up to see him.

"He dried me out. Got me back up on my feet, made me feel like a man again. The doctor he paid to help dry me out was Walker Phillips. Bill Bruck gave me a job. It wasn't at the mortuary—he was just starting that out. He also ran a hardware store. I worked there for about fifteen years, then went to the mortuary. About that same time two new people came to town. One was Eldon LaSalle. The other was Owen Mott.

"Mott came in from another county and was an appointed sheriff. I don't know if it was a coincidence or if there was some money that changed hands. All I know is that Mott did not seem overly concerned with Eldon LaSalle. And LaSalle gave the appearance of being someone who wanted to do good in the community. He paid for the building of the Chamber of Commerce. That was in the early days of his citizenship.

"Then came the fire. It was the fire that killed a man named Clinton Cole and a little boy. Mott led the investigation and ruled that it was an accident. I don't know why, but I never believed that. Maybe it was just the way Mott looked when he talked about it. The other man who had a strange look about it was Bill Bruck. I never questioned Bill. I never felt I had that right. I figured whatever he knew was his to know, and he had a good reason for knowing it. They did the autopsy and found that the little boy who was burned to death was a kid who had been taken from his home sometime earlier that year."

"That was supposedly my brother," Steve said.

"That's where I would have left it but for Walker Phillips. I was going to church regularly then and had straightened out my life to the point where people thought of me as a pillar of the community.

Some sort of moral example. That's a laugh. If only they could have seen inside me.

"But one night Walker Phillips came to see me. He had been drinking heavily. That's not something he used to do. So I knew there was something wrong. He proceeded to spill his guts to me. He asked me not to say anything to anyone, but that he had to talk to somebody. You know, I think deep down maybe he wanted me to talk about it. Maybe he wanted to be caught. You think strange things when you're drunk. Believe me, I know.

"So I listened. And this is what he told me."

Hendrickson paused. "I'll take that water now, if you don't mind."

"Sure." Meyer left the office for a moment, leaving Steve and Bethany alone with Hendrickson.

"You shouldn't have come here," Hendrickson said. "It can only end badly for you now."

Tiny mice feet clawed Steve's spine. The man no doubt spoke the truth.

Meyer came back with the water and Hendrickson drank. He cleared his throat and seemed to be gathering his strength, like a weight lifter about to do the clean and jerk.

"The boy in the fire was Eldon LaSalle's own son."

Steve almost slipped out of his chair. He saw Meyer's eyes filling the thick lenses of his glasses. Even Bethany seemed stunned.

No one said anything for a long moment. Then Hendrickson continued. "Eldon LaSalle came to these mountains after building that place he calls Beth-El. He was able to keep tight control over the information flowing out of it. I don't think anyone even knew he had a son until years later, a son named Johnny. Only Walker knew the truth. The truth about Eldon LaSalle's son."

Hendrickson took another sip of water in what was obviously an ordeal.

"He brought Walker up to the place in secret to examine his son. It was clear he was not the son LaSalle wanted as his heir. He was retarded. I guess that's not the term you're supposed to use now. I can't keep up. He was not perfect, let's put it that way, and that was all that mattered to LaSalle. Sometime up there Walker made his deal with the devil. I don't know all that was involved after that, how much money may have changed hands. But Walker was in deep.

"I sometimes wonder why LaSalle didn't just kill poor Walker. I know Walker has two daughters who he was estranged from. But he loved them. They came to represent the only good thing he'd ever done. Maybe LaSalle told Walker if he ever spoke about anything, he'd deal with the daughters. At the end, I don't think it would have taken much to scare Walker into doing anything."

Suddenly Hendrickson's eyes narrowed. "If this gets out, they may try to kill Walker and those two girls. You've got to promise me you'll take care of that."

Meyer deferred to Steve.

"Mr. Hendrickson," Steve said, "I wasn't entirely up front with you. Yes, I talked to Dr. Phillips, but he shot himself before I left. He's dead."

Hendrickson closed his eyes, paused, nodded. "Then there's no use holding this thing close to the vest," he said. "Walker told me that LaSalle had found a boy to his liking, and wanted him to be his only son."

Steve had a sudden thought about a TV mini-series he'd seen once. A Stephen King story about a demon who came to an island community in the middle of a storm when no one could get out. He came to take away one of their children, to become his apprentice demon. It was chilling, and as Steve recalled the demon won because the town didn't stand up to him with collective faith.

"What happened next was horrible," Hendrickson continued, "but Walker, for reasons known only to him, went along with it. I do know that in the next few years Walker became quite wealthy. But his drinking got worse.

"Cole had become a problem for LaSalle. So it was arranged. Cole and the boy died in a fire that was set by someone from LaSalle's own group. Walker performed the autopsy, but there was still one other role that had to be played."

"Mott," Steve said.

Hendrickson nodded. "And now you know what's been hidden all these years. I'm a coward for not coming forward before."

"That deputy," Steve said, "Oderkirk. He was killed, wasn't he?"

"I don't know," Hendrickson said.

"You didn't suspect?"

"I've given up suspecting."

"I think Oderkirk started asking questions Mott didn't like."

"That may be." Hendrickson was a deflated balloon now. He seemed to sink inside his suit.

Meyer clicked off the tape recorder. "This is all hearsay," he said. "I believe it, but we need to have direct evidence."

"We can exhume the boy's body, do a DNA match," Steve said. "He's buried in Indio. We'd still need LaSalle's DNA. He predates the databases. I don't think he has a record."

"We've got enough for the feds to go up there with a search warrant. They're going to need a whole team for this one. I better call those two guys in LA."

"What about Mott?" Steve said.

"We have less than nothing on Owen Mott," Meyer said. "We're going to have to tread very lightly around that one."

"And what about me?" Hendrickson asked.

"No one needs to know we've spoken," Meyer said. "In the warrant affidavit you will be an anonymous citizen informant. That's enough to get us through their gates."

Bethany spoke. "But will you be able to get out?"

When the interview with Hendrickson was over, Steve and Bethany filled in gaps with Meyer for another hour and a half.

Meyer might have gone for another two, but Steve finally said, "That's it for the night, Meyer. Have you thought about what you're going to do with us?"

Apparently he had not. He took his glasses off and rubbed his eyes.

"I'll help you out," Steve said. "You're going to secure a couple of rooms at that Hyatt we saw near the hospital. Under your name.

You're going to spring for the meals and some clothes for Bethany. We'll kick back there, if you don't mind. At least until the feds come riding in to town."

"Which may be sooner than you think," Meyer said. He opened his cell phone and made a call, turning his back and walking to a corner of the conference room. A moment later he was back.

"Just half an hour more," he said. "Issler and Weingarten just got here."

"Already?" Steve said, "How many speed laws did they break?"

"Doesn't matter. They're feds."

"All right," Steve said. "But I want you to bring us another bag of Milanos."

"Nice to see you again, Mr. Conroy," Agent Issler said. Weingarten gave him a nod.

"I missed you guys," Steve said.

"I guess you're ready to help us nail LaSalle?"

"I am so ready."

"Then we need to move fast," Issler said. "I'm going to need statements from both of you."

"Mr. Meyer has it all on tape," Steve said.

"Just some things we need for ourselves. We'll put it all together."

Steve looked at Bethany, who seemed ready to fall asleep. "I'll give you half an hour," he said. "Then we go into Mr. Meyer's version of witness protection."

It was eight thirty when Steve settled into a room at the Hyatt, with a window that looked out at the mountains. In the moonlight they were but an outline, peaceful in repose.

Quite an illusion, Steve thought. You'd never know that death was everywhere out there.

He disconnected the hotel phone and fell into a solid, dreamless sleep.

SEVENTY-TWO

It was almost noon when he awoke. The room was quiet but for the hum of the air pumping in. Peaceful. His leg was sore but not unbearable. Best of all, he was outside of Verner and all that it represented.

He wondered how Bethany was doing. What she would do now. How do you get back into life when the only life you knew was the bizarre world of Eldon LaSalle?

Maybe he could help her find a job somewhere. Get her some support. Just like he got in recovery. Hers was going to be a recovery from a living death. She'd need some group for that.

He flicked on the TV to catch the news. Today would be a nice, slow day. Take it easy. He'd make sure Bethany got a good lunch and would charge it to the room. He'd check in with the DA later, find out what the latest—

The TV came on to the hotel channel. Steve advanced to the next channel.

Which could have been the All Hell Has Broken Loose network. With a banner underneath her that said *Verner, California*, a female reporter with hair flapping in the breeze was saying, "... know so far. At approximately four thirty this morning, agents from the Bureau of Alcohol, Tobacco, and Firearms served a federal search warrant at the enclave of religious cult leader Eldon LaSalle. We don't have all the details yet, but one of the agents has been shot by a high-powered weapon. We understand the agent is in critical condition at Traynor Memorial Hospital. Since then, it's been something of a standoff here. As you can see behind me, more and more vehicles and agents are arriving on the scene. We don't know how many people are inside the compound, or what arms they have, but agents are making this a very careful—"

The backdrop was ATF central. Steve flipped to the next channel. A talking head was on a split screen with a male reporter. "... status of several women. There are reports of a hostage situation, but we haven't been able to confirm. Negotiations appear to be underway. I spoke to one of the agents, who did tell me that the situation is stable for the moment, but it feels like something could blow at any time. What nobody wants is another Waco situation. Again, early this morning federal agents—"

Steve put the remote down, plugged in the hotel phone, and called Bethany's room. She picked up immediately.

"Have you seen the news?" he asked.

"News?"

"There's an army outside Beth-El. An agent's been shot. It looks like a standoff."

"Oh no."

"The other women are apparently being treated like hostages."

"Dear God." It sounded like the truest prayer he'd ever heard.

"We've got to get up there. You have information that can help, about the insides, about—"

"It won't do any good," she said. "He will kill them all."

Steve said, "Get dressed." Meyer had been good enough to find fresh clothes for both of them, though Steve's selection was from the jail's overflow. But this was not going to be a job interview.

He called the DA's office next. The receptionist put him through to Meyer.

"Are you okay?" Meyer asked.

"Oh yeah, but what about you?"

"The town is at a complete standstill. The highway's closed down, traffic everywhere."

"I need to get up there with Bethany. We know the inside."

"I can't get to you from over here. I'll see if I can get somebody on your side to pick you up."

"I'll be ready."

"I hope so," Meyer said.

SEVENTY-THREE

The scene was straight out of a Bruce Willis movie. ATF and FBI, fully armed, were set up along the highway at several points. Two choppers hovered in the sky, over a bevy of law-enforcement vehicles, strategically placed.

Steve held Bethany's hand as an agent showed them, along with Mal Meyer, to the command post. The heart of the CP was a black SUV with a full complement of high-tech equipment in the open back.

Agent Issler was on his phone as Meyer brought up Steve and Bethany. The noise from the choppers mixed with the scratchy sound of electronic voice feeds and the general din of a full-on cordon.

Steve saw someone else he recognized in the back of the SUV. The guy who'd taken him on the ride, at gunpoint, that night at his law office. He wore black sweats, headphones, and was sitting in front of a laptop. When he saw Steve, he nodded like it was old-home week.

Issler clapped his phone shut and looked at Steve. "So what have you got?"

"She was on the inside," Steve said. "She can give you a layout."

Issler said, "Can you start now?"

Bethany nodded.

"Then I'll have you talk to Agent Malone." He indicated the man in the SUV.

Bethany squeezed Steve's hand. "It'll be all right," he said, and helped her into the back of the vehicle.

"Nice to see you again," Malone said to Steve. "Glad you're okay."

Okay, Steve thought, was a highly relative term. His leg still hurt when he put pressure on it.

To Issler he said, "What's the latest?"

"We have one agent down. Don't know how many inside, except we think Eldon LaSalle is dead."

"What?"

"Johnny LaSalle is negotiating. We think it would have been Eldon if he was alive."

"What's Johnny saying?"

"He wants a lot of things he's not going to get."

"And if he doesn't?"

"I think you know."

Steve gave a quick look to the cordon. "How you going to keep this from being another Waco?"

"What kind of a question is that?" Issler said.

"Realistic."

"We're talking."

"How long you going to talk?"

"Mr. Conroy, if you'll just hold tight."

"Do you know if there's a Sienna Ciccone in there?"

"Who—"

"She's someone you're definitely going to want to talk to. She's in on it."

Steve took a step back. From where he was he couldn't see any of Beth-El. Only the side of a mountain, dotted with a few agents with rifles. A lot of potential death any way you looked at it.

"Let me," Steve said.

"Let you what?" said Issler

"Talk to him."

"I don't think that would be a good idea."

"What could it hurt?"

"It could hurt a lot."

"It could help too. I'm the closest thing he's got to family."

At which point Mal Meyer, whom Steve had forgotten was there, said, "Yeah, family who almost got you killed."

"Let me talk to him," Steve said. "You'll be listening. You can cut it off whenever you want. Just let me talk to him once."

The agent paused, then opened his phone and turned his back. He paced a few yards, talking.

"What are you thinking of saying?" Meyer asked.

"I don't know exactly," Steve said. "I guess I'll just have to think on my feet. As long as I can stand on my feet."

Issler came back. "Let's go," he said.

The negotiator was a man, about forty, with striking gray eyes and short hair the color of ash. Almost Steve's height, he looked in tremendous shape, with broad shoulders and thick arms. He wore a dark blue T-shirt and matching jeans and a fully featured Sam Browne belt.

Issler introduced him to Steve. His name was Maxson.

"So you're the brother and the lawyer?" Maxson said.

"That's right," Steve said.

"That's not bad. You understand that we want to keep him talking?"

"Yes," Steve said.

"Now listen carefully. I do not have command authority. LaSalle knows this. You therefore cannot ask me to make any decisions. Clear?"

"Yes."

"We just want him to talk. You're a lawyer, you know how to ask open-ended questions, that's what I want you to do. We'll be listening. If things go sideways, we're going to get you off. The longer we can keep things status quo, the better for everyone."

"Okay."

"He's doing his best to come off cool. He's pretty good at it. Keep him that way."

"Okay."

"There's one hostage in there who needs medical treatment. We're exchanging some food for her."

"Her? Do you know her name?"

"Sarai. That's what he gave us."

"Can I talk now?"

"Just remember," Maxson said. "Keep him talking."

SEVENTY-FOUR

"Hello, Johnny."

"Well, this is some sort of miracle! Praise the Lord!"

"How are you doing?"

"No, babe, how are *you* doing? Where you been?"

"Let's talk."

"Not with all the feds listening in. How you doing, Maxson?"

Steve looked at Maxson, who was listening on a headset. Maxson shrugged.

"What I say's confidential," Johnny said. "So come on up and we'll talk in person."

Maxson shook his head.

"I don't know if they'll let me," Steve said.

"Sure they will," Johnny said. "Maxson's my bud. Tell him I'll let two of the ladies go just so I can talk to you."

"Sienna," Steve said. "Let her go."

Maxson looked like he would bust a vein in his forehead.

"Have 'em call me back in five minutes with an answer," Johnny said. "In five minutes the deal's off the table."

Click.

"Absolutely not," Issler said.

"Two hostages," Steve said. "That's a pretty good trade for some talk."

"How do you know it's just going to be talk? How do you know you'll even come back?"

"It's worth a try," Steve said.

Issler and Maxson exchanged looks.

Steve caught something there. "You're going in, aren't you?"

Issler said nothing.

"Call him back," Steve said. "Tell him I'm coming up."

"No—"

"I'm talking as his lawyer. He still has the right to counsel. Now you don't want to be violating any constitutional rights, do you?"

"You're not seriously—"

"I am seriously."

Issler said, "Wait here."

The wait felt like an hour. When Issler came back he said, "You talk at the gate. You bring the two hostages back with you. Then we talk about the next step."

"That's the deal?"

"That's it. Are you clear?"

"Clear."

Issler handed Steve a phone. "Press and hold 2. That comes to me. How do you feel?"

"I didn't know you cared."

"You don't know me very well, Mr. Conroy."

SEVENTY-FIVE

They dropped Steve fifty yards from the front drive. He walked the rest of the way, limping slightly. He noticed then that it was quieter. The choppers were gone. Part of another deal, maybe?

All he knew was that he was very much alone at the moment.

He got to the drive and walked up the gravel to the iron gate. Behind it stood one of the LaSalleites—the one named Axel, Steve thought—and he looked hyped up. He said nothing as he pressed a button on the gate box.

Slowly, the gate opened.

As Steve stepped through he noticed that Axel held a handgun. Probably a semiauto 9mm.

"Put your hands out," Axel said.

Steve complied. Axel patted him down with his left hand, letting him know with each slap who was in control.

"Let's go," he said, and nodded for Steve to move ahead.

They walked up the winding road without a word, until they were almost to the clearing where the house could be seen.

At this point Axel put the gun to Steve's head. Held it against his temple and said, "You will get this if you do anything you are not told to do. Clear?"

"Yeah," Steve said, his throat as dry as the ground beneath his feet.

"Then keep walking."

They approached the house. About ten men, all holding mean weapons, watched. Every face seemed to hold the hope that he could be the one to do the honors, to blow Steve away when the order came.

Axel took him into the house, down the hall, and into the library where Steve first met Eldon LaSalle. Now it was Johnny standing by the fireplace, alone.

He smiled. "Leave us," he said.

Axel withdrew and closed the door behind him. Johnny folded his arms and faced him. "You are one crazy dude, I got to give you that."

"Crazy?" Steve said. "Or am I anointed?"

Johnny said nothing. For once his blazing blue eyes, so secure and confident every other time Steve saw them, had a thin glaze of doubt.

"How'd you do it?" Johnny said. "How'd you get back here?"

"You really care?"

"I just want to know."

"Like you said, a miracle."

"Now that's funny, because we're going to need more of 'em. There's going to be some shooting soon. There's going to be a little apocalypse here."

"Let the hostages go."

"It's too late," Johnny said.

Steve went to him, within arm's length. "Let me help get you out of this."

"Out? You think there's going to be an out?"

"There can be."

"In your dreams, Brother."

"What happened here?" Steve said. "How'd it get to this? What happened to Eldon?"

Johnny looked into the fire, smiling ruefully. "Oh, man. One never knows, huh?" He put his gaze on Steve. "Let me clue you in on a little something. Our father, our real father, didn't kill himself. Eldon did it, set up a fake suicide."

Steve's blood went cold.

"Listen," Johnny said. "You have to make it on your own in this world, and if they try to stop you, you have to stop them. The official story is that Eldon shot himself yesterday. That he was afraid of the feds. He showed weakness. And now I have stepped in to save Beth-El."

"What do you mean the official story?"

"I think a clever lawyer like you can figure that out."

Steve said, "You did it. You killed him."

"Hey, you really are clever, aren't you?" Johnny started laughing. A lost laugh. The laugh of a dead man.

Steve waited for the laughing to stop. When it did, Johnny just breathed slowly, watching flames. Watching the fire under that grotesque bas-relief of the stoning of the man. It all reminded Steve of hell.

"Johnny," he said, "listen to me now. Do you remember Cody Messina?"

Johnny looked at Steve, frowned. "Whoa. Yeah. I haven't thought about him in ... where'd you come up with that?"

"Don't you remember that day you saved me from Cody Messina? He was going to pound my head down my neck if I didn't give him my Mountain Dew, that's what he said, and then all of a sudden he got a Mountain Dew can to the head. You threw it at him, Robert. Then you told me to run and later I found out you jumped on him and bit him good."

Johnny looked off, seeming to remember. "You called me Robert again," he said.

"Do you remember that?"

"Yeah, now I do. I do remember that. And it's funny."

"What's funny?"

"I still drink that stuff. Got cases of it."

"You were my hero then. You were on the right side then. You were my protector. I loved you more than anything when we were kids. That's been killed. That's what I hate the most. I hate that it was taken away. You took it away."

"Me?"

"You sent me off to die. Just like that."

Johnny peered into Steve's eyes. "Would you believe me if I told you I didn't send you off to die?"

"You, Eldon, whoever. You didn't stop it."

"Would you believe me if I told you that wasn't true?"

"No."

"Eldon ordered it, but I got to Neal. I told him not to do it. He was going to take you a long way away. He wasn't going to slab you."

"You expect me to believe that?"

Johnny met his eyes. "Yeah. I do. After I took over, I was going to bring you back. Steve, yeah, I used you. I tried to buy your loyalty. Then I had to guarantee it when you started getting cool feet around here."

"So you guaranteed by having Mott plant coke in my car, just so you could pressure me into staying."

"Then Eldon got all whacked over you."

"You could say that."

Johnny said, "But Steve, I want you to know something. In all of this, man, I really did want to see you again. I did want my brother back. Can you believe that much?"

"I don't know, Johnny," Steve said, "but I do know you need somebody to talk to the feds, be in between for you. We'll get out of this together."

"I'm not giving myself up."

"Just the hostages. Give them up and I'll stay. You made a deal to let two go. Let them all go. Show good faith. Do that much, one step at a time. And that includes Sienna."

Johnny shook his head. "She wants to be with me. I'm sorry about that."

"Let her go. Let them all go. We can get it back, Robert. The way we felt about each other. Don't do this thing. I'll stick with you. I'll be your lawyer and your brother."

Johnny shook his head. "I'm not going back to the joint. And you know that's the only place I'll be going."

"If you do this, if the women here die, there's something worse that's going to happen. There's a justice out there that's going to rain down on you."

"My brother, are you getting godly on me?"

"Listen to me! I don't know what it all means, but there has got to be something like that for something like this." Steve paused and looked hard into Johnny's face and knew he was talking to himself now. "I don't want to lose you again, not this way. I want to get you back. I want to make it right. I didn't call out when they took you. I let it happen. I want to make it right ..."

Johnny did not answer. He looked into the fireplace, the flames flickering in his eyes. He stood like that for a long time.

Then the door opened, and two men with guns drawn came in. One was Axel. The other was Bill Reagan.

"What's up?" Johnny said.

Reagan walked up to Steve and hit him with the butt of his gun. Steve hit the floor.

SEVENTY-SIX

"Whoa, whoa," Steve heard Johnny say.

"He killed Rennie," Reagan said. "Rahab helped him. She shot Neal. She's down there spilling her guts right now!"

Steve's head was spinning in a tight spiral. The left side of his face felt numb.

"Let me do him," Axel said.

"No, me," Reagan said. "Downstairs. In front of the women. Let them see."

"Shut up, both of you," Johnny said. He grabbed the front of Steve's shirt with both hands and pulled him up.

Steve blinked a couple of times.

"Is that true, Steve?" he said.

"How would he know?" Steve said. Then he knew. "Mott. You've got Mott down there monitoring everything."

"Let me!" Reagan said. "Let's get rid of him now!"

"Steve," Johnny said. "Is it true?"

"Yeah, it's true," Steve said. "So what? It doesn't change anything."

"See?" Reagan shouted.

"Shut up," Johnny said.

"We do him now!" Reagan said.

"You want your chance? I'll give it to you. But when I say, not before. Got it?"

"But—"

"Got it?"

Reagan heaved a breath, then snarled, "All right."

"I'm sorry it has to be this way, Steve," Johnny said.

SEVENTY-SEVEN

Darkness and cold.

The darkness Steve could partially understand. He had a hood over his head. A black hood like they gave to Saddam before he was hanged. Like they used to do all the time when hanging was the punishment meted out in these good old United States.

The cold was the cold of a stone basement. A prison cell maybe. Or dungeon. They had marched him down here and he heard a door lock. Hands cuffed behind him.

So much for heroic stands. So much for his influence over his long-lost brother. So much for his life finally amounting to something more than the day-to-day quest for a buck or a fix.

He tried to feel his way around the enclosure, kicking out with his foot. He thought all sorts of things might be waiting for him. Bear traps. Rats. All the finer things of life set up here by Eldon LaSalle. And now Johnny.

Brother love was not all it was cracked up to be.

He heard some crackling. Like major electric wires. Popping sounds.

No. Not electricity.

Gunfire. Distant but clear.

We're all dead now, he thought.

He tried to gauge the time as the shooting continued. Ten minutes or thirty? More? He couldn't tell.

Then the sound stopped as suddenly as it had begun.

Back in silence, he wondered if this was just some calm before more storm. Or something worse. What if the feds lobbed in gas or something? Or bulldozed the place with tanks?

If that happened, what could he do with his head bagged and hands shackled?

More time passed. Not good. He was starting to feel the internal pressure of nature's call. A final indignity before death?

Then something at the door. Someone trying to get in?

"Anybody in there?" a voice shouted. "This is ATF. Agent Larson. Anybody inside?"

Steve moved toward the sound, shouting through his hood. "Yeah! One guy!"

"Can you open the door?"

"No."

Pause. "Stand back."

Steve heard a grinding of some kind. Someone cutting through steel. Then a chinking sound, like chains falling off. And a burning smell wafting in.

He heard the door open.

"It's all right," the voice said, and there followed the sound of footsteps, maybe three sets.

Then his hood was removed.

It was dark in the room, with faint light coming through the open door. Three silhouettes stood in front of him, guys with helmets.

"Conroy?" the man said.

"That's me," Steve said.

"Good to see you."

"What's happened?"

"The place is secure. Let's get you out. And get those cuffs off."

SEVENTY-EIGHT

They checked Steve out and had him sit in the back of an ambulance. He couldn't see anything outside but bursts of activity from federal agents, a blur of dark jackets with *ATF* in yellow on the back. It was now about six p.m. The smell of guns had finally dissipated in the wind.

Issler came by, looking tired but relieved.

"How many got out?" Steve asked before the agent opened his mouth.

"All the hostages. Thank God they were in a bunker, like you."

"What about the men?"

"Three custodies. The rest, no."

"Johnny?"

Issler shook his head. "This has the marks of death by agent. They fired the rounds. We had to go in. Bethany helped enormously. We still don't know why the women were unharmed. Or why you don't have a hole in your head."

Steve said, "Mott. Sheriff Mott. You need to—"

"Mott's dead."

"What?"

"One of our guys went with your DA, Meyer, to question him. He took off. They caught up to him heading south. He pulled over and ate his gun."

Steve said nothing. His hands shook. "Talk to a woman named Joyce Oderkirk. Her husband worked for Mott. Mott, or one of the LaSalleites, took care of him when he started asking questions about an autopsy."

"Anything else?"

"Is one of the women Sienna Ciccone?"

"We don't know all the names yet. Who is she?"

"Someone you'll want to talk to."

Issler nodded. "There's one more thing. I can't let you have it because it's evidence, but there was a shoebox we found inside that had your name on it and something inside. We thought maybe you could explain a rather cryptic message."

"I'll try."

Issler stepped away from the ambulance for a moment, then came back holding a gray shoebox. On the box lid was a yellow sticky note with the words *For Stevie from Robert.*

Issler removed the lid. In the box was a single can of Mountain Dew.

"So what's that all about?" Issler asked.

"I think—" Steve had to pause. Hot tears pushed against his eyes. He took a long breath. "I think it means my brother saved my life."

Issler requested Steve wait in the ambulance. Might have some questions to be answered.

Steve didn't have any pressing plans at the moment. His body was buzzing with what he supposed was post-traumatic stress. Like he couldn't believe it was over, really over.

That Robert was dead. And Eldon LaSalle. And most of the others.

He decided small-town life was not for him. LA was a lot safer.

At some point he dozed off on a gurney.

Issler woke him up. "We have a sticky little situation here."

"How's that?"

"There is a Sienna Ciccone."

"You talk to her?"

Issler shook his head. "She said she won't talk to us until she talks to you. She wants you to act as her attorney."

Steve blinked a couple of times to clear his head. "Now there's a twist."

"Yeah, you want to explain it?"

"I better talk to her."

"Tell me what this is about first."

"Agent Issler, I hate to pull lawyer-client privilege, but there you are."

"What privilege? You're not even – –"

"It's *Gideon v. Wainwright.* It's the US Supreme Court. You get to have the attorney of your choice before you talk, and right now that's me. You don't want to run afoul of the Supreme Court now, do you?"

Issler sighed. "I need a vacation."

SEVENTY-NINE

"Surprised I asked to see you?" Sienna said. She and Steve were sitting in the back of a black Yukon, one of the command post vehicles. Issler had ordered they be left alone for a few minutes.

"You could say that," Steve said.

"I don't suppose you could really act as my attorney."

"Would you really want me to?"

"I would trust you in any circumstance. Does that sound crazy?"

"Uh. Yeah. There's just a tiny bit of baggage that would prevent me from giving you adequate representation. Knowing you're a consummate liar might color my judgment."

She nodded weakly. "No argument there."

"When you came out to my office that day, it was all part of the setup."

"Yes. Johnny wanted me to be around you, assess you."

"How did you know I was going to be evicted from my office?"

"I didn't. That just happened. I used it. I'm good at using things."

"Oh yeah. Very good."

Sienna said nothing. Steve didn't know whether to feel pity or scorn. A cold stone sat in his chest. He was silent too.

Finally Sienna said, "Can I tell you a story?"

"Does it have a happy ending?"

"I don't know the ending yet. I know the beginning real well. It's about a girl brought up to be a good Christian. She had a father and mother who made sure she went to Sunday school and church. She got the Bible drummed into her so she knew it backward and forward. Our little story was all roses until the girl turned sixteen. By then the mother had died and she was alone with her father. It was tough on both of them. They didn't know how to talk to each other. The girl, she had something in her that just ... wasn't good. One night she sneaked out to be with her boyfriend. Ha. Boyfriend. She knew him all of a week. They went out driving and had vodka and then she had her first ... experience."

She gave Steve a quick look, then cast her eyes down.

"When she got home, her father knew. I don't know how he knew, but he did. It was in his eyes. He could smell my breath and . . . oh, I guess you know who the story is about now, don't you?"

"I was taking a wild guess."

Sienna took on the faraway look of remembering, spoke slowly. "I couldn't stand the look in Dad's eyes. He was a mechanic. Cars, trucks. Hard worker. Such a strong, good man. We had a fight that night. A big one. There was just something in me that didn't take to what he wanted me to be. We screamed so loud. And he slapped me. I ran out of the house. I was going to run away. I did, for a couple of days."

She stopped, took a deep breath. "When I finally came back, it was too late. He was dead. They said it was his heart. He'd had heart trouble before, but it wasn't a coincidence. I knew that. Bored yet?"

"I'm still listening," Steve said.

"I got out of town. Too many eyes looking at me. Went to another state, got a job, finished school, got to college. Slept around. Got accepted at DeWitt. More of the same. Then I got on an appeal project at school that first summer, and went out to Fenton to help a prisoner with his appeal. His name was Johnny LaSalle."

Another pause. This was obviously an effort. Steve waited for her to go on.

Sienna said, "You've heard the stories about women who get fixated on prisoners? I think there's a name for that. There's something about a different world that you can be a part of, because somebody in that world wants you to be part of *them*. Maybe he's got some savior thing going on. Then there was just the attraction."

She shook her head and seemed to be searching for words.

"I can see how it might have happened," Steve said. "You were messed up. But you're smart, Sienna. How could you let him drag you into this thing?"

"I'll tell you how," she said without hesitation. "It's like my dad always told me. There's an enemy who wants to bring us down, and if you open the door, he'll take the invitation."

"Enemy?"

"The devil."

"What, you're saying you were possessed by the devil?"

"No. But I felt like I was possessed by Johnny LaSalle. And when I was with him, even when I thought I was totally in love with him, there was a part of me whispering to get out, get away. I should have listened. Just like I should have listened to my father. I want to be able to listen again."

He started to wonder if she was just feeding him more lies, setting him up for her trial, manipulating him to her side. She'd mouthed so many cool, stiletto lies. "Shouldn't be too hard. You just do it."

A pained smile curved her mouth. "If it was only that simple. I didn't listen the whole time I was with him. We set you up. We lied to you. To your face. At first I could do it, but then I started to ..."

"To what?"

She looked at him. "Have feelings."

"You sound like a Hallmark card," Steve said.

"I guess I do. But I'm saying it anyway. I was pulled in two directions, and Johnny seemed to know it. His pull was stronger in me. When they took you off that day, the day you saw Johnny and me in the window, I was about ready to die myself."

"Not much help," Steve said.

"Then Johnny told me it was all right, that you were just going to be taken away for a while. Until Eldon was ... removed. By then he had some feelings too, if you can believe it."

Steve said nothing.

"You know the rest," she said.

"It's not over yet," Steve said. "The feds think you were a hostage. As soon as they start questioning you, things might get hairy. Even for a good liar like you."

"I'm through with that."

"Sure," Steve said, not at all sure of anything. "I strongly advise you get a lawyer, preferably one who is not me."

Sienna shook her head. "I'm going to tell the FBI everything it wants to know about Beth-El and the LaSalles."

"That could lead to a conspiracy rap. Get representation."

She smiled. "Still holding up the finest traditions of the bar, huh?"

"At this point, Sienna, I'm holding on for dear life. But there's one thing I'm not able to do, try as I might."

"What's that?"

"Hate you."

"You don't?"

"No."

"I'll take it."

Steve thought she meant it, really meant it this time, in spite of the past. Maybe that was the best way to leave it. "I know a guy," he said. "Good federal defense lawyer. I'll send him your way."

She shook here head. "Forget it. I'm talking. If I go away, I go away. I guess I'll never practice law, though, huh?"

"Most states'll let you, even after a conviction, when some time passes. Who knows? Maybe going through all this will make you a better lawyer. Maybe I'll be a better lawyer too."

"There's no doubt in my mind," she said.

"One more question," Steve said.

She waited.

"All that time you were lying to me," he said, "and giving me the line that you were a good girl and all, did you ever think there might be a God looking down and thinking, *Hey, I do not like what she's doing.*"

"All the time," she said without hesitation. "Call it perverse, but there it was. And still I went on. Now I'll have plenty of time to beg him to forgive me."

"Well," Steve said, "I hope he does. I guess we all need that in one way or another. So I really hope he does, Sienna."

"He will," she said. "That's the only thing I'm sure of now, the one thing I have to hold on to."

"Then hold," Steve said.

EIGHTY

Three days later, Steve stopped at the Sheridan Arms and found that his old apartment was still for rent.

"You come back!" Jong Choi said, not asking a question.

"I come back," Steve said.

"Oh! You know seven? You call cops." He produced a card from a drawer and handed it to Steve.

The card was LAPD. A detective named Holmes. Not Sherlock. Lee.

"Seven?" Steve said.

"Arrest," Jong Choi said.

"The kid in number seven?"

Choi nodded vigorously.

Steve went out to the courtyard and called the number. Holmes was in. Told him that Chris Riley, Numba Sev'n's real name, had been caught with a lot of hot stuff, including Steve's computer. So Numba had turned thief, and was now residing in the county jail. And, Holmes wanted to know, would Steve come in and make a statement?

Yeah, he would. And as he clicked off the phone he decided something else. He didn't know where it came from, but there it was. He would go down to the jail to see the kid. Try to talk some sense into him.

He'd tell him a story, about prisons and cons, about the way they end up by staying stupid. He'd give the kid one shot because there aren't too many breaks in the world. Steve had been given one. So he'd pass it along to somebody else.

It didn't make much sense. Steve knew the odds. But he also knew he just had to do it.

He heard a mew at his feet.

Nick Nolte padded around him with a feline nonchalance that said, *I didn't really miss you but I'm glad you're back anyway.*

"I love you too," Steve said as he picked up the cat. "Come on and give me a hand. I mean, a paw."

He started moving some of his belongings into the apartment. Managed to get half the stuff in before Mrs. Stanky stuck her head out as he walked by and carped about needing some Milk of Magnesia as if he'd never left. He assured her he'd get it.

Then she said, "Get rid of that cat."

He was home.

Jong Choi helped Steve with his last item, the old trunk. It had been with him the whole way, through every ugly turn and every ray of light. He put it against the bare wall where he once had a sofa.

When he was alone at last, Steve opened the trunk. The photos and papers were scattered around, a random pattern that seemed to match his own patchwork life.

He found the picture of Robert in his train pajamas. The cereal picture. Looked at it for a long time.

Then he got on his knees. He put his hands together over the trunk. And just like when he was five years old, stumbling over words but putting his whole soul into it, he said a prayer for Robert Conroy.

And somewhere in there he said a prayer for himself. It felt good. It felt like he was talking and someone was really listening. It freaked him not at all.

He'd tell Gincy about it in the morning. Gincy would show him what to do next.

When Steve finished his prayer, he lay on the carpet and looked at the ceiling. Full circle. For better or worse he'd landed back in LA.

For better or worse.

He knew then there was one more thing he had to do.

EIGHTY-ONE

He knocked tentatively on Ashley's door. He hoped the shock wouldn't curl her hair. He hoped a lot of things. It was close to evening and she might not even be home.

But she was. She answered in jeans and a crimson sweatshirt, looking like the Ashley he'd known in law school.

"Steve!"

He put his hands out. "Tah dah."

"I can't believe you're—come in."

He tried not to look too relieved as he walked through the door.

"You're limping," she said.

"Have you been following the news?"

"It's all over the place. The ACLU's already filing wrongful-death actions against the government. You weren't inside, were you?"

"Oh yeah."

They went to the living room. He sat on the sofa, like he'd just come back from court ready to spend an evening with his wife. He remembered doing that. Remembered they had some good times amid all the bad.

He missed even the bad now. Because she had been there with him. At least she'd been there.

"I'm not taking you away from something, am I?" Steve said.

"Not at all," she said.

"Or somebody?" He let the implication hang in the air.

"No."

Now Steve tried not to look too happy.

"I'm so glad you're all right," Ashley said. "Can you tell me about it?"

He opened his mouth but nothing came out.

"If you can't right now," she said, "that's fine. Maybe you need—"

He was crying.

"Steve."

"I'm sorry. I'm—" The tears kept coming. "Sorry." He got up and almost ran to the kitchen. He tore off a paper towel and put it to his face.

He felt Ashley's hands on his back. "It's okay. Go ahead."

He did, for about a minute, full out. When it was over the paper towel was soaked. All the time Ashley just stood there, touching his back.

"Man, I'm sorry," Steve said.

"No."

"I don't know what happened there."

"It's okay."

He turned to face Ashley and she hugged him. Held him.

Steve said, "Would you consider doing something?"

"What's that?"

"Would you let me take you for a hot dog dinner?"

She stepped back and looked at him. "Hot dogs? Are you serious?"

"I just got this wild idea."

She shook her head, then smiled. "Fries too?"

They drove to Jelty Park, where the carnival was. He parked the car without a word and looked at her.

"Remember?" he said.

She looked pleased for a moment. Then her face got serious. "Steve—"

"I know. No obligation. Just hot dogs. Deal?"

She paused. "Deal."

They went in, lights all around, got their dogs and fries at the stand. After that it was talk and even laughs.

An hour passed, then another. They rode the little roller coaster and played a few games. Steve won a stuffed tiger at the milk-bottle throw and gave it to Ashley. She said it reminded her of Steve when he was in trial. "A real tiger," she said. He liked that.

Then it was cotton candy and the Ferris wheel. They stopped at the top, looked down at the lights of the carnival and the San Fernando Valley. It was a warm night. The breeze carried the scent of eucalyptus, dry grass, and a touch of LA perfume from the freeway.

Just before the descent he caught sight of the ride at the end of the park. He turned to Ashley. "Let's go on that next," he said.

She looked where he pointed. "What, the Zipper?"

"Yeah."

"I thought you hated those rides," she said.

"I want to try it," he said. "I want to try it with you."

"Really?"

"Really."

The wheel slowed as they neared the ground.

"The Zipper makes me nervous," she said.

"Have a little faith," Steve said.

Ashley looked at him as if trying to read his thoughts. Steve held her gaze. The colored lights reflected in her eyes like a neon dream. A dream of good things.

She smiled then and took his hand.

"Let's go for it," she said.

ONE

I.

Hey, buddy! Long time! Tracked you down after reading your blurb on the Prominent Alumni page. Prominent! You made it, buddy. I always knew you would, though it was all pretty crazy back there freshman year. Remember that? Wild times, oh yes. How'd we ever make it out of the dorm!

So I found your law firm website and then you and here I am! I'm in town! We have a lot of catching up to do. Call me, man. Can't wait to see you.

Sam Trask vaguely remembered the name at the end of the email. You remember guys named Nicky, even if you don't think about them for twenty-five years.

Nicky Oberlin. That's how he'd signed the email, along with a phone number.

The tightness in his chest, the clenching he'd been feeling for the last few weeks, returned. Why should that happen because of one random email? Because it presented a complication, a thing that called for a response. He did not need that now, not with the way things were at home.

Sam took a deep breath, leaned back in his chair in his Beverly Hills office, and tried to relax. Didn't happen. He kept seeing his daughter's face in his mind. She was screaming at him.

A quick knock on his door bumped Sam from his thoughts. Lew poked his head in. "A minute?"

Sam motioned him in. Lew Newman was Sam's age, forty-seven, and wore his sandy hair short, which gave his sharp nose and alert eyes added prominence. When Lew was with the Brooklyn DA's office he was known as the Hawk, and Sam could see why. He would've hated to be a witness about to be pecked by the Hawk's cross-examination. He was glad they were partners and not adversaries.

"We're going into high gear against the good old US of A this week," Lew said.

Sam nodded. "Got it on the radar." The FulCo case was by far the biggest Newman & Trask had ever handled. Potentially a billion at stake. That thought gave Sam's chest another squeeze.

"Cleared everything else?" Lew said.

"One matter to take care of."

"What's that?"

"Harper."

Lew rolled his eyes. "Hasn't that settled?"

"I'll take care of it."

"Please do."

"I said I would, okay?"

Lew put his hands up. "Just asking. I get to ask, don't I?"

"Of course. Sorry."

"Need you, buddy. I know things haven't been the best with—"

"I can handle it, Lew."

His partner nodded. "How's Heather doing, anyway?"

Sam did not want to talk about his daughter, not now. "We're working on it."

"Good. She'll pull through. She's a good kid."

Sam said nothing.

"So on Harper—"

"Lew, please—"

"Let me just say this once, okay? We do have a business to run, and—"

"You want me to get rid of the Harper file ASAP."

"That would be nice. Can you settle?"

"Not right away."

"Why not?"

"I need more discovery or it'll be undervalued."

"Come on, Sam. What about your value to the shop?"

Always preoccupied with the cost-benefit analysis, Lew was. Maybe that was what really had changed for Sam in the last four years. After his conversion, a little of the drive for the dollar had gone from his life.

As if sensing he'd stuck a foot over the line, Lew said, "Look, I trust your judgment, of course. But a quick settlement surely is going to be within the ballpark, give or take, and what's the problem with that?"

"No problem at all. Girl goes blind, we can toss her a few bones and move on."

"Come on, I don't mean that. Just think about it for me, will you? Harper off the table. I love you, sweetie." He made a golfing motion. "How about eighteen next week?"

Golf was always the way Lew made up. "Sure."

"I love you more," Lew said, then left.

For a long time Sam swiveled in his chair, as if the motion would gently rock his thoughts into some cohesive order. But it wasn't happening, because Sarah Harper was not a case he wanted to expedite.

The tightness came back. Come on, he scolded himself. No heart attack. You're not even fifty years old yet. Guys like you don't die before fifty. He kept in shape, ran three miles every other day, didn't have too many extra pounds. But he knew there was no guarantee. One of his old friends from UCLA Law had just gone to the cooling rack after playing pickup basketball.

One minute Tom had been a hard-charging partner at O'Melveny, and boom, the next he's an obit in *California Lawyer*. It could happen to anyone.

Sam rubbed his chest and looked back at the monitor. Nicky Oberlin. He tried to remember the face that went with the name. Didn't come to him.

Truth was, a lot of that first year at UC Santa Barbara up the coast was lost in a brain fog. He was still a long way off from a sober life then, and most of what he remembered of freshman year was a dorm known for grass and beer and late-night parties.

So this blast from the past was hearkening back to days he'd just as soon forget.

Was he the guy who came into his dorm room one night, hammered to the gills, and tried to roll out Sam's bed—while Sam was still in it? A lot of crazy things happened back then. It was a wonder any of them passed their classes.

Yeah, that might have been Nicky, a little guy with a moustache. But then again ... brain fog.

And in the fog, like the trill of a night bird, a faint vibration of unease. Oberlin had sent this to Sam's private email address. It wasn't posted on the firm's site. It would have taken some doing to find it. Apparently, Oberlin had. Which bothered him no end. It was like ... an intrusion, and by a guy he really didn't know.

He closed his eyes for a moment and expressed his favorite prayer of late, for wisdom. Having a seventeen-year-old daughter who seemed determined to throw her life down the toilet necessitated divine intervention on a daily basis.

Now he needed wisdom for his professional life. The Harper family had come to him in their hour of greatest need. He would not drop the ball.

He took a deep breath. This was not what he thought life would be at this point in his career. He thought he'd be at the pinnacle of his profession, able to coast along at a hardworking but smooth pace, with his wife and kids along for the ride.

Instead, he was tighter than a hangman's rope and wondering if the American dream was imploding on him.

He didn't need any more tasks or obligations, no matter how small. With a touch of his index finger he deleted Nicky Oberlin's email.

He hoped Nicky wouldn't take offense.

2.

Heather Trask wondered if he would be the one.

He had the right look. She liked long hair that hung down wavy, especially if it was blond. He had great style too, judging from the way he tapped the table with his hands. He played drums for a band called Route Eighteen.

And he clearly had his eye on her. Always gave her a half smile whenever their eyes met.

Would he be the one, her first time, so she could get it over with?

Roz, who was holding court as usual at an outdoor table at Starbucks, was already well schooled in the guy department. She'd burned through three boyfriends in the last year. Heather hadn't had even one yet. Roz was older than Heather by only two years but had a worldliness Heather could only admire.

Heather also loved the way Roz could cut and color her hair any which way, without a thought. Right now it was short and hot pink. Heather wasn't quite ready to chop her shoulder-length tresses and go from brown to a more luminescent tone. Maybe she would once she got out of the house.

Maybe then she'd feel like she really fit the puzzle. The pieces at home were all jumbled. She wasn't a piece there; she was a hole. The church thing wasn't going to happen for her, and her parents' disappointment made her feel like an alien presence in the home she grew up in.

Depression washed over her again. She'd been feeling so much of the dark side lately. She was using it in her songs, which Roz said were bordering on genius. Still, it was like a big, black weight on her, and she was sick of it.

Her mom and dad's solution? God. Jesus. Church.

Why couldn't she get into religion? It just didn't click, the tumblers didn't fall. Something was wrong with her brain. It wasn't a Trask brain, and she could see that thought in her parents' pained eyes with every new confrontation.

She needed to get out of there. They'd be much happier and she could finally see if there was something in this world that made sense. She could get on with things she should already have gotten to at seventeen.

So, she wondered, would her first time be with the drummer?

There were eight of them around the black iron table, crammed in and chattering away through a haze of cigarette smoke. Heather didn't really like smoking that much but did it anyway. Image. The hard part was covering up the smell when she got home.

Big Red cinnamon gum was good for the breath part. As far as her hair and clothes, well, she just told her mom it was because she'd been at Starbucks at an outside table. You just couldn't get away from the smoke out there.

She didn't think her mom totally bought that, but at least she didn't press the issue. Her dad was the one who would've made the big deal, but he was always so busy he never noticed.

"They could've taken the geek-rock crown from Weezer," she heard Drummer Boy saying. "But they turned to slacker romanticism."

Oh, no. Was he one of those pretentious, know-everything-about-music types? The kind who couldn't shut it once you got them started?

"Their last CD was nothing but lo-fi jangle and lush fuzz."

Yep.

"Detached and boring," Drummer Boy concluded loudly.

Just like you, Heather thought.

Drummer Boy brought his chair over to her side. He smiled at her and said, "Are you Jamaican?"

"What?"

"'Cause j-makin' me crazy."

She closed her eyes.

No way he'd be the one.

Maybe she should just let it be random and hope for the best.

Or maybe there wasn't going to be any *best*. What would she do then?

3.

"Don't worry, I'm not one of *those* kind of wives, complaining up and down about how much time her husband spends at the office."

Sam took a root beer from the refrigerator, turned to face his wife. "But a little complaining every now and again never hurt, right?"

"Is that what you think I do?"

"Not in so many words, but lately ..."

"Lately what?" She put her hands on her hips.

Uh-oh. Sam called that the Gesture, but not to Linda's face. The Gesture always raised his macho hackles. His wife was smart and insightful, and she could usually see through him. Drove him crazy sometimes. And when she was angry, and her hazel eyes caught the light, they sparked like flint on stone.

"Hints," he said. "You drop hints."

"What, would you rather I hit you right between the eyes?"

"Maybe a little more directness *would* be a good thing."

"Maybe I don't want to add to your stress, okay? Did you ever think of it that way?"

"Of course." He stepped over to her to kiss her. She gave him her cheek. "Don't pout," he said.

"When you deserve these lips again, you'll get them."

"How about I bribe you with my stunning culinary skill?"

"I'm listening."

"I'll cook up some steaks."

"You get one lip for that," Linda said. "Both if the steaks come out right."

"You drive a hard bargain."

"Take it or leave it."

"Take it. Now pay me on account."

She kissed him. A short one.

"You have inspired me with visions of things to come," Sam said. "I shall cook masterpieces."

"For you, me, and Max."

"Where's Heather?"

Linda paused. "She's out."

"With who?"

"Let's not."

Dead giveaway. "Not that Roz girl."

"Sam, I know—"

"I thought we told her—"

"Sam, please. We've been through it with her and it just leads to more anger."

Indeed, his circuits were charged. They sizzled with a high current whenever the subject of Heather's associations came up. "Who's in control around here? I don't want her seeing that girl."

"Heather is seventeen and pigheaded, like someone else I know."

She said it in a lighthearted way, but Sam wasn't into being light at the moment. "What if she wanted to go out with a serial killer?"

"Sam, Roz is hardly a serial killer."

"She's trouble, is what she is."

"That's a little harsh."

"Is it? I saw her at Starbucks one day, hanging out with a bunch of lowlifes."

"How did you know they were lowlifes?"

"Come on."

"What happened to the presumption of innocence?"

He ignored the dig. "Where do they go, these two? They go to concerts—who knows what kind of music these bands are playing. The lyrics. Have you heard some of the lyrics out there?"

"Is this from the man who used to be a poet?"

"Hey, we didn't write anything like they're doing today."

"You know who you sound like?"

"Who?"

"Our parents."

"That's depressing." Sam went to the living room and plopped on the sofa.

"Don't pick up the remote," Linda said.

He picked up the remote. "I'm just going to check the news."

Linda snatched the remote from his hand, sat next to him. "I'm just as concerned about our daughter as you are. So we need to talk about how to handle this. We need to be together when Heather gets home."

"We have to rehearse? Is this a play or something?"

"It's called parenting."

Sam shook his head. "I think I've got it figured out."

"What?"

"Parenting."

"Oh, do you? Pray tell, what's the secret?"

"Lowering your standards," he said.

Linda hit him with a pillow.

Sam put his head back on the sofa. "You're right."

"Hm?"

"It is complicated, isn't it? I mean, I'm in the delivery room one day and out comes this innocent little package."

"Yes, I was there too."

"Innocent and pure and it's the greatest experience of my life. And I say to myself, I'm going to protect her and love her and be there for her, and when she's little she can't get enough of me. Then one day she turns thirteen and it's like some mad scientist flips a switch in her brain."

Linda stroked his arm. "It's called growing up."

"It's called the pits on a platter, is what it's called. I feel like an innocent bystander. I was standing there, trying to love her like always, and now I'm being shut out of her life."

"As my mom used to say, this too shall pass."

Sam felt the mild pressure of tears behind his eyes. "I just want her to be happy. I want her to make the right choices. I want—"

"Sam?"

"What?"

"What you want is to make it all happen yourself."

"No—"

Linda sat up. "I know you. It's good what you want for her, but you can't make it happen. You have to let God in on this."

"Like I don't know that?"

"But do you?"

"Sure I do."

She gave him the *come on now* look, but not the remote.

4

In the study, Sam tried to get thoughts of Heather out of his head by preparing for tomorrow's deposition. It would be the crucial moment in the Harper case. His questioning of the expert who would testify that the emergency-room doctor had not made a terribly wrong diagnosis would set the stage for everything to come.

In a medical malpractice case, the testimony of experts was the key to the trial, because juries looked upon them as the high priests. Most jurors, in a medical emergency, would be willing to entrust their lives even to an unknown doctor. They entertained a willing suspension of belief that a doctor might be subject to the imperfections of mere mortals.

Lawyers who sued doctors, on the other hand, were often seen as bottom-feeders, responsible for everything from higher insurance premiums to acute acne.

Sam knew he would have a double burden if the case went to trial. In his opening statement, he planned to face the issue head-on. He would be up front with the jurors about tort reform and frivolous lawsuits.

Last trial he had, in fact, he'd asked the jurors on *voir dire* if any of them disagreed with the proposition that most lawyers are greedy ambulance chasers. Only a seventy-year-old grandmother, whose son was the DA of Kern County, raised her hand. But Sam walked through that door to elicit pledges that the jurors would treat the case before them with an open mind.

And although he'd won that case, for a fifteen-year-old boy who broke his neck diving into a river at an unsafe resort, the experts from the other side almost swayed the jury the other way.

Which was why the deposition of the experts was so important. If they came off as credible and competent, the basis of liability could disappear like a dandelion in the wind.

So Sam went over his questions carefully, designing them to build in a solid, inexorable fashion. He'd have to be on every one of his toes, because Larry Cohen, the insurance company's lawyer, would protect the doctor with every bit of legal firepower at his disposal.

Cohen was a near legend in the litigation community. At sixty-one, with a full head of silver hair and the frame of a football player—he'd been a standout linebacker at Colorado State—Cohen had not lost a case in twenty years.

It was Sam's hope that by undermining Cohen's expert in the depo, the Harper case could be settled for a fair amount. Then everyone would be happy—Lew, the Harpers, even Cohen himself, for it would be another file off his desk and wouldn't count as a loss in court.

Two hours flew by like two minutes. The only interruption was Max, his twelve-year-old. Max still liked to give his old man hugs before going to bed, and Sam took every one. Who knew how long that would last? In a few months Max would turn thirteen, and then what? Would the same mad professor that got to Heather flip a switch in his son's brain too?

How he prayed not.

Sam took a break at ten thirty and jumped online. He scanned the headlines at Google News, then made a quick stop at his email.

In the middle of the list he saw another message from Nicky Oberlin.

> *Hey man, just following up. Hope you got my email! We have GOT TO get together, my friend! Don't let me down! Call me now!*

A faint queasiness rolled through his stomach. A feeling, ever so slight, that he was being pushed. Sam never like being pushed.

He deleted the message, hoping this would be the last time he would hear from Nicky Oberlin.

Still, his eyes lingered on the screen for a long moment after the message vanished into the ether, as if another of its kind would suddenly appear, only this one not so friendly.

Presumed Guilty

James Scott Bell,
Bestselling Author of
Breach of Promise

Murder, betrayal, and a trial that feeds a media frenzy.

Can one woman stand against the forces that threaten to tear her family apart?

Pastor Ron Hamilton's star is rising. His 8,000-strong church is thriving. His good looks and charisma make him an exceptional speaker on family values. And his book on pornography in the church has become an unexpected bestseller. Everything is perfect.

Until a young woman's body is discovered in a seedy motel room. The woman is a porn star. And all the evidence in the murder points to one man: Ron.

With the noose tightening around her husband's neck, Dallas Hamilton faces a choice: believe the seemingly irrefutable facts—or the voice of her heart. The press has already reached its verdict, and the public echoes it. But Dallas is determined to do whatever it takes to find the truth.

And then a dark secret from Dallas's past threatens to take them all down.

As the clock ticks toward Ron's conviction and imprisonment, and an underworld of evil encircles her, Dallas must gather all her trust in God to discover what really happened in that motel room ... even if it means losing faith in her husband forever.

Softcover: 0-310-25331-4

Audio Download, Unabridged: 0-310-27819-8

Pick up a copy today at your favorite bookstore!

No Legal Grounds

James Scott Bell,
Bestselling Author of
Presumed Guilty

How far will a man go to protect his family?

Attorney Sam Trask will go farther than he ever dreamed, even in his worst nightmare. Because his worst nightmare is about to come true ....

At age forty-seven, attorney Sam Trask finally seems to have his life in order. The dark years of too much drinking and all-consuming ambition have given way to Christian faith. His marriage is strong again. Everything seems finally on the right track.

Then a voice from the past comes back to say hello.

Suddenly Sam faces a danger more real than he ever imagined—danger from someone who will not rest until Sam's life comes crashing down around him. Desperate, Sam seeks protection from the law he's served all his life. But when the threats are turned on his family, and the law seems powerless to protect them, Sam must consider a choice that strikes at the heart of his life and faith—whether to take the law into his own hands.

Softcover: 0-310-26902-4

Pick up a copy today at your favorite bookstore!

ZONDERVAN®
.com

Three ways to keep up on your favorite
Zondervan books and authors

Sign up for our *Fiction E-Newsletter*. Every month you'll receive sample excerpts from our books, sneak peeks at upcoming books, and chances to win free books autographed by the author.

You can also sign up for our *Breakfast Club*. Every morning in your email, you'll receive a five-minute snippet from a fiction or nonfiction book. A new book will be featured each week, and by the end of the week you will have sampled two to three chapters of the book.

Zondervan *Author Tracker* is the best way to be notified whenever your favorite Zondervan authors write new books, go on tour, or want to tell you about what's happening in their lives.

Visit *www.zondervan.com* and sign up today!

ZONDERVAN®

ZONDERVAN.com/
AUTHORTRACKER
follow your favorite authors